TALES OF
PLANET MAGNAE

I0611232

JASON TEJIRI BOJE

TALES OF PLANET MAGNAE

Copyright © 2024 by Jason Boje

Second Edition: May 2026

Self-Published by: Jason Boje

Cover Design by: Getcovers

Interior Layout by: Jason Boje

For inquiries, please contact: jasontejiriboje@gmail.com

I. HISTORIES OF SUFFERING PLANETS

HUMANITY being punished for its hubris in some way or another has been a tale as old as time. But never had it been to the extent experienced by the humanity of the MG Galaxy. Centuries had passed, yet the mankind of that universe would struggle with the advancement that would come so easily to other human races in other universes. After a series of constant setbacks, it seemed they would never bring forth the transition between the Fourth and Fifth Industrial Revolutions they so desperately sought, unable to combine man and machine without monumental drawbacks. Their advancements in space travel, however, continued exponentially.

Mankind travelled off Planet Earth and far into the MG Galaxy, using the resources collected from newly explored parts of the galaxy. A simultaneous blessing and curse similar to that of the past, which brought on a booming technological advancement. A synergy between man, machine, and the stars that the humanities of previous ages would have never been able to predict.

Hundreds of years following these vast advancements, humanity saw itself taken back to square one. War, pestilence, famine, and natural disasters in the form of the same technological boom that initially improved their lives tenfold. Earth had been destroyed beyond comprehension, to the point that humanity of this universe's present no longer had a single soul living on it. Using the last remnants of their damaged spacecraft, humanity relocated to their last bastion of hope, the only other habitable planet throughout the galaxies. Even then, on Planet Magnae, humanity's luck grew worse. Misfortunes of barbaric pre-modern proportions were soon to come.

Magnae, the human race's planet of refuge following these constant misfortunes, was similar to Earth. Its skies were darker, so much so that one could see the stars of space even in daylight. As opposed to the healthy greens and yellows of Earthly grass, Magnae grass fields alternated between maroon red, blood orange, and, in rare cases, gold. The billions that populated a once thriving Earth dwindled to the hundreds of thousands that populated a mostly empty Magnae. But these last remnants of humanity were not alone in the cosmos. Human beings had company on their new planet. An extra-terrestrial company that they were not fond of in the slightest.

***

Large ferocious waves of water as thick as blood crashed against each other as the world as he knew it succumbed to the wrath of a deadly flood. Murky saltwater was all there was to be seen for miles without a spot of dry land or respite. But somehow, despite all the death and destruction the flood caused, Emmanuel Ekib held on for dear life. A tall, dark-skinned man with kinky, curled hair and a heavy-set brow, on any other day, Emmanuel would have seemed like a foreboding individual. But then, as he hung for dear life on a stray piece of wooden debris, he looked the image of a weak and timid man, desperate to preserve his life.

A large body of water washed over, swallowing him whole as it plunged him into the sea below. Emmanuel struggled to keep himself afloat as he braved the violent waters. He closed his eyes with a tightness, whimpering as he clung to the debris until the skin around his arm went raw. He prayed to whatever universal essence would listen to and allow him to survive the flood.

Eventually, the waves calmed. Much to his surprise, his pleas and prayers were heard. Perhaps the universe was not completely and utterly cruel.

Overwhelmed with relief, Emmanuel swam back up to the surface, making his way back to the safe dryness of shore. But what he was met with onshore put a hamper on his relief. He looked around him in awe to see the previously flooded Magnae seem to dry up instantaneously, leaving behind charred, barren lands where sandy beaches and vibrant jungles used to be.

Emmanuel rose, still covered in dirty water, coughing and spluttering on the floor. He looked across the barren land he had stumbled upon and saw an interesting-looking man.

The man's skin had an unearthly glow to it. One that at first glance would not raise any alarms, but upon further inspection, was blatantly inhuman. The man was dressed in golden silk in contrast to Emmanuel's grey-tattered tunic. The gold of his cloak matched the aura surrounding this beautiful alien abomination.

"The Divinity," Emmanuel whispered, his voice shaking in fearful recognition. Crippled with fear, he clutched his chest, his heart beating at an inhuman pace. It was just his luck that the one being he wished to see the least happened to be the first one he came across after having his life saved. He backed away and made a panicked run for it before he could be seen.

Emmanuel ran away from the barren shore and towards the mainland of his nation. Or at least, what was left of it. Not a single building or structure was left standing. His home village of Polarven had been decimated.

Oddly, Emmanuel was impressed at how easily this post-medieval land had been destroyed to the point of resembling an ancient prehistoric one. He could count on one hand the amount of other human beings he saw alive. Like him, they either choked and spluttered on blood-soaked seawater or wandered around, minds frayed and wondrous at the sight of their desecrated mainland.

"What's happened to everyone?" he muttered to himself. He continued to trudge through the land, cold, hungry, thirsty, tired, and defeated. As he walked past dozens and dozens of trampled villages, he stumbled upon an area that remained intact and thus piqued his interest. A cave, with a trail of water leaking from the darkness.

Emmanuel walked through the cave, so dark that one could barely make out the rock crevices that surrounded them. He followed the trail of glowing water until he reached the end of the cave, where he was met with a sparkling pool of water within a deep crater on the rocky floor.

He gasped with excitement and rushed towards it. He cupped his hands, using them to shovel water into his mouth and onto his face. The water helped to wash him clean and quench his dying thirst. He splashed more of it upwards, smacking his face and filling his mouth. Before he could fully satisfy his thirst, Emmanuel stopped his shovelling.

He froze, beginning to feel an odd sensation throughout his body. The sensation made his skin itchy and irritant, prompting desperate scratching. As Emmanuel scratched, all parts of his body that the water had touched corroded his skin lightly.

4

Emmanuel winced in pain, but this pain was soon replaced by an even stranger sensation. A sensation of immense power within himself. Emmanuel looked at his arms, which grew heavily scarred but bulging with muscle.

"What?" Emmanuel whispered as he observed his newly charred and powered body.

"You're forbidden from doing that," said a voice from behind him.

He turned to see The Divinity, who looked at him in deep shame. For a split second, he forgot about what he had just experienced, reverting to shaking with fear as he looked at the divinity. He backed away from the godly figure, quivering.

"This world has received enough punishment," stated The Divinity. "Do not make matters worse."

Emmanuel gulped down a heavy lump in his throat as he stared at The Divinity in awe. A silent tension filled the crisp cave air. He dropped to his knees to beg for forgiveness, but on his way down, he noticed what was in front of him. On the left hand of The Divinity, there was a small scar. Upon taking sight of the scar on The Divinity's hand, something seemed to change within him. He looked at the scar, then looked back at his arms. His expression changed from one of fear to one of stoic resolve.

Emmanuel stood back on his feet, much to The Divinity's surprise. He confronted the fauxangel with hatred in his eyes. This one simple act of standing up would go on to become the most important event in Planet Magnae's history. One that would be retold again and again, decade after decade.

***

A century passed after this event. In a tall, weathered building, a room full of people dressed in dark crimson leather and metal-adorned military wear were positively thrilled at the chance to hear another retelling of this story. These beautiful young recruits sat eagerly on wooden stools, surrounded by walls decorated with charred golden weaponry. They listened to one of their leaders read from a book titled - The History of Emmanuel Ekib.

"...And when Emmanuel Ekib saw that cut on The Divinity's crude alien hand, that was the day that mankind realised-"

"That false gods can die!" shouted a particularly excited male recruit, pumping his fist in the air. The other recruits laughed at and cheered for the assertion. The interrupted leader with the book seemed less than amused, prompting the recruit to sit back down in shame.

"That was the day mankind realised we were no longer at the mercy of our so-called angels," said the leader. "The day we found out The Divinity could be hurt and so could his peers. The day we were no longer at the mercy of their cruel judgement, for we had developed the ability to fight back. Now tell me, war recruits. Do you plan to waste this ability?"

A female recruit bursting with passion leapt out of her seat, slapped her left hand against her heart, and used her right hand to salute.

"No, we don't, sir!" she exclaimed. The officer slammed his book shut and looked at her and the other recruits with a sense of pride.

"You're fucking right, you don't!" he exclaimed back. The recruits rose from their seats in a series of incomprehensible patriotic jeers and chants. Once again, Ekib's story had invigorated them into action.

***

Moments later, twenty of these recruits, whether they be soldiers, medics, tacticians, or scavengers, stood in front of a huge wooden door at the front of the stone building. Most were equipped with knives, axes, and blades alike and looked desperate to use them.

The wooden doors opened, allowing them to sprawl onto an enclosed, makeshift battlefield – charred, barren land with only wooden stock boxes and stacked piles of bags of raw meat to use as cover. Waiting for them on the battlefield were a group of forty or so older and rougher-looking degenerates, equipped with large dull blades. The soldiers of the group descended upon them with knives and swords, their blades encased in a fiery energy. The two groups of fighters wasted no time in ruthlessly hacking and slashing at each other.

Standing on the balcony of the grand stone building were a series of leaders from this military branch, overlooking the recruits. The most focused of them was Keith Best, aka The Head Foreseer, a large, bald, muscular yet pot-bellied, domineering man of over fifty.

The Head stood sternly as he watched the battles that took place. He turned around to look at his subordinates, only to be irritated at the fact that the other Foreseers were not as focused on the battles as he was. At the time, Planet Magnae was in such a dire state that he and his ilk of military men and women were the closest thing humanity had to a world government. Or any kind of organised leadership.

The door leading onto the balcony burst open, and through it came the second most important man of this branch. Alexander Lang, The Vice Foreseer. Lang was a slender, dark-haired, and eloquent-seeming man of well over forty, though he did not look a day past twenty-five. As the Vice Foreseer joined The Head and the others, he was followed by a short, scrawny man in an old lab coat.

The Vice Foreseer greeted the other Foreseers with a hearty handshake and then directed his attention towards his leader. "Evening, sir," he said as he and the Head shook hands.

"Evening," The Head greeted back.

"How are the recruits doing against the prisoners?"

"Very good. They seem more ferocious than ever. I think they'll benefit from a continued increase in training regime intensity."

The Head Foreseer glanced over to the scrawny man who accompanied the Vice Foreseer. He furrowed his thick eyebrows at him.

"And who do I have the pleasure of meeting?"

"This is Doctor Smethwick," introduced The Vice Foreseer. "He's going to be working with us for a short while, helping to make sure that the recruits stay at peak human strength. He wants to study them first before he gets to work."

"I'm mostly interested in seeing the top ten recruits as soon as possible," added Doctor Smethwick.

"You came at the right time. Our top twenty is training right now," said The Head, gesturing down at the recruits fighting the prisoners. "And there goes one of our top ten."

The three men looked towards a young woman with curly jet-black hair on the battlefield. A honed scavenger, the second a prisoner had his body gored with a blade of fire, she collected every spare item he had, from cigarettes to knives, looting all she could off of the body almost as fast as it hit the ground.

"She's top ten quality?" Smethwick asked with uncertainty.

"Just about," said The Head. "Not as talented as most, but works five times as hard. That's why we call her Queen Triumph."

The Head Foreseer pointed towards a group of recruits fighting on the other side of the field.

A large brute of a man threw his much smaller comrade far across the battlefield, the short and stout man launching towards an unfortunate prisoner. The last thing he saw was two knives plunging straight into his eyes.

Two recruits could be seen a short distance away from them. One sank a poison-covered knife into a prisoner, and the other used a spear to cut and slash another.

"Those are recruits nine to six. Soldiers and scouts. Ageless, Bone Ripper, Slow Poison, and Spirit Crusher."

"Interesting nicknames," muttered the Doctor. "What am I working with in terms of a Top Five?"

A malevolent smirk came across the Head Foreseer's face. He nodded downwards to the heart of the battlefield.

"That's number five, *Silent Memoir*. Quiet yet brutal. You can't take your eyes off a soldier like him for even a second."

A prisoner stumbled over a bag of raw meat on the edge of a battlefield in a desperate attempt to escape. He heard something rustling near him, but when he turned around, nothing could be seen. Suddenly, his right leg was slashed, seemingly out of thin air. Then his torso, then his arm, then his throat. As he dropped dead to the floor, a pale brunette stood over him - Silent Memoir himself.

"That fine young woman over there is number four, *First Ranger*. Doesn't engage directly in the combat, but she's a great leader with remarkable intuition."

The doctor looked to see the tall, tanned, and stoic First Ranger organising other recruits on the battlefield. Upon her instructions, they flanked a large group of prisoners, overwhelming and immobilising them. The doctor nodded, impressed.

"Over there is *Heart Stealer*. When he's not busy being a womanising fuckup, he's being one of the best warriors I've seen in a while. Which is why he's number three."

On the battlefield, the strikingly tall and dashingly handsome Heart Stealer took on three prisoners on his own. They cut and slashed at him, but he dodged all of their attacks with a swift fluidity, then returned cuts of his own with his miniature axe, efficiently taking them all out.

From a ledge of stacked crates above Heart Stealer, a spry young woman jumped down onto the red-sand thoroughfare with fists full of gauze. She ran through the battlefield, attending to any of the wounded soldiers she came across. In a matter of twenty seconds, she managed to wrap up the wounds of four injured soldiers without breaking a sweat or making a mistake.

"Number two, right on cue. They call her *Recruit Infinity*. She's like an engine. An endless supply of stamina. A very rare talent when it comes to medics."

"Oh my," gasped the Doctor. "If that's your number two, I'd love to see your number one."

The Foreseer pointed right into the very middle of the battlefield. Right there was a dark-skinned young fighter with short afro hair, the infamous Dagim Chibuike. Two inches below average in height but well above average in muscle mass, Dagim wielded a sword heavy enough to need two men to lift it. A sword lathered in a thick corrosive gel of energy and layered over with the purest flames engulfing the blade to an inch above the hilt. He used this impressive feat of Planet Magnae blade science to completely separate a prisoner's torso from his legs in a gruesome display of his strength.

"There he is. Dagim Chibuike, our number one recruit." The Head introduced proudly. As he said this, Dagim cut across three more prisoners with one heavy swing, spreading fire and blood through the general vicinity. Then, through two more with another wild parry with energy residues flicking off the blade and burning into the ground below. A prisoner cried as he tried to run away from him. Dagim grabbed him by the shoulder, spun him around, and impaled him on his sword. He lifted his sword and the man to the sky with one hand, then ripped his body off the blade with another. He dumped the body onto the ever-growing pile of prisoners beside him.

"We call him Puer Diablo, or as he's more commonly known - *Devil Child*," The Head said with malicious excitement. The doctor watched Dagim continue to rampage through the battlefield in horror and intrigue.

"So-, so…so *he* will be the one to receive the Ultimatum Source when the time comes. Correct?" asked the doctor, nervous beyond reasonable measure.

"Correct. He's been the top recruit for a while. He deserves it," confirmed The Head. "He'll be the one who destroys those damned alien tyrants once and for all."

The doctor nodded, unable to take his eyes off Dagim, frightened yet delighted by the prospect of this recruit consuming the Ultimatum Source. The Vice Foreseer, however, seemed uneasy when he heard the Head say this. He looked down at Dagim, who was charging around with a psychotic smile on his face.

The Vice shook his head and sighed.

II. DEVIL CHILD

DAGIM Chibuike only loved one thing more than the energy he felt during a fight. The energy amongst his ranks after returning from one.

The *Puer Diablo* burst into the recruit dining room with the pompous swagger of a galaxy-conquering demigod. Like most other rooms within the confines of that weathered branch building, the stone walls vibrated with the same fiery energy that covered the recruit blades, decorated with medals and paintings of Magnae soldiers past.

Filling the room were the shouts of many recruits hustling around mossy tables as they celebrated another brutally successful training yard massacre. Dagim pounced atop one of these tables, addressing his comrades with passionate shouts louder than their own.

"Freedom, power, strength, life! All things we greatly desire, all things we greatly possess, but not to the extent that we deserve!" Dagim bellowed at the top of his lungs. "But once this is all said and done, we will have taken them wholly by blood and by force!"

The recruits clapped and cheered, galvanised by the sentiments that poured out of him.

"May those nasty other-worldly creatures pray to their mothers. Because once we are done with them, their disgusting devotion to their alien ideals is all they will have left!"

Another bout of patriotic cheers came from the recruits who raised their drink to Dagim. He hummed a quiet tune.

"Droregen de simvi par vrey! Droregen de simvi par voo!" sang Dagim, praising the strength of humanity and their fearlessness in the face of adversity in Magnae Second Tongue.

"Droregen de simvi par vree! Droregen di mas eh vel schru!" the recruits sang back, singing about how what he said was the truth and that adversity would only make them stronger.

Dagim clapped his hands and danced on the table as the entire room continued to sing in their planet's second tongue. As the recruits danced and cheered with him, one of them moved her way to the front of the crowd. The bright, bubbly, and red-haired Roisin Indermill, aka Recruit Infinity.

Roisin took centre stage in front of the table that Dagim stood on. She cleared her throat, taking her turn to address the crowd.

"Also, whilst we're all here, I want to remind you of the gala event we're having later this week. Tell your townspeople and make sure you're all there," she informed them. Some of the recruits groaned at her announcement. "And try to wear something nice. You don't want to look scruffy on what could potentially be the last time you're seen by the public."

"Anything for you, Roisin!" shouted one of the female recruits. People in the crowd laughed, causing Roisin to blush and chuckle. The recruits soon went back to drinking their drinks and singing their songs.

***

13

Later, Roisin sat at a table with Dagim, who devoured a plate of meat. The two greeted each other with smiles.

"You did well out in the fields today," she complimented. "I saw you cut down three at once."

"Funny, because you were fixing some of our own so fast, I barely saw you at all!" Dagim quipped. "How do you maintain that for so fucking long? You have an iron lung you never told anyone about?"

Roisin's rosy cheeks grew rosier as she smirked from the flattery. "Everyone has their talents."

She looked across the table to see the two other recruits sitting opposite them. One of them was a large, burly man absentmindedly eating a particularly chewy piece of meat. The other was the pale, slim, and melancholic-looking Stefan Machin, aka Silent Memoir. Stefan stared down at his plate, a glossy yet lifeless look in his eyes.

"Stefan, are you coming to the gala?" asked Roisin. He gave her a stifled nod in place of a verbal response. A response the male recruit next to him seemed aggrieved by.

"You just gonna ignore someone when they are talking to you?" he asked. Stefan tilted his head towards the recruit. He fixed his eyes on him in a discomforting manner.

The male recruit became frustrated, shoving Stefan by the shoulder. In response, Stefan unsheathed his knife and stabbed it into the table. The blade landed in between the fingers of the recruit, cutting his ring finger slightly. The recruit grabbed Stefan by the collar, threatening to beat him.

"Break it up. Now," Dagim ordered.

"He's the one making people uncomfortable. It's not my fault this cunt won't talk!" the aggressive recruit shouted.

"It's not the cunt's fault he *can't* talk," Dagim said.
The recruit looked back at Stefan, who blinked slowly and lethargically. He took his hands off him.

"Sorry," the recruit grunted.

Stefan shook his head, using this as his cue to leave the table. Dagim sighed, focusing back on his dinner, chowing down aggressively as he listened to the disgruntled recruit awkwardly grumbling in the background.

***

After evening dinner, Dagim walked through the chipped metal corridors of the recruit dorms. The Devil Child saw himself surrounded by his comrades who drunkenly stumbled by him. Acoustic strumming and beating drum tunes played through the air as the sound of partying recruits threatened to burst his eardrums.

He paid no attention to them and their festivities, looking towards one of the large posters nailed to the wall instead. The one scroll that captured his attention stated the effects of *The Ultimatum Source* in Magnae Second Tongue. Dagim read the scroll attentively, attempting to cram all the information at once.

"Oi! Dagim!" he heard a voice call him.

He looked around him to see Hugo Stacey, aka Heart Stealer, standing in front of a random door room with both of his arms around the shoulders of two giddy female recruits who stood to the side of him. The tall, dirty-blonde recruit had a shit-eating grin plastered across his drunken, smug, yet handsome face. Another recruit came out of the room to stand behind Hugo, proving to be as giggly and scantily clad as Hugo's other girls.

"Evening, Hugo," Dagim said.

"There he is! The Devil Child himself! In the flesh!" Hugo exclaimed with glee.

"Are you having a good night, Hugo?"

"A very good night! A very good night indeed."

Hugo looked towards the girls and raised his eyebrows at them suggestively. Two of them giggled at him, though the third rolled her eyes and pushed him away playfully. She gestured at the other two to come back to the room, the three of them leaving Hugo to talk with Dagim.

"As much as I'd like to, I don't think I can handle all three of them on my own," Hugo chuckled, giving Dagim the same suggestive look.

"I'm sure you'll manage," Dagim scoffed.

"Come on, man, those girls want to see the Devil Child's true fire."

"I'd love to. But my mind is elsewhere at the moment," Dagim said. Hugo noticed the poster he was staring at, a sly smirk on his face.

"The Ultimatum Source!" Hugo marvelled. "You'll have the strength of ten men as opposed to your usual five. How do you think you'll use it when you receive it?"

"I don't know," Dagim said. "But I know whatever powers it'll give me, they'll be fucking special."

Hugo watched as Dagim's eyes were intensely focused on the text. He could hear heavy, excited breaths escaping from his nostrils. He smirked.

"That's what I love about you, Dagim!" Heart Stealer said. "The raw energy! Can't wait to see it in action once we get on a *real* battlefield."

Dagim nodded, continuing to read the writings over and over. As the two recruits looked at the scroll, they were being observed around the corner by another recruit. Frederica Rasmussen, aka First Ranger, peered from around the corner, sending a piercing glare towards Dagim. Her perfectly sculpted eyebrows hung over two dark, smoky eyes which shot envious daggers at the back of Dagim's head. As far as Frederica thought, neither Dagim nor Hugo were aware of her watching them. But Dagim knew. She did it so often that he could sense it.

"Let her watch," he thought, scoffing in his head.

***

Dagim did not blame Frederica. He, too, was one for eavesdropping on the conversations of those superior to him. Earlier that day, he had overheard a discussion between the Foreseers with his ear to the outer walls of their meeting rooms. It was forbidden for recruits to even walk down the corridors that led to the meeting room, never mind stand outside the door and listen in. But Dagim found himself curious enough to flout these rules. What he heard interested him more than anything.

"How are the Westfield Gambit battle plans looking?" the Head Foreseer had asked.

"Pretty good if you ask me, I had one of the top recruits familiarise herself with it and adapt the plan to suit the strengths of her team on the battlefield," Dagim heard the deep and measured voice of Foreseer III respond. Dagim assumed he was talking about the plans Frederica helped formulate. She did have her uses, even he would have admitted so.

"Suit their strengths on the battlefield," scoffed The Head.

"Is there something wrong, sir?" asked Foreseer III. Dagim heard The Head Foreseer slam his hand on the table, with great force, as if Foreseer III had said something wrong. A silence took up the room for a few seconds before The Head spoke again.

"These kids have never been on a real battlefield before, they have no strengths on it to 'suit'!" exclaimed The Head Foreseer.

"Don't you think our soldiers are skilled enough?"

17

"They *are* skilled enough. One of the best recruit classes we've ever seen. But they not only lack the mentality for it but an appreciation for why we fight," The Head explained. "They've never even seen what the enemy is truly capable of. Only a small portion of them have fought a real fauxangel. Hell, if it weren't for the inconvenience of age, I'd have us on the battlefield instead."

Another silence took up the room. Then, one of the Foreseers cleared their throat to speak. "Forgive me, sir, but I believe you are mistaken," Dagim heard the weathered voice of Foreseer IV cautiously utter. "We have the most passionate group of recruits yet, but that's hardly an issue. These young men and women have been hardened by the death and destruction that comes with facing those prisoners day in and day out. They are ready."

"Really? Is that why I see them jumping and dancing all over the fucking place after every training battle? Is that why they drink like fish and fuck like rabbits daily?" protested The Head Foreseer, his exclamations silencing his subordinates. "As far as I'm concerned, anyone who is enthusiastic when faced with the prospect of death in battle may be too naive to engage in it."

Dagim listened to another few moments of silence, the Foreseers rescinding any arguments immediately. He waited until the next person talked, and it was the Head again.

"Any soldier worth their salt can kill a bunch of rapists, murderers, and thieves in a controlled training environment," scoffed The Head. "It takes a true fighter to go up against *real* alien menace. To engage in combat against The Divinity's fauxangels themselves."

"Yes, you're right, sir," Foreseer IV agreed.

"I hope to hell I'm not, actually," said The Head. "For all of our sakes."

With that, the conversation was over. Dagim rushed to evacuate the premises before he was caught eavesdropping. Ever since he heard that conversation that afternoon, it stuck with him. What he heard had infuriated him to no end. Did The Head not think that they were capable of fighting this war? Was that how he behaved now, celebrating them to their faces but denying their worth as soldiers behind closed doors? Did The Head think that little of them? Did The Head think so little of *him*? Surely not.

Whether he did think that or not, Dagim was prepared to prove him wrong. He *did* understand what they were fighting for, and he was ready to face The Divinity and his fauxangels. He was more than willing to kill any alien threat, no matter how powerful and godly they may be.

He was the Devil Child after all.

III. TO FORESEE

NOT one day went by where Quinn Trepanier, aka Queen Triumph, did not work herself to the bone. Though like the other female recruits, she did not fight in battle, she still trained much harder than most who did. The Magnae Forces' top scavenger worked herself as if she were competing for Dagim's spot at the top of the ranks. From as early as five o'clock, she spent her mornings in the training room, beating at an old bag hanging from the ceiling. She beat away at it, a few paces in front of the blade-fire replenishment station and a few paces behind the standard weightlifting station. Her body was soaked with floods of sweat as the skin on her knuckles peeled and bled.

Two hours later, Frederica entered the room to see her hard at work. Quinn paused her intense session to greet her with a nod. "Frederica."

"Good morning, Quinn," she greeted her back. "You're here even earlier than usual."

Frederica stationed herself and her sack of training equipment on a wooden bench across from Quinn. She stood back up and stretched her leg in an unorthodox manner, pressing her left big toe on the floor and twisting her calves and thighs around. Quinn gazed at her muscular legs in envy before snapping herself out of it.

"Of course. I have to, if I want to remain a top ten recruit," Quinn said. "I don't know what I will do if I get dropped."

"Ego can't handle being number eleven?" Frederica asked.

"Pockets can't handle it," Quinn corrected. "The extra pay fucking helps."

"I'd be more concerned about whether your *body* can handle this, Quinn. Overworking's real."

"Well, it's better than underworking, isn't it?"

Frederica stopped her stretching with an abrupt planted foot. She jutted out her left leg, twisting it around and flexing the muscles as her gaze locked in on Quinn. "You should focus on working smarter instead of harder. Instead of focusing on a million powerful combinations…"

Frederica delivered a swinging roundhouse kick to the bag, fast enough to startle Quinn, who jumped as the bag swung back her way. "...you should consider focusing on only a few efficient training techniques."

Quinn watched as the punching bag continued to swing back and forth wildly. She was surprised by how violently Frederica was able to cause the bag to swing with such a powerful yet low-effort strike.

"I'm not sure if that makes much sense, but you're six spots ahead of me for a reason," she said with a smirk.

"Mhm," Frederica agreed, her face as stoic and expressionless as usual.

***

The two girls engaged in an early silent training session for the next hour and a half. At eight-thirty, the rest of the top ten recruits showed up on time for training to begin. As the rest of the recruits poured into the room, they all took up different positions.

21

Dagim, Hugo, and Bone Ripper walked their way over to the weight training area. By this point, Quinn was doing crunches in the corner next to Frederica, who worked on her sickle with a whetstone as she sat by the benches at the energy flame station. Once it had sharpened, she placed the tip of the sickle inside a red-hot slit of a hole in the stone bannister beside her.

Bone Ripper picked up a large kettlebell made of stone and swung it back and forth, impressing the two. Though at six-foot-seven and two-hundred and fifty pounds, it was far from the most impressive thing any of them had seen him do.

"If only you were as pretty as you are strong," Hugo joked. Dagim laughed.

Quinn groaned. She never found Hugo funny. She never found him all too interesting either, so she could not understand why so many of the other female recruits fawned over him. Though that might have been a lie on her part. She could somewhat understand, he was incredibly good-looking, she had to admit. Aside from that, she could not stand to be around Hugo. The way he was always trying to crack jokes and show off irritated her, and he was too cocky and flashy. How a person like that could be seven spots ahead of her and the second-best soldier in the entire branch was what she truly did not understand.

Bone Ripper grunted at Hugo's remark whilst Dagim laughed. Frederica looked over to them and scoffed. Dagim noticed this and walked to join her. He nodded to greet her, but she did not return the gesture. Quinn sighed. Not a day went by where those two did not subtly butt heads in one way or another.

"Sickle. Strange choice of weapon," Dagim commented. "Especially for someone who isn't a soldier."

"A little more nuanced than a giant fuck-off sword, isn't it?" Frederica responded. Dagim let out a condescending laugh. His smile showed camaraderie, but his eyes told a different story.

"I should get to sharpening my giant fuck-off sword, shouldn't I? Need to stay number one," he said. Frederica sighed under her breath as she glared at him through the corner of her eye. She returned to preparing her sickle. Dagim sneered as he looked down at her.

Quinn knew what went on between them. Frederica did not like that Dagim held the top spot and did not think he deserved it, and Dagim did not like the fact that she thought this. Quinn did not get why Frederica would have any frustrations regarding this. Who cared if Frederica was not the top recruit destined to utilise The Ultimatum Source? She should have been grateful that she had a firm place in the top five recruits. Unlike Quinn.

***

In the evening, Quinn looked like a completely different woman. Her skin glistened, though not from sweat this time. She shone with the pampered glow of the green silk dress she wore. Her curly black hair was twisted to perfection, and her green eyes popped even more than usual. She walked with brisk confidence as she entered the grand hall of the Magnae Forces' Main Building.

Foreseers, soldiers, and civilians alike occupied the marble floors and white-cloaked tables of the room, dressed to the nines for a black-tie event. Children played with random pieces of cutlery, dressed in their poorly fitted suits, whilst the adults discussed with the Foreseers and the elderly enjoyed their food quietly at their tables. The three scores of men and women in this room were amongst the richest and most free of the humans on Magnae, most of whom funded

23

their military operations through construction, cloth manufacturing, and food production enterprises. Yet even their fine suits and dresses were tattered at the seams and littered with holes. Even they had struggles.

The recruits sat on uncomfortable yet stylish oak benches lined in the other half of the room as they drank together. Quinn saw Dagim sit with Hugo and Roisin on a bench opposite Frederica and Stefan.

As Quinn approached them, her face scrunched as she saw Hugo. Not just because it was Hugo, but because he had reached into his blazer and brought out a small glass container with a severed finger in it.

"Hugo, you can't bring that out here! Put it away!" Roisin reprimanded.

"What on Magnae is that?" asked Frederica. "Is it-"

"A finger? Yes," answered Hugo. "The latest of the tokens I've collected from prisoner kills."

"Maybe instead of heart, they should call you *Pinkie Stealer*," Dagim mocked. Roisin and Stefan snickered. Hugo rolled his eyes.

"Whatever, it's my thing," he said with a shrug. "Imagine all the much cooler shit I can take from those glowing alien fiends once we slay them all."

Frederica rolled her eyes away from Hugo in disgust. She directed her attention to Quinn, who sat down next to her on the bench.

"Alright, guys?" Quinn greeted as she looked over what everyone was wearing. The boys all wore suits. Dagim's was baggy around the legs, Stefan's was poorly fitted around the arms, but Hugo's was tailored despite it being worn out, naturally. Like her, Roisin and Frederica wore silk dresses, Roisin's pink, and Frederica's black. Roisin looked like a stunning picture in her dress. Frederica also looked good, but it was clear from her body language and the sour expression on her face that she hated being dressed this way.

"Alright," Dagim greeted her.

"Oh, hey, Quinn!" Roisin said, chipper as ever, with a wave to match. Quinn waved back at her and the others. The only person not to greet her with a hello, a wave or even a simple nod was Hugo. He had been laughing ever since she arrived at the benches.

"What's so funny?" demanded Quinn, already frustrated before she even heard the answer.

"Oh, nothing, just your presence," Hugo chuckled.

"What? What the fuck does that even mean?" she asked.

"Pay attention to your surroundings, you're the only person sitting here who isn't a top-five recruit," Hugo pointed out. Quinn looked around. He was right. She hated that he was right.

"So?" scoffed Quinn. It was clear she was more bothered by his assessment than she liked to let on.

"So, leave?" suggested Hugo, tapping her shoe with his. Quinn's tense jaw gaped open at Hugo's candid command. Her eyes narrowed into a glare. Hugo laughed at her expression as the others watched awkwardly.

"Don't you ever talk down to me like that! I'm still a top-ten recruit!" Quinn shouted down at him.

She knew good and well that Hugo intentionally said things like this to push her buttons, but oftentimes, she could not stop herself from reacting.

"Last time I checked, the top ten isn't quite the top five," Hugo said.

"You won't let me sit here, but you let him?" Quinn protested, pointing a finger at Stefan. "He can't even talk!"

"Don't be like that, Quinn!" Roisin said. She looked over at Stefan, but saw the comment did not faze him. He simply stared ahead, unsure of how to respond to the situation.

"The difference is that he's good and you're not!" Hugo said. Quinn could feel her skin flush red and hot as the frustration built within her. She had reached her boiling point and assumed a fighting stance.

"You want to see who's good? Come over here and see who's fucking good!" Quinn challenged. Hugo looked at Dagim and laughed. Dagim shrugged, staying out of the confrontation.

"You scared?" goaded Quinn, fists raised and threatening to pound in Hugo's face. Hugo did not flinch, his smug smirk persisting.

"Yeah, I'm scared," Hugo said. "Scared I'll accidentally beat you within an inch of your life because I'm rank number three and you're rank number ten, soon to be eleven because you're shit-"

Quinn refused to let him finish his tirade, swinging a punch at his face. The blow never landed. Hugo stood up to dodge it, then used his leg to swipe at her feet. Quinn found herself knocked down to the ground and once again at the mercy of Hugo's mocking laughs. The others at the bench shared looks, wondering if anyone was going to step in and stop the oncoming fight. Dagim raised his hand to the others as if to say, "Let them finish."

Quinn launched herself back up to her feet at an alarming pace and delivered another punch to Hugo, this time connecting it with his face. The cocky blonde was surprised to see the blow hit him, stumbling over onto the floor in disorientation. Quinn jumped on top of him and started to strangle. The struggle between the two recruits soon gathered the unwanted attention from many of the folk of the gala, who watched on in judgment. The Head noticed the reaction from the general crowd. He did not look happy.

Dagim and Roisin struggled to pry Quinn off of Hugo before The Head Foreseer came over, but were unable to quell Quinn's wrath. Frederica and Stefan joined in, but even with their help, they could barely get Quinn to release Hugo from the chokehold.

The Head Foreseer marched his way over to the situation. With one powerful glare from his steely blue eyes, he made Quinn unhand Hugo and climb off of him. Quinn made eye contact with the Head Foreseer's furious stare. Behind him, she saw many of the gala's affluent yet poorly-clothed attendees looking on at her in shame. Quinn felt butterflies twist in her stomach as the shame of how she was acting finally dawned on her.

With haste, she left the gala and exited the building.

***

Later that night, Quinn could still feel the embarrassment from her outburst at the gala. She tried not to think about it, instead choosing to concern her mind with taking care of the other kids of Iqra House. She was sitting on the cluttered, dirty-carpeted, wooden-toy scattered floor living room of the orphanage, attempting to plait the hair of a restless young girl who sat in front of her. A series of erratic children ran past the two, laughing and screaming as they kicked the wooden toys about the room. Seeing this, the girl was eager to join in and ran away from Quinn mid-plait. Quinn sighed as she watched dozens of children run around the house like headless chickens.

A sweet, jet-black haired woman entered the living room, making sure to carefully avoid all of the racing kids. Iqra Frazier was used to kids rushing around her house like this. She took a seat on the floor next to Quinn.

27

"Would it kill her to stay still for five goddamn minutes?" Quinn complained to her.

"She reminds me of you at that age," Iqra said. Her face had grown wrinkled and folded up on itself, giving her a constant look of happy squinting eyes that accommodated her warm smile. Quinn smiled back. Iqra's happy, squinted eyes scoured around the walls of the foster home. They were a dull cream colour, dirty, moulded and peeling. Just the sight of her home's poor condition visibly upset her. Quinn noticed this, which in turn, visibly upset her.

"Don't worry, I'll receive my next payment at the end of the week. I'll get it all fixed," Quinn assured her.

"Are you sure you can?" asked Iqra. "I don't want you to waste all of your money on us."

"Shouldn't be a problem. "As long as I keep my rank, I'll have more than enough, so don't worry about that."

Iqra's warm smile returned to her face. She leaned down to cradle her head against Quinn's shoulder.

"When are you leaving to fight the fauxangels?" Iqra asked.

"We don't know yet, but probably soon. I can feel it," answered Quinn. Iqra nodded her head slowly as she stared into space. "Once we do, you won't see me until we've won. Until we've completely beaten the fauxangels for good."

Iqra's face grew worn with worry. "Please be safe," she said. "I don't know what we would do without you."

Quinn crossed her heart in an exaggerated manner, amusing Iqra. She spent the rest of the night caring for Iqra as the two sat with each other in the living room. Throughout the night, Quinn could not stop herself from looking at the scattered mess of the room around her. If only for the sake of Iqra House, she needed to keep her rank. She needed to stay useful to the Forces.

Aiza Armstrong did not look like a Foreseer. Whilst most of the other Foreseers were stuffy older men, she was a younger woman with a charming look about her. This, along with the blasé attitude she held towards her duties, made her rank the lowest at VII.

She had already suffered the boredom of sitting through a long Foreseer meeting the other day, and now she was faced with another one. She sat on a sturdy wooden chair adorned with studded metal along the sides and a golden slab on each armrest as she tucked herself and her chair closer towards the round table. There was not much else in terms of furniture in this dark, desolate room. There was not much in terms of company either. Sitting beside her on the table were most of the other Foreseers. She had the misfortune of sitting next to Foreseer IV, the stuffiest of them all, though she also sat next to Foreseer III, a tall, rugged and messy-haired brute of a man and a sight for sore eyes. Sitting across from her was Foreseer VI, the only other woman on the council. Though with her gruff, masculine demeanour, towering height, and low voice, she fit in better with the men than Aiza ever could. Next to her was Foreseer V, an unremarkable entity of a man. Neither the Head Foreseer nor The Vice Foreseer was at the table yet. The others had been at the table for over half an hour, so Aiza wondered what the hold-up could be. In the meantime, the other Foreseers discussed with each other.

The Vice Foreseer entered the room, but The Head did not follow. Aiza had suspicions regarding this meeting already. With no sign of The Head, the other Foreseers continued their discussion even though the Vice had made his presence known, and it was customary to stop talking when done so. Aiza found this interesting.

29

The Vice loudly cleared his throat to talk, but still the conversations continued. It took a brash clapping of his hands to quieten everyone down and draw attention towards him. With everyone sitting down and quiet, The Vice gestured at a man to come inside the room.

A tall man in a long sky-grey cloak entered the room with a tiny glass knife in his hand. The Vice ordered him to shut the door firmly, to which he obliged.

"What's the meaning of this?" asked Foreseer V, looking at the cloaked man.

"You must all draw blood whilst in this sacred room," stated The Vice Foreseer. "Because what I am about to tell you cannot leave it."

As soon as the command left his mouth, he was met with distrustful eyes. But regardless of this, they all nodded in agreement. The cloaked man moved between each member of the table and granted them a small incision underneath each of their fingernails for blood to leak out in slight droplets. With every Foreseer cut, he left the room without another word. The Vice Foreseer wiped the blood from his fingertip across the table. With a faint mark of blood streaked across, he crossed his arms together and started the discussion.

"As you all know, Dagim Chibuike, aka Devil Child, is our top recruit by a considerable margin. Meaning that when the time comes, he will be the one to consume the power from the Ultimatum Source and help seal our victory," said The Vice. "This is a serious problem."

"That sounds like the exact opposite of a serious problem," scoffed Foreseer VI. The Vice Foreseer scowled at her as if what she had said constituted treason. She sat up in her chair, feeling the need to explain herself. "You're telling me you had us draw blood because you're worried that what might be one of our best soldiers ever is going to collect the power that may help us...win?"

"I agree with VI," said Foreseer IV. "Dagim is charismatic, patriotic, respectful of his superiors, and has an incredible fire within him. I can't think of a better recruit to receive it when the time comes."

"That 'incredible fire' is the exact reason I'm worried," said The Vice. "Do you know why he is called Puer Diablo? The Devil Child?"

"Because he's a ferocious fighter," answered Aiza. To her, it was an obvious question with an obvious answer. She had seen Dagim fight and kill prisoners in the battle yard. There was nothing angelic about the way he operated. The Vice laughed at her, however, as if she had just said something ridiculous, though she could not yet see why.

"I meant the real reason. Does anyone know?" asked The Vice. The room went silent. Through the silence, the Vice Foreseer waited to see if anyone was about to answer. When no one did, he answered it himself.

"When going through the potential recruits years ago, The Head Foreseer and I were reluctant to take Dagim on. For on the day of his birth, his mother died, and his father was crippled in two separate events of misfortune," The Vice told them. The other Foreseers were made slightly uneasy upon hearing this. For once, Aiza paid attention during a Foreseer meeting.

"Not only did this child come into a world like this from unfortunate circumstances, it's always seemed like something was 'unhinged' inside him, even from an early age. Something we should be concerned about," The Vice stated.

"What are you suggesting?" asked Foreseer III. The Vice gulped as he stared deeply into his eyes.

"I don't feel safe granting exceptional amounts of strength to a person who carries this much negative energy about them," The Vice exasperated with gravity.

Aiza could no longer take the look on his face seriously and giggled. This directed the attention of the others towards her, especially The Vice and his exasperation. Now she would have to explain herself.

"He's a rowdy cunt who had a shit childhood!" laughed Aiza. "If we worried this much about every soldier who fit that description, we'd have no bloody recruits left!"

The other Foreseers laughed at Aiza's remark to her surprise and amusement. The Vice was not pleased by this in the slightest.

"You're telling me this does not seem a little contrived to you?! You don't think it's a coincidence that on that day we were gifted a soldier who on paper was seemingly perfect but was born and raised under dire circumstances?!" The Vice impugned. "Not a part of you worries this may be a gambit by the godly alien threat we fight? To place what would be our undoing right underneath our noses until the day it chooses to destroy us?"

The laughs that Aiza had prompted disappeared. She let out an awkward cough as she looked down at the table.

She had to admit that when he put it like that, it might be worth worrying about. But Aiza was not fully convinced. Surely, they had every reason to trust their top recruit with the power that would help them win the war against the fauxangels, right?

"I *do* see where you're coming from," accepted Foreseer VI. The other Foreseers seemed to be of the same tune.

"All I am saying is that this is nothing that we should take lightly. Agreed?" asked The Vice Foreseer. The others nodded in agreement, though somewhat unenthusiastically.

While Aiza nodded, she was still not convinced. Dagim Chibuike a threat to their war effort and the planet? To her, Devil Child was a blessing to the North Magnae Forces. But something told her to keep her thoughts to herself and go with the flow.

"Look under your fingernails and remember. I do not care if it's your wife, the godfather of your children, or the Head himself," The Vice told them all. "As far as everyone else is concerned, this discussion never happened."

IV. TYRIAN PURPLE

LIKE Dagim, Roisin loved being on the battlefield. Though for entirely different reasons. Whilst Dagim loved the thrill of battle and passion for fighting for a good cause, Roisin's enjoyment came from aiding in the care of those who did. It came from the fact that with every wrap of a bandage and injection of an antidote, she was helping the people of her planet, and to a greater extent, mankind in its entirety. Nothing swelled her heart more than knowing that Recruit Infinity was making a difference. But Roisin knew her days helping the people of Magnae would not last forever. They were numbered.

Roisin sat anxiously on a table in a dull, cramped doctor's office. Her eyes were fixated on the walls, where wooden shelves of medicine vials were situated. Though they acted as proof of the doctor's legitimacy, the sight of them made her nervous every time she visited. For a second, she wondered if it might have been a better idea to see the official Magnae branch doctor, Doctor Smethwick. But if she went to Doctor Smethwick, there was no doubt that word would spread amongst the ranks about her visits. She could not afford to let any of the Foreseers know about her visits here, not a chance. So, Doctor Curtis Shaw would have to make do.

The short, stubby doctor rifled through a disorganised drawer of items in a small cupboard in the corner of the room. No matter how stressed or anxious Roisin felt, she always giggled when she saw him doing that. He looked like a troll foraging for gold. From the cluttered pile of medical supplies, he retrieved a box container, one usually used for cigars. Doctor Shaw opened up the container, revealing a syringe of greenish-blue liquid. Roisin rolled up the sleeves to both arms of her Magnae Forces jacket, then braced herself. This was her fifth visit in five consecutive weeks. She knew the drill.

Doctor Shaw gave her a shot in her left bicep, then another in her right. Roisin's face scrunched and twisted something ugly upon receiving both shots. She stamped her foot on the floor multiple times to mitigate the pain, breathing in and out as she calmed the fits that came with it.

"Phew!" Roisin shouted, her foot slamming against the floor. Her twisted face relaxed, returning to its usual glow. Doctor Shaw raised his eyebrows at Roisin and shook his head. Roisin sighed. She could tell what he was about to bring up again.

"Are you still working with The North Magnae Forces?" he asked.

"Yes," sighed Roisin. Doctor Shaw pushed the bridge of his glasses, lowering them down as if to make sure Roisin saw the disappointment in his eyes clearer.

"I can't just stop. I'm needed now more than ever!" Roisin insisted.

Doctor Shaw did not seem all too swayed by this argument. "Roisin, if you continue to do this, your muscles will worsen. You could permanently lose the use of your arms," he stated. "Do you understand?"

Roisin looked down at the floor in shame and anger. She knew he was right to remind her, but that did not mean that she wanted to hear it.

"Well, that's why we have this special stuff," Roisin said, gesturing towards a large crate in the leftmost corner of the room labelled *R.I. Medicine*.

"That's true," sighed Doctor Shaw. "But there are limits to it. You have to rest. You have to stop working on the front lines, or you will suffer the consequences."

"That is simply not an option," Roisin asserted, putting her foot down figuratively and literally. "I'm the best medic on the field. I'm the second-best recruit. Hundreds of other recruits look up to me. The public is counting on me. I'm Recruit Infinity."

"And if you continue to be stubborn, your arms will deteriorate, and you will be nothing," Doctor Shaw warned her. He was not one to beat around the bush, something Roisin thought she would appreciate in her doctor. But at the moment, all he was doing was irritating her. She angrily rose from her seat, grabbed her crate of medicine and left Doctor Shaw to his rudimentary medical office.

***

When leaving Doctor Shaw's office, Roisin always made sure to take the long route back to the Magnae Forces Main Branch Building. Usually, she would trek past the land of this wheat farmer and then take the second main road out of the Balndan Settlement. Through that road, she could split off through a bush town and sneak into the back den of the training building at night and carry her crate to her room before anyone could spot her. During her long journey from the farm to the back den, Roisin would often lose herself in her thoughts. The journey was long enough to give her enough time to lament her existence and curse her arms and body for failing her, and get it out of her system so that she could return to the recruits with a smile on her face again. But tonight, Roisin would not get to delve into her thoughts. Her attention was preoccupied.

As Roisin crossed the path of the farmer's blood orange field, she saw the farmer by the matching red barn, a half-mile away from where she was walking. She watched the farmer try to lock up his barn, struggling to do so due to the rustiness of the lock. As usual. But what was not usual was the woman in a silk silver robe who emerged from within the wheat field. The regal-robed woman stood up lethargically and trudged her way towards the farmer, who still fiddled with the lock with his back turned. Roisin narrowed her eyes. For some reason, she felt she had seen this woman before, or at least someone like her. Curious, she watched on.

The silver-robed woman walked up to the back of the farmer until she was close enough for him to feel her breath on his neck. The farmer turned around, only just noticing her presence.

"Fuck me!" the farmer exclaimed, startled into a jump. He calmed down a little once he saw it was just a woman in a robe. "Can I help you, ma'am?"

The silver-robed woman did not answer him. A warm, charming smile crept across her face, but as the smile stretched, it reached inhuman levels of wideness. The farmer raised an eyebrow at her. A radiant glow buzzed through the top layer of the woman's skin as she pointed down to the ground below the farmer. It was with this action that Roisin finally realised why she recognised this woman. With a point of her finger, the fauxangel ignited the floor.

"No!" Roisin screamed as she watched the man burn down to an awful pile of corrupt flesh. The fauxangel smiled down at the burnt remains of the victim and then sprinted away from the scene. Roisin felt a piercing pain in her heart. She should have known. She should have known a fauxangel when she saw one. She beat herself up internally for having let that happen. She should not have let one kill someone in her presence so easily. Roisin rushed her way throughout the rest of her journey, desperate to get back to the main branch and inform the Foreseers. She assumed if one fauxangel made themselves known, then it was only a matter of time before others did. She was right.

As she rushed through the side fields of the Balndan Settlement, she was forced to watch as dozens more male and female fauxangels in long silver robes would burn down huts and murder civilians. Entire neighbourhoods were engulfed in flames from the fauxangel points and gestures.

Roisin's heart wept for all the villagers she found herself unable to save during her journey. She had considered listening to Doctor Shaw's advice, but that could no longer be the case. Not now, not ever. The people needed the Magnae Forces, and the forces were in dire need of Recruit Infinity.

***

An hour later, not only did all the Foreseers know about the fauxangels resurfacing, but the entire North Magnae Forces were already preparing to face them head-on. The Head Foreseer stood with the other Foreseers in a spacious, dark underground room carved out in a cave. Hundreds of recruits stood in front of them waiting for orders. Behind The Head was a man-made lake of water. It looked like the very same water Emmanuel Ekib had washed himself in a century prior, as depicted in their history books.

"Earlier this night, we received word of a dozen fauxangel sightings. Do you know what that means?" The Head asked rhetorically. "It means they have once again set foot on our plane. It's the end of a quiet period and the start of another fauxangel war!"

To the Vice Foreseer's surprise, the recruits held off on their usual jingoistic chants and listened to The Head.

"I don't care what you've done! I don't care what rank you are! I don't care what you've killed and how many of them! Know that you are not ready! Know that what you will be facing out there is nothing compared to anything you have seen, currently see, or will ever see in your entire fucking lives!" The Head bellowed. "Do you understand me?"

"Yes, sir!" the recruits shouted back in unison.

"All of you will be hurt, a lot of you will be crippled beyond repair, many of you will die, many more of you will wish you had died. But all of that means fuck all because you know you want to be on that battlefield more than anything. You're itching for it. I can feel the energy thumping through your passionate young hearts. You know you're going to go out there and show The Divinity he has no right to rule over this land the way he does. Right?!"

"Right, sir!"

"Right?!"

"Yes, sir!"

"Droregen de simvi par vrey!" The Head sang out with vigour.

"Droregen de simvi par vrey!" the recruits sang back, a choir of unbridled passion.

The Foreseers dispersed, allowing the recruits to come forth towards the lake of water. As opposed to the leather military jackets they wore in training, all the recruits were dressed in sturdy crimson armours of flexible metal protective gear. Each soldier unsheathed their weapon and formed into a line, waiting their turn to have them enhanced with fiery energy.

Roisin saw Dagim, who was first in line. He washed his sword in the water. The water enchanted the blade, damaging it on the surface yet hardening it with extra strength and power. She watched as Dagim placed his sword in its scabbard. He looked down into the shining light at the bottom of the lake, and there it was - The Ultimatum Source itself, a strange essence of magical glory that had once given Ekib the ability to fight back against The Divinity.

Consuming the source itself would no doubt give the wielder enough power to do what Ekib could not and finish The Divinity. But its power was so immense and fear-inspiring that it was kept as a fail-safe, only to be used by the top recruit in the direst moment of the war. That recruit would be Dagim.

Roisin saw the feverish look in Dagim's eyes as he looked down into the bottom of the lake. One day, he would have all that power to himself, so she could see how it excited him so much. She was glad it was Dagim of all the recruits who could have ended up at the top. Ever since they met as kids in Lagrogh Village, she saw the fire in his eyes and knew how much it burned in his heart. If there was a person she could trust to help them win this war, it was him.

***

After all the soldiers washed their weapons, they all charged out on foot, following The Head and The Foreseers as they bombed through the fields away from the branch building and towards the mainland.

"They're likely to show up in open spaces, the outskirts of settlements. Split up into the assigned areas and be careful when you engage the enemy," The Head said to the legions of recruits behind him. "Fifth and fourth squad will help me clear the area of any civilians and kill any fauxangels we come across. The third squad will set up traps. But be careful about it, it'll get dark very soon. Second and First squads are the only ones who should engage the enemy directly and follow Frederica's plan!"

Frederica remained stone-faced and focused on the road ahead of her with intensity.

"Does everyone know what they're doing? Is everyone familiar with the meet-up point?" asked The Head. He was met with a series of incomprehensible voicings of approval from all of the recruits. "Good. Let's go!"

Once they passed the farm, the recruits dispersed into five groups of twenty, ready to complete their tasks.

***

Frederica lay vigilant on a hill, overlooking a thick field of tall grass as crimson as her battle gear. She watched as her squad of soldiers, the figurehead of which being Hugo Stacey himself, all crouched as low as she had and slinked their way through the grasslands.

Frederica's measured stoic gaze morphed into a widened, panicked stare as she saw what lay ahead of them. Five fauxangels, silver-cloaked and golden-skinned, marched forward monotonously.

Flattening her body as she hid on her hillside location, Frederica's chest vibrated against the charred grass, her heartbeat reaching unprecedented rates of rapidity. She had gone over their attack plans at length and reiterated each clear instruction a dozen times over, yet a part of her feared that a concoction of panic and inexperience would have them forgetting every single one. She was about to see whether those fears were warranted.

The quintet of fauxangels marched further into the grasslands, closing in on the five soldiers' concealed positions. They walked with an air-headed grace about them, gentle winds blowing through their silky locks of hair.

41

Although they looked like taller, stronger, better-looking, and more evolved humans, from the way they behaved, one would assume they were lacking in agency. Especially from the way they walked without direction or purpose.

No matter how much they looked like humans, Frederica and any Magnae soldier worth their salt could identify those creatures from their gaits alone.

One of the five fauxangels shifted his vacant gaze over to a nearby tuft of ruffling grass. Before he could waltz over to inspect it, a human adversary lunged out of hiding, ready to enact the first step of Frederica's plan. With his blade reverberating with a quiet, potent energy surrounding it, one of Frederica's five performed his soldierly duties, dragging the searing hot blade across all five of their necks as he sprinted by them. Whilst this would have killed any human, not a single one of the fauxangels dropped dead.

The North Magnae soldier returned to his comrades amongst the tall grass, watching as all five fauxangel's opened necks leaked with their blood, a syrupy liquid that shone a tyrian purple. These thoughtless creatures simply touched at the rapidly healing wounds on their necks in unison. If their gaits were not proof enough of their lack of humanity, this certainly was. As they tapped at their healing necks, the same soldier who delivered the initial blow took advantage of their lack of awareness, picking one of them and continuing his attack. His blade burnt through this first fauxangel's neck, slashing it enough times to kill a human man three times over. His dozenth blow finally achieved its goal with the fauxangel's neck wounded too severely to heal as he became the first to fall to his death. The soldier rushed back to the rest of the squad following his successful attack. An attack that instilled a sense of urgency within these human-esque creatures.

42

As the second one of the fauxangels raised its finger, the soldier knew to sprint in the opposite direction with haste. The ground beneath him burst into flames as he narrowly escaped the fauxangel's conjured blistering attacks, avoiding scorching burns on his feet by a fraction of a second.

As the fauxangels pressed forward, Frederica's squadron made themselves known, rushing out of the bushes with the intent to kill. Of all of them, Hugo launched into the attack with the most excitement, believing it was his time to shine. He reached for the metallic projectile device on the side of his scabbard next to the left twin of his dual axe blades.

Known as a *Bronze Bullet*, the cylindrical device was the furthest development in Magnae weapon technology, allowing the soldier who wields it to shoot just one singular high-powered bullet at their enemy. The recruits were taught only to use this device in very rare emergency situations, though it was clear that Hugo had no respect for these rules. Heart Stealer pulled the trigger, impulsively firing his bullet through the skull of the first fauxangel he saw.

"Oh yeah!" Hugo screamed with pleasure as he watched the creature's head explode into a fleshy purple mess. Chunks of alien brain matter decorated the blades of grass.

"Those are for emergencies only," Frederica grumbled furiously, giving him a death glare from over the hill. She seethed at the fact that, had Hugo heard her grumbles, he probably would have dismissed her with a flippant quip such as, "It worked, didn't it?"

She was glad it did work. For his sake. With another fauxangel dead before further direct combat had even been attempted, Frederica raised her hand, giving a firing signal of her own. Fifteen more Magnae soldiers sprang up from alternate hiding places in different sections of the long red field. With burning steel in each of their hands, they closed in on the fauxangels, swarming them with a sea of fire as their human adversaries tripled in threat.

A minimum of three soldiers attacked one fauxangel at once. All but Hugo, who saw it fit to roam free. He abandoned his duties with blatant disregard, sinking his blade into whatever fauxangel he saw fit in a series of freestyle attacks up and down the fields.

"He's going to give me a fucking aneurysm," Frederica whispered through a hoarse voice and gritted teeth. For a second, it seemed Hugo's reckless divergence from pre-approved battle plans was bearing fruit. This did not last.

Hugo attempted to sever one of the fauxangels by the wrist but miserably failed. The fauxangel knocked Hugo's dual axes out of his hands and dropped him to the floor. It pointed to burn the floor beneath him, and he instinctively rolled out of the way. The male recruit who had been standing beside him, however, was not so lucky and was burned alive for his efforts. The recruit screamed in agony, horrifying Hugo. The cocky smirk his face once had was wiped clean. Strangely, Frederica was glad about this. It was about time he started to take all of this seriously. Yet again, that did not last. The frustration he elicited from her doubled as she saw him lying on the floor, yet to process his very recent failure.

"Get the fuck back up," Frederica demanded. Hugo awkwardly picked himself back up to his feet as if he could hear her. He fumbled about the battlefield as his fellow soldiers hacked and burned the swarmed fauxangels, spraying tyrian blood dozens of feet into the air.

One soldier found himself in a compromising situation, a fauxangel having knocked the blade out of his hand and forced its slimy gold fingers around his neck. Hugo rushed to his aid with a reinvigorated energy, only to be stopped dead in his tracks. The point of a fauxangel finger sent a wild burn to the grounds below him.

"Shit!" Hugo shrieked, jumping in fear as he dodged the bundle of flames. He threw himself to the side, his body slamming down hard. It sang with piercing pains, though was grateful it was not dancing in flames.

Hugo helplessly watched as the other recruits worked to finish off the rest of the fauxangels. Every part of him wanted to join in, but a newfound fear seemed to be freezing him in place. Frederica's anger at his incompetence had progressed to confusion and frustration, fighting for supremacy within her migraine-ridden head. What on Magnae was he doing? He was never like this on the battle yards.

Hugo looked to the left of him and saw a burnt soldier groan as they dropped to the floor. This only crippled him with further building fear.

***

A Magnae soldier finally managed to break through a fauxangel's neck with his blade, killing the final one. The squad collectively let out a sigh of relief. Thirteen of the twenty soldiers remained. A great number of soldiers were lost, but a successful battle by any measure. Even with Hugo's failings.

Suddenly, a man could be seen from afar. He held his hands behind his back and calmly stared at the group. They witnessed a rare sighting of The Divinity himself.

"No way," Frederica muttered, rising to her feet in awe. Never in her life had she seen The Divinity in the flesh. Never in her life had she wanted to. Against her better judgement, Frederica leapt down from her vantage point, falling over her own feet as she sprinted in a desperate attempt to reach her fellow recruits.

The recruits on the main battlefield shared blank, fretful looks. Not a single soul in crimson uniform knew how to proceed. Each pair of eyes lasered in on their fellow man in hopes of a plan being suggested by any of them. None had the answers they desperately sought.

The Divinity smiled. "Good evening."
Syphoning gusts from the air around them with golden energy, the head fauxangel surrounded himself in swirling winds as he conjured up an avatar of a giant pair of hands, prepared to deliver a backhand slap to be heard across the galaxy. Frederica arrived, metres away from the soldiers, as the hand of the false God prepared to strike them down.

"Ground! Now!" she gasped in a breathless order, being the first to follow her instructions. The remaining soldiers dove to the floor to avoid the crashing winds. Hugo, however, was still too frozen in fear to move. The North Magnae Forces' third-best recruit was smacked down by the hand as he came crashing to the floor. He was knocked out.

As the hand of 'God' swiped back and forth, the soldiers lay flat on the ground. Frederica turned around and attempted to use her bronze bullet to shoot The Divinity, but she missed by a long shot. Other soldiers followed her lead, only to face the same issue. Their efforts were hopeless.

"Back! Back!" Frederica shouted as she gestured at the others to retreat. The surviving members of the squadron obliged, scurrying away and escaping on all fours.

Frederica groaned as she lifted the unconscious Hugo onto her back, pushing herself to crawl away with his added weight. She looked back to see The Divinity. For reasons unknown to her, he was not following them or following up on his attack. He smirked to himself, staying put as he allowed their escape.

Frederica did not understand why he chose to do that.

But she was grateful that he did.

V. SIGN

STEFAN travelled back to camp early. As of that point in time, it was only a series of craft tents on a grassy hill that the Foreseers were just about finishing up with. He and his squad were forced to make a retreat from an impromptu battle with the fauxangels they found themselves up against. By the end of the battle, half of the squadron was dead or injured, only two fauxangels were killed, and Stefan had already made use of every single one of his throwing blades. Stefan wondered whether some of the other squadrons fared as hopelessly as his in their fights. He soon found his answer.

An overlapping collection of fervid jeers could be heard from afar. Stefan saw over the hill's horizon, where a dozen recruits returned from battle. They were led by Dagim, who raised his sword to the sky. Impaled on the sword were the mangled heads of two fauxangels. An old woman and a young man, stacked like a revolting shish-kebab with tyrian purple sauce. Dagim laughed menacingly as he waved about his fauxangel-decorated sword for all to see. Whilst some of the other recruits cheered him on, the Foreseers did not seem as pleased. Especially The Vice.

Stefan watched as the blood dripped down from the old fauxangel's decapitated head, trickled off of Dagim's sword, and landed on the floor in thick droplets. You would not think that such a crass and violent image would put a smile on Stefan's face. But it did. Because to him, that signified hope. Proof that their fight against the fauxangels would not be in vain. That hope was all they had nowadays.

"Sixteen kills may be much less than you are usually used to, but when it comes to the fauxangels, this is an impressive number for a first battle," The Head told the entire camp when they all returned from their battles. "This gives you more than enough time for relaxation, but in a few hours, you will have to get back out there. For now, you will take shifts patrolling areas of the land we marked on the map so we can figure out their next location. Those of you not on a shift can rest. Good job, everyone, and good luck moving forward."

***

Come night, the camp was properly set up with all the tents lined in a row across the hill as well as a stone structure. On the outskirts of the camp, Stefan joined Dagim, Roisin, Hugo, Frederica, and Quinn around a campfire. All their battles had taken place hours ago, and the recruits as a whole were still dejected, downtrodden, and despondent. Even Dagim, who by his display with the sword had won an emphatic victory, was low on energy. Their first taste of real war had left them tired and quiet, not a single word nor breath to be heard over the crackling fire.

"Oh, come on, guys, at least try not to look too down! We just had our first *real* victory!" Roisin said, breaking the silence. She was met with no response. No one else shared her enthusiasm.

"Cheer up, you lot! Think about what we'll be able to do when we win the war!" Roisin said. "Like my cousin, for example. She's been looking to start a family in the Capital Settlement. Once we've cleared the land of fauxangels, she can actually do that safely! What about you, Quinn? Got anything like that?"

49

"Uhm," muttered Quinn, like a student not expecting to get called on. "I guess when we're done with all this, I'll have more time to look after the kids at Iqra House."

"See? We have lots to be excited for!" Roisin beamed. "What about you, Stefan?"

Stefan reached into his jacket and brought out a rough piece of paper. He opened it to reveal a highly detailed pencil drawing of a beautiful young girl. His lovely Anais.

"Girlfriend?" Dagim asked. Stefan nodded proudly, a slight twinkle in his soft, brown eyes. The best girlfriend he could have ever asked for.

"Hugo, you're up next!" Roisin said. Stefan and the others turned to him. Hugo stared into the flames of the campfire, a shell-shocked expression about him. Not a single whisper left his mouth.

"Don't you have something cocky or smart-arse to say?" Quinn goaded, thinking about their fight at the gala.

Hugo continued to stare into the fire, not blinking or moving. The others looked at each other with concern. Stefan was aware of why Hugo was acting this way. Even though his squad had won a victory and killed all their fauxangels, Hugo had frozen up when he was needed the most.

Not only did he fail to do his part in helping them, but he passed out and had to be carried back to the camp by Frederica during their retreat.

"Since when did he become such a fucking liability?" Frederica had commented when their squad came back to camp. Stefan did not know, but it concerned him to see the usually arrogant Heart Stealer so stifled.

"Frederica?" Roisin asked, moving on from Hugo.

"I don't like discussing family and friends," said First Ranger.

Roisin nodded. "How about you, Dagim? Who from your family are you most excited about returning?"

"I don't have anyone from my family I still want to see. Anyone alive, that is," Dagim said. Roisin's jovial expression turned sour.

"Oh, well, what about friends from back in our neighbourhood?" asked Roisin.

Dagim shook his head and laughed.

"Nah, I don't keep in touch with any of them either," he said. Roisin's mouth twisted a little. She gave up on getting an answer from Dagim.

An awkward silence filled the air. Once again, all that could be heard was the crackling of the campfire.

"I don't need all of that anyway," Dagim added after a while. "Once we win this war, my life's purpose will be fulfilled, and I'm more than satisfied with that alone."

Roisin smirked at Dagim's sentiment. She rested her hand against the small of his back as the group returned to their silent fire-watching.

Stefan observed Dagim, whose thick eyebrows gave his wide eyes an intense flavour. Stefan enjoyed observing the other recruits, Dagim most of all. He was such an interesting character to him. In both a good and a bad way. There was always something going on.

As the fifth-highest-ranked recruit and a man with a skill for silence, Stefan would often spy on the recruits higher ranked than him to learn as much as he could. He did this with Dagim, especially, seeing as he was number one.

The next morning, Stefan would observe Dagim again through his tent. He sat on a log outside of one of the tall, pointy white craft tents around the corner. From this angle, he could watch whatever Dagim would be doing in his tent. An odd hobby of his, he would often have to admit to

51

himself, but one he could not help but keep on doing every chance he could. That day, he caught something strange.

Stefan saw Dagim venture into his tent early that morning, coming from a late-night battle. But an hour later, another figure went into Dagim's tent. A man in a black leather mask. Stefan sat up on his log to get a better look into Dagim's tent, and what he saw happened so fast and randomly that he could not believe it.

The man equipped a knife and charged towards a resting Dagim who lay on his tent's hammock. He pressed a knife against Dagim's neck. Dagim stopped it, but not before it drew blood, granting him a small cut. Dagim overpowered the man and pushed him off.

The man stumbled, then lunged forward at Dagim with the knife again. Dagim dodged two slashes but was brought down by a powerful push kick to the chest. He landed back on his bed, and the masked man approached him knife-first. As he went in for a stab, Dagim grabbed him by the wrist and twisted, spraining it. The masked man screamed in agony. He headbutted Dagim, who landed back down on the bed, disoriented.

With Dagim distracted, the masked man ditched the attack and escaped the tent. Confused and also a slight bit disoriented, Stefan reacted late, jumping up from his position.

"Fuck off!" the masked man shouted, barging Stefan over with all his might. Stefan fell, his body slamming against the log. He gasped with pain as he felt his kidney smack against the wood. By the time he gathered his bearings, the masked man was nowhere to be seen. Stefan looked back into Dagim's tent to see him still holding his head and reeling in pain from the headbutt. Someone had just tried to kill Dagim in front of Stefan's very eyes.

Stefan's eyes scoured around the campground. It was still too early for most people to be wandering about. So apart from him, no one saw what had just happened. He scratched his head in confusion. He resolved to keep a mental note of this event. It made no sense now, but he had a feeling it would become clear to him soon.

***

That afternoon, Stefan marched with a squad of soldiers throughout the abandoned village town centre. The area was empty, the brown buildings that occupied it having been scorched black and grey with burns. The fauxangels had made their mark there already.

The group marched down a cobbled road, eyes on high alert and weapons at the ready. Stefan always made sure to stay at the back of the group whenever he went on patrol missions with a squad. Not only to keep an eye on everyone and make sure that they were safe, but to make it easier to do what he was about to do.

Stefan distanced himself from the group slightly, trailing off and letting them walk ahead of him. As the rest of the squad walked down the cobbled square, he ventured down a road past a destroyed tavern.

He stepped inside the red-carpeted interior of an oak-polished worship building. He walked through the middle of two long rows of church benches and to the back towards an oak-carved drawing of The Divinity on the back wall. Another day, he had seen a series of cloaked spiritual cultists praying to it. A very strange set of individuals, to the point of being almost as inhuman as the fauxangels.

Stefan was not concerned about the imagery of The Divinity. He was only concerned about what was underneath it. Waiting for him by the back wall was a beautiful young woman, short of stature, pale of skin, dark of hair and

53

freckled of face. The young woman's smile lit up the entire room and left Stefan smirking and elated. He was delighted to see her. His lovely Anais.

When the two were close to each other, they embraced one another in a caressing hug, followed by a soft kiss. But as Anais pursued to turn the kissing into fondling, Stefan stopped her. He removed her hands from his body and shook his head. Anais scrunched her eyebrows at him, wondering what she had done wrong.

"We won't be able to keep doing this for much longer," he said to her in sign language. Stefan was not deaf, but Anais was. Having lost his ability to speak in his childhood, this was the only manner in which the two could communicate. "It won't be long until we have to move camp."

"So?" Anais signed back. "Then I will move also."

"I don't want to have to make you do that," Stefan signed, his hand movements slow and measured.

"And you won't, it will be my choice!" Anais signed back, her hand movements quicker and more exasperated. Stefan sighed.

"This is too dangerous, Anais."

"And you fighting against higher powers isn't?"
Stefan sighed again. Ever since he joined The North Magnae Forces, Anais had always had a problem with it. No matter how many times he reminded her of how good a soldier he was and how he was unlikely to die as gruesome a death as she thought he might, she never listened. She always remained immensely protective of him, something he both loved and loathed about her.

"I don't want you dying for a cause on behalf of people who don't understand you and who probably don't even treat you well," Anais signed. "If money is the issue, I will help you find a job where you are safe and respected. We'll figure it out together."

"I'm not being forced to do this," Stefan assured her, his hand movements were bold and definitive. "I enjoy it, I believe in it, and if I don't do it, *nowhere* on this planet will be safe."

Anais sighed and clasped her face in her hands. She latched onto Stefan and gave him a warm hug.

Stefan hated making her feel this way, but it had to be done. He wanted to do his part in helping the war effort against the fauxangels. Anais would have to live with that.

***

Hugo was always known as the Golden Boy of his hometown. The people of the prestigious town of Lantrusta would always brag about how Heart Stealer was one of their own. Ever since he was a young boy, he had a skill for anything physical. Sports, fighting, sword-showmanship. The people of Lantrusta had urged him to join the forces due to these skills. And so, he did. For most of his life, Hugo was glad that he had joined. Less out of a passion for fighting and a wish to defeat The Divinity and his fauxangels, and more because of the reputation it gave him.

When people heard that he had risen to the rank of the third-highest recruit in the most recent North Magnae Forces class, they showered him with praise and glory. Men considered it a privilege to train with him, and the women considered it a privilege to sleep with him. For Hugo, life after joining the Magnae Forces was heaven.

Going through these thoughts in light of recent events, Hugo could not help but feel like a fraud and a failure. His first taste of real war, and he had crumbled completely. He could not put his finger on why that had happened. One second, he was shooting the head off of a fauxangel with his bronze bullet and facing the others with bravery. The next second, he was crippled by fear just by seeing what they were capable of. Then, when The Divinity showed up, he got even worse. All he could remember was being knocked out cold by his energy winds and waking up hours later in camp. He saw the faces of the other members of his squad when he came back. When Frederica had gone on a tirade, cussing him out for being *ineffectual,* he did not even try to argue back to her. He felt like he deserved it. Apart from Frederica, the other recruits on that squad were not angry at him. If anything, they were more disappointed. But to him, that reaction was even worse.

Hugo tried not to let his failures in battle bother him as he marched towards one of the camp's craft tents for breakfast. He entered the white-cloaked enclosure to see many foreseers and recruits getting their morning food. With a plate of food in his hand, Dagim stood next to Ahmed Lal, aka Ageless and Brendon Rohlta, aka Bone Ripper, by the table with all the meat portions. Hugo joined them.

"Alright, Hugo!" Ageless chuffed as soon as he saw Hugo join them. Ageless was a strange-looking young man. He had the tanned, chiselled, handsome and very well-structured face of an imposing man, but the body of a short, lithe one. He looked quite the picture standing next to Bone Ripper, a beast of a man in every sense of the phrase. "You collect any new tokens from the enemy, Heart Stealer?"

"No, nothing like that, unfortunately," Hugo answered. It took all but two seconds for Ahmed to pick up on the fact that Hugo had lost his usually cocky demeanour. It took him no longer to realise this amused him.

"Oh yeah, I heard how you did with the others in the Fred squad," commented Ahmed. "Not a good look, mate."

"Yeah, I had some difficulties," Hugo said, shaking his head. Ahmed could barely contain his laughter.

"It's alright, Heart Stealer. Maybe not everyone's cut out to be a soldier, eh?" Ahmed chuckled, failing to contain his laughter. Brendon laughed along with him. Dagim did not laugh but let out a light scoff. Hugo's jaw tensed in the face of mockery. His sullen face morphed into a look of irritation. He latched onto Ahmed, grabbing him by the collar and lifting him.

"I'm still twice as good a soldier as you'll ever be. Never forget it," Hugo spat.

"Maybe back in training," Ahmed laughed. "But we're in a real war now. And so far, I can see you can't hack it."

Hugo's grip on Ageless' collar loosened, his face coloured with embarrassment. He tried to think of a rebuttal but came up short in terms of any responses. Hugo let go of Ahmed and dropped him back to the floor. He picked up his plate and buried his face in the meat portions for his breakfast. Hugo fixed up his plate and turned away from the mocking duo and towards Dagim.

"How are you doing, Dagim?" Hugo said. But Dagim did not hear him. He was not even looking in his general direction. Dagim's gaze was instead focused on the Foreseers, who all ate at the fruit and carbs table on the other side of the crafts tent.

Dagim's sights were specifically set on Foreseer IV, who discussed with The Head. Dagim noticed a bandage around Foreseer IV's wrist, the sight of which aggravated him greatly. His face scrunched with a constipated rage as if he was struggling to contain an immense amount of anger within him.

"You good?" Hugo asked. He placed a hand on Dagim's shoulder, to which the Devil Child immediately smacked off. "What's going on with you, Dagim?"

Dagim marched over to Foreseer IV and throttled at his neck. Hugo's mouth gaped open in surprise. That was the last thing Hugo expected him to do. That was the last thing anyone in the crafts tent expected Dagim to do.

VI. TUMULT AMONG RANKS

THE second-in-command Foreseer noticed the five-fingered vice the top soldier had around the neck of one of his closest subordinates. He threw down his plate and marched to the situation.

"Unhand him right now!" The Vice Foreseer ordered. Dagim continued to strangle Foreseer IV regardless.

"Devil Child! Compose yourself this instant!" ordered The Head Foreseer. Dagim did not listen, strangling Foreseer IV even harder. Foreseer IV choked, struggling to pry his hands off his neck. He looked into Dagim's eyes, which were widened and bloodshot with fury. The Head and Vice Foreseer jumped into action, tearing Dagim off Foreseer IV by force. Dagim grunted with the wild anger of a rabid dog as he pushed both Foreseers away from him.

"What is wrong with you?!" The Vice Foreseer asked.

"What is wrong with me?! What is wrong with him?!" exclaimed Dagim, pointing a finger at Foreseer IV. "He tried to kill me in my sleep this morning!"

The Head Foreseer darted towards Foreseer IV in shock. All the other soldiers who occupied the tents turned to observe the scene Dagim had just created.

"What is he talking about?" asked The Head.

"He tried to kill me in my sleep!" Dagim repeated.

"And what reason would I have to do that?!" asked Foreseer IV, disgusted by the accusation.

"He snuck into my tent during my sleeping shift wearing a mask!" Dagim accused. "He tried to cut me up but wasn't good enough to finish the job, explaining *this*."

Dagim pointed towards the bandage on his wrist. The Vice Foreseer's eyes shifted anxiously.

"This is from when I injured myself whilst clearing the Raynor Forests of fauxangels. Any squad can vouch for me being there," explained Foreseer IV. "This is a serious allegation and one I do not take lightly."

"Raynor Forests. That sounds about right," said the Head Foreseer. "Why would you think it was him? It could have been a thief or a prisoner who snuck onto the camp?"

The Head Foreseer looked at Dagim sternly, but his glare remained fixated on Foreseer IV. His breath was hot with anger. The Head shook his head.

"I don't have the time to deal with this bullshit!" he shouted at Dagim and Foreseer IV. "We'll figure this out later. We have work to do now."

The Head Foreseer walked back to the crafts table to eat his meat and carb-heavy breakfast. Dagim's glare remained on Foreseer IV, who left to walk out of the tent with The Vice Foreseer.

"What the hell was all that about?" Hugo asked Dagim. Dagim gave Hugo one look and scoffed. He left the tent. Hugo shrugged. Perhaps he would find out later. He had other things to worry about. Like what Ahmed had said about him. Was he right? Could Hugo not hack it? Could the infamously cocksure Heart Stealer not back it up when it came to real battle? He had to wonder.

When the Magnae Forces fought on the battle yards during training, Hugo prided himself on how well he could kill prisoners. Apart from Dagim, he had the highest battle yard criminal kill count. He always left a training session with his axe blades blood-soaked and his body itching to fight some more. So why, after he faced the fauxangels, did he leave with his axes clean and his body dreading the thought of going back out to fight? What would the people of Lantrusta think if they knew how pathetically he performed? What would Magnae think as a whole? Hugo feared he might have lost his edge. He assured himself he had not. His actions told a different story.

***

Hugo sat on a log outside his tent, fretting from morning to afternoon. He was only pulled out of his train of wrecked thought when Foreseer III approached him with a stern look on his face.

"We believe there might be a fauxangel congregation in a settlement a few miles from here," Foreseer III told him. "Meet at the rover. We're leaving in twenty."

Hugo nodded in response to the order. Only a few moments after Foreseer III left, the thought of going back to battle started to make Hugo queasy again. His nerves got the best of him, his throat feeling thick and constricted, and his skin beading with sweat. He ran behind his sleeping tent and heaved into the grass below it, colouring it with the vomit of his meaty breakfast. He looked around to see if anyone saw him. No one else was close by. No one but Stefan. Hugo groaned once he saw the mute man's face. Stefan was always lurking around. Of course, he had to see him like this.

"You're not going to tell anyone about this if you know what's good for you," Hugo warned. Stefan did a "*My lips are sealed*" sign in response.

"Hilarious," Hugo grunted sarcastically, wiping the vomit from his lips. He could no longer deny it now. He had lost his edge.

***

Frederica was a dreamer, in both the figurative and literal sense of the word. Figuratively, Frederica was a visionary who, through her work in the North Magnae Forces, hoped to carve out a good future for humankind. In the literal sense, Frederica would often have odd dreams every night that would pain her mind. Her most recent one was the oddest of them all.

Frederica found herself within a golden palace. The shiny, polished interior of the castle was coloured silver and gold. The palace had the minimalist layout of godly regalness, a scarcity that both added to the beauty and gave credence to a godly figure's lack of need for material possessions. Or that was Frederica's interpretation of the space, at least. The floors were carpeted by sheets of coated metal, and the walls were indented with carvings in alien languages. After observing the room, Frederica came to a realisation. She was not a tangible figure within this construct but a vague essence watching the palace from above like a deity. It made Frederica feel both powerful and insecure in her sense of being. She blinked and suddenly, a large, imposing throne of gold and marble appeared in the middle of the palace out of thin air. Upon the seat sat The Divinity. Frederica had always found the appearance of The Divinity morbidly marvellous. She was fascinated by how human he looked despite his gold-tinted skin, with his long brown hair and deep blue eyes.

Two of The Divinity's fauxangels, a strapping young man and a vibrant-essenced woman, had also transferred into the area from thin air. Both waited on The Divinity hand and foot, one of which fed him an odd golden paste and the other who warmed him with a light fire emitting from their hands. The food, the plating, the vibe of the room, the expression on the fauxangel faces, even the way The Divinity chewed - everything about this scene was immensely fascinating to Frederica. For a moment, she forgot she was in a dream and felt as if she was truly observing their godly enemy himself at his most intimate.

The Divinity stared at the floor. He was sombre, chewing and blinking slowly, flattening the gold paste with a lack of energy as if he were automated.

"We lost sixteen today," sighed The Divinity. "The humans may very well win this war."

"Worry not, my divine. They may outnumber us, but they don't even begin to compare when it comes to power," said the female fauxangel as she warmed her lord's feet.

"Do not underestimate them," warned The Divinity. "They have an unquenchable spirit about them, especially when they believe what they are doing is right."

"I've always envied their passion for life," sighed the female fauxangel. She, too, looked like one who could easily be mistaken for a human. With her frizzy light brown hair, Frederica was quick to notice how much she resembled her late aunt. The species of the fauxangels intrigued Frederica to no end, especially with their many similarities to humans. Frederica hoped to learn all about them one day.

"And their innovation," The Divinity continued. "Trust humans to find a way to replenish the ancient lakes of the cave. Our forces are struggling against those weapons."

The Divinity waved away the male fauxangel who was feeding him the golden paste. The fauxangel drew the plate of gold away from his lord, bowed, and left the room. The Divinity gestured at the female fauxangel to sit on his lap.

She did so with glee, playing with his silky brown hair. The Divinity sighed.

"We wouldn't have to fight if humans understood even half of what we do," he complained to her as she met his hair with more comforting touches. "Judgement is necessary. It's our duty to guide them. It's their duty to obey. But they refuse our control at every turn."

The female fauxangel nodded in agreement as she patted him on the head. Frederica found these sentiments curious. Was this how The Divinity truly felt? That his actions were not only righteous but an act of endearment towards humanity? It was a common thought amongst humans that this was just what fauxangels used as an excuse to cause carnage. Emmanuel Ekib had every right to start the fight back against The Divinity. The Magnae Forces had every right to continue it.

"But no. They've been relentless from the very moment they became capable of hurting us. They completely lost any semblance of honour. Like a bastard child disobeying his mother when he sees that his father doesn't respect her," The Divinity spat with vitriol.

"Do not worry, they will learn in time," the female fauxangel assured him. "They refused to allow us to do so gently, so we shall continue to do so forcefully."

Frederica could not recall what happened in the dream past that point. But what she had seen and heard concerned her. She always had realistic-seeming dreams, but never one so vivid. Despite all logic pointing against it, a small part of her was convinced that the events she had dreamed may have actually happened.

***

The wave of worry and concern that Frederica's odd dreams gave her was enough to cripple her for an extra hour every morning. But after these feelings subsided, they would be replaced by a need to work to the best of her ability.

Frederica spent the morning within the dark enclosure of the most secluded war tent on their campsite.

She sat hunched over a wooden table in the tent. Using a dip pen, she scribbled onto a sheet of paper titled *CONTINGENCIES*. If her dreams were trying to tell her anything, she assumed that it must be that their efforts against The Divinity were weighing on his mind and forces. Meaning they ought to multiply their efforts and attack.

An hour into her contingency writing session, Frederica was joined within the tent by The Vice Foreseer. Frederica's perpetually stoic expression broke, her face beaming with delight as she set her eyes on him. Whenever the Vice greeted her with a smile and wave of his, it was as if something cold within Frederica melted for a moment.

"Oh, hello, sir! How are you this morning?" Frederica greeted, swivelling her body to face him properly.

"I'm fine, thank you for asking," said The Vice. "What are you working on?"

"Oh, it's nothing," Frederica downplayed with a nervous chuckle. "I was just thinking of safety plans in case The Divinity decides to gather enough energy power to flood the world again. Bunker reinforcement plans and stuff like that. Better to be safe than sorry, you know?"

"Very true," The Vice said, smiling at Frederica. He nodded his head, then pointed a measured finger in her face.

"You see, this is what I've always liked about you, Frederica. You consider the factors that others don't. Your intelligently proactive nature never fails to amaze me," The Vice Foreseer complimented her. Frederica's dark, tanned face blushed a bright red. She looked downwards, stifling a smile. She did not wish for The Vice to notice how pleased his approval made her, but there was no hiding it.

"But it also makes me wonder. Why are you stuck at rank number four? Why not number one?" asked The Vice Foreseer.

Frederica's smile dropped from her face like a ton of golden bricks. Bringing up that topic of discussion was a sure-fire way to dampen First Ranger's mood.

"I ask myself the same thing. I work hard, I come up with the battle plans, I lead effectively," she said to him. "I suppose if I were a front-line soldier or an ace medic, I'd deserve the higher rank."

"I don't believe that. And I don't think you do either," said The Vice Foreseer.

Taken aback, Frederica's eyes darted up from the floor and into his. She had always thought that. That she deserved to be the top recruit. That she would be more suited to Dagim's position. That damned arrogant Devil Child whom she wished she could tear off his pedestal. This was the first time that anyone had ever said it out loud, including her.

"It should be you who receives the Ultimatum Source when the time comes," said The Vice Foreseer, impassioned. "If we let that reckless animal Dagim receive the ultimate power, he may very easily win the war. But what he'll do with it afterwards will destroy us."

Frederica nodded, enamoured. She could not agree more. Dagim was the ultimate soldier, that much she could admit. But he did not have the temperament to be a wielder of power even greater than Ekib once had. She saw him as impulsive, reckless, too bloodthirsty, unable to compose himself, and too quick to anger. Frederica was convinced that if Dagim wielded ultimate power, Magnae would be doomed.

Something in the back of her mind told her she needed to do something about him. She did not know what.

"If there's a recruit who can win this war and save us all, it's you," stated The Vice. "Wouldn't you agree?"

"I haven't agreed with anything more in my life!" Frederica blurted, embarrassed by how quickly it came out. The Vice smiled.

"Good, because we can kill two birds with one stone," he said. "I can guarantee you the spot as the top recruit, but only if Dagim is removed from the equation."

Frederica stared into space, a face plastered with consideration, breathing out of her nose. Dagim out of the equation? Did that mean what she thought it might?

"Just something for you to consider," The Vice Foreseer added, noting her apprehension.

"Alright," Frederica said. The Vice exited the tent, leaving Frederica to her thoughts. She struggled to compose herself, rapidly tapping her pen against the table.

***

"Dagim out of the equation?" Frederica still pondered to herself quietly, late into the afternoon. She wandered around camp, thinking. There was no way The Vice Foreseer was genuinely suggesting she kill him. But if that was not what he meant, then what was? The whole situation puzzled Frederica to no end. What if he *did* mean that he wanted her to kill Dagim? Would that be the right thing to do? The fact that she was even considering it worried Frederica. But perhaps she had to. How else could Dagim be taken out of the equation?

Speak of the devil, Dagim returned to the camp on foot, with tyrian blood on his sword once again. Tired and out of breath, he walked past Frederica in the camp. Dagim took a seat on a log across from where Frederica was standing. He

67

reached for a cloth behind the log and used it to wipe fauxangel blood from his sword. As Dagim cleaned his sword, he was approached by The Head Foreseer. Usually, Frederica hated how thrilled The Head seemed to be in Dagim's presence. But today, Frederica noticed a different energy about him as the two men came face to face.

"Successful battle?" asked The Head. Dagim nodded with exhaustion. "Good. Come with me."

Dagim followed The Head Foreseer, who marched towards the front of the camp where a stone structure had been built. There, all the other Foreseers stood. Frederica's gut told her that something bad was about to happen.

The Head Foreseer reached into the crate behind him and picked up a sword and shield. He clanged them together to get the soldiers' attention. The clattering of the blade and shield alerted many of the recruits who wandered around the camp. The Head Foreseer continued to smash the metal weapons against each other until every single recruit who was currently at the campsite gathered into a crowd.

"Pay attention! Now!" screamed The Head. The entire camp looked towards their leader, who, within a moment's notice, had entered a state of rage that seemed all too random. Not a single pair of eyes drifted away from him, especially Dagim, who looked him up and down in confusion. The Head Foreseer glared at Dagim. He nodded at the other Foreseers. The Vice Foreseer and Foreseer IV grabbed a hold of him and put him down on his knees.

"What are you doing?!" Dagim exclaimed. Frederica's eyebrows furrowed, wondering the same thing. But no one answered the question. Dagim attempted to struggle out of their grasp, but they restrained him.

Without prior warning, The Head sent a powerful kick straight to Dagim's stomach, shocking the other soldiers.

Dagim grunted something fierce, keeling over only for The Head to kick him again.

"This is a lesson in respect and humility!" The Head shouted at the other recruits. He continued to belt Dagim's stomach with kicks of fury to the point where Dagim started to cough up blood. Frederica's mouth gaped open slightly. The other recruits could hardly believe what they were seeing.

An outraged Roisin and Hugo had moved to the front of the crowd to come to Dagim's aid, but were stopped in their tracks by one glare from The Head. "Get back in line. The lesson isn't over yet," he ordered.

The Head kicked Dagim in the side and swiftly turned to face the crowd of soldiers.

"This man, one of your *comrades*, had the utter gall to not only physically attack, but also accuse one of your Foreseers of attempted murder. And with not a shred of proof to his claims!" The Head chastised, kicking Dagim again. As they held him in place, The Vice and Foreseer IV looked down at Dagim, not a morsel of remorse on their faces.

"This is a man I trust with my life. A man I trust with your lives," said The Head, gesturing to Foreseer IV. "The last thing I need is some insolent shit sowing seeds of doubt within my ranks in the middle of a war!"

The Head crouched down next to Dagim and stared him in the eyes. Dagim grimaced.

"You think because you're number one, you can accuse who you want and attack who you please?" The Head asked him. "Have some fucking respect!"

The Head kicked Dagim a final time, this blow being stronger than the others, causing him to spit up more blood. He stormed away, followed by the other Foreseers.

Dagim dropped to the floor and squirmed in pain. Roisin, Hugo, Stefan, and Quinn all rushed to his aid. Frederica remained idle.

"Oh my! I can't believe he did that!" cried Roisin. The group helped Dagim get back on his feet as he grunted heavily.

"What was that even about? Who tried to kill you?" asked Quinn. Dagim refused to answer, pushing his mates away from him. He growled in anger and hobbled away. The four exchanged perplexed looks with each other.

What she had just seen made a mark on Frederica. It made her feel compelled to take some sort of action. But she was not sure what she was to do. All that she was sure of was that she could no longer pretend she did not know what The Vice was asking of her.

She knew exactly what he required.

VII. DIABOLUS

DEVIL Child sat on his bed with a pensive glare focused on nothing in particular. The potent heat of pure anger radiated off of Dagim to the point of palpability. The pain from the Head Foreseer's beating mixed with the shame of the spectacle that was made out of it infuriated him enough to burst a blood vessel. He held his sword as he pierced it into the wilting scarlet grass below him. His grip tightened until his inner palm matched it in colour. Every instinct in his body told him to pull the sword out of the dirt, march into the Foreseer's tent and cut every single one of them from belly to brain. It was what they deserved. How dare they try to kill him and condemn him for defending himself? Dagim wanted to make them rue the day they ever decided to trifle with him, but now was not the best time to do so. Now, he could only complain to himself.

A ball of energy formed out of thin air within the confines of Dagim's tent, capturing his attention. The energy took hold of Dagim's eyes, preventing him from looking away despite his efforts to do so. Through it, he saw a female fauxangel emerge. The godly creature presented itself to the Devil Child, shocking him to his core.

This fauxangel appeared different to others. Instead of glowing, her skin had a dark aura around it, and instead of standing, she floated. Everything about this fauxangel was otherworldly, aside from its frizzy light brown hair. Dagim stood up for a better glance at the fauxangel. As he looked her up and down, she smiled.

"You didn't look too good out there. Are you okay?" the special fauxangel asked him. Dagim was too shocked to respond. "Look at the way you're treated here, despite all that you do. How sad. My heart weeps for you, Devil Child."

Dagim narrowed his glare at the fauxangel, sighing out of his nose. He picked up his sword and assumed a fighting stance.

"Don't try that," warned the special fauxangel. "Unlike your Foreseers, I will succeed in killing you."

"Kill me? How do you know they want to kill me?" Dagim asked.

"I know many things. I'm a very learned woman."

"Then do you know *why* they want to kill me?"

"Dagim, I can't talk to you if you keep waving that sword in my face."

"Do you know why they want to kill me?!" Dagim repeated angrily. The special fauxangel laughed.

"Because you're the Devil Child," the fauxangel told him. "They believe you to be cursed. They don't trust you with the Ultimatum Source, and they'd rather get rid of you than take any chances."

"I find that hard to believe," Dagim scoffed at her.

"Your mother died after your birth. Your father was crippled and blinded on the same day," said the fauxangel. "Maybe not a curse per se, but at the very least, a concerning set of circumstances for their best soldier."

Dagim's grip on his sword loosened. For a brief second, he defrosted a slight bit. She might have been a fauxangel, but what she was saying was not exactly far-fetched. Perhaps she might have been worth listening to.

"Ridiculous," Dagim scoffed, attempting to push the notion out of his head.

"I know, you're not nearly as special as everyone treats you," she scoffed. "But there's someone here who is, and you're going to help in getting them to hear me out."

Dagim's face twisted with weary confusion. He had never felt this way before, so unsure, that is. What was going on right now? What was this fauxangel saying to him? How was he to respond to these claims and statements?

"And if I don't?" asked Dagim.

"Oh, nothing. You'll continue to stay here and risk the shame of being killed by your people," the fauxangel laughed at him. Dagim looked her up and down with a scowl.

"You think this is funny?" asked Dagim.

"Not at all. You can be of great help to us," she answered. Dagim blinked rather quickly, tightening his grip on his sword again. The fauxangel rolled her eyes. "Trust me, Dagim, I swear to The Divinity himself. It is in your best interest to help me. If you don't and stay with these humans, you are finished."

Dagim lowered his sword. He stared into the fauxangel's intoxicating eyes. They seemed to put him at ease, speaking to him in a way. He took a deep breath in, deciding what course of action he should take.

"I don't give a shit about what my Foreseers want to do with me!" Dagim asserted with fervour. "I don't fight for them, I fight for freedom! For power! I fight to protect the people of my planet from unholy alien creatures like you!"

Dagim lifted his sword with power and might. With a mighty swing, he launched his blade towards the fauxangel's neck, roaring all the while. The ball of energy returned, blinding him, and allowing her to escape before the blade reached her.

73

Dagim breathed out heavily as he placed his sword back in the dirt. He rubbed his hand against the back of his head. His body language and facial expression screamed uncertainty. Blood-curdling screams suddenly echoed through the camp.

"What the fuck is going on?" Dagim grunted with frustration, rushing out of the tent.

***

Dagim left his tent to see the soldiers being terrorised by two male fauxangels of a similar appearance to the special fauxangel he had just seen. Except their skin was dark, charred, and smoky, and they moved as if they were mindless. A series of soldiers attempted to attack the divine creatures but were killed when the fauxangels sent several burns underneath them.

Dozens of soldiers succumbed to the blue fire the special fauxangels conjured, to the horror of the soldiers who only narrowly escaped it. Dagim saw Foreseers helping up The Head, who suffered from burn marks on his left leg. From what The Head had done to him, he should have been happy to see him like this. But he was not. He was devastated.

The top recruits stood in a star formation with Frederica at the forefront, clasping her hands together.

"Soldiers! Maintain Marly formation one and attack in waves!" Frederica ordered. "Ready? Go!"

The top recruits charged at the two fauxangels, screaming passionately. They ran in an unorthodox manner, maintaining the star formation as they switched positions. The formation confused the fauxangels, who attempted to send several burns down their way. Two soldiers were burned down. The rest prevailed and engaged the fauxangels in combat.

74

Stefan and the series of recruits that surrounded him made efforts to sever the hand of one of the fauxangels with their blades, but were knocked aside by a powerful swing. The fauxangel floated out of the way of the next wave of recruits that attempted to attack him.

Hugo and two accompanying soldiers reached the second fauxangel, but he created a partition of fire on the floor, blocking them. The first soldier leapt over the partition and started a relentless cutting campaign. He was unable to break through his skin and was forced to retreat.

Dagim, still injured from his beating, ran into the action, but the pain surging through his body prevented him from charging all the way. He rested his body against his tent, cursing under his breath in Magnae Second Tongue.

The fauxangels floated higher into the air and distanced themselves from the recruits. They caused the floor to combust in random areas across the camp in a spread-out, blue-flamed attack. The soldiers panicked and dashed throughout the camp. A dozen were too slow and were burnt. Hugo hyperventilated as his legs buckled to the floor. He cradled his head in his hands.

"It's okay, you can hack it. It's okay, you can hack it. It's okay, you can hack it," Hugo whispered to prepare himself. Hugo picked himself back up from the floor and darted his way towards the nearest tent. He quickly returned with as many Bronze Bullets as he could find. He threw them on the floor to random recruits. Quinn snatched up one of the Bronze Bullets off the floor.

"Hugo, you're a lifesaver!" Quinn exclaimed.

"I am," muttered Hugo. Hugo began to look less panicked. He confidently stormed his way closer to the fauxangel and shot the Bronze Bullet at it.

The bullet spiralled towards the fauxangel at a blistering pace, zoning in for the kill. Yet the split second before it hit the fauxangel, it managed to catch it before it reached him, discarding the bullet as if it had posed no threat to him whatsoever. The panic returned to Hugo's face. He sprinted away from the battlefield.

The two fauxangels stood next to each other, back-to-back. They created a four-foot wall of blue fire to guard them, burning a great number of soldiers in the process. The other soldiers looked up at them, seemingly defeated until…

…Dagim powerfully leapt over the wall of fire, lunging himself towards one of the fauxangels with his sword in attack position.

"Die!" Dagim screamed at the fauxangel, disregarding any pain he had experienced.

The fauxangel caught Dagim by the neck and strangled him. Dagim's sword dropped to the floor. The other soldiers looked on in horror.

With incredible speed, Dagim reached to grab the Bronze Bullet he had tucked at the back of his tunic trousers. He pressed it against the fauxangel's head and shot it dead.

Both Dagim and the fauxangel dropped to the floor with a thud. The other fauxangel looked over to his dead comrade. They were distracted long enough for Roisin to shoot the fauxangel in the ribcage. As soon as the fauxangel dropped to the floor, many soldiers rushed to kill it, butchering it mercilessly with their blades.

Dagim lay on the floor, too tired to move, the pain from the beating still apparent. He turned his head to see the other soldiers tearing the organs out of the fauxangel's body. The sight of the suffering fauxangel amused Dagim to no end. He chuckled, which gradually turned into a maniacal laugh.

***

Hours later, soldiers and Foreseers alike made efforts to mitigate the destruction caused by the battle earlier. They built new tents and cleaned the grounds of the burnt bodies of dead soldiers. Dagim watched on as all the Foreseers did the brunt of the work. He did not move a single muscle. He had done enough for them today, especially considering how they treated him. The Head noticed and made his way towards him with a calmer disposition about him.

"You did good out there," complimented The Head. "If it weren't for your bravery, we could have been defeated in our very own camp."

"I know," Dagim said, glowering at him. The Head lifted his head upwards, glowering back.

"If you're waiting on an apology for what I did, you're going to be waiting a very long time," The Head asserted. "Things like that happen during times like these. Get over it and focus on your next task. Understood?"

"Understood," grunted Dagim. The Head grunted back at him, then turned his attention towards the other recruits in the camp. He made his way over to Hugo, who stood next to Quinn.

"Heart Stealer."

"Yes, sir?"

"I saw you run away from battle earlier," commented The Head. Despite Hugo being taller, it seemed like The Head was looking down on him purely from the disappointment he saw in his eyes. Hugo tried his damnedest to avoid eye contact with The Head's disappointed glare.

"Keep this shit up, and you'll be nowhere near rank three," The Head snarled down at him. "You'll be doing nothing but clean the land of fauxangel parts with the low-levels down South."

Hugo dropped his head in shame. Dagim knew how he felt. He was not happy with The Head at the moment, but he knew the pain of disappointing him.

Quinn turned towards the Head. "Well, whilst we have you here, there's something I want to discuss, I-"

Before Quinn could speak her mind, The Head pushed past her and walked away.

"Oh," Quinn said. "Guess I won't be discussing anything then."

"Looks like we're all on his bad side," Dagim grunted, walking away.

***

Even later, Frederica walked through the camp with a handful of the night's portions. She noticed Dagim sitting far from camp, distanced from everyone else. She walked over to Dagim, sneaking up behind him. She noticed his attention was focused on the stars.

Frederica slowly and quietly unsheathed her sickle. Unbeknownst to Dagim, she stood over him, like a predator prepared to attack its prey. Frederica paused. She heard the subtle crunch of stale grass. She turned around to see Stefan had snuck up behind her. He smiled at her.

She quickly placed her sickle back in its scabbard, the noise it made alerting Dagim, who turned around.

"Oh. What do you two want?" Dagim asked.

"Nothing, I was just leaving," Frederica said to him.
She left the two at a brisk pace. Dagim's eyes squinted at her suspiciously as she made her way back to camp. He shook his head as he watched her leave. Was she trying what he thought she was trying? The list of people within the North Magnae Forces that he could trust was shrinking by the day.

Stefan remained in the same space, staring blankly at Dagim. He nodded upwards at him. Stefan handed him a note he had written.

"Before the attack on the camp, I saw a burst of energy flash from within your tent. What was happening?" the note read. He peered back up at Stefan, who raised an eyebrow at him. He scratched his hair and sighed.

"Don't worry about it," Dagim told Stefan. "I'll tell you later."

Stefan gave him an understanding nod. Dagim appreciated this. Any other person, and he was sure they would either press him further directly or do so secretly. He crouched down to take a seat and joined Dagim to look over the dark evening horizon.

Considering he had a lot on his mind, He did not necessarily want company. But with Stefan silently by his side, he felt the quiet of being on your own coupled with the warm feeling of companionship that came with spending time with a brother in arms. The best of both worlds.

As Dagim looked over the horizon, he noticed a figure running towards them from afar. He tapped Stefan on the chest, gesturing the mute towards the figure. The two watched it run closer and closer, startled by its erratic movements.

Following the man over the hill came hundreds of other men and women. As they came closer, it was clear who they were. They were a series of fauxangels, led by none other than The Divinity himself. The pair looked to each other in fear as the legion approached, sprinting and chanting.

"Droregen de simvi," Dagim muttered to himself.

VIII. ARM OF GOD

THE soldiers of the farthest breached North Magnae Camp stood in the perilous presence of The Divinity and the thousands of fauxangels who outnumbered them in an intimidating show of force.

By the time Dagim and Stefan had rushed back to warn their comrades, the fauxangels had already arrived, swarming them from one side, as the faction that followed them swarmed the Magnae Forces from another. With soldiers still suffering from the earlier attack on the camp that wounded many, the forces of humanity could do nothing but stand there defensively as the fauxangels enclosed them from all angles. Any fight on their part was pointless. Their fate was in the hands of The Divinity and whatever his fauxangels were planning to do.

The Head Foreseer stood at the forefront, a brave foreboding stance in the face of the threat despite their hopelessness. Even his perpetually fearless expression twitched, a millimetre of uncertainty peeking through. Even he knew the situation was grim and highly unlikely to end well for him, the Foreseers, and most of all, the recruits.

He watched on helplessly as The Divinity floated down towards him, his consort of alien foot soldiers encircling them closer and closer until the two heads of the separate species and their humanoid armies were mere metres away from clashing.

"Head Foreseer, Keith Best," The Divinity said snidely.

"Head Prick, The Divinity," The Head Foreseer derided.

"I don't know if you've noticed, but you're heavily outnumbered," The Divinity chuckled.

The Head scoffed. "That hardly matters. Each of my soldiers is five times the fighter than any of the alien fodder in your ranks."

The Divinity laughed. "I wonder, would you sing the same tune if we all decided to attack you this very moment?"

The leader of the angelic extra-terrestrial army raised his finger, pointing it at The Head. The legions of fauxangels behind him followed suit, raising their fingers too. The soldiers of Magnae flinched in collective terror of the fauxangels sending a thousand burns their way. The human ranks bustled, almost collapsing into a stampede mess as each took a cautious step back.

The Divinity laughed again. He put his finger down, returning his arm to his side. All the fauxangels did the same, putting the nerves of their human opponents at ease.

"You'll be happy to know that my legions of holy fighters here do not plan on attacking you."

"What the hell does that mean?"

"This is nothing more than a show of force," The Divinity explained to The Head. "We want to show you how thoroughly you will be defeated once we carry out a proper attack in the near future."

The Head Foreseer's eyebrows crunched together, perplexed as could be. As The Divinity raised his finger once more, The Head and the Magnae Forces backed away, fearful of his actions in spite of his words. As opposed to the burning fire they anticipated, he conjured a blinding light to the side of the fauxangel army. Led by The Divinity, every fauxangel exited the area, using the blinding light as a portal. Once the last fauxangel had left through the portal, the light vanished without a trace.

A collective wave of relief washed through the area, cleaning all members of The North Magnae Forces of the stifling, helpless terror that had swallowed them up as a whole. Such terror was replaced with the same perplexion that marked The Head Foreseer's face throughout that entire interaction.

"What was the meaning of all that?" The Vice asked.

"I don't know," The Head grumbled with frustration. "I have no fucking clue."

***

Stefan sat himself on one of the hundreds of steel-plated seats that circled the outer perimeter of a very large room, scarcely lit by a solitary energy light fixed to the ceiling. This was a room Stefan did not know of before being seated next to Roisin in the final row. They were part of the last section of soldiers who had been urgently ushered in for an emergency forces meeting.

All soldiers in all their seats surrounded a bronze table in the exact centre of this brutalist room. Each Foreseer sat around this table as The Head spoke. This was the focal point of the room as the meeting droned on.

"And I'm not sure why The Divinity chose to threaten us with attacks to come rather than just attack. Let's just be glad that was all he did," said The Head as he continued his lecture to all who listened. "But we still shouldn't take the threat lightly."

Both the Foreseers and the recruits nodded in unison, The Head's cue to continue. "Failure to prepare is preparing to fail, as they say," he said. "Understand that we are no longer engaging the fauxangels in direct combat. Instead, we'll be using ancient guerrilla tactics. Take special note of the Underground Contingency Plans."

Each one of the recruits attended to the pen and paper before them, writing down what The Head suggested. Stefan, most of all. He sought to draw out the plans from memory as opposed to simply taking notes.

"Shit," Stefan heard Roisin wince under her breath. He turned to see her grinding her teeth as she used one arm to clench at the other, gripping nails into her pained flesh.

Stefan took up the pen and paper that lay on the sleek metal desk. He glanced at Roisin, who grunted in quiet pain as he wrote a message for her. He tapped her shoulder, showing it to her.

"Are you okay? Do you want me to take you to Doctor Smethwick after this?" Stefan's note asked. Roisin smiled.

"I'm fine, don't you worry about me, sweetheart," she assured him with her rosy-cheeked affability. He did not tell her, but he knew she was lying. That was the third time he had seen her wince and grasp at her arm that day.

A few more lectures were held, detailing the finer details of their plans moving forward. The full extent of their sneak attacks on the fauxangels and how they would conduct them was explained. Following its conclusion, the Foreseers left the room, followed by all of the recruits.

Stefan tucked the notes from the meeting into the breast compartment of his crimson battle wear, holding them close to his heart as he left the room last.

***

Before the first of their newly assigned *fauxangel sneak attack missions*, Stefan saw it fit to take on another solo excursion while he still had the chance. The fifth-ranked Magnae recruit sat with his legs crossed and eyes closed, surrounded by grass charred black and miscellaneous pieces of broken metal and wood. What was once the bustling marketplace of Vohdkaz Town was now a testament to the dangers of being attacked by fauxangels. He was the only lifeform in the area.

Sitting amongst the wreckage of his hometown calmed Stefan in a way most would not understand. Most other soldiers who came from parts of the planet that had been destroyed would refuse to talk of such places and would not dream of returning regularly. But Silent Memoir would spend all of his days in this part of the land if he could. Like most Magnae locations, the skies were so dark you could see the stars at noon. But in almost no other places did the stars shine so bright, their sight so vivid it seemed you could reach out and hold them. As Stefan opened his eyes to peek at the stars above, he felt as if he had been thrown out of the atmosphere and allowed to float through the cosmos.

Stefan surveyed his ruinous surroundings. He could not remember exactly where the house he grew up in would have been. Yet the memories were as vivid as the stars above. Most being of the constant trouble he would get himself into as a wayward child with no supervision.

He could see the women at the cloth vendors who, after purchasing a new dress, he would make awful comments about their looks until they ran away crying. Sometimes they would abandon their dresses, which he would sell back to the vendors and wait for another woman he could repeat the cycle with. He could see the old men walking to the wells to collect water, the same men he used to hurl blood-stained rocks and disparaging insults at for his amusement. He derived sadistic pleasure from watching them fall and injure themselves as they cursed him back. He could see markets of tenders he used to cheat out of money and swindle out of their food. At the time, he appreciated being able to feed himself without having to pay, even after said tender went out of business due to his actions. He could also see the exact place where a fauxangel had chosen to punish him for all of this unruly childhood behaviour.

"That glib tongue gets you into a lot of trouble, doesn't it?" the menacing fauxangel asked him that day. "Shall we fix that?"

When the fauxangel sent a burn to the surface of his tongue that day, Stefan thought he had been sentenced to die. Even with all the injuries he had sustained over years of being a top soldier, the most pain he had ever experienced in his life was the fauxangel's burn on his tongue. The pain did not kill him, but it did cripple him. For that was the day he lost his ability to speak forever.

At times, Stefan felt as if he deserved it. The civilians of Vohdkaz Town certainly felt that way, with those that he terrorised rejoicing at the depression his new disability had bestowed upon him.

If it were not for meeting Anais, he did not know how he would have coped. Like most Magnaeans, he saw The Divinity and the fauxangels as alien creatures posing as deities. In contrast, he saw Anais McIntosh, the love of his life, as an angelic deity posing as a normal human being. She was a deaf young woman similar to him in age who lived in the same town and was kind enough to teach him how to adjust to his new life as a speechless man. It was as if she were sent by the real God himself. She taught him to communicate without words and to find joy in being kind and loving. There was no one he appreciated more, no one he considered more responsible for making him a more honourable man.

Despite the damage done to his speech, Stefan was strangely glad it had happened. He thought it changed him for the better. Others did not understand that he honestly would not have liked his life to have gone any other way.

***

Roisin Indermill sat in the backseat of a rover, surrounded by a squadron of recruits. All the other recruits packed with her on the scarcely cushioned aluminium-built seats were soldiers, Hugo being the most familiar face she saw. Roisin was the only medic fit for such a mission.

Their next destination was a marshland, to conduct the first of many *ancient guerrilla* missions The Head had assigned. Roisin could hear the rickety mechanical mechanism that pulled the turning roll wheels of the vehicle squelch with moisture the further they travelled. She would not have been surprised had these wheels sunk into the ground before they even reached their hiding spot.

"Why do you keep grabbing at your arm?" Hugo asked Roisin. The question shocked, confused, and then shocked her again. She had not even been conscious of the fact that she was clasping it. His bringing it up had made her acutely and retroactively aware of how many times she had done so in just the last hour.

"What's wrong?"

Roisin's baby blue eyes widened. She would have to make a mental note to control her reactions, calming her face and assuming a neutral state. But she could not help but feel concerned about how frequently people were noticing the pain she was in. Stefan had even offered to take her to the doctor earlier.

"There's nothing wrong with me," she grunted, sounding more defensive than she had intended.

"Alright," Hugo said, picking up that it was a topic that would only cause frustration for both if he probed further.

86

Everyone who had been selected for this particular mission had been riddled with nerves in the lead-up to it. But none as much as Roisin. She had done a good job in keeping the pain and degeneration of her condition at bay using Doctor Curtis Shaw's medicine. But a decent portion of said medicine was destroyed during the attacks on the camp.

To make the situation worse, the current mission was sprung upon them by surprise, so Roisin saw herself unable to find a good hiding place for her to take the medicine on the rover. She resolved that she would have to deal with the suffering pains of her arm for however long this mission would be. A great risk to take.

Roisin smirked at the irony. The only medic on this mission, whose only job was to keep the soldiers healthy and undamaged, was having a hard time doing the same with herself.

IX. GRANULATE P

HUGO Stacey was quite pleased with himself. What was previously a common feeling for him to have was becoming rarer by the day.

The shame and humiliation of his constant failures on the battlefield saw him determined to rid himself of the crippling fear and incompetence he was becoming known for. As they conducted their marshland mission, he was desperate to prove he had not lost his edge. He did not disappoint.

Not many soldiers could say they defeated a fauxangel without the aid of another soldier's blade. Yet Hugo was able to destroy two on his own with one risky manoeuvre. Launching himself out of the murky water he was concealed in, Hugo had waited for the perfect moment for a set of wandering fauxangels to align when he conducted his impressive attack.

Lining up the shot perfectly, Hugo fired a Bronze Bullet through the neck of one fauxangel, exploding its throat as the bullet continued to soar through the air until it landed in the second creature's eye. The burning energy of twin blades sank into the fauxangel's injured eye, cutting and searing the wound further. Hugo dug in until the second was dead.

To say the other soldiers were impressed was an understatement. In one move, he cut their work in the marshlands down by a quarter, without alerting any other fauxangels to their position. They celebrated him, singing songs of his praise as they travelled to camp on the rover journey back. Hugo's smile gleamed from ear to ear. For the first time in a while, he felt like Heart Stealer.

***

Hugo and the other recruits returned to their new place of stay. A spot of land in their temporary camp, hidden in the driest area they could find in the deepest valley the marsh had to offer. Many recruits cluttered around him, wanting to hear the tale of his double-fauxangel kill. A few of these were adoring young women of the cleaning stations who were much to his liking.

Hugo dismissed them all. "I'll tell you all later. I need to get some rest," he insisted as he hurried past them.

Hugo Stacey, aka Heart Stealer, passing up an opportunity to brag about his excellence in battle whilst in the company of beautiful female recruits, was suspicious and out of character. If any of them had followed him into his sleeping quarters, they would have found out why.

Hugo scuffed his boot against the dry mud of the enclosure floor, passing by the spear that held up his tent. He ignored the beckoning embrace of the warm hammock he had told the others he wished to rest in, his eyes on a spot in the dirt under it. Hugo used his knife to carve out a small hole in the dirt below. With the hole cover removed, he could reach far down into the dirt and retrieve a tiny bag of chalky purple powder. It was his dozenth time holding it, yet Hugo marvelled at the substance as if it was his first time setting eyes on such a thing. Granulate P was an illegal substance, great for calming one's nerves yet boosting their energy simultaneously.

"Gorgeous," Hugo whispered.

This substance was all that stood between Hugo and *losing his edge*, as he liked to call it. It rid him of the intense anxiety attacks he had developed recently, allowing him to engage on the battlefield as if they were never a problem.

Hugo tucked the bag of Granulate P into the back part of the flexible metal of his crimson trousers. He would need it if he wanted to survive the next mission. Or thrive during it as he did the last.

As Hugo was about to leave his tent, a fit of paranoia struck his heart. Fluttering near the right side of his tent, flapping beneath the cloth, was a note. A note he had no memory of leaving there. Had someone been in his tent? He hoped to God that was not the case.

"Must've flown in due to the wind," he thought, calming himself down. Whether it had been blown in or left there by someone who snuck into his tent, it made him curious. He picked it up.

"What the fuck is this?" Hugo muttered as he read the note. Or at least tried to. The note was almost illegible and written in a language he could not understand. It was not English, nor Magnae Second Tongue, nor did it even resemble anything a fauxangel might have written. It might as well have been gibberish. Hugo scoffed, tearing the note and dashing it to the floor as he left the tent.

***

Hugo failed to make it far as he exited his tent. The second he stepped a foot out of it, he accidentally knocked himself against another recruit.

"Of course, you of all people just happened to be aimlessly bumbling about my area of the camp," Hugo complained as he rubbed the pain in his head the bump had caused. He had clashed with Queen Triumph.

"Shut up. I was *not* bumbling about," Quinn said. "I was specifically looking for you."

"Really? What's made me so lucky?" Hugo asked with a sardonic flair. Quinn shook her head, regretting having come. "Well, Trepanier? What is it you had to ask me?"

"People are saying you performed some amazing double-kill on a pair of fauxangels by yourself. But you haven't shared the details with anyone who wasn't there," Quinn said. "So, tell me. How did you do it?"

Hugo ran a hand through his blonde, wavy hair as he cockily winked down at her. "If I didn't tell those wonderful girls of the cleaning station, why would I tell you, *scavenger girl*?" he asked.

"You're rude," Quinn scoffed.

"As if you're ever nice to me either," Hugo scoffed back with a smirk.

Quinn rolled her eyes at him as she passed a hand down through her long black hair.

"I'll have you know, by the way, that the energy on the blades you probably used to get that impressive kill on those fauxangels was scavenged from dangerous territories by me," Quinn scolded.

"So?" Hugo asked.

"You should be nicer to the *scavenger girl*," Quinn insisted.

Hugo chuckled. "I'm sorry, do you expect me to kiss your feet for having done your only job?" he mocked. Quinn's face twisted into a belligerent grimace. Hugo's eyes narrowed in on her as it did.

"Weird. You're even more beautiful when you scowl like a monster," he commented with a smile.

"Funny prick," Quinn scoffed in sarcastic anger. She had grown tired of his quips and comments, leaving him to storm elsewhere.

But he truly meant it. He did think she looked beautiful. He found the way her thick, dark eyebrows scrunched over her striking green eyes to be adorably endearing. He *also* knew that she would interpret the comment oppositely, as a mockery of her looks. But he would not tell her the truth. Her misinterpretation was what made it so funny to him.

As Quinn walked away, Hugo was glad he did not waste any time collecting the drug. She might have entered his tent if he had not left it at that exact moment. She would have seen that he was taking Granulate P. No one could find out.

As Hugo thanked his lucky stars that his substance consumption had not been uncovered, the fierce winds doubled in strength. A sudden airflow hit his face, bringing with it a note similar to the one he had seen in the tent. Another small page of gibberish writings.

"What even are these?" Hugo complained under his breath as he swatted it away. His eyes travelled in the direction he saw the paper had come from. They focused once they caught wind of another piece of paper flying with the wind from the same location.

Hugo saw a series of tents in the corner of the camp. One of these baker's dozen in that section had to be the origin of these pestering papers. If he was not mistaken, he was almost sure one of those was Frederica's tent.

***

"Tell me what you know about the Ultimatum Source," The Head Foreseer ordered as the opener to their conversation, refusing to beat around the bush. He sat on the hammock in Dagim's tent as his top recruit stared back, his body lackadaisically leaning on his sword dug into the dirt.

"It's a source of power at the heart of the manufactured mixture of the water that the great Emmanuel Ekib found in a cave pool, and harvested fauxangel energy. It's hidden somewhere The Divinity and his forces would never be able to find. It contains so much raw, potent power that it's dangerous for normal people to even feel the rays of its light on their skin, never mind hold it," Dagim answered.

"Correct," The Head Foreseer sighed with satisfaction. "But you left out the most important part."

"Oh, I thought it went without saying," Dagim said before revealing it. "As the top recruit, I will be the one who consumes it, either in case of an emergency or conclusion. Either once we reach a stage in which we cannot win by normal means, or once we're ready to deliver the final killing blow to The Divinity."

Dagim expected The Head Foreseer to be satisfied with this answer, though he acted otherwise. The leader of the Magnae Forces rose from his hammock seat. His bright eyes were sunken, holding dark circles as they pierced through Dagim. Dagim stood up straight as The Head closed the distance between them. He could feel the furious breaths emitting from his nostrils brush against his skin.

All of his instincts told him he was to be struck by The Head Foreseer. He could not shake the feeling that he was in for another beating, despite having not done much to warrant such a thing.

"Some say you're not ready for The Ultimatum Source," The Head said. "Others say you never will be."

"They're all wrong," Dagim asserted.

"They fucking better be," The Head scoffed. "Because you might need to consume it earlier than any of us would have ever anticipated."

Dagim started to breathe heavily through his nose. Intense emotions stirred within him. There was the typical grandiose excitement that grasped at his soul whenever his future of utilising The Ultimatum Source was brought up. A hair-raising, heart-pumping, head-spinning, thoroughly arousing energy grew within him until it was as potent as the source itself.

But a new emotion took hold within Dagim along with this excitement. An emotion that was foreign to him.

Fear.

X. OCULAR DECEPTION

IT was a well-known fact that one of the most important skills for a soldier to possess on the battlefield was keeping one's mind in the present. Whether it was against violent prisoners in the training yard or fire-conjuring fauxangels amid genuine battle, a soldier was expected to have cleared their mind of all but one thing. Killing the enemy.

As Dagim spread the fires of his swinging sword through hidden spring attacks in the jungle that day, his mind journeyed elsewhere. He was incapable of focusing on the present as thoughts of the special fauxangel who had appeared in his tent many nights ago occupied his mind.

Everything about her and her visit intrigued Dagim from start to finish. Everything from her dark energy to her snarky attitude. The way she so casually teleported in and out of his tent. Her flippant mention of information she should have had no access to. Such as the conspiracy to kill him, which at the moment had been resigned to an unspoken myth or false rumour around the forces.

"You're not as special as everyone treats you...but there is someone here who is."

That was what stood out to him. He had not the faintest clue who she was referring to, the topic becoming a major cause of concern for him.

Dagim recalled having agreed to tell Stefan about it when he asked, but ended up doing no such thing. He had yet to tell a single other person of that encounter. He wanted not to have to think about it at all moving forward. Yet as the days went on, her face took a commonplace of stay in the recesses of his mind.

"Because you might need to consume it earlier than any of us would have ever anticipated."

Another line that constantly played through his mind. That was the closest he could get to pinpointing the advent of these anxious thoughts that bothered him so. Previously, any mention of his future status as the consumer of the Ultimatum Source and the soldier who would win this war would fill him with vigour. But with what had been occurring around him, the fear this prospect brought with it was all that permeated within the Devil Child's psyche.

***

Dagim returned to camp in a cleaner, less-injured state than a fauxangel battle would typically leave him. Something many recruits preferred, but Dagim despised.

The current North Magnae battle plans included hiding out in ponds and forests, surprise attacking fauxangels to achieve one or two kills, and immediately retreating before their alien adversaries could retaliate. A cowardly battle tactic, Dagim thought, that, despite being safer for their forces, frustrated him.

He was in the perfect mood to finally engage in a confrontation he had been holding himself not to, as he marched towards the Vice Foreseer's tent. The second-in-command military leader loured as he found the infamous recruit waiting for him outside his tent that afternoon. The tall man's haughty upturned nose turned downwards as Dagim glared up at him.

"Is there something I can help you with, Devil Child?" The Vice scoffed.

Dagim mirrored the same intimidation tactic The Head had used on him in his tent the other day. He quickly closed the gap between the two of them until only an inch of tension-filled air lay between their gazes.

"I'll never forget," Dagim muttered menacingly. "You people tried to fucking kill me. I'll never forget."

Dagim saw The Vice Foreseer open his mouth to respond to what he predicted would be an eloquently spoken string of lies and excuses.

Before he got the chance, Dagim barged into him, 'accidentally' knocking him with his shoulder. The Vice lost his balance as he struggled to keep on his feet, slipping as if the dry marshland had been replaced with ice.

"My bad," Dagim laughed. He made himself scarce, marching away from The Vice before he could retaliate in word or action.

"Insolence," The Vice Foreseer spat in anger as he watched Dagim stride away. "We'll snuff it out eventually."

The Vice Foreseer would barely enjoy a brief moment of respite before yet another young soldier would invade his personal space.

"Vice! Vice! Vice!" a frantic young recruit pestered him as he ran to his tent.

"What's making you so frantic and bothered?!" The Vice asked angrily. "Spit it out, soldier!"

"We have to gather up as many troops as we can in as many rovers as we can for a wide sweeping search. The Head's orders."

"What for, exactly?"

The frantic recruit took in a long breath. "I think one of our squadrons has uncovered parts of a fauxangel sanctuary."

The Divinity lay sunken in his throne, his hair a brittle mess, his skin worn and tired, and his eyelids half-closed over a pair of nigh-lifeless orbs. The golden skyscraper-ceiling sanctuary of his seemed to lose its essence in accordance with this leader's state of mind and body. Both the colouring of his walls and the glow of his skin had paled until they were a duller, uninspiring shade of yellow.

The Divinity that sat in his chair was a far cry from the impressive leader who had threatened the Magnae Forces with legions of fauxangels weeks prior. He wallowed in solitude, no servants around to feed him paste. He muttered musings to himself from sunrise to sundown.

"It won't be long until the humans realise the legions of godly warriors that I threatened them with were a falsehood," The Divinity said, speaking his fears out loud as if doing so would mitigate the hold they had over him. It did not. He pulled at his wilting hair, grasping a fistful of the physical embodiment of stress.

"They are yet to know of that power of mine, but it won't be long until they figure out it was nothing more than an empty showing to dampen their morale. An ocular deception," he lamented. "It won't be long until they notice the discrepancies between the number of men I claim to have and the number they face and take down in battle!"

The Divinity scratched at his peeling, dry skin as his anxious thoughts doubled. He glared into eternal nothingness, biting down hard as he shivered in his seat.

"They cut, shoot, and burn through my men with such disgusting ease," he continued to mutter to himself feverishly. "I can't allow this to continue any longer. I can't allow humanity to believe that they can defeat a god."

***

The inside of Frederica's marshland tent was more organised than the temporary stay of her fellow recruits. Two thin metal pillars held up the cloth as opposed to a spear or whatever discarded weapon the other recruits could find to do the same in their living quarters. Its main fixture was the hammock that occupied the middle of most other tents, being folded up and put to the side in place of a large wooden desk for her to conduct her writings on.

Frederica put ink to paper as she wrote another series of notes. With a subtle irritation about her, she used her other free hand to force the paper down onto the desk.

She believed she saw Hugo having picked up one of these notes. When he found himself unable to read it, however, she saw him dismiss it and carry on with his day.

Frederica invented her very own language in her head, using it to write all the things she wished to note down yet keep to herself. Thus, if anyone did stumble upon her notes like Hugo had, they would have no way of deciphering them. Frederica praised God for Hugo's lack of curiosity on the matter. Whilst he, or anyone else, would have been unable to translate the notes, she still thought it best that as few people as possible found them. Their writings were different ideas on how she could end Dagim's life.

Frederica sighed as she continued to write. She must have come up with twenty potential ideas on how she could get rid of him without drawing attention to herself, each written out with detail. None were good enough to execute yet. She had no idea how The Vice wanted her to go through with this. Of all the plans she could think of, not a single one negated the monumental risk of killing their top recruit without it somehow being traced back to her.

"Tiresome," Frederica sighed to herself, wiping her forehead with the latest note of plans, then crushing it into a ball. Relieving her of sweat was the only use such paper had any more as she grew tired of writing and planning.

"These will make for a good fire," she scoffed as she dumped the remainder of her notes into a metal bucket.

***

As Frederica left her tent an hour later, she saw the marshland camp to be much emptier than when she had resigned herself to it the previous morning. Hundreds of wandering recruits and multiple Foreseers had dwindled to tens of recruits and one or two lower-ranked Foreseers. The Head and Vice were noticeably absent.

Frederica searched the camp, looking for someone to explain what had occurred whilst she locked herself in her tent all day. She found Roisin sitting on a log by a patch of pink pondwater as she practised dismantling and reassembling a syringe.

"Afternoon, Frederica," Roisin greeted, smiling. "Have you packed your stuff for moving yet?"

"Moving?" Frederica asked.

"When those squadrons return from their search missions, we'll be moving camp again."

"Search missions?"

"Yeah, search missions," Roisin said. "They might have found parts of a fauxangel sanctuary."

Frederica's sour mood worsened. Whether it had been due to incompetence, accident, or spite, she did not appreciate this being the first time she was hearing of such an important mission. She crossed her arms tightly, her body fidgeting as she suppressed the rage this revelation elicited.

"And why wasn't I told any of this?!" she asked, doing a poor job of concealing frustration.

Roisin glanced up at her with soft, concerned eyes. "I'm not sure," she answered. "I think it had something to do with

100

the message The Vice wanted to give you as he was rushing to get on the second scout team."

"He had a message for me?" Frederica asked.

"A soldier asked whether they should retrieve you from your tent to join in on the search squads. He said you were busy with a specific mission he assigned to you," Roisin explained.

Frederica's world froze. Her tawny brown skin flashed pale as her heart all but stopped beating. She had to force herself not to gulp.

"Did he tell you what the mission was?" Frederica asked. She wiped the side of her face, removing the neurotic sweat that dripped down her head.

"No, just that it was confidential and that you should still keep working at it, even with his absence. He wouldn't tell us the actual mission itself. No matter how many times we asked," Roisin said. That final sentence calmed all of Frederica's woes.

"Right, I'll get back to working on it then," she sighed with relief.

Roisin smiled, the cheerful redhead returning to her syringe assembly practice. Frederica left her to it, resigning herself to her tent once more.

Due to her and The Vice having not discussed it in a while, Frederica hoped that perhaps The Vice had forgotten about or discarded such plans. Especially with the lack of progress she was making regarding them. But it was clear that it was not the case. She was still expected to kill Dagim discreetly. Now, she was at a crossroads. Was she to follow the orders of the second-highest in command of the force and one of her idols, or was she to trust every gut instinct that told her that doing so would lead to dire consequences?

On one hand, she agreed that Dagim was dangerous. The time in which he might be required to consume the Ultimatum Source was drawing closer, and she could not afford to let a man of his character hold such power. On the other hand, her doing so could cause unforeseen issues for her career, the forces, and humanity as a whole.

XI. MY ORIGIN

AS Quinn co-led the search of the 'sanctuary sightings' that her squadron was sent to piece through, she was disappointed. All they were able to uncover were discarded pieces of gold stone scattered across fields, as opposed to the imposing building they expected to find. Either The Divinity had known they were coming and thus relocated or destroyed the building that was supposed to be there, or their scout sources were mistaken. Either way, the only benefit that came from that search was her ability to scavenge and harvest more resources to provide burning energy for their blades and materials to construct more Bronze Bullets.

Aiza Armstrong, the lowest-ranked Foreseer and the other co-leader of the search team, joined Quinn as they trudged through the maroon dust that had poisoned the air of these barren lands.

"What a great use of our time," Quinn coughed sarcastically as she waved the dust out of her face that infiltrated her eyes and mouth.

"I wouldn't call it a waste. Look at that extra good stuff," Aiza said, gesturing at the dented metal container Quinn held by a sturdy handle, the bronze box glowing with energy.

"I could have collected twice as much in half the journey," Quinn complained as she tapped the box, the fauxangel energy squelching within it as it stirred.

Aiza shrugged. She swivelled around for a moment, taking in their general surroundings. Behind her were the twenty other recruits who had joined them on the search. Behind them was a vast empty wasteland of scorching sands and the occasional blackened cactus.

"Seems like everywhere you go nowadays you're likely to find the ruins of a former settlement rather than an intact one," Aiza commented.

Quinn's eyes hit the floor. Her face grew weary with concern. "I hope Iqra House is alright."

"Iqra House?"

"The orphanage I grew up in. The one I send most of my recruit pay to," Quinn explained. "With us travelling so far and moving between campsites, I've not been able to check if they are. I probably won't until this is all done."

"Try not to let it worry you too much," Aiza advised.

"It's hard not to," Quinn sighed.

Aiza studied her as they walked further onward. The usual overly aggro expression she held on her face had faded, worry and sorrow being worn in its place. It melted her heart to see Quinn hold such a countenance.

"Keep scavenging as well as you do, and we'll have enough energy to kill every single fauxangel," Aiza said with a playful smirk. "We might even win this war by the time your next recruit payment gets to Iqra House."

"A hopeful thought," Quinn said, weakly smirking back.

＊

Quinn and her search squad arrived at the North Magnae Forces' new hidden campsite just as the soldiers were setting up the last of the tents. She found the site to be quite the downgrade from their camp on the marshlands. The grass there was drier and fuller, but the area was colder and the winds even heavier. But it was further away from any form of civilisation, thus far from breaching fauxangels.

Quinn spent the next quarter of an hour searching through the camp to find her belongings. Her tent and sleeping quarters had been set up by someone else whilst she was on her search mission. A gesture she was initially grateful for until she realised that meant she would have to find out which one of these identical-looking fixtures was her own. She only paused her sweeping search through the camp when she overheard an interesting conversation being had by a couple of female recruits in the midsection of the camp.

"What are you doing waiting outside of Heart Stealer's tent?" the raven-haired girl asked her blonde comrade. Her lighter-haired friend sat on a log with her legs crossed outside of what she assumed was Hugo's new tent.

"Another one of Hugo's fangirls," Quinn thought to herself, rolling her eyes at the pair.

"I'm waiting for him, obviously," the blonde scoffed at her raven-haired friend.

"What for?" raven-hair asked.

"You *know* what for," the blonde giggled suggestively.

"Gross," Quinn thought.

"Lucky," raven-hair laughed, envious.

"I thought you didn't like him? You said he was too cocky and everything," said the blonde.

"Doesn't mean I wouldn't get with him. He's a pretty man," raven-hair laughed. "That sniffle he's got recently pisses me off, though. Couldn't deal with that in bed."

"Oh yeah. He *has* been sniffing a lot lately," said the blonde. "Do you think he's ill or something?"

Raven-hair laughed, shaking her head. "There are other reasons a person might sniff too much," she commented with a wink of an eye. Her blonde friend was not quite picking up

105

what she was putting down. Quinn, on the other hand, knew exactly what she was referring to.

"Oi!" the blonde squealed as Quinn pushed past her and her friend.

"Excuse me, ladies," Quinn said as she swung open the flaps to the tent.

Hugo stood in the middle of his sleeping quarters holding an item in the air as he inspected it. As soon as Quinn stepped foot inside his tent, he slid it into hiding, safe within his pocket.

"What are you up to?" Quinn asked as she closed the flap behind her.

"Nothing that's any of your business," Hugo said.
Quinn glared at the crimson-mesh pocket that held the item Hugo was hiding from her. She could have sworn she saw a small bag containing something purple within his grasp.

"That better not be Granulate P in your pocket," she said. Hugo's signature grin stretched to both sides of his face, amused at the accusation.

"Where the hell did that even come from?!" he laughed.

"You spent your first few real battles either frozen in fear, nearly pissing your pants, or running away from a fight. Then, all of a sudden, you returned to being your usually brash self, killing fauxangels with ease," Quinn explained. "I think that might have to do with the purple bag in your pocket."

"What are you on about? Where would I even get Granulate P from?" Hugo scoffed.

"I don't know, why don't you tell me?" Quinn asked.
Hugo's smile waned, his well-groomed eyebrows levelling his gaze into a glare. "Get the fuck out of my tent, Quinn."

Quinn stood firm, intending to do no such thing. When she finally did move, it was in the opposite direction to his orders. She lunged towards him, ready to take the bag of powder out of his pocket by force. As her hand reached for Hugo's pocket, he caught it tightly within his grip. She attempted to thrust the other hand towards his pocket, only for Hugo to grab hold of that one with his other.

With both her prying arms in his grasp, Hugo pulled Quinn close to him. Quinn saw her face close enough to his to have kissed him. Almost no space existed between her and his charming grin.

"You're even more beautiful up close," Hugo whispered. Quinn felt her cheeks flush red as she stared into his sparkling eyes. She cursed herself a million times over, embarrassed at how she was being made to feel and how her body showcased it through the redness of her cheeks.

"Could you let me go, please?" Quinn stuttered, avoiding further eye contact.

"Of course," Hugo happily obliged, unhanding her. Awkward and flustered beyond belief, Quinn marched out of the tent without questioning him further.

"That was close," Hugo sighed the second he was sure she was out of earshot. He spent the next minute using a knife to cut a hole in the ground to hide his Granulate P.

***

The Divinity lay underneath a raining cloud of pure bright energy, allowing it to shower him with its replenishing goodness. Two female fauxangels stood to either side of him as he washed himself back to health, the three of them being the only beings in the Planet Luxurae sanctuary. Simply being in this area would be enough to blind a human, yet The Divinity felt at the top of his form as the droplets of energy soothed his skin.

"Ah. You have no idea how wonderful this feels, ladies," The Divinity said as he bathed.

107

"I'm glad you're enjoying it," fauxangel one said.

"It's good to see you back to your best, my lord," fauxangel two said.

"I apologise if my recent behaviour gave you and the people cause for concern, ladies. The Magnae Forces and their wiping out of your brethren had reduced me to an anxious, depressed shell," The Divinity admitted. "I was only able to break myself out of said shell by remembering one thing."

"And what was that, my lord?"

"My origin."

As The Divinity stepped out of the showering replenishment of falling energy, the cloud disappeared into thin air. His hair had returned to its full luxurious length, and his skin had regained its extra-terrestrial golden glow. He opened his eyes, beaming down a wondrous smile at the two of them.

"Do you know how I, and by extension you, and all my other wonderful creations came to be?" he asked with a raise of his eyebrow.

Both fauxangels stared up at him with wide, curious eyes as they shook their heads. "Tell us! Tell us!" they pleaded in unison. The Divinity was more than happy to do so.

"It's a very simple but powerful story," he chuckled. The Divinity cleared his throat and regaled them with the tale.

"Millions of years ago, on this planet that we consider home, Luxurae, my first ever memory was being born out of a heart of a fiery ball of light and bred out onto the planet as a man grown. The universe was my father, the light itself was my mother, and the galaxy was my purpose. As soon as I stepped foot on Luxurae, I was aware of my abilities, capable of using them, and knowledgeable of the purpose father and mother had given me to carry out with said powers. Do you know what I did first once I was able to utilise these powers properly?"

"You created our brethren?" fauxangel one guessed.

"That's right. I created you and all the others," The Divinity confirmed. "An ability I no longer possess, unfortunately, unless through ocular deception. Once this small planet of ours was populated, mother and father chose to take the heart of it away from me."

"A shame," the fauxangels agreed in unison.

"Thankfully, they left me with an abundance of alternative powers. Once the planet was sufficiently populated, do you know how I used my powers next?"

Both fauxangels ran through their minds for answers. The Divinity patiently waited for one of them to work it out for themselves. After a while, one of them did.

"Travelled our galaxy to find other lifeforms to guide!" fauxangel two answered with excitement.

"Exactly! Very good!" The Divinity confirmed with joy. The fauxangels glanced at each other and then back at him, delighted with the praise and encouragement that came with the story. The Divinity leaned in, the fauxangels focusing further as he continued his telling.

"The humans of Planet Magnae call us aliens, acting as if we are hellspawn from a backwards planet. They call us fauxangels, a pathetic attempt at branding us as fake deities similar to those of their ancient human tales. But we're much higher than even real angels are. We're *gods*," he said with a glint of pride in his eyes. "Gods with the purpose of ruling over and governing lifeforms incapable of successfully doing so themselves."

"Lifeforms such as the humans of Planet Magnae," fauxangel one said, her mouth twisting as if the mention of them put a bad taste in it.

"Correct. Lifeforms such as the humans of Planet Magnae," The Divinity said. "Which is why I've being reinvigorated with a newfound source of energy that has me determined to win this war and put them back in their place."

Using the powers he had spent the past few moments informing them about, The Divinity conjured up a ball of light, transporting a large item to show off. The female fauxangels watched as the floors beneath were stained with dark maroon human blood. They watched as The Divinity conjured up a pile of human carcasses in front of them. The corpses of Magnae men, women, and many children.

A few had their heads decapitated. A few had their limbs severed and welded onto other parts of their bodies with energy. A lot of them had been scalped and tattooed with marks of heresy. All suffered from burn marks and profusely bleeding orifices.

"Is that from your attack this morning, sir?" asked fauxangel two, staring at the pile with lustful delight.

The Divinity smirked. "Yes," he answered. "Isn't it beautiful?"

XII. PAIN AND POISON

AIZA Armstrong, aka Foreseer VII, perused the camp with concerned eyes. That evening, she had seen twice as many soldiers return to camp from battle with injuries as she had ever seen on a singular evening since the war had started. It was only to get worse.

Half an hour later, Aiza saw the camp flood with panicked recruits, rushing in pairs as they carried the burnt and bruised bodies of unfortunate soldiers on makeshift gurneys constructed from long tree branches and cloth. The vast majority of these battered and bruised bodies were deceased recruits who had fallen in battle. They were being carried back to camp, she assumed, to receive a proper burial by the higher-ranked Foreseers.

On one of these gurneys lay Quinn Trepanier. Aiza's heart skipped multiple consecutive beats as soon as she recognised her. Her woes quelled and her body calmed as she was carried closer. She saw that though Queen Triumph's eyes were winced shut, she was still breathing. Thankfully.

"Drop her here, let me get a look at her," Aiza ordered. The recruits listened, carefully dropping the gurney and standing by as Aiza crouched down to talk to Quinn. The curly dark-haired young soldier ground her teeth together in pain. Aiza found the root cause of it. An ankle that had not only been twisted, but marked with fauxangel burns and scraped bloody.

"How did you get an injury like this from scavenging?!" Aiza asked.

"I didn't get it from scavenging," Quinn winced through her gritted teeth. "I got myself a blade and a Bronze Bullet and fought alongside the soldiers."

"Now, why the fuck were you fighting alongside the soldiers?!" Aiza asked, infuriated. Quinn took in a deep, laboured breath before she provided her with an answer.

"Remember when you told me we might be able to kill all the fauxangels by the time I was set to pay the orphanage again? To cheer me up and all?"

"I do, yes."

"Well, I tried to speed up that process."

"Why would you do such a thing? Were you trying to get yourself killed?"

"Of course, I wasn't," Quinn sulked like a petulant child. "I thought if I joined a soldier squad, I could help put an end to this war quicker."

"Yes, I'm aware of that. *I* want to make sure you're aware of how fucking ridiculous that was," Aiza scolded.

"I'm aware of *that*," Quinn pouted.

Aiza studied Quinn's leg. She looked at the two recruits who stood by. "Take her to Recruit Infinity," she ordered.

They picked up Quinn's gurney again before she had even finished giving the command.

"It's not that bad of an injury, is it?" Quinn asked, desperately hoping the answer was no.

"With Roisin's help, it'll heal enough for you to walk without assistance in a few weeks, but probably still hurt about a month after. All in all, you'll be fine," Aiza answered. "But it does mean you won't be able to scavenge for a while."

Quinn smacked her hand against her head. "Fuck my life," she groaned as they carried her away.

***

Aiza ran ragged around the camp all evening, attending to the many issues that had sprung in the camp following this flood of gurney-ridden soldiers coming from many failed battles. With The Head Foreseer, The Vice, and multiple others still out on their sanctuary search missions, it was up to her to take up the chains of command and establish order in this hectic space.

From organising their evening tasks to giving speeches to boost morale, to aiding in the wound-tending duties due to the lack of medics they had for the amount of soldiers who were injured, Aiza was put to work like never before. She had a newfound appreciation for her rank as the lowest Foreseer that day, not imagining having to deal with all of this regularly like The Head and The Vice did.

As Aiza marched towards the very outskirts of the camp, towards a large forest of black-leaved trees, she found the most unique of issues to resolve. Despite it being another task piled onto her overflowing plate, she found it refreshing due to its uniqueness. She approached Stefan, who stood at the edge of the forest, arguing in sign language with an adorable-looking young woman, short and stout. Aiza had never seen this woman before, but one thing stood out to her. She wore no crimson. Therefore, she was not a recruit of the North Magnae Forces. Therefore, she had no business being this close to camp.

Aiza interrupted their conversation, pulling Stefan aside. The second Stefan laid eyes upon her, Aiza began to angrily sign at him.

113

"Who on God's red Magnae is this?!" she asked him in sign language. She was one of the few in the North Magnae Forces who had bothered to learn sign language. Not out of a profound kindness of her heart and sympathy for Stefan, but so that she could communicate with him without having to bring a pen and paper for him to write tedious notes with.

"Apologies, Foreseer VII, I'm in the process of trying to get her to leave," Stefan signed back.

"Who is she, though?" Aiza signed with frustration.
Stefan sighed. He glanced at the cutesy girl who frowned back at him.

"This is my girlfriend, Anais. She's been keeping up with our war effort, tracking our camp movement and travelling close to each campsite."

"Why would a non-recruit go through so much effort for such a dangerous task?!"

"Because she wants to make sure I'm safe," Stefan signed. "And she loves me."

Aiza peered over at Stefan's girlfriend standing behind him. Anais glowered at her. Such venom radiated from the deaf girl.

"I have a lot to deal with at camp, with *this* being the least of my worries," she signed. "I'm going to go now, but I expect this girlfriend of yours to be miles away from our camp by nightfall."

Anais shook her head in defiance. Stefan rubbed his nose. "Easier said than done," he signed.

Aiza shook her head at both of them. "Stefan, if I see her around any of our camps again, you'll end up in a world of trouble," she threatened through sign language. "If the Head finds out, he'll consider what you're doing as knowingly putting a member of the general public in danger. He'll end

114

up giving you a worse 'beating of subordination' than the one Dagim got."

Stefan sighed. "Alright, I'll get her to leave," he signed.

***

Speak of the Devil Child, when Aiza returned to camp following her scolding of Stefan, Dagim was the next recruit she saw herself having to attend to. Aiza held out a metal bucket for Dagim, one he filled to the brim with painful wretches of expunged vomit for minutes on end.

"I haven't seen anyone this ill since Foreseer III during that Enigmaetia Ocean trip," Aiza commented. "I hope you're not seeing intergalactic mirages too."

Dagim could hardly respond to her quip. His eyes were bloodshot red, his throat sore and coughing out the last remnants of sickness.

"Was it something you ate or drank?" Aiza asked.

Dagim answered. "Some piece of shit nectar I drank at dinner," he coughed. "I don't know what the diners put in that shit, but it's been making me throw up all fucking day."

This answer confused Aiza. The dining section and by proxy, the food and drink in it, was held to the highest standard of hygiene and cleanliness by The Vice himself. From a thorough check of his medical records, she could not remember Dagim being allergic to anything that would warrant such a sickness. She had enough time to think about what may have been causing it as Dagim continued to throw up some more. By his third vomiting session of the hour, she came to the right conclusion. She had seen similar sicknesses both hurt and kill a few soldiers back in her day. The blackish speckles throughout his expunged sick combined with the protruding neck veins gave it away.

This specific brand of vomiting was a result of someone ingesting the poison that could be extracted from the black leaves of dying poisonous Magnae trees. Dying jungle trees specifically from the Minoai Region, not too far from their current camp. In most cases, ingesting this poison would kill an unfortunate soldier. But not Dagim.

Aiza figured it must have been just about enough poison to make him sick, but not enough had been in his drink to kill him. Whoever did this was too cautious with the amount they put in, for fear of it being obvious in the victim's drink. Ironically, the amount of secreted drops you would need to make sure you killed your target would be too much for a covert assassination, as the poison would rise to the surface and blacken the drink. The greatest amount you could put in without traces of it being found was exactly two drops. Drops which only had a chance of killing its target seven out of ten times. These chances were much lower if said target was particularly strong. This proved Dagim had been the strongest target possible, as all it had caused him was a series of painful vomiting sessions.

"When I find out who made that awful drink, I'm going to pull out their entrails and strangle them with them," Dagim said. The threat sounded weak, his voice and body trembling.

Aiza grunted in response. She could not think of any recruit who would want to poison their top comrade. She could think of some Foreseers who would, however.

Her mind travelled back to the ritual with the blade underneath their nails. The one The Vice Foreseer had forced them all to do, to bind them to an agreement that constituted them not speaking to anyone outside the room about their discussion, not even The Head himself. What were they discussing that day, exactly? It took her a while to remember.

"You're telling me this does not seem a little contrived to you?! You don't think it's a coincidence that on that day we were gifted a soldier who on paper was seemingly perfect but was born and raised under dire circumstances?!" she vaguely remembered The Vice arguing. "Not a part of you worries this may be a gambit by the godly alien threat we fight? To place what would be our undoing right underneath our noses until the day it chooses to destroy us?"

Aiza looked back at Dagim, who had cleared his stomach through purging vomit. Had The Vice Foreseer already acted on those worries? Had a recruit attempted to kill Dagim on his orders? The answer became obvious to her the more she thought about it.

Aiza remembered agreeing with the premise, but not being on board with his worrisome rhetoric. She found it preposterous that he had tried to kill Dagim because of it.

She considered whether she should be the first Foreseer to break the ritual agreement and expose this plot.

XIII. DAMNED SOURCE

SICKNESS had plagued Dagim for an entire day. Whilst his comrades had suffered and struggled in lost battles all day, he found himself incapable of helping them. He spent over twenty hours stuck in his tent, throwing up blood and failing to keep strange fever dreams at bay. He did not know why that drink had made him so sick, though he heard Foreseer VII had her theories. What concerned Dagim more was the effect this sickness had on him. Even after the physical symptoms of the sickness passed, its unforeseen effects on his mind persisted.

He would see apparitions everywhere, all around him, at random times of the day. Sightings of a woman who was not there. The special fauxangel, the dark-aura woman who had teleported into his tent that day, talking of finding someone special amongst the recruits, ran through his mind now more than ever before.

"She's not here anymore," Dagim would groan to himself now and then. He felt he had to remind himself, or else he would be swept away by these tricks of the eyes and mind. Or else he would do something he would regret.

***

In the evening, Dagim sat on the sleek metal seats in the relocated emergency meeting room. This time, he did not sit by the stands looking on at the meeting. This time, those many seats that circled the focal point of the room were empty. Dagim was at the head table with all Foreseers, included in that day's set of secluded discussions. The only other recruit to be granted this privilege was Frederica.

The Devil Child had found the discussions of the meeting thus far to be exceptionally uninteresting, his impatience quickly getting the better of him.

Without shame, he chose to interrupt these discussions, bringing up the topic he had been itching to speak of since the moment he sat down that day.

"Isn't it about time I consumed that damned Ultimatum Source already?!" he shouted as he rose from his seat.

As soon as those words left Dagim's mouth, he scanned the table to gauge the opinions of the most important faces in the room. The Head seemed unconcerned, leaning back in his chair. The Vice seemed perturbed, his jaw clenching. Foreseers III to VII held mixed expressions that he could not determine were more positive or negative. Of all the people around the table, Frederica was the most blatantly against it. The glare she always seemed to have directed at him held twice its usual dissatisfaction. He did not have to guess what she, of all people, thought about it. She rose from her seat to let it be known.

"Now is not even *close* to the right time for you to consume that *damned source*," Frederica asserted with quiet venom. She had a skill for making her pent-up frustration seem measured as opposed to the righteous anger it stemmed from. A skill Dagim was well aware he did not possess.

"When will it be then? When hundreds more of our soldiers are killed?!" he argued.

"In due time, Devil Child. It's called the *Ultimatum* Source for a reason, not the *impulsively consume whenever you see fit* source," Frederica chastised.

"What a load of shit," Dagim scoffed. Frederica shook her head at him as if he were her child who had just greatly disappointed her.

"First Ranger is right, there's no reason to be in such a rush, Devil Child," The Vice Foreseer added with all the smug pomposity he could manage. "We were making good progress with wiping out the fauxangels until very recently."

"Well, we aren't anymore," Dagim scoffed. "The camp constantly smells of burnt soldier flesh nowadays."

"The Ultimatum Source is the final solution, and we're not at the final stage," said The Vice.

"That's right," agreed Foreseer IV.

"Fine. If you don't agree with me that the time is now, maybe it's not," Dagim said. "But it is coming very soon, that is a fact you cannot fucking deny."

"I see where he's coming from," Foreseer VII, aka Aiza agreed.

"I don't," scoffed Foreseer III.

"Neither do I," said Foreseer V. "Like The Vice said, you seem to be in a rush."

"Why am I being treated as if I'm acting unreasonably for wanting to end this war?" Dagim asked.

"I'd like to understand that too," Foreseer VII added. The Head sat back in his chair quietly, the gruff bald man's piercing eyes floating between the other faces in the room. He sat saying nothing as he let their argument play out.

"It's still far too early to warrant unfolding the plans we have for The Ultimatum Source," said Foreseer VI.

"Clearly," scoffed Frederica.

"What would warrant unfolding those plans then?" Dagim asked with building frustration. "If The Divinity showed up and rained literal hellfire on our camp itself, you probably still wouldn't say the time was right."

"When that day comes, I will quite literally force the source down your throat myself if that's what you want. Until then, calm down," Frederica snapped at him.

"I reckon if it was you who was the top recruit, you'd be singing a different tune."

"Perhaps. But unfortunately, we're stuck with you, so such hypotheticals are irrelevant," Frederica insulted back.

"Just stop talking," Dagim scoffed.

"This is starting to sound like you just want the Ultimatum Source's power for power's sake!" Foreseer III accused.

"Come on, give the young man some credit here," Foreseer VII defended.

"Exactly," Dagim said.

The Vice rolled his eyes. "Listen, the rest of us are on the same page here. You're not ready, and it's not the right time," he asserted. "This discussion is pointless. The matter has already been settled."

"Far from it!" Dagim exclaimed. "Why don't we hear what The Head thinks before we say that?"

All pairs of eyes violently darted towards The Head, who sat in the focal chair, as unmoved as he was when the discussion had started. Every member of the secluded meeting waited for his answer with bated breath. Dagim most of all. The Head Foreseer zoned in on Devil Child alone as he gave his answer.

"They're right. You're not ready," he answered. "And even if you were, it isn't the right time."

Dagim could hardly believe what he was hearing. He could not determine what irritated him more, The Head's final verdict being in direct agreement with The Vice's, or the look of quiet contentment it had put on Frederica's face.

"Didn't you tell me I might have to consume it much earlier than expected?" asked Dagim.

"I did," said The Head.

"And what's made you change your mind about that?" Dagim asked.

The Head shrugged. "You heard The Vice," he said with calm determinism. "The matter has been settled."

The Head rose from his seat with a laboured sigh. He would hear no further discussion, making his way for the room's exit without so much as looking at any of the other Foreseers for confirmation.

The meeting adjourned. Its conclusion left Dagim feeling dissatisfied and disgruntled, to say the least.

***

Come nightfall, Dagim sat up on the mattress of his tent bed, having not gotten even an ounce of sleep. Nighttimes were so peaceful at camp. Lying in a tent, one could get the impression the world had gone still. If the forces themselves were not to be called to action, with no fauxangel sightings at night, every soldier would seize the opportunity to fall into the deepest sleep the human body could and wake up refreshed and maximised. Dagim was not able to take advantage of this prime opportunity to rest his body and mind. As usual, thoughts of the events of the day prevented him from doing so.

He heard a ruffling of tent cloth. With the quiet of the night disrupted, he measuredly turned his head in its direction, conscious of any danger he may have to deal with.

The rough, lantern-jawed head of his weathered leader popped through the opening flaps. Unexpectedly seeing that smile alone in the dead of night could strike fear into any man's heart.

122

"The Devil Child is wide awake," The Head chuckled as Dagim rose from bed in intrigue. "Come with me. Now."

***

Dagim stood across from The Head Foreseer, deep within a crater of exposed bedrock in a stone field miles away from camp. The two of them were the only members of that branch of The North Magnae Forces both awake and off-site. Dagim had asked no questions of The Head from the moment they snuck out of the camp quarters to the moment they stepped foot on the bedrock. He understood that he was to just follow The Head's lead and observe.

Dagim watched as The Head worked on the ground in preparation for something he could not yet figure out. Firstly, he carefully placed a pair of pincers to the side. Secondly, he had worn a pair of metallic gloves so rough, thick, and sturdy that Dagim could hardly believe one could still move their fingers around in them. After making sure his heavy gloves were properly fit, he picked up the pincers with one hand, using his spare hand to press down an even smaller crevice in the middle of the bedrock. A circle formed in the dirt as the crevice flipped over as if the mound of natural dirt had been a mechanical device of human creation. On the other side of the flipped circle was a thin layer of potent golden energy, buzzing as if it were a swarm of pink bees. The Head used the pincer to break off a piece of this golden energy, a clinking sound as he picked off a cluster of granules.

As he stepped away from the crevice hole, it flipped over once more automatically. Using the pincers to drop it, The Head placed the energy granules in the palm of his thick-gloved hand. He reached out to Dagim, showing off what he had collected.

"What's that?" Dagim asked.

"I think you know," The Head smirked. Dagim had only to think for a few seconds to realise that he did.

He felt the air being siphoned out of his lungs and his heart threatening to escape his chest. For the second time that day, he could not believe what The Head was suggesting.

"Now? You want me to consume the source now?" Dagim asked, riddled with uncertainty.

"Only a small portion. To see how your body reacts," The Head said. He could not help but laugh at how apprehensive Dagim had become. "Besides, weren't you just raving today about how you want to consume the full thing?"

Dagim gulped away the swelling lump in his throat, taking in a deep breath through his nose as he forced his nerves to calm themselves. "Get it over with," he grunted.

The Head approached Dagim carefully as he pinched a granule of golden energy. Dagim tilted his head back, opening his mouth wide. It took every ounce of self-control for him to stay still as The Head brought the small piece of the source closer to his mouth.

"Don't swallow, just let it pass through you," The Head said. "Let it drop into the heart of your soul."

Without further deliberation, The Head dropped the granule. Dagim allowed it to fall down his throat without as much as attempting to swallow or ease its difficult passing. Despite the deep discomfort it caused, he followed The Head's direction, remaining completely still. He felt it pass through his body until all of a sudden, he could feel its presence no more.

The Head stepped back to observe Dagim as he closed his mouth and lifted his head upright. He watched as his top recruit braced himself, putting on a mask of prepared bravery as he waited for whatever changes to his body were to occur.

Thankfully, or not depending on how one looked at it, these changes were minor. But for the slightest taste and smell of blood in his mouth and nose, and constant subtle stirring at the heart of his stomach, Dagim felt relatively normal. On the whole, he found it to be a thoroughly underwhelming experience, considering he had just swallowed a piece of raw power.

Dagim glowered at The Head with seeking eyes of confusion, the older, muscled man chuckling back at him.

"You were expecting much more to happen, weren't you?" The Head guessed.

"Understatement," Dagim stated. "Weren't you?"

"Nope, I knew barely anything would happen," The Head said. "That's all I expected."

Dagim crossed his arms firmly, his blackened eyes sparkling with curiosity as he waited for an elaboration on his leader's part.

"The tad bit of discomfort you showed from that morsel proved something to me. Frederica and the Foreseers were right, you truly aren't ready to consume the full source. It's not quite the right time. But the fact that you just showed no further adverse symptoms proved something else..." The Head stated with building anticipation. "...I was also right after all. You *will* be able to consume the source much earlier than expected. If I were you, I would double the intensity of my battle training to prepare."

"Right," Dagim muttered. His eyes lowered, fixating on the dirt below as he processed it all. Even the adverse symptoms he did show were fading. The stirring in his stomach had slowed, his nose had cleared, and the taste of blood in his mouth became strangely sweet. That waning sense of pride that had been dampened within him as of late swelled with a renewed vitality.

"You've heard the mutters circulating among our forces about you and the source?"

"I have."

"And what do they say?"

"Something along the lines of me being a wild animal of a man with a cursed life who will ruin everything and everyone if I consume the source."

"Do you believe the first part to be true?"

"First part?"

"The part about you being a wild animal of a man with a cursed life?"

Dagim shrugged. He did not want to say that he believed it was true, but he could not honestly state that it was not.

"I believe it," The Head said, answering his question, much to Dagim's surprise. "But my belief in it is why I believe the opposite of the second part. I think a wild animal of a man with a cursed life is the perfect recipient of that Ultimatum gold. The only men fit to consume such a source are men like you and me."

Only men like him and The Head? Devil Child was not sure what to make of that. "What do you mean?" he asked, stumped.

"There's a very specific set of reasons as to why our planet is the way it is. Reasons that explain why, as humans of the 31st century, we live in a sparse, ungoverned society that our ancient ancestors would consider a technologically-regressed hellhole," said The Head. "And it's not just because of The Divinity's awful rule and the fauxangel attacks that come with it. Do you know what the other reasons are?"

Dagim's head shook. He had not given the state of their planet much thought further than the deep will he had to protect it from The Divinity's fauxangels. The other pervading issues of their nigh-empty wayward and barren world were hardly a point of rumination for him.

"Most of humanity's problems stem from a lack of a gut understanding of the raw power within man that causes us to improve and thrive. Instinctual incompetence, I call it. Our ancestors reached fantastic technological heights that we might struggle to *ever* replicate. But in a way, I'm glad it's like that. They cultivated immense power that caused human destruction through both their few successes and many failures. Due to a mixture of overreliance on their tech and an understanding of their capabilities on an intellectual level, but not an instinctual one," The Head explained in detail.

"I see," Dagim said, though he struggled to take it all in. He pieced enough together to see the direction The Head was pointing him to, as he waited for more clarification.

"I was a child with too much violent energy growing up, just like you were. I was arrested multiple times before I was ten. I joined a bunch of older boys, thugs of the street, and ended up killing my first fauxangel with them at twelve. I got up to all sorts of shit. The type of shit a kid gets into when they have no family or community to guide them. Just like you did," The Head told Dagim. Revelations that increased the amount of respect he had for him.

"But it was that same intense, awful, violent energy that fuelled my passion to become Killbroker, the best soldier of my recruit class. It's the same energy that allowed me to rise to the rank of Head Foreseer and lead all of Planet Magnae," The Head continued. "But an even greater fate awaits you. You've always known that."

Dagim was speechless. Those mixed emotions of pride, fear, and vitality stirred within once again. The Head gripped Dagim by the back of his neck, holding him tight like a father would whilst bestowing urgent wisdom onto his son. Dagim rested a hand on one of The Heads as the two men locked passionate gazes.

"Do not be ashamed of what you are and how you came to be this way," The Head advised. "If you truly wish to save humanity, you must embrace the awful power within you, Devil Child."

XIV. LIMINAL LIGHT

POISON. A couple of drops of a secreted poison from a jungle leaf not too far from camp was how Frederica had tried to kill Dagim a week prior. A series of plans she set in place once she gained access to the prepared meals of the top ten recruits on the morning of her assassination attempt. Her caution had gotten the better of her. If she had wanted to make sure he would succumb to the vile black substance, she should have mixed in more. But then the poison would have risen to the top, increasing the chances that Dagim or someone else, for that matter, would notice it in his cup.

All First Ranger had succeeded in doing was putting Devil Child through a day's worth of intense pain and sickness of the body and mind, which he quickly recovered from. Yet despite her failure, Frederica could not shake the mountain of guilt that weighed down on her shoulders.

Knowing what she had done, she was unable to even face the majority of her fellow recruits. Ironically, the only recruit she had interacted with during that point in time was Dagim himself, through that secluded meeting the Foreseers had about the Ultimatum Source. Other than that, Frederica had made it her duty to avoid Dagim or anyone close to him. From Roisin to Hugo to even Stefan. She used this situation as a reason to respond to a request that had been asked of her before, but she had never got around to. She took part in the Magnae Forces recruit relocation scheme.

The task of protecting the ruinous towns, the last remnants of civilian settlements, and other village establishments, from orphanages to schools to bars, was a responsibility strictly for the South Magnae Forces. But with their dwindling numbers in the war, desperate times called for many South Magnae Forces to join the fields of combat along with their North Magnae counterparts. As a way to cover these losses, high-ranked recruits of the North, such as Frederica, supplemented the guarding ranks in place of the three mid-to-low-ranked recruits of the South who joined the North's armies.

***

Swapping out her North Magnae crimson battle wear for South Magnae navy blue, Frederica's daily tasks differed. Instead of planning most battles and observing a few, she would organise which squads should defend which civilian area at which time of the day. On alternating days, she would join these squads, aiding in the menial tasks of cleaning the streets of burnt items and dead fauxangel victims. She enjoyed these days much less than the others.

Frederica was never one to be disturbed by constant death and destruction. She understood it as a natural consequence of living in a cruel world and a dying planet. Yet the strength of her stomach was tested through her work with the South Forces. Even someone of her constitution could not deal with the sights in the towns they patrolled through.

Whether it was The Divinity himself or his fauxangel ranks, their alien adversaries had a sick sense of humour when it came to displaying their human kills. That week, it seemed that the fauxangels chose to target humans aged ten and under for their killing sprees. It also seemed that they opted against their usual burning fires, choosing decapitation as the mode of execution for these child victims. Hundreds of these decapitated heads were placed in every pond, lake, or river close to a civilian settlement. Not only did that mean the waters of most villages were contaminated, leaving little for them to drink, but it meant Frederica and the South forces would have to fish out every youthful skull to clean the water with many civilian onlookers. A very effective morale dampener, even for those as strong as Frederica thought herself to be.

One of the heads reminded her of her late nephew Denis. The only other Rasmussen she got along with, since she was the only person who bothered to take care of the young boy. If he had not lost his life in the Disquiet Sea years ago, she could imagine his head being one of these found in ponds.

For the first time since the start of the war proper, Frederica could honestly see humanity losing. She considered not just the prospect of the fauxangels beating them, but the high likelihood that her generation would end up being humanity's last.

***

Back at the North Magnae Forces, Stefan surveyed the outer perimeter of their camp. He did not consider it wise to call Aiza's bluff. When Foreseer VII threatened to tell The Head, he knew she meant business.

Every day, Stefan would travel alone along the outer regions of their camp, searching far and wide for any tent, re-purposed abandoned building, or makeshift shelter in the forests that Anais might have been temporarily living in. He did not find a single one this time. For once, she had listened and taken herself far away from North Magnae camps. He sighed with relief.

He did not see his girlfriend, but he did see another familiar face. Hugo Stacey, who was joined by a not-so-familiar face. Heart Stealer and a rough man were talking.

Silent Memoir utilised his exceptional skill of sneaking up on others without leaving even a trace of sound to get a closer look at the scene. He hid himself amongst the trees as he watched Hugo and the non-recruit stranger collude. By the time Stefan had reached a position close enough in the forest to eavesdrop, they had finished their discussion. He came just in time to see the transaction that followed. As Hugo handed the man ten magenta-coloured, triangle-shaped coins, the man handed him a small bag of purple powder. Silent Memoir's past as a troublesome swindling child saw him easily able to identify the drug that had just been placed into Heart Stealer's hand. He watched Hugo tuck away his newly purchased Granulate P.

As the man left, exiting to the other side of the forest, Stefan realised his face was indeed familiar. He had seen the same man a few days ago. The last time he had seen the man was also during one of his outskirt searches for Anais. The man was also colluding with another recruit he knew well at that time. But this was the first time he had realised what was obvious with hindsight - the man was a substance dealer. His soft brown eyes narrowed with suspicion.

Stefan picked out a spare piece of paper and a small pencil from his back pocket, using it to quickly scribble down a note. With the note written, he emerged from hiding.

"Oh shit, Stefan," a startled Hugo gasped as he stepped in front of him. "What are you doing out here?"

Stefan slammed the note against Hugo's chest. The tall blonde recruit picked it off and read it.

"You just purchased Granulate P, didn't you? Don't bother trying to lie about it. I saw you exchange money for it with my own two eyes."

Hugo bit his lip nervously. Stefan could tell from his scanning eyes that he was searching for the right lie that would get him out of this situation. He could tell from his defeated sigh after that he was unable to come up with something and so could only come out with the truth.

"You caught me, I've been taking Granulate P! Heart Stealer's a druggie, I've been exposed!" Hugo admitted with frustration. "And unless you want me to go back to freezing on the battlefield, you better leave me be, mind your business, and not tell a single other fucking person."

Stefan palmed his hand against his face. He would have berated Hugo if he had the voice to do so. Instead, he composed himself as he wrote another note for Hugo to read.

"Are you getting some for Roisin?" Stefan's note said. Hugo scratched at the crown of his head. "No," he answered, blunt and bewildered. "What's Roisin got to do with this?"

Stefan's lips pursed downwards in disappointment as he wrote a final line on the last piece of paper he had brought with him. He dashed it to Hugo upon completion.

"I saw Roisin make a deal with the same man you did," it read as Hugo stared down at it. He looked back up at Stefan in disquietude.

***

"That's enough for now. If there aren't any spiritual cultists in the area, we'll start on Austral come sunrise," Frederica told the members of her South Magnae squadron.

The navy-clad men and women dispersed, leaving the river to return to their stations as civilian guards. It was a job well done. Though it would have been done better had they

133

not had to relocate a group of praying spiritual cultists in the area.

Frederica remained by the river, mourning the loss of the youthful corpses they had taken out and buried. As she did so, First Ranger was met with a sudden shock of instantaneousness. A light forming from the molecules in the air. The light blinded her at such an alarming pace that her vision was taken away from her before she had even realised what was happening. Panic set into Frederica, her heart dropping as her eyes closed.

The light faded just as quickly as it had formed, and Frederica was able to open her eyes again. She was surrounded by a liminal space of blinding light whiter than the one that had sent her into this trance. Frederica felt as if she had been transported outside of the universe itself, her surroundings cold and absent. Then a person teleported in front of her. A female fauxangel with a wry smirk.

As opposed to the typical fauxangel complexion of glowing gold, her pale skin vibrated with a dark, encompassing aura. Her hair was a brown frizzy mess.

"Treacherous. They're all so treacherous," this special fauxangel said to her.

"Sorry?!" Frederica uttered with muddled trepidation.

"Kill them all. It's all they deserve. You know it's true," the special fauxangel said in an excited, sensual whisper. "You know it."

The blinding light attacked her face again, taking her out of the dream-like trance and back to reality. The liminal light had vanished, the dark-aura fauxangel leaving with it.

"What was that?!" Frederica panted, scrambling by the riverbed as she gathered herself. Two things came to mind.

Either the guilt of the attempt on Dagim's life, combined

with the depression brought on by the decapitated child heads, had started to fracture her mind.

Or over-exposure to fauxangel energy had sent her well and truly mad.

XV. HOLY LITERATURE

TO be healed was a wonderful thing. Quinn thought as much as she sat on Roisin's medical table.

While not surprised, she was impressed at how quickly Roisin was able to heal her mangled ankle. All it took was some initial cleaning, the on-and-off removal and application of a cast and one final day-long treatment session using massages and high-grade ointment. The now profusely reddened but clear and clean skin on the area where the wound once was, hurt almost as bad as the fauxangel fire that had damaged it in the first place. Still, it would be bearable enough for her to walk, sprint, and even jump. She would be back to scavenging in no time. She was also impressed at how easily Roisin had been able to make the tent that was provided for her into a cosy medical room. Especially with the shelves of books and supplies that hung from the tent's ceiling via a strong thread.

"I don't think I saw you take even a single break during that last session," Quinn said, delighted as she felt the healed skin on her ankle. "You're called Recruit Infinity for a reason."

"You recovered quite well. You're called Queen Triumph for a reason," Roisin complimented back with a cheeky smile. Quinn laughed, nodding her head as she moved her ankle joint some more.

Quinn left Roisin's tent in a mood as chipper as her newly healed step. Her next destination should have raised her mood higher. In theory, at least.

The early hours of that morning had Quinn and several other recruits clumped together in clusters as they filled the marquee tent at the heart of the camp. A pair of Foreseers toiled with the gruelling task of keeping the clattering recruits in an orderly line. Grasping recruit hands breached the barrier between the Foreseers and their desks of boxes. The few recruits who bothered to stand in the queue were the first to receive the cash-filled envelopes in each. Each would disregard the patience they had held up to that point once the envelope was in their hands, tearing it to get their pay.

By the time Quinn had reached the front of the queue and received her envelope, most other recruits had collected their cash and made themselves scarce. She bit her lip, consumed by anticipation as she carefully opened it. Sour disappointment was all that awaited her. The measly seven magenta coins she had expected to be there at the very least were absent, only three existing in their place.

"This can't be real," she sighed, the emptiness of the envelope disgusting her. Three pitiful pink isosceles and nothing more.

Quinn peered across the emptying marquee in search of someone with enough authority to explain the insultingly low pay she had been given and why. Foreseer III leaned by the front desk. The tall, toned, and tired-looking recruit leader stood there, his eyes glazed.

"Excuse me," Quinn called out as she approached him.

"Yes," Foreseer III sighed, already regretting having the conversation before it had even started.

"I have a question about my recruit pay."

"Unhappy with it?"

"Yes. I'd like to understand where the rest of it went," Quinn said as she showcased the cash.

Foreseer III leaned over, his forearms flexed and knuckles pressed down as he studied the envelope. An eyebrow was raised at Quinn.

"I don't understand. What's the problem?"

"Last time I checked, three is less than half of seven. Why did I receive such a severe pay cut?"

"We've cut out redundant funds, reallocated them towards increased weapon manufacturing capabilities," Foreseer III explained. "A sacrifice you should deal with if you don't want us to keep losing this war."

"Half my pay wasn't a redundant fund," Quinn scowled.

"You were out of commission. This will make up for all the blade energy and bullet material that went unscavenged during your absence," Foreseer III argued. "If I were you, I'd get used to that pay. Consider yourself lucky if it even rises again before this war is done."

Had there been no witnesses, Quinn might have acted on the impulse her body and mind were begging of her, and forced his mouth shut with a punch.

"The money I earn here goes straight to the Iqra House Orphanage. One of the last properly-run civilian establishments on Magnae!" she explained. "It's not going to stay that way on three fucking mag-coins!"

Foreseer III sighed deeply out of his nose. "Well, you should have thought about that earlier," he grumbled. "Imagine if you had just kept scavenging and not thrown yourself into a battle that wasn't even asked of you. You'd have never been injured, and you'd still have your orphan money."

"This isn't right," Quinn cried. "I shouldn't-"

"Do me a favour and get the fuck out of my face before I break yours," Foreseer III ordered with a snarl. "I'm tired of you damn entitled recruits."

Quinn was just as surprised by his candid threats as she had been by the drastic pay cut. "Unbelievable," she muttered in defeat as she left the marquee tent.

***

Dagim was primed and ready for war. The small portion of the Ultimatum Source he had ingested in combination with the passionate words of wisdom The Head Foreseer bestowed upon him that day had replenished his virility. He took every chance he could to fight in a battle. Not a morning or afternoon went by where he was not engaged in combat, and not an evening went by without hours of gruelling self-directed training.

It was a miracle he had not torn his tent to shreds as he practised violent swings of his great sword. He visualised the savage killings of dozens of fauxangels, frothing at the mouth as if he was currently in battle. The special dark-aura fauxangel that had plagued his mind was the most common victim of these fantasies. He imagined gutting and scouring her a million times over.

***

Dagim and the squadron of warriors who joined him proved to become disconcerted by the constant losses in battle North Magnae had been experiencing. Together, they took great risks to aid in the slow process of reversing it. Efforts to catch groups of fauxangels off guard had taken them to the strangest of places to fight and search. It took them to what could only be described as a plane of fire.

Miles of blood-orange rocky land scorched so hot by the sun that steam rose from the dirt every time one took a step. Standing in the same position for too long saw you likely to burn your feet worse than being a victim of a fauxangel's attack. The Devil Child did not mind. He would walk through literal hellfire if it meant he could get his sword bloody.

Dagim sank his sword through the scarred stomach of the only fauxangel he had managed to find that day. He received boundless pleasure from watching the humanoid alien choke on the blood that pooled in his mouth, not minding the vile tyrian purple liquid sprayed over his crazed face. He twisted his great sword, skewering the creature as he held him in place.

"Your bastard leader's next," Dagim threatened, reaching for his Bronze Bullet in its scabbard. He forced it into his victim's mouth and yanked at the trigger. He enjoyed the mess of fleshy confetti that resulted from it, the dark-red skies speckled with fauxangel rain.

With his Bullet spent through the fauxangel's head, Dagim was the only life moving in the area, not counting the sizzling plants that shrivelled under the belting sun.

"Where did the rest of them go?" he asked himself as he turned left and right.

An unceasing desire to track down and kill this wandering fauxangel had consumed Dagim. Therefore, he had chosen to depart from the group he had come out with when he chased after it. He assessed that they must have continued with the search through the plains of fire. He grunted, placing his sword back in its scabbard as he looked around for a squadron to regroup with.

***

Dagim's sense of direction failed him that day. It was as if the universe had conspired against him meeting his fellow recruits again. The bottom of his recruit boots had been burned down a layer from the miles of scorching rock he had marched up and down. An hour into his wandering walks, Dagim had completely given up on finding a squadron. He had chosen not to make the journey back to a camp, staying in the scorching area. Something else had caught his eye, shining in the distance as he trekked the fields of fire.

When thinking of the areas most affected by the misfortune of humanity and fauxangel attacks, Fay Nation came to mind. The plains of fire Dagim walked upon did not make for a healthy and stable ground to claim as land and build on. So naturally, his curiosity was piqued as he eyed a fully intact building hidden on the underside of a shallow cliff from afar. After minutes of marching and climbing down, Devil Child was at the doorstep.

It was not the grandest of structures up close, but Dagim was impressed that a building of such fine stature was still standing in an area like this. It reminded him of tales he had heard of the Earthly Roman Empire countless centuries ago. It sported polished white columns that held up a flat, indented roof and golden-numeral metal plate decorations over the doors. Dagim had spent enough time admiring. It was time, he thought, to see whatever was still standing in this refined abandoned building.

Dagim's wonder and awe diminished once he walked through the corridors of the building. The walls were different shades of red and grey, marked with dirt, burns and blood, and every piece of furniture had been charred and broken to pieces. The interior did not hold a candle to the beauty of the exterior, like a very gorgeous person with a severely lacking personality. Dagim smirked, recalling Quinn having half-jokingly made that same observation about Hugo once around the campfire.

As Dagim walked through the building, grimacing at the monument of internal destruction, his curiosity remained

141

high. He had seen mouldy clumps of golden paste in the corners of the front room, telling him this was an abandoned fauxangel sanctuary. As lacklustre as the location proved to be, he knew he could derive some valuable information from searching it.

With a calm face, he thrashed and tore through the building. Rampant destruction being second nature to him, he ruined the building's shoddy interior further, smashing and breaking any items or pieces of furniture that cluttered his search and emptying the room. After the twentieth trinket smashed to the side and the fourth burnt chair broke against the wall, Dagim found something of use.

"What do we have here?" he muttered to himself as he parted a pile of charred scrolls to find a book vibrating with weak fauxangel energy.

"Humans versus Deities: The True History of Magnae Struggle," Dagim read the title aloud. An intriguing title. Devil Child could not remember the last time he sat and read a book so thick. Its contents were twice as intriguing as the title, as Dagim sat in a corner of the room and indulged himself in its tales.

***

Several hours and countless pages later, Dagim's mind had been expanded more than ever before. He had only read about a quarter of the daunting book, flicking between different sections, focusing on the most interesting parts, and skim-reading the rest. His head throbbed with a thick essence of pain, as if all the knowledge he had just consumed had been physically filed away in a container within his brain that was threatening to burst.

As Dagim shut the book, he paused for a moment to think. He did not know for sure whether the intriguing revelations contained within that book were the *true history* of Magnae's struggle. All he knew was he had to share what he learned with someone else as soon as possible.

***

Hugo stood by the seating logs at the end of the camp, arms folded as he watched the congregations in the site's midsection. His eyes fixated on Roisin. The charming flame-haired medic was her usual bubbly self, pleasantly fraternising with her fellow recruits. Hugo thought of her in a different light now, dubious as he observed her every step.

What did Stefan mean when he said he saw her making a deal with the same man? Was Roisin taking Granulate P as well? That seemed unlikely. She was not a soldier. She also was not the type to supplement her body with unsavoury substances. Yet Stefan had sworn he saw her talk with his very same dealer. Perhaps it was a health thing, Hugo considered. He had seen her grip at one of her arms now and then. Maybe she was secretly taking something to ease the pain? He was not sure how right he was. He needed definite answers but knew he would get nowhere if he asked her directly. He would have to either snoop around or catch her in the act, just like Stefan had done with him.

Hugo turned to the side as he heard heavy footsteps bounding in his direction. He watched as Dagim hurried his way across the south camp. He joined his side with a bag.

"Hey Dagim, have you spoken to Roisin recently? I-"

"Could you remind me of everything we've learned about the origins of The Divinity and his fauxangels?" Dagim asked, interrupting him with urgency.

Hugo laughed. "Why? Are you repeating Recruit School?" he mocked. "Or are you a spiritual cultist now?"

"Answer the goddamn question," Dagim insisted.

Hugo sighed. "Fine," he said as he thought about it for a moment. His lips pursed as the cogs turned.

143

"Well?" Dagim urged with raised brows.

Hugo rubbed his chin. "Well, for starters, The Divinity is this god-like alien from the planet Luxurae, who formed millions of years ago out of the heart of a light-"

"That's right, he's said to have *formed* millions of years ago," Dagim interrupted again, his excitement uncontainable. "But other sources describe otherwise in detail. Other sources cite him as being *created*, not formed. As if he were a creature by design. They also say he was not born millions of years ago. He was created *way* later."

Hugo scowled at Dagim as if he had gone insane. "What the hell are you talking about? What other sources?"

Dagim revealed the reason he had been carrying the bag around. He opened it and picked out an old book. Hugo laid eyes upon *Humans versus Deities: The True History of Magnae Struggle*. He noted the faded fauxangel energy it vibrated with.

"I found this in an old abandoned fauxangel sanctuary. The whole place had been trashed from the inside, and I had to turn it upside-down whilst searching for any leads on The Divinity's forces. Once I did, I found this book hiding underneath all the rubble," Dagim explained.

Hugo turned the book from side to side, inspecting every corner. "From the energy around it, we know one thing for sure. A lot of fauxangels had their slimy gold paws on it."

"I think whatever fauxangels stayed at that sanctuary must have been guarding that book, keeping it hidden until they either died or were forced to abandon the home before they could take it with them."

"Why would they want to hide this book?"

"For one, if the history in this book has any reality to it, it further exposes The Divinity as a fucking fraud. He claims to be a deity. A god older than multiple human civilisations.

But what if he's truly just an abomination *created* a couple of centuries back?" Dagim suggested.

"How exactly does it say he was created?" Hugo asked.

"It doesn't go into specifics," Dagim said. "It's filled to the brim with so many vague alternative stories of how we were told things happened in the past. It's dense but at the same time, really fucking shallow."

"How's it any use to us then?" Hugo asked.

"The information in here could be pieces of history that we've been lied to about for years!" Dagim exclaimed.

"It could also be lies, miscalculations, or straight-up fiction," Hugo dismissed.

"Could be," Dagim sighed. "But if it isn't…"

Devil Child trailed off as he flicked to the back pages of the book. He stopped at a list of names. All the authors who had contributed to the alternative knowledge within the contents of the book were there.

"Look," Dagim said, tapping at the page.

Hugo filed through the compilation of names credited in the back. One name immediately stood out.

"Ryland Best," Heart Stealer read. "Best. Why is that surname familiar?"

"I think he might be related to Keith Best," Dagim answered. "Or as we like to call him, The Head Foreseer."

XVI. QUESTIONS AND CONTINGENCIES

THE Divinity and his fauxangels. This race of aliens kept Dagim wide awake at night, in light of the glowing book and its contents. Nothing else had entered his innermost thoughts for days on end. Despite Hugo's scepticism, Dagim had only grown in his belief that the tales in the book were the true hidden history. He had no way of confirming, but for a powerful gut instinct that told him he was right. As far as he was concerned, the book held truth. The Divinity and his fauxangels were not gods who travelled to Planet Magnae to bestow their holy rule. Dagim would not be surprised if the fauxangels had only been created shortly after humanity had set foot on this planet in the first place. Humans predated Luxuraeans. He knew it.

Dagim needed answers. The teachings of the book were not enough to quench his newfound thirst for knowledge. After a battle that morning, he sought out the closest person he could find to the one author's name they recognised.

***

Dagim sat by a desk of bladed weapon crates draped over with a crimson robe and scattered with the most unorganised set of documents he had seen in the largest tent on camp. He stared across at The Head Foreseer, whom he had handed and told of the book moments ago. The Head rustled at his greying beard as he skimmed through the pages, seeing the information for himself.

"You say you found this hidden in an abandoned fauxangel sanctuary?" The Head questioned.

"Under burnt furniture inside a building under a cliff in Fay Nation," Dagim confirmed.

"If even half of this is true, it changes everything," The Head said, poking the pages. "We need to find out as much as we can with this book. Especially when and for what reason it was written."

"That's why I came to see you," Dagim said. He stood up, leaning over the scattered papers as he gestured at the book. "Look at the back where it credits all the authors," Dagim said. The Head nodded as he flicked to the back page. He pointed out the name he and Hugo had noticed.

"Ryland Best. Any relation?"
The Head pinched the skin at the side of his bald head as he thought. "I think so," he said.

"You think so?"

"Yes, I'm not sure. Something tells me that could've been my father."

"Could've been? You don't know?"

"He wasn't in my life growing up. I was raised by just my mother for a few years and the streets of Chastmensta after that. Before my mother died, I'd only heard stories about my father and who he was," The Head explained. "All I knew was that he was an adulterer who left us to go do some work or research for the fight against the fauxangels. I can't remember what my mother said his name was, though."

"I think there's a good chance your father was Ryland Best," Dagim asserted.

"Seems that way," The Head said.

"So where do we go from here?" asked Dagim.

"First of all, I'm going to do some digging on my family history. Find out more about my supposed author-father, Ryland Best," The Head said. "In the meantime, keep this book quiet around camp. Only talk about it if specifically asked. Don't want to create too much of a stir until we've found out more."

Dagim nodded as he rose from his seat. He left the book on The Head Foreseer's desk, leaving the tent to attend to his soldier duties. Before he opened the tent flaps, another thought burst into his mind.

"There's one other thing about the book we need to look into," Dagim said.

"And that is?"

"I finished reading it a few hours ago, and I noticed something big was missing."

"Yes. What was it? Spit it out."

Dagim cleared his throat with a grunt. "From the very first page to the last, there's no mention of Emmanuel Ekib," he said. "Not even the moment when he found the pond water and realised The Divinity could be hurt. Nothing."

The Head leaned forward, cracking his knuckles as his brow lowered. "Strange," he muttered, picking up the book to inspect it once again.

***

The Head's orders not to indulge the others at camp in these discussions were futile. Had he told Dagim beforehand, perhaps they could have kept what they were discussing low. But Hugo was under no instructions to keep such information quiet. A few conversations here and there spread the news quicker than fauxangel fire. By evening time, the few people who had heard of the glowing book and its alternate history had told a few others who had told a few more and so on until the book's contents were common knowledge amongst half of the North Magnae Forces.

Dagim grumbled under his breath as he witnessed the largest concentration of chattering recruits congregating at the centre of the campsite. He heard the same common words and phrases crop up in each of these overlapping conversations. Fake history, fauxangel lies, and no Ekib.

Dagim approached Hugo, cutting across his path as the third-ranked recruit made his way to the dining tent.

"Hugo, have you been talking to other recruits about the book I found?"

"Was I not supposed to?"

"Would've preferred if it was kept quiet, but there's no going back now."

Hugo gave Dagim a one-shouldered shrug as if to say, "Oh well."

The two watched the excitable rumour mill that had been made of their recruit quarters turn around.

"From what I've heard, most of the camp agrees with you," Hugo noticed. "The book was hidden in an abandoned fauxangel den for a reason. There must be some truth to it."

"Not good. We don't want people jumping the gun."

"Do you not believe the book might be the truth anymore?"

"I do, but that's just my gut feeling. Nothing's even been confirmed. The Head's still looking into his family records to learn about Ryland Best," Dagim asked.

"Let's hope we learn a lot soon," Hugo said. "People are already asking me many questions that neither of us can even hope to answer yet."

Dagim ended the conversation in non-verbal agreement. The bustling nature of the camp that day refused to dissipate. Even as the questions and accusations that the glowing book prompted had quelled, chaos brewed amongst the recruits. Worried murmurs had turned into visible panic. The curious commotion that had coloured the general aura of the area had been gradually darkening. Its origin came from the front end of the camp. As Dagim and Hugo walked towards the commotion, they knew the North Magnae Forces had just experienced their second major shock of the day.

The two recruit men stood on the perimeter edge of the main camp. The root cause of the camp commotion was laid out in front of them. Multiple squadrons of soldiers returned to camp with their battle wear burnt and fear in their eyes. A few wore deep scars on their faces, others held broken weapons stained with their blood, and some carried fire-crisped and bloody-dismembered bodies of their less fortunate comrades on their backs.

Though they were injured, they did not trudge back to camp as if returning from a lost battle miles away, a sight that had become increasingly common in the weeks gone by. They ran with fear, indicating that whatever threat had attacked them was ever-present.

Without a single word from either of them, Dagim and Hugo broke into action, ready to deal with whatever their comrades were escaping from. They stormed their tents and the weaponry marquees, collecting all the battle equipment they could before rushing out into the outskirts of the camp. As other soldiers saw them, they followed suit, Silent Memoir being one of them.

***

With his sword in hand and blazing with red-hot energy, Dagim led the crimson emergency squadron. He sprinted onto the raspberry fields his injured comrades had escaped from, with Hugo, Stefan, and a few other weapon-clad male recruits behind him.

Dagim's eyes lasered in on the threat ahead of them. Two wounded soldiers with limps sprinted from the grasp of two older male fauxangels.

As Dagim, Hugo, Stefan, and their squadron reached the area, two things became abundantly clear when assessing the couple of fauxangels. One, their burns sent blue fire like the fauxangels who had shown up at the first camp breach. The ones that were lackeys of the special fauxangel who pestered Dagim in his tent and his mind. Two, they were unbelievably fast. An effortless flick of one of their fauxangel wrists conjured up rapidly rising blue flames that engulfed both fleeing soldiers. Their bodies were burnt so thoroughly that they became piles of ash before two steps could be taken.

"Enough of that shit!" Dagim screamed as he and his soldiers ran close enough to attack the fauxangels.

Using a circling swarming formation, the eight members of this brave squad spun around the agile blue-flamed alien menaces. Their rapid, erratic movements were enough to avoid the constant rising flames the fauxangels buggered the lands with. But only just about. They kept their formation, running in spinning circles as they stepped forward to reach striking distance.

Dagim was the first to land a blow, slashing his sword against a fauxangel chest. A shallow scratch was all he was able to land as he dipped back into a side-stepping formation before a flame could reach him. Another soldier wished to apply another attack to the same area Dagim had, rushing forward with his sword. He landed a more devastating attack, drawing fauxangel blood. His efforts would have been better spent elsewhere, as he was touched by the fauxangel, a bloody hole burning into his heart as the creature's flame-covered finger touched his chest.

Regardless of what he had just seen, Hugo took his chances. Wild swishes of his axe pushed the other fauxangel back as he tried to cut him, but failed to land a single blow. He gave up his attacks, rushing away before he could be met with the same burning fate as the last one fired. The soldier who desired to follow up his attack was much less fortunate, being burned the second he stepped out of formation. In a matter of a minute, their chances of victory had been significantly lessened.

"Fuck it, let's do this," Dagim said, skipping past all the plans he had for this battle in his head as the emergency trump card forced its way to the front of his mind. One glance at Hugo had the recruits on the same page.

"All-Star Bronze Contingency?" Hugo asked. Dagim nodded.

"All-Star Bronze Contingency in three!" he ordered the remaining soldiers. "One! Two! Three!"

Dagim, Hugo, Stefan, and the remaining soldiers took a bold risk, halting their constant movements and planting their feet on the ground. With quick draw and no care for aim, all the soldiers released their Bronze Bullets from their scabbards, blasting the copper-coloured projectiles out of their cylindrical casings with panicked pulls of five simultaneous triggers pointed at the duo.

One of the fauxangels was successfully killed by this attack, two lucky bullets having made their way through one ear and out the other, leaving a hole through the side of his head. The other had been caught by the other three bullets, all to the gut and torso. But he still clung to life.

Stefan saw to put an end to this. As the fauxangel lifted his finger, Stefan's side steps to avoid his blue fire were done with such speed that it looked as if he was walking on air. Three of his energy-laden throwing knives were flung into the three bloody bullet holes on the fauxangel, putting an end to its defiant rise.

"God," Hugo sighed with relief as they watched it take its final breath. The five soldiers took a moment to gather themselves post-battle. They had killed two high-grade fauxangels in such a short matter of time, yet none of them felt good about this result. Not even Dagim.

That was the third time a set of fauxangels had exposed and breached an area of theirs close to camp. This time, they had gotten too close. All were aware of the low likelihood that they would be able to survive a fourth breach.

XVII. EMBRACE

THE three highest-ranked male recruits and the two other surviving soldiers walked through the raspberry fields of the outer camp region. They stumbled upon a part of the field where the original conflict had blossomed. They saw a few injured soldiers groan as they rolled on the floor, a rover parked to the side, a collection of hundreds of fire marks burnt into the ground, and a litany of corpses, three being fauxangels, and twenty-two being Magnae soldiers.

"Let's get to work then," Hugo sighed.

The two other soldiers attended to the rover, making sure the energy fuel capsules were full enough for the journey back to the main camp, and the mechanism that pulled the wheels forward would be able to handle the load back.

Dagim, Hugo, and Stefan cleaned the battlefield of their comrades. The few who were injured and awake were eased into the backseat of the rover. The dead bodies were gathered in a pile to be buried. Some soldiers seemed to be dead initially but would prove to have either been unconscious or comatose upon inspection. The sight of one of these cases caused Dagim's heart to burn.

"Roisin," Dagim gasped as the body was presented to him by Stefan. Her North Magnae armour had been destroyed, falling off her in metal chips that exposed her shins, arms, and parts of her midriff.

"Is she alive?"

Stefan placed a careful finger on her neck. He nodded yes, that simple gesture filling Dagim with wild relief. Dagim took Roisin off of Stefan's arms, reviewing every part of her body for signs of serious or potentially fatal injury.

"Is that a fauxangel burn?" Dagim asked, using his head to point at Roisin's arm.

From the bottom of her elbow to just underneath her shoulder, the area's skin was dark in contrast to her peachy complexion.

"It doesn't look like one," Hugo said, wincing with subtle disgust. The trio studied Roisin's arm, noticing the blackened marks had not stained any other part of her body. Closer inspection proved the injury to be a series of continuous bruises as opposed to the aftermath of fauxangel burning.

Stefan's eyes shone with sudden realisation, with Hugo's doing the same soon after. The two gave each other a look, privy to information that Dagim was not. Information they did not share, and a look Dagim could not decipher. He was not interested in doing so anyway, the only concern in his mind being Roisin's well-being as he forced the tears not to leave his eyes.

"At least she's still breathing. Thank God for that," Dagim sighed, counting their blessings. "Who's the best medic at camp after her?"

"Well, there's Doctor Smethwick, but I think he left after the pay drops," Hugo sighed.

"What about the recruit medics?"

"I'm not sure who's second."

"Whoever it is, we need to get her to them quick," Dagim said. "Let's not waste any more time. Pile the bodies in and take the rover back to camp."

Dagim rushed to the rover with Roisin in his arms, his two comrades watching. Hugo and Stefan shared another look before separating to follow Dagim's instructions.

***

Frederica returned from her weeks of civilian guard service amongst the South Magnae Forces, re-joining the North Magnae camps. Upon her arrival, she had decided she would keep herself locked in her tent for a short while before attending to her old duties of organising and observing battles. Her brief stint of madness at the riverbed had left her severely shaken up even weeks after the fact. The image of the fauxangel woman with the dark aura, chanting about how she should never trust and only kill, replayed in her mind during every waking hour. She had wanted to keep to herself until her mind was clear once again. But she could not remain idle for long. She threw herself back into work, involving herself in Magnae camp affairs as if she had never left.

A lot had happened in her absence. Worried retellings of how fauxangels with blue fire almost seized their camp echoed through the ranks. If that was not enough to think about, she heard murmurs about new fauxangel history. A special book had been found and brought back to camp.

A book that claimed most of the history they knew about The Divinity was fake, a claim that, though Frederica found initially ridiculous, she was starting to consider when she saw how many recruits and even Foreseers believed it. She did not understand and was deeply interested in finding out more. The inconsistent ramblings of the other recruits around the camp did nothing to clear the confusion for her.

When The Vice Foreseer asked to speak with Frederica privately in her tent, she hoped he would enlighten her as to what they had learned concerning this book. Unfortunately, he had chosen to discuss other matters.

156

"Why on God's red Magnae is Devil Child still alive?!" he asked as he stood over her with imposing vexation.

Frederica gulped. "I've been meaning to speak to you about that," she said. "I no longer want to be a part of any plans to end his life."

The Vice Foreseer shuffled as he increased in indignation. "You were more than happy to give me the impression that you could follow through, First Ranger. May I ask why?"

Frederica believed honesty to be the only policy in this scenario. "I did try to end his life a few weeks prior. A few drops of poison in his drink," she answered. "It failed to kill him and only succeeded in poisoning my mind with guilt."

The Vice Foreseer squinted his eyes. "What is there to feel guilty for here?" he asked. "What we're doing is just! Weren't you in agreement that an animal like Dagim could not be trusted with ultimate power?!"

"I don't care. I don't wish to be responsible for the death of one of my comrades. Animal or not," Frederica asserted.

The Vice Foreseer let out a deep, frustrated sigh as he leered over Frederica. First Ranger clenched with a subtle anxiety when she looked over his face, the very picture of exasperation.

"The fauxangels are grinding out the last bit of hope we have of winning. Soon, the emergency glass will be broken and Devil Child will be bestowed with superhuman abilities greater than anyone in history has ever held," The Vice warned. "When that day arrives? Chaos."

"It's a risk we'll have to take," Frederica said. "Worst case scenario, he uses his powers to save mankind, and then we'll have to deal with whatever chaos he brings afterwards. I've made peace with that."

Frederica expected to be beaten over the head with continuous lectures or strong words of further indignation. She did not expect The Vice to accept and walk away.

"We'll see how long that peace lasts," The Vice chuckled in a whisper as he left the tent.

Frederica's shoulders relaxed, relieved for him to be out of her sight. But not even up to five minutes later, Frederica's tent was intruded upon by another stern-faced Foreseer. One of a lower rank and opposite gender.

"Hello, Foreseer VII," Frederica said, surprised to see Aiza burst into her sleeping quarters so suddenly.

"Hello, First Ranger. Or should I start calling you Foreseer VIII, considering the way you've been colluding?" Aiza blurted out. "What's this about animals and poison?"

Both the tanned colour and stern confidence that Frederica wore on her face drained, leaving her looking like a pale, frightened child. Aiza nodded, the look telling her everything she needed to know.

"You were eavesdropping?" Frederica asked, attempting to appear more frustrated than she was frightened.

"I've had some theories of my own about Dagim's sickness that day. And I've been keeping my eyes and ears out for suspicious activity," Aiza told her. "I decided to take a trip to the back of your tent once I saw The Vice walking towards it to hear for myself. And what do I hear? That my theories were valid."

Frederica scoffed. "Then what do you plan on doing about this?" she asked boldly.

"Do me a favour and file away the iron-lady act," Aiza mocked. "We both know you'd crumble if I went and told the camp about your little assassination attempt."

Frederica pouted. She could not deny that she, in fact, would. "I'll ask you again, then," she said, insisting on maintaining that *iron-lady* tone about her. "What do you plan on doing about this?"

Aiza's eyes travelled up to the top of the tent as she dwelled on the thought. Frederica tensed herself to prevent her body from shaking as the Foreseer's gaze lowered.

"I think I'll keep it to myself," Aiza decided. Frederica's eyes threatened to pop out of her head in surprise.

"Genuinely?"

"Yes. Do you want to know why, Frederica?"

"Why?"

"Because you not only showed guilt for what you have done, but you put your foot down, making it clear that the plans were over. It takes resolve to tell The Vice Foreseer to fuck off," Aiza said with a hint of pride.

Frederica felt a cool breeze wave over her, her anxieties leaving as the words left Aiza's mouth.

"But do you know what I want you to do in return for my favour?" the Foreseer asked right after.

Frederica's anxiety returned faster than it had left as she considered what Aiza could suggest of her.

"What?" she asked.

Aiza laughed. "I want you to expose The Vice. Let everyone know about him and his plans to kill Dagim."

"You can't be serious?" Frederica gasped. She considered that almost as bad as exposing herself.

"I am," Aiza insisted. "And if you don't, I'll go back on my promise and let everyone know about your little poisoning habits."

Aiza did not give Frederica the chance to argue her way out of it. She aggressively patted her on the shoulder, spun around, and marched out of her tent.

"You've got to be fucking joking," Frederica muttered to herself, exasperated.

It was evening time, and the camp was quiet but for the few recruits who started the process of packing their items in preparation for their next camp move the following morning. Hugo, too, kept himself busy, pacing up and down the camp as he reached the seats around the campfire. They were empty, apart from a few choice recruits.

It had been quite a while since Heart Stealer was able to sniff some Granulate P, and to say he was going through the effects of withdrawals would have been a great understatement. His hands had been too clammy to keep a hold of his cup at mealtime. His mind had been too frayed to hold a steady conversation. His body had been too plagued by jitters to hold himself together. His last Granulate P stash had run out. He used the final batch during the last battle he fought with Dagim and Stefan, and his recruit pay would see him unable to secure more.

"Why did I get hooked on that shite?!" Hugo had whispered to himself a dozen times that day.

A part of Hugo was glad he had run out. He could not continue taking Granulate P after seeing Roisin's injuries a few days prior. He and Stefan had shared a look that day, and though they both said nothing to each other, they were thinking the same thing. Whatever deal Roisin had made with the substance dealer was probably to supply her with something to deal with her bruised, degenerating arm. A condition none of them had known about, which had to be an intentional omission on Recruit Infinity's part.

Seeing Roisin in that state made him feel guilty about his substance habits. At least she was trying to counteract a degenerative condition. He felt as if his excuse was weak in comparison. Cowardice in battle was hardly an ailment.

Hugo sped up his pacing walk. Sweats and shaking made it disgustingly uncomfortable for him to lie down at night. This was the best he could do to keep his body fresh.

After an hour of constant walking, his legs ached, but the sweats had been cooled by the air, and the shaking had passed. For the time being, at least.

***

With his body having returned to feeling normal, or at least as normal as it could be, Hugo put an end to his constant movements by sitting by the campfire. He stared at the crackling campfire in front of him. He would have allowed himself to space out and lose his mind in the flames had there not been a rarer and more intriguing sight there: Quinn Trepanier shedding a tear.

Hugo could not believe his eyes at first as he saw the headstrong girl he spent most of his time engaging in vitriolic spars of insults and mockery with, bawling her eyes out. With concern etched on his face, he stood up, walking across to the seat beside her.

Queen Triumph had been so preoccupied with her wailing that she had not noticed Hugo sitting beside her until he tapped her on the shoulder. She took sight of him, removing her hands from her head to reveal a red face with quivering green eyes.

"What's wrong?" Hugo asked, genuinely concerned. Quinn did not believe him to be so. "Leave me alone," she grunted, clearing her eyes.

"I want to find out what's up with you first," Hugo insisted.

"Hugo, fuck off. I'm not in the mood for your damn quips and insults," Quinn said.

"Neither am I, I'm honestly asking," Hugo said, soft of tone. "I've never seen you get like this before."

161

Quinn searched his eyes for signs of hidden ridicule. Finding none, she let her woes be known.

"You know Iqra House? That home I grew up in?"

"Sort of."

"I got a letter from her today. She says they're thinking about shutting down soon."

"What? Why?"

"My recruit pay was the only thing that kept them afloat. It got cut due to my stupid fucking injury, and now they're struggling to keep the walls from crumbling down!" Quinn ranted. "All those children could be left without a home, and it'll be all my fault!"

Hugo watched Quinn's jaw clench. Her eyes squirmed as they coated themselves in more tears.

"That's rough," Hugo sighed, shaking his head in solidarity. Quinn sniffed away a tear as she nodded back. Hugo found himself wanting to put an arm around her to console her, but was conflicted as to whether it would be the right move. He decided to test the waters, reaching over to embrace her. Surprisingly, she accepted this embrace.

"It's not your fault," Hugo consoled. "It's not like you asked to be injured like that. Or for that prick Foreseer III to cut your pay."

"But it still happened. And it wouldn't have if I just did my actual job," Quinn sighed.

"I think it's sweet, you know," Hugo chuckled. "You wanted to help your old home so bad that you were willing to do something as fucking stupid as fight fauxangels with no experience. It's lovely."

Quinn's eyes surveyed Hugo from one end of his wide, charming smile to the other.

"I can never tell when you're being serious or not," she said, a sly smile forming on her face.

"That's part of the fun. Most of the time, I am serious. You just assume I'm not."

"Really? Like when?"

Hugo paused as he thought of an answer. An interesting one came to mind, but he was visibly reluctant to spit it out.

"Hmm? Are you gonna tell me?" Quinn asked, smirking as she prodded him for the answer.

Hugo sighed. "You know when I joke about how strangely beautiful you look when you're irritated with me? Well, I'm never actually joking," Hugo admitted with an embarrassed chuckle.

Quinn felt her cheeks blush hot. Just like they had during their last encounter in his tent. "Yes, you are. Shut up," she chuckled, equally embarrassed.

"I'm not, I swear. I can't think of a pair of eyes I enjoy staring into more than yours. Honest to God," Hugo chuckled. "Even when you're fuming, cursing me out, and trying to force your hands into my pocket, I can't help but dive deeper into those eyes. They're amazing."

Quinn's eyes had dried from tears yet shone with a glint. She had no response but a warm smile. A smile that Hugo reciprocated as he stared at her with longing eyes of his own.

What happened next surprised both. Neither even thought about what they felt compelled to do before they did it. Once they did, they could hardly fathom it was happening. Heart Stealer and Queen Triumph, notorious rival recruits, locked lips in a passionate embrace by the campfire.

Even with all the trials and tribulations that had been hampered upon the North Magnae Forces, Hugo and Quinn felt as if there was not a single thing amiss.

As the two recruits kissed, both felt as if, for the time being, everything was right with the world.

XVIII. RELEASE

ROISIN was used to watching people she had treated wake up from her tent hospital bed and greeting them with a smile. She was appalled when she found herself doing the opposite. She had woken up that morning in her tent's hospital bed, being greeted by a disappointed frown and a shake of a head. For the first time in a while, she had seen the pudgy face of Doctor Curtis Shaw in front of her.

"Doctor Shaw?!" she gasped, almost throwing herself from her hospital bed. "What are you doing here?!"

Doctor Shaw sighed, adjusting his glasses as he shifted himself closer to the bed. "What have you done to yourself, Roisin?" he asked, his voice laced with lamentation.

His question drew Roisin's attention to her most affected arm. The state it had reduced to was a visual shock. Never had it appeared to be so blackened and bruised. Never had it felt so wilting and weak.

"I think it's safe to say the medicine didn't work for as long as I hoped."

"I'm surprised you even had enough to last this long."

"I didn't. I had to get more from a less *reliable* source."

"And why would you do that?!"

"You know why. So that I could keep my strength up and continue my medical work."

Doctor Shaw's exasperation as to the lack of care she took of her health seemed to transform into anger. "Didn't I warn you something like this would happen if you continued your work with the Magnae Forces?! You're lucky you haven't lost it yet!" he scolded her.

"I know, sorry," Roisin sighed as she rubbed her arm.

"You're lucky I arrived in time to give you the treatment you needed!" Doctor Shaw exclaimed.

"How *did* you even get here in time? I never told anyone in the Forces about my disease, nor the treatment for it you gave me," Roisin said.

"Roisin. They've had me on standby since the day you moved to the first war camp," Doctor Shaw revealed.

"What?!" Roisin exclaimed, sitting up with a scrunched face. "Have they known about my condition all this time?!"

"I have," said a gruff voice, making themself known. Roisin watched as The Head Foreseer strolled into the tent, taking up a position next to Shaw.

"Sir," Roisin greeted uncomfortably.

The Head grunted, as disappointed in himself as Doctor Shaw was in her. "I shouldn't have let you go on this long."

"Why did you?" Roisin asked.

"You're head and shoulders above any other medic recruit we currently or have ever had. I thought that as long as you kept taking your medicine, I could risk keeping you among the ranks," said The Head. "I was fucking wrong. My foolish decision to let you carry on could have cost you an arm. Or worse."

"True," Roisin muttered, lowering her head.

"I'm sure you know what I'm to say next, Roisin."

"I do, unfortunately."

The Head took in a laboured breath, signifying the reluctance towards what he was about to confirm.

"Roisin Indermill, aka Recruit Infinity, as of now, you are no longer a member of the North Magnae Forces."

Roisin nodded. She accepted her fate with dignity as a single tear dropped from her eye.

***

Keith Best, aka The Head Foreseer, grumbled like the disgruntled older man he had so quickly become throughout his life. He was a far cry from the rambunctious ten-year-old boy who slept on the streets as he mourned his mother. The kid who would pick bloody fights with kids much older and bigger just to feel something.

Sometimes it felt as if those days were only a short while ago. So many years had passed, so much had happened. Younger him, who roamed the slums of Rogh Nation, would have never guessed these would be the types of problems older him would have to face. Being forced to release the best medic recruit his forces had to offer at a time when soldiers were being injured every second was just the icing on an ever-growing, stressful cake.

Soldier morale was plummeting faster than a meteoroid. Not to mention that despite countless nights of research, he still had not found any more information on Ryland Best or made any headway in determining what was true from the glowing book that was stirring hectic ruminations throughout the camp.

He amassed an immense amount of self-control to prevent himself from releasing his stress in the way his instincts wanted. Violently lashing out in a fit of glorious rage to be heard on the other side of the planet and across the galaxy.

He sat behind the desk of his tent, seething. Little did he know that his day was about to become twice as stressful.

Of all the things The Head Foreseer knew Frederica Rasmussen for, timidity was not one of them. He glared with bewilderment as he saw her half-peering into his tent.

"First Ranger!" The Head exclaimed, gesturing at her to come inside. First Ranger approached his desk with caution.

"Sir," Frederica said. The cracking of her voice reminded him of Roisin's when he released her earlier. "There's something you need to know."

The Head huffed out of his nose like an enraged bull. He knew whatever it was, he would not enjoy hearing it.

***

Dagim cleaned his sword of the viscous tyrian fauxangel blood that stained it. As he sat outside the weapons tent, he appreciated the rare peaceful vibes that encapsulated the camp. It was not often that one would sit down and relax, enjoying the silence of the surrounding Magnae site. It was a rare calming treat. One that was abruptly disrupted.

"The Head Foreseer's gone fucking mental!" Dagim heard a recruit exclaim. His attention was drawn towards a building crowd of recruits clambering together in a rush to reach one point of the camp.

"I think he might kill him!" another said.

Dagim stuck his sword in the ground. He took up a brisk jog as he followed the crowd to the end of camp, to see what those exclamations were referring to.

As Dagim arrived at the scene, he struggled to push to the front of the crowd. He could not make it further than the exact middle of the congregation, with recruits pushing and shoving their way about this area of the camp to get a better look. As the commotion stilled, Dagim was able to get a clear view of what was occurring.

"You treacherous cunt!" The Head Foreseer screamed as he leathered The Vice's face with his tenth vehement blow. "You dared to do such things?! Under my nose?!"

The two men were in the midst of a brutal fight. From what Dagim had observed, it was less of a fight and more of a one-sided beating of pure savagery.

"I'm sorry I didn't tell you of my plans," The Vice Foreseer coughed through a mouth flooded with warm blood.

"You're going to be sorry you ever fucking met me!" The Head threatened as he readied up another blow. The Vice Foreseer's handsome aquiline nose was turned into a broken mess after being met with a swinging headbutt that sent him crashing down to the floor.

"Please, sir. Allow me to explain myself," The Vice begged, holding both his mouth and nose to stop the blood from staining his clothes. "You'll understand why I chose to do such-"

The Head struck The Vice with a roundhouse kick across the face. The second most powerful man on North Magnae had been reduced to a blubbering, coughing, red-stained mess as he clung to the floor. Dagim's hatred for The Vice Foreseer and the attempts he had made on his life saw him delighted with being given the opportunity to watch him grovel in pain. The second-hand embarrassment of seeing such a previously great man be so woefully taken down a peg was too much, however. Even he had to admit.

The Head Foreseer crouched down to The Vice. "I don't want to hear your explanations, I want to see you get out of my fucking sight!" The Head screamed in his pathetic, wounded face. "You're no longer The Vice Foreseer of the Magnae Forces! You're nothing! Now get the fuck out of camp before I goddamn kill you!"

The Vice Foreseer nodded, meekly agreeing. The crowd of onlookers parted ways as he left the camp.

He ran away from all the Foreseers and recruits, dripping with blood and shame.

Once the former Vice was out of camp, The Head forced his way back into his tent, shouting and thrashing all the while. The recruits of the camp were in shock. Dagim knew if he asked most of the other recruits, all he would receive were conflicting stories about what had occurred that would only take him further away from the truth. He searched for the first Foreseer he could find. Once he located her, Dagim approached Aiza, who had been watching from the very back of the crowd with a blank stare.

"What was all that about?" Dagim asked her.

"You were right," she answered. "The Vice Foreseer has been trying to kill you."

"I knew it," Dagim said. The vindication he felt in having his suspicions confirmed was not as pleasurable as he anticipated it would be.

"He's had plans to make sure you don't consume The Ultimatum Source. Plans he made some of us Foreseers swear not to tell anyone. Not even The Head," Aiza explained. "But what most didn't find out until recently was that those plans involved trying to murder you."

"And people were acting like I was fucking making it up," Dagim grumbled.

"He was responsible for both the things that had almost killed you. The masked man and the drink that made you sick," Aiza added. "He's been very busy."

Dagim's jaw clenched. "Was anyone else involved in this?" he asked.

Aiza pondered for a few seconds before answering. "No. Just him," she lied.

XIX. THE SKY

AS the recruits of the North Magnae Forces continued the slow progression that was their relocation to another base, Dagim experienced that rare quiet about camp. The camp's quiet did not originate from any peace that had been bestowed upon it. Quite the opposite. It had grown emptier and colder.

The Vice had not been the only Foreseer to lose his job the previous day. Foreseers IV, V, and VI had been shown the door. They had been lucky to keep their jaws intact, unlike The Vice. Though Foreseer IV was given two black eyes for playing the part of the knife-man in the first Devil Child assassination attempt.

Only two other Foreseers kept their jobs and faces intact. Foreseer III and Aiza, Foreseer VII. Aiza, after The Head found out she was the one who insisted on Frederica telling the truth about The Vice, and Foreseer III being the only Foreseer to manage to convince The Head he had no prior idea of any of the Vice's wrongdoings.

Dagim was still unsure of why Aiza had not just told The Head herself. He heard she had eavesdropped on The Vice attempting to manipulate Frederica into aiding him in his unscrupulous plans, and that Frederica refused, but The Vice kept pressuring her. Then, Aiza had pressured her to expose him to The Head.   The entire story marred Dagim with scepticism. From what he had seen around the camp, Frederica was The Vice's favourite recruit, and he was her most trusted advisor. With the constant distrust and disdain she held for him, he was surprised that she would expose said favourite advisor to save his life. There was something he was not being told. Information being held. Not from The Head. He believed that once again, both he and the force leader were being kept in the dark. Frederica, on the other hand, he made a mental note to be warier of.

Dagim passed by a sturdy rover on its way out of camp. Its energy capsules were being filled by two recruits with golden canisters. Its back was being loaded with crates for storage by a few other recruits and Foreseer III. Hugo and Quinn were among the several prepping the rover, smiling as they aided each other in heaving a final crate onto the bed of the vehicle.

"Afternoon, guys," Dagim greeted, stopping to talk.

"Afternoon," they greeted in unison with simultaneous smiles. The pair were in a much more positive mood than anyone else at camp.

"Have either of you seen Roisin?" Dagim asked.

"Not since she got sent to the hospital," Hugo answered.

"She's *still* at the hospital?!" Quinn asked. "Will she be alright?"

"Only if they fix her arm. It looked like it was rotting last time we saw it," Hugo said.

"Oh shit," Quinn gasped. "Let's pray she ends up well."

"Yeah, let's," Dagim sighed.

That was when he noticed what he was surprised he had not picked up on when he first started talking to them. Since they had loaded the last crate on the rover, Hugo and Quinn had wrapped an arm around each other's waists, holding each other tight in the way young lovers would.

171

"Didn't know you two were so close," Dagim said, smirking. With the surprise he saw on both of their faces, it was as if they too had not realised that they were holding each other so tightly. Both blushed.

"Yeah. We are, aren't we?" Hugo chuckled.

"Yeah," Quinn agreed in a sweet and awkward way. Dagim laughed. For the first time in such a long time, he honestly laughed.

"I don't know why, but I'm not as surprised by this as I'd have thought," he chuckled. "You two make a *very* interesting couple."

"In a good or bad way?" Quinn asked.

"Both. Mostly bad," Dagim chuckled. Hugo scoffed. Quinn rolled her eyes.

"Interesting that you think that. The universe seems to disagree with you," Hugo said.

Dagim's eyebrows furrowed. "What are you on about?"

"Look at the sign celebrating us as a couple," Hugo joked, pointing to the skies. "A shooting star. Coming out just for us."

Dagim and Quinn followed Hugo's finger, their eyes searching the dark skies. Among the beautiful stars that speckled the morning sky, a burning sphere of potent light energy barrelled through it like a raging comet of divine beauty. Hugo smiled down at Quinn as she observed it, expecting her to send a smile back. All he was met with was a face marked by confusion and worry.

"That's not a shooting star, Hugo," Quinn uttered.

"What? What else could it be?" Hugo asked.

The trio searched through the skies to find where the first comet of burning light originated. Their eyes took them west, where more energetic spheres barrelling through the air rained from above. Dagim followed the trajectory of each

172

one. The 'shooting star' Hugo pointed out landed in a field over the horizon, creating a small fiery explosion in its wake. A second one of these balls of energy landed in a yellow pond a half-mile away, drying up the water at the heart of its source as it sank through. A third landed a few metres away from them, burning a hole through the earth.

"I think our planet's being hit with a meteoroid attack," Dagim observed with a grumble.

"It's being hit with a meteoroid attack?!" Quinn repeated, the thought panicking her.

"That hasn't happened in years," Hugo scoffed.
He could not deny it anymore when the energy spheres started to strike areas in their general vicinity. Especially when one had struck through some of their ranks.

The bulbous ball of energy burned itself through the neck of Foreseer III, decapitating him. Its residue injured the man at the wheel of their rover, claiming its second life.

Dagim, Hugo, Quinn, and any recruit who had been even a few metres away from the rover ran to find safety as more hurtling spheres descended upon their position.

***

The recruits at camp devolving into cluttered masses of panic and chaos had become a commonplace sight throughout this portion of the war. But never had such fear and disorder been so present as when the light-energy meteoroids began to rain down on the main thoroughfare of the camp.

Several recruits and a Foreseer had been killed, and more deaths were soon to come.

Dagim could hardly see anything as he rushed through the camp. With the constant running of his fellow recruits, screaming and crying to and fro, he had lost track of Hugo and Quinn. Whilst most recruits were sprinting to shelters to hide or rovers to escape, Dagim was struggling to reach the

173

weapons tent. He assessed that where light energy attacks came, a legion of fauxangels would follow. He needed to be ready in case he was right.

Dagim played a dangerous game as he ran through the camp. He had to step over the bodies of dead, burnt, and bleeding comrades who had been struck by energy meteoroids. He saw the scorched torsos and incinerated faces of Bone Ripper, Ageless, and other top recruits as he made his way through the chaos. He had to avoid being knocked over by alive comrades who rushed aimlessly from all directions. He watched them fall over each other whilst making sure he was not in the firing line of the meteoroids that were claiming their land and men.

Dagim flinched, his body poisoned with fear as he heard the explosive energy of a meteoroid landing a few inches behind him. Another landed a foot ahead of him, burning half of the fleeing group that had been in front of him into a fleshy crater in the ground. Dagim forced himself to press forward regardless, desperate to get to the weapons tent. But God must have been playing another one of his cruel jokes. The second Dagim reached the tent, a massive meteoroid obliterated the structure, the explosion shooting him back as he crashed to the floor.

As Dagim gathered himself, he looked upwards to see a series of meteoroids all falling towards his position. Each meteoroid plummeted in a way that if he were to try to run out of their way, he would risk not escaping in time and being struck. All he could do was crouch and pray none would strike him. He dove to the ground in cover, hands over his head as if he were a scared child. Each of the meteoroids struck positions close to him. Two behind him, one to the left, two to his right, and another one in front of him. The only one that came close to killing him was a smaller one that skimmed past his leg, leaving a burn.

"Shit!" Dagim cursed as he watched a patch of flesh on this leg blacken and crack at record speeds. He smacked himself, ignoring the pain as he got on his feet and bounded forward into a sprint. He followed the rest of his surviving comrades in fleeing the camp.

At this point, he had dozens more bodies to step over, as well as fields of burning tents and more meteoroids, each seeming to get smaller and more precise as they struck the land around him. Dagim sprinted forward in a zig-zag formation. He could not remember a time in which he experienced more fear than in these moments.

He was one of the last few recruits who had not either already fled the camp or succumbed to the meteor energy.

*****

Dagim had escaped by the skin of his teeth. A sprint across the fields, a long time holding his breath underwater as he passed through the ponds, and a second sprint towards a cave enclosure was what it took for him to get to safety. He sat precariously in the minuscule enclosure he had forced himself into for shelter. He stared out of the crevice, watching as the meteoroids continued to fall.

As Dagim adjusted himself uncomfortably in the cave, he realised he would have to get used to his position for a while longer. If he took the risk of stepping out of this cramped cave spot for even a few seconds, he ran the risk of being destroyed by the balls of spherical energy that had increased in firepower to the point they left not an inch of the land in front of him unburnt.

After an hour of staring at the raining hellfire, hoping to see it end but never getting his wish, Dagim's eyes were treated to a different sight for once. He saw who he assumed was the obvious culprit of this meteoroid attack.

The Divinity conjured himself from thin air, emerging out of one of the balls of lights that rained from the sky, just like he had been said to do in his origin story.

Dagim seethed at the fact that he could not bound out of the cave and attack him. He resented watching the glowing humanoid soar through the skies amongst the meteoroids that were his doing. The fauxangel leader floated through the air above barren lands with his arms outstretched. With his body drenched in blood and wounds on his hands, he looked like a messianic figure. Or the devilish imitation of one.

Dagim watched The Divinity chant something unintelligible. The more The Divinity chanted, the more meteoroids fell from the sky.

XX. THOSE WHO REMAIN

DAGIM trekked the concrete plains of an unknown territory as he searched for surviving recruits. The Divinity's meteoroid rain-fire had destroyed the lands around him. He could no longer notify any major landmarks that would have hastened his search. Everywhere had been reduced to rubble, twice as barren and burnt as even the worst nations of Magnae. He had made several attempts to trace his journey back to camp and failed each time. It was as if all signs of the North Magnae Forces had been wiped off the map.

Tired and hungry from a day's worth of aimless trekking, Dagim fuelled his journey on willpower and spite. When he had left the cave and started his journey, he vowed not to stop walking until he stumbled upon another recruit he could reconnect with. It had been twenty-two hours since he forced that promise on himself.

"God," Dagim muttered. The burn wound on his leg itched and flaked, matching the dry parched feeling that was agitating his throat and mouth.

By hour twenty-three, he was growing unable to fulfil the promise he made to himself. He stopped walking, on the verge of giving up.

Just before he could have collapsed, he caught sight of a damaged rover. He waved the vehicle over weakly as it slowly drove towards him.

Dagim felt as if he was on one of his missions, cramped in the backseat of a half-broken old rover, sitting amongst his fellow recruits, some injured-bodied, some familiar-faced, and some both. Of the twelve recruits in the back, and the three in the category of 'both' was Stefan, who slept. Silent Memoir snored, though Dagim was surprised at how he could sleep peacefully with three burn marks across his chest. One of the only other familiar faces wore no crimson or Magnae battle armour. Dagim took notice of Roisin's civilian clothes as she sat across from him.

"You're no longer part of the forces?" Dagim observed.

"You saw my arms after that fauxangel breach. It was about time I faced reality and gave up my duties as Recruit Infinity," Roisin chuckled through the pain.

"It's a shame," Dagim sighed. "You were the best of us." Roisin smiled weakly.

"Doesn't mean I can't help out here and there!" she said, desperate to keep the little optimism present. "Who do you think convinced Maeynation Hospital and Verloen Village to send out rovers to collect you guys?"

Dagim looked around at all the soldiers packed alongside him, including Stefan, who had fallen into a deeper slumber. He took note of the faint residue of an ointment Roisin applied to the raw energy burns that pained Silent Memoir's chest. It was yet to start the healing process.

"You're lucky you got released a couple of days before the meteoroids hit."

"I know, right? I heard the North Magnae Hospital was one of the first places to burn down," Roisin said. "What even happened anyway? Why was a meteoroid attack mostly focused on your camp?"

"The Divinity," Dagim answered.

"You saw him again?"

"Yeah, I saw him calling them from the sky and encasing them with his energy. He was all bloody and injured, so it probably took a lot of his power. Hurt him and all, but it was worth it considering the damage he did."

Roisin contemplated. "Do you think that's why no one's spotted him for a while? Was he building up enough energy to do all that?"

"Yes, and with the injuries they gave him, I won't be surprised if it's why he goes into hiding again for another while," Dagim grunted. "The cowardly prick."

Roisin twirled a lock of her ginger hair, her darling blue eyes vacant yet fretful. "How many other recruits do you reckon survived?" she asked, staring at nothing.

"I lost track of them, but I think most of the other top recruits probably found a way to escape like I did," Dagim said. "I'm not so confident about the lower-ranked recruits and older employees. Especially The Head."

"If there's anyone who's survived, it's him," Roisin said.

"Yeah. He's the one person I trust to be fine," Dagim agreed. "He better be."

***

Days had passed since Dagim's conversation with Roisin in the rescue rover. He never imagined he would have to climb into a hole in the ground and crawl through a tunnel to reconnect with the rest of the Magnae Forces, but that was exactly what Dagim did that morning.

The moist, nasty tunnel led Devil Child towards The North Magnae Forces' new base of operations. The cosy atmosphere that came with the open air of the camps they moved to and from was replaced by drab interiors and a stale underground ambience. He saw many recruits recovering within the first of many rooms of a charmless series of

179

subterranean bunkers. Black metal walls, black metal floors, dimly lit sources of energy stuck to the walls in a poor effort to brighten up the area, and no furniture but for the few crates of items they had managed to salvage.

As Dagim moved through the boundless plain room that was the bunker main, his body refused to settle down until he had locked eyes with The Head Foreseer again.

"Devil Child," Dagim heard The Head's voice, sounding much gruffer than it typically would. He shifted to the side to see the leader of the forces walking towards him. He had sustained a burning injury to his neck, the reason for the voice change.

"You're alive. Good," Dagim said as the two rough men shook hands.

"You're alive. Even better," The Head said, smiling. Dagim gestured at the bundles of recruits going about their day in the bunker. "The ranks seem much emptier now."

"They are. Doesn't help that Foreseer III's dead and I happened to fire three other Foreseers on the same week that all of this was set to happen," The Head said. "It's just me and Aiza. And since she's on a mission, it's just me set to handle all of this shit right now."

Dagim's eyes squinted a touch as his mind tracked back to the savage brutality The Head had dealt upon The Vice that day. It seemed The Head could read his mind, a rare look of guilt about him as he cleared his throat.

"I think it's long past the appropriate time I gave you a well-deserved sorry," The Head said. "I never believed you when you said there were people in our ranks with plans to kill you. I can't apologise enough for that."

Dagim smiled. "The beating you gave The Vice Foreseer was enough of an apology."

The Head Foreseer boomed with laughter. The damage to his throat gave his chuckles a scratchy sound that somehow made him seem world-wearier.

Dagim and The Head straightened up, both becoming serious again following their brief amusement.

"I saw The Divinity fly through the sky from the cave I was hiding in. He was the one who called upon those meteoroids," Dagim said.

"I figured as much. He's probably returned to hibernating after such an attack, hasn't he?" asked The Head.

"I thought the same. We won't see him for a while," Dagim said. "But when next we do, I think it's time I finally take in the full power of the Ultimatum Source."

The Head broke eye contact with Dagim. "That's another thing I wanted to talk to you about. It's going to be a no-go on those sped-up plans to have you consume the Ultimatum Source."

"Huh? Why?!"

"The cave we kept the source in has been sealed shut following the meteoroid attacks. Rocks have blocked the entire entrance and clogged the pool. We can't even see where the source is under all of it, never mind reach it."

Dagim clenched his fists "Just our fucking luck!" he exclaimed with frustration. "But the source is still intact, though, isn't it?"

The Head shrugged. "We have a team of recruits going through the process of removing the rock and clearing the cave without damaging anything. It'll take a while before we're anywhere near able to retrieve it."

"Fuck!" Dagim exclaimed, grinding his teeth hard as if he were trying to cultivate white dust. "Everything's gone to fucking shit!"

"You're telling me," The Head scoffed. "We lost a great number of recruits ranked in the top one hundred, including seventy per cent of those ranked in the top twenty. Not even the top ten was completely safe."

Dagim knew as much, having seen Ageless and Bone Ripper's corpses during his dash through the meteoroid-scorched camp that day. His closer friends in the top ten also came to mind. He knew Roisin was no longer a part of the forces and thus had not been a victim of the attack, and that Stefan was severely injured, albeit breathing the last time he had seen him. He did not know about the rest.

"Heart Stealer, First Ranger, and Queen Triumph. Are they all alright?" Dagim asked.

"Frederica and Quinn are fine. Any injuries they sustained, they're quickly recovering from," The Head informed him. "I wish I could say the same for Hugo."

***

Dagim burst into the medical room, denting the metal door with the amount of force he applied. He had done this to every medical room he came across, his destructive impatience once again getting the better of him. Finally, he entered the right room. Hugo's room.

Dagim was met with an empty space, but for a flat hospital mattress propped up by a steel mound and a solid blocky chair near it. Hugo lay on the mattress, unconscious. Quinn sat on the chair, doting over him as she rubbed his hand. She turned to Dagim with an expression that could only be described in one word. Devastated.

"What's wrong with him?" Dagim asked as he fixed himself by her side. Quinn sobbed as she squeezed Hugo's hand tighter.

"He's alive, but he won't wake up," Quinn cried. "We've tried everything. For *days*. He just won't wake up."

Dagim's eyes wavered as he fell to his knees. He rested a hand on his comrade as he struggled to keep looking at his comatose face. A fringe of wavy blonde hair spilt over a crusted bandage wrapped tightly around his head.

"How did this happen?" Dagim asked.

"After the chaos hit the camp and the meteoroids started falling, Hugo grabbed me by the arm and we ran together to the first rover we could find. He got behind the wheel and drove like crazy over the fields," Quinn said. "We were about to reach the underside of this mountain for shelter when a meteoroid struck the front of our vehicle. Both of us flew out of the rover."

"My God," Dagim sighed. "Surprised you didn't get badly hurt, too."

"I was lucky. If I lift the hair on the back of my head, you'll find a permanent scar to remind me of that day. But other than that, I'm fine," Quinn said. "Hugo cracked his head very badly, and I haven't seen him open his eyes again even once since then."

Dagim gripped the sheets draped over Hugo tightly, his hands balling into a fist as he dug his nails into his palms. "He's not going to stay like this forever, is he?" he asked.

Quinn sighed, parting her curly black hair out of her tearful eyes. "He's not likely to wake up anytime soon. That's all the doctors have said," Quinn lamented. "In the meantime, all we can do is hope that he eventually does. That he *ever* does."

"That's better than nothing," Dagim said sternly. "He'll be alright. He *will*."

He grunted, tightening his fists as he suppressed any disquietude within him. He wore a bold face. For both Quinn's sake and his own.

183

XXI. THEORY

FREDERICA was grateful for how Aiza had given her the choice to expose The Vice's plans in the manner she saw fit. An ultimatum would be a better term for it rather than a choice. Ironically.

With Aiza keeping schtum about her involvement in the plans to kill Dagim, Frederica had told The Head her involvement only went as far as The Vice insisting upon her helping with it and her refusing. She used the poison plants and a note he left for her as proof. With The Head furiously raging at him, any effort on The Vice's part to insist the truth, that she had been involved from the start, would be hard to believe. But as far as she knew, The Vice had not even attempted to expose her back. He uttered not a word about her part in the poisoning, not mentioning her once. It was why she still believed in her heart that he was an honourable man deep down. Because he kept quiet about it, Frederica kept quiet about it as well.

She wished to thank Aiza for allowing her to do so, but could not find her. According to The Head, Aiza survived the meteoroid shower with no injuries sustained. Thus, as one of the healthiest and least damaged members of the forces following the recent tragedies that fell them, she went on a scouting mission to assess the status of the fauxangels. An important mission she was taking a while to return from.

First Ranger despised dishonesty, especially when it was used in the way she had, to divert suspicion and attention from one's crimes. But the North Magnae Forces did not need to be more frayed than they already were at that point. The situation had kept her safe, but increased her guilt.

***

Frederica ate in the dining area of the underground bunker. Their complete lack of furniture or most other items meant the recruits had to hold bowls and cups either in their hands or rest them on the floor where they sat, with no chairs and tables to speak of. Frederica picked at the burnt pieces of the dry meat that was their meal for the day. An unappealing one, but they were not spoiled for choice.

Frederica sat in complete solitude, confining herself to the most secluded corner of the room. Not out of her still present guilt, though that played a part, but due to health reasons. For the past few mornings, she had been cursed with the most debilitating headaches she had ever experienced in her life. She was so rife with pain that she could hardly stand staring at the lights in the room, never mind engaging in conversation with dozens of chattering recruits. She knew not the origin of such brutal head pains. The only injury she had received from her escape during the meteoroid attack was burns around both ankles. She had no injuries to the head like the likes of other soldiers, such as Quinn, and to a much greater extent, the comatose Hugo. Such harrowing headaches had to have originated from elsewhere.

Frederica could only remember one time in her life when she had experienced such piercing migraines. That dreaded break in her sanity at the riverbed where she saw that mind-breaking vision of the dark fauxangel in the liminal space. Thinking back on that moment increased the intensity of such painful migraines. She thought it might be in her best

185

interest to analyse what had happened to her that day, though she avoided doing so. She took this same attitude with the headaches themselves, wincing and grunting in quiet pain every once in a while, whilst pretending they were not there the rest of the time.

The Head entered the dining hall, his heavy boots echoing as he stomped to the front. He interrupted their dry dinner, pounding a fist on the wall to grab their attention for an announcement.

"As some of you have heard by now, The Divinity was responsible for the meteoroid attack. The obvious bad news is that it's wiped out a majority of our forces. *But* the good news is it took a great toll on him, and he'll need to hibernate for a while. I think this is the perfect opportunity for us to hibernate too," The Head announced. "Apart from a few roaming squads who will be tasked with protecting civilians, none of you will patrol the lands for fauxangels anymore. None of you will fight in battles. None of you will engage with any fauxangels in any way. From now on, we'll only be gathering information and building our strength. From now on, we're keeping things low."

With his short announcement over and done with, The Head left the room. The recruits murmured amongst themselves, sharing their thoughts. Some of the soldiers seemed belligerent, greatly disappointed by the fact that they were *hibernating*. Others seemed overly relieved. You could separate those two groups, Frederica thought, between the stronger and more stupid recruits, and the weaker, more cautious ones. Frederica was in the middle. She would have liked to use this opportunity for them to pressure The Divinity and strike whilst he was out of commission, but she understood that it might not have been the best time. They had no access to the Ultimatum Source, with what was left of the excavation team making slow progress when it came to carefully digging out the cave. Without the source, they had no hope of killing the head of the fauxangels. Especially with the lower number of soldiers at their disposal.

But Frederica saw how this hibernation time could end up being very useful. As The Head said, they could use it to rebuild their strength and gather more information that would help them defeat the fauxangels once their strength had returned. Frederica knew which piece of information she wanted them to delve into most. The alternate history from that glowing book, written by Ryland Best, among many others. She had not yet looked into it, but she knew the answers to their problems were tied to that information.

***

The Divinity lay underneath his shower of gold once more. This was not as pleasant a replenishing bath as it had been the last time he enjoyed the facilities of Luxurae. This time, his wounds were deep, blood leaking from multiple orifices on plain, dry, coarse, aura-less skin, vibrating with no energy. The gold water he washed in was stained tyrian from his scars, scrapes, and rotten flesh.

As opposed to the two subordinate female fauxangels who had attended to him the last time he was here, The Divinity practically cowered in the presence of the fauxangel who stood over him as he bathed and healed. A fauxangel with a much more potent aura than his, covered from head to toe in dark energy. An enigmatic woman with pitch-black eyes and a crisp white smile. The entity that had breached the cryptic dreams and strong minds of both Devil Child and First Ranger, soldiers of the North Magnae Forces. Or as the highest fauxangels of Planet Luxurae knew her, Theola.

"You lost this much bodily energy from completing just *one* hellfire attack, younger?" Theola scoffed. "And you're supposed to be *the most powerful fauxangel*."

"When they brand me with that title, they're not including you, Theola," The Divinity acquiesced. "If they knew of you, they wouldn't have branded me as such."

"Obviously, younger," Theola scoffed. "I don't need assurances from my lesser."

"You're right, sorry, madam," The Divinity sighed.
Theola kissed her teeth at him.

"This is why you measure out your strength. Even if you want to create devastating attacks, you can't ignore the toll it will take on your body. Don't be fooled by your own dogma. You are not a god," Theola lectured. "Why do you think I'm not sending out the blue-flamed batch anymore? If I created just a few more of that calibre, I could wipe out an entire section of humans. But if I did that, it would harm my body to the point of killing me and potentially disrupt my cycle. You should be thinking in the same way."

"Yes, of course, sorry, madam," The Divinity said.
Theola scoffed. She stepped to the side and waved her hand. Dark energy formed at the tip of her fingers, smoking off of each of her fingernails as it floated in the air. Each tendril of energy combined to create a black portal. The Divinity sat up, the portal's appearance startling him.

"Where's that portal taking you? Magnae?" he asked, worrisome of tone. Theola nodded. The Divinity's face twisted. "What business do you have on Magnae?"

"I want to collect important intel during your absence, of course," Theola scoffed. "I'm seeing how long it's looking to be before I'll need to step in."

The Divinity scrambled out of his bathing comfort, his mind and body in anguish as he reached out a begging hand to Theola.

"Just wait. Allow me to continue this war when I'm well, I wish to be the one who ends it," The Divinity pleaded. "I'm close to carrying out your will! I've almost broken the humans and *their* will. They will fall soon!"

Theola laughed and sighed simultaneously. "Don't worry, younger, I'm not to take away any of your glory," she assured. "I'm not going to attack. I'm just going to observe."

***

"Devil Child! Silent Memoir!" The Head had roared into the sleeping halls of the top five recruits at the crack of dawn. "Get to the meeting room! Now!"

Dagim and Stefan ambled into a meeting room that early morning. An area as black, metal, and lifeless as the rest of the bunkers. Only in this room, they had the privilege of actual furniture, seating themselves on one end of an obsidian table. Three people sat on the other side of the table. The Head, Frederica, and a woman who said "Morning, Stefan!" to him in sign language.

Stefan saw what he assumed to be an interpreter there, a woman who could translate his sign language into spoken words to save the time he would spend writing notes to communicate. This job could have just as easily been done by Aiza, he thought. But no one had seen her since she left for her scouting mission.

Dagim's eyes were directed at Frederica instead. Typically, he and Frederica would set the tone during one of these meetings by giving each other glares of hatred. A non-verbal indicator of their rivalry and a precursor for the brutal arguments that were to be inevitably had between the two of them. Only at that moment, Frederica averted Dagim's gaze completely. His suspicion towards her grew, though he did not know what exactly he was suspicious of.

"Right. Frederica came to me with a lot of new information, so we have a shit ton to discuss right now," The Head said, starting the meeting off with pace. "Dagim, you've read all of that new history book, haven't you?"

"I have," Dagim confirmed.

"Good," said The Head. "And Stefan, do you know why I've called you here?"

"No," Stefan signed. Every time he used sign language during that meeting, the interpreter would repeat what he had said out loud for the rest of the room to understand.

"Sifted through a bunch of records last night and of all the surviving soldiers, you scored the highest in historical knowledge back in Recruit School," The Head revealed. "Are you still as highly informed as you were back then?"

"I am. Me and my girlfriend, Anais, used to read many tales together every night before bed. It was our very own couple's tradition," Stefan signed. Dagim smiled, finding Silent Memoir's fun fact sweet. Frederica was unmoved.

"Very nice," The Head scoffed.

"You two can help consolidate the new pieces of knowledge I learnt," Frederica said.

"We could," Dagim agreed. "Let's hear them then."
Frederica sat up straight, clearing her throat. "Firstly, I'd like to hear both your thoughts on the *No Ekib* Theory."

Dagim thought about it for a short while. "It sounds far-fetched, so I'm not completely on board with it. But I do find it fishy that such a book never mentions him at all," he said.

"People have always had theories that Emmanuel Ekib was not who he said he was. That's bound to happen with any ancient tale with minimal proof," Stefan added. "It's much more likely that either his story was omitted, or his role in history was intentionally downplayed."

Frederica nodded, satisfied with the answer Stefan had given.

"Interesting," The Head said, rubbing his grey beard. Frederica leaned forward, her fingers intertwined in a formal fist. "Ever since we first arrived in this bunker, I've written and sent letters to any surviving historian I could contact. I must have sent close to fifty, but I only got about fifteen back," Frederica said. "But all of them had the same answer to my questions. There was not a single piece of tangible evidence that one could directly point to and prove Emmanuel Ekib's story of using the lake from the water to fight back after The Divinity's flood."

Confusion started to filter through the air, showing itself on each man's face.

"And what does that suggest?" The Head asked.

"Three things, potentially," Frederica said, holding up three fingers. "One, that it was a fabrication. Two, anything proving it's happening has been destroyed, intentionally or otherwise. Or three, his importance in Magnae history has been greatly exaggerated and overemphasised."

Frederica waited a couple of seconds for the information to digest before continuing. "Of those three potentialities, which do you reckon is the most likely?"

The Head grunted. "It's either one of the last two. Proof being hidden or the history being not as it seems."

"I agree," Dagim said. Stefan had nothing to add to this thought yet.

"Out of those two, which is the most likely one?" Frederica asked.

"Because it was kept away by fauxangels, it would make me think Ekib's history was being hidden as well as The

Divinity's less God-like origins. But from what I saw of the book, no pages were ripped out. It remained in its entirety. Meaning the human authors had reason to omit his history too," Stefan signed in detail. "So, I reckon a mix of both the last two theories is reality, but I'm leaning more towards the overstating his role side of things."

"I'm leaning in the same direction," Frederica said. "We need to determine what Ekib's true role was from the little proof we have of his past."

"From what we learned in history, he was the first man to use the potent energy of the fauxangels against them after The Divinity punished the world with the flood. He was the first man to take in powers close to the modern-day Ultimatum Source. The first man to prove The Divinity could be hurt," Stefan signed in elaboration. "What does it say in the book, Dagim?"

"The flood is mentioned, the lake is mentioned, and so are a series of potent power sources similar to today's Ultimatum. It was said that a group of travellers in collaboration with scientists at the time were the ones who figured out how to harvest alien energy and planned a month-long attack in which they finally struck The Divinity and found out he could bleed," Dagim explained.

"Which is along the lines of what a few historians told me has been a somewhat valid theory. Nothing confirmed, but a valid theory," Frederica said.

"Alright, so assuming the books are right, and the historians are valid, who was Emmanuel Ekib? What did he actually do?" The Head asked. "Why do the North Magnae Forces history books tell us this grand tale of him taking it all on if there's no proof and it might not even be real?"

"Useful soldier propaganda, perhaps," Frederica said. "Maybe it started as a slightly edited version of the inspiring folktale of whatever Ekib *actually* did and blew out of proportion over the years."

"Or, maybe the authors and historians are the ones with the false information," Dagim suggested.

"Also likely," Frederica admitted. "But I'm more inclined to trust the word of historical scholars over headstrong soldiers. For now, at least."

"What we need to do is find out more information about the actual authors of the book. Find out what they either knew or thought they knew at the time and how they arrived at their conclusions, whether they were accurate or not," Stefan signed.

"Which brings us back to Ryland Best," Dagim said, glancing at The Head Foreseer.

The Head cracked his knuckles, a determination about him. "Yes, it does. I'll have to do a lot more digging on that family of mine," he said. "A lot more."

XXII. WOMAN OF THE SHADOWS

YOU could count the number of times Quinn had left Hugo's side on one hand. She would have starved in that room if other recruits had not come to her with food and water each day. The only times she would leave Hugo's side were to use the bathroom next door. For most of each day, she would sit by his bed, holding his hand. She wanted to be the first person he saw once he woke up. That moment seemed unlikely to come anytime soon.

Quinn had to laugh at the cruel irony of it all. For the years Heart Stealer and Queen Triumph had known each other since Recruit School, they hated each other. At least that was what they told people and themselves. It was obvious to some that such *hatred* was nothing but a thin layer of aggression, shielding themselves from the tension they felt in each other's presence. She found it funny that once that layer was finally removed, once they embraced said tension and connected, he had been taken away from her.

She refused to accept that this would be the state of it. It did not matter what the medics and doctors had suggested. She believed that one of these days, he would wake up. One of these days, he would be able to envelop her in his strong embrace again.

Now embedded into the recent culture of *hibernation* amongst the recuperating forces, Quinn was rarely asked for. Aside from the pleas to get her to eat, drink, or intermingle with the other recruits, there were no duties asked of her. This meant that Quinn would only see two people most days. Her comatose lover, Heart Stealer, and one of the few soldiers who she allowed to visit them, Devil Child.

"Morning, Quinn," Dagim greeted that day, walking into the hospice with a chair of his own. He sat it down and sat beside her.

"Morning, Dagim."

"How's he doing today?"

"Same as always. Maybe a little better than most days, actually."

"What do you mean?"

"I've gotten better at using the feeding funnels, so food and drink are going down easier," Quinn explained. "Guess that doesn't mean he's doing better, but it's something."

"Yeah, it's something," Dagim agreed, twiddling his thumbs in an uncharacteristically anxious way. He watched as Quinn reached over to fix his hair over the bandage. Just a swipe of her hand, and it was as good as if Hugo had woken up to style it himself. Dagim scoffed. Even in such a state, Hugo Stacey's hair managed to look perfect.

"When was the last time you left this room, Quinn? And I don't mean for food or bathroom breaks."

"You know the answer to that, Dagim."

"You haven't left since Hugo was first brought here, have you?"

She nodded. Dagim shook his head. "You're going to need to leave for once today," he said. "How would you feel about taking a break and helping me out with something?"

Quinn shook her head. "I don't know if you've noticed, but I'm not exactly in the mood to do anything else," she snarked as she began to stretch out Hugo's legs for him. A practice she needed to do multiple times daily, so the muscles would not wilt away for however long he was to be out.

"I know. If this were just some random mid-level-importance mission, I wouldn't have come here for you," Dagim scoffed.

"It's really important, is it?" Quinn asked as she did the same exercise with Hugo's arms and neck.

"It's crucial, so I need you to say yes," Dagim emphasised.

"Then it depends," Quinn sighed. "What do you want me to do?"

"What you do best, obviously," Dagim said. "Who else is going to help me scavenge and search?"

***

Quinn travelled outside of the bunker's hospice halls for once. She joined Dagim and Stefan, watching her step as she walked carefully behind them. For the first time in ages, recruits of the North Magnae Forces breathed fresh air into their lungs as they travelled above ground.

Of all places these literal breaths of fresh air could be taken, it had to have been the plains of fire. Dagim led the way through these scorched orange savannahs, Stefan nimbly following, Quinn being the least coordinated of the three of them. She worried that every next step she took would end up being the one that burned through her boots and would scar her feet.

"This is the general area where I found the glowing book," Dagim said.

"Didn't you say you found it in that building below the cliff we just passed?" Quinn asked.

"Yes, but we've already turned that place upside down enough times. There's nothing more to be found in that building," Dagim said.

"What are we searching for now?" Quinn asked.

"Anything that can point us in the direction of any fauxangel knowledge, big or small," Dagim said. "If we can uncover anything new that we haven't seen before, I'll consider this mission a success. This area holds secrets for us to expose. I can feel it."

Stefan skipped forward with increasing speed. Quinn steadied the movement of her feet and eyes, synchronising them with optimal focus. She kept her eyes peeled for anything that fit Dagim's descriptions.

***

The Divinity sat upon the flat ceiling at the top of a great tower. A golden monument of peak fauxangel construction. With a hand crushed against the bottom of his chin, he sulked, muttering to himself as he stewed in his misery. Several of his wounds from his energy hellfire attack had been healed and sealed, yet several others insisted on bleeding more. He covered a vague, sullen gaze over the pale, empty sunflower-coloured fields of Planet Luxurae's most bountiful land. Only a handful of his fauxangel subordinates could be seen below. A simple collection of beautiful, golden, and happily mindless folk that on any other day would have made him appreciative of what he had. He could not bring himself to feel that way as he conversed with himself, fermenting with fury.

"Theola. The great woman of the shadows. The voice from behind the curtain. The one above all," The Divinity muttered, listing her many titles with building envy and resentment. "I can't let her undermine my greatness. I simply *can't*."

His eyes darted over to the side of him. He considered conjuring up a portal and stepping through it, just as Theola had done during his healing bath. He wished to follow her, to see whatever she was planning to do on Planet Magnae at the least and to stop it and take over from her at the most. But he could not act on these considerations.

Reluctance and fear left him rooted to his spot, sulking on the gold town tower.

The Divinity looked down at the family of fauxangels. Just the sight of them seemed to alter his thoughts. In an instant, his mind changed.

He conjured up a portal of light.

***

Hours ago, Quinn was afraid to traverse the plains of fire without Dagim and Stefan having to practically hold her hand and guide her through. She had found her groove since then. Not only had she learnt how to step through the lands without fear of burning her feet, but she also gained the confidence to travel alone and without guidance.

She had split up from Dagim and Stefan to conduct her own focused search. She allowed her instincts to take her wherever they chose on this journey through orange grass and stone. They took her to a forest. Quinn wanted to ask herself why she had felt compelled to travel there until she immediately noticed the answer to her question smoking in front of her. A tree with burning leaves.

An equally frightening and beautiful sight, the type one would expect to see the spiritual cultists of the land worshipping. Quinn celebrated her instincts for having taken her there. For underneath the burning tree was a revelation that was somehow twice as intriguing.

***

It took a while for Quinn to relocate Dagim and Stefan again. The two of them had found no luck in finding fauxangel signs that could lead to uncovering secrets and had decided to use their time hunting heat mammals in jungles for food to bring back to the bunker. She laughed, understanding why Dagim had insisted that she join them.

When Dagim and Stefan arrived, their eyes lit up, blazing as brightly as the leaves.

"This is definitely a sign," Dagim said. "When have you ever seen sustained combustion like this without a source?"

"That's not even the part I wanted to show you," Quinn said. Using an emergency knife she had tucked away in the back of her armour, she parted the charred leaves on the floor. She pointed the tip of her knife towards a pile of glowing fauxangel energy. Though glowing may not have been the appropriate word. The energy was dark in colour, the substance vibrating with a black aura.

"This is something special," Quinn said.
She enjoyed the fascination on Stefan's face, his calm brown eyes shimmering and his sweet smile as wide as one could be. She found Dagim's reaction strange, however. From the look he held about him, one would assume he had just seen the ghosts of his late parents.

"What's up with you, Dagim?" Quinn asked.

"I don't think you realise how important a sign this is," Dagim told her.

"Why? What does this suggest?"
Dagim rubbed the sides of his coarse afro hair as if the thought of informing them stressed him out. Stefan and Quinn's collective attention was grasped with an iron grip.

"Stefan, remember ages ago, near the start of the war proper, when you said you saw something strange happen in my tent and I told you I'd tell you sometime?" Dagim asked.

Stefan frowned, nodding. He appeared more serious than he had been before, yet twice as excited.

"What's this?" Quinn asked, confused.

"One day, a fauxangel teleported into my tent. One that looked nothing like any of the others. Only the special, blue-flamed ones came close to looking anything like her, but she'd stand out even among them. She had messy hair, pale skin, and a very dark aura," Dagim revealed. "A dark aura of the same shade as this fauxangel energy."

Dagim thrusted an aggressive pointing finger at the pile of energy residue as if it were the mark of the devil. Quinn crossed her arms, keeping her attention on him instead of it.

"The fauxangel that left behind this residue teleported into your tent at camp?" she asked. "Why? What did she do?"

"Mocked my life. Laughed about how my birth killed my mother and crippled my father. How I'm the Devil Child who the Foreseers were planning to kill. And how I was not as special as everyone treats me," Dagim said, recalling the conversation with a sour expression. "Then she asked me to help her locate someone within our ranks who *was* special. After telling her no, I tried to cut her with my sword, but she teleported out of there. I haven't seen her since, unless you count my dreams."

Stefan blinked slowly. Quinn shook her head. "And why didn't you tell anyone else about this encounter until now?" she asked.

"I didn't trust anyone at camp at the time. I think you should remember that someone had just tried to fucking kill me," Dagim complained. "Then after a while, I forced myself to put it out of my mind and focus on my tasks. But now I realise that was wrong. I should have been thinking and talking about it all the time. This dark-aura fauxangel woman is the key to us learning so much more."

"First things first, then. Let's collect the energy, bring it back to the bunker, and talk about it there," Quinn said. "Others need to see this as soon as possible."

Stefan agreed, being way ahead of them. He opened a compartment to his battle wear, taking out gloves and wearing them.

He collected the first clump of dark fauxangel energy.

***

The first person the trio showed the dark fauxangel energy to was the person who had the most vested interest in being updated following their return. Frederica had been waiting for them at the front of the halls to the top five sleeping quarters, itching to hear any news. They did not disappoint as they showed and told all they had found and discussed at the burning tree.

"Oh my God. This…this is insane," Frederica stuttered. She had the same face Dagim had when Quinn had first shown the dark fauxangel energy.

"Is that face contagious?" Quinn quipped to Dagim. Stefan laughed.

Frederica grabbed Dagim by the shoulders, her fingernails burrowing into them as her crazed eyes burrowed into his.

"What's your damn problem?!" Dagim asked.

"That dark fauxangel you said teleported into your tent and left that energy by the tree! What did she look like?! Describe her again!" Frederica shouted.

"Calm down," Dagim scoffed, thrusting himself out of the grasp of her crazed hands. He cleared his throat to answer. "She had messy frizzy brown hair, pale skin, and an intense dark energy radiating off of her."

"It's her," Frederica gasped. Her body slumped, and her legs grew weary as if she had the energy extracted out of her.

Quinn and Stefan dove into action, supporting her before she crashed to the ground.

Dagim was tired of her theatrics. "Is there something you know about this fauxangel?!" he asked.

Frederica gave him a lethargic nod. "I've had otherworldly visions in the past. Ones that have had me questioning my sanity," she revealed to the others. "Most of these visions featured this dark fauxangel."

XXIII. THE CYCLE

THE Head, Dagim, Stefan, and Frederica sat at the black table for their next intel meeting. They were joined by the sign language interpreter and the newest member of their knowledge collection team, Quinn.

Days ago, Frederica told of the visions in which she saw the very same special fauxangel who attempted to coerce Dagim, giving them quite a bit more to discuss.

"Theola," Frederica started. "From the many names I've come across during my research, Theola is the one that came up the most."

"That's the name of the dark fauxangel who's messing with both of our heads?" Dagim asked.

"Most likely. That's what I've heard," Frederica answered.

"You don't sound sure," The Head said.

"None of the historians or scholars I've been keeping in contact with could confirm that such a fauxangel was real, nor offer me any information on her," Frederica explained. "Of the dozens of sources that I've been able to contact in the past few days, the only people who had the faintest clue were these groups of spiritual cultists I found. The type who worship fauxangel energy."

"Not the most reliable of sources," Quinn scoffed.

"But our only sources. The only people who claimed to have seen her," Frederica said. "The only people who could comprehend what Dagim and I have experienced."

"Let's hear them out," Dagim insisted.

For the first time since they had laid hateful eyes on each other during recruit school, Dagim and Frederica were in full agreement.

"Whether they're reliable or not, we could learn something from hearing what they had to say," Stefan signed.

"Maybe," scoffed The Head. "What did you learn from these cultists then, First Ranger?"

Frederica reached for a box of papers on the side of the table. She picked up the first few pages out of it and placed them in front of her for reference.

"They say she's a fauxangel with more power and authority than The Divinity," she said.

"More than The Divinity?" Quinn asked, sceptical.

"That doesn't sound right," Dagim agreed.

"They say she's *the woman of the shadows*. A powerful fauxangel that even most of the creatures on Planet Luxurae know little about. The voice behind the curtain who truly guides their people," Frederica continued. "They say that whilst The Divinity was responsible for the creation of all the fauxangels, she is the outlier. That her origin predates The Divinity himself."

Frederica carried an essence about her as she read her notes, like the information was as exciting and fulfilling as if she were the one hearing it all for the first time.

The reception she received from relaying such information did not match.

"To be quite frank, I don't care what *they* say," said The Head as he sat up on his chair. "It sounds like a steaming pile of shit to me."

"Yeah, spiritual cultists *say* a lot of things. Like how they think we should give up the war and accept the fauxangels as our rightful rulers," Quinn added in agreement. "Not much that comes out of their mouths is worth listening to."

"What parts do you not believe?" Frederica asked.

"Pick any part, it all stinks of the same flavour of bullshit," The Head scoffed. "I reckon there's a more rational explanation for the dark energy and the woman you and Dagim saw than there somehow being a secret woman with more power than the most powerful creature in the galaxy."

"Like what?" Stefan signed.

"I don't have an explanation myself, but I reckon it exists," The Head answered.

Frederica ignored the rest, focusing on Dagim. "What do you think?"

Dagim shrugged. "I'm not sure. I'd need to hear more about this Theola."

Frederica flicked over to the next page on the pile in front of her. She read it carefully, the room growing silent as they waited for her to take in her notes. She glanced up from her pages again, looking at all of their awaiting faces.

The Head and the three recruits watched as Frederica opened her mouth to speak. No words came out as her lips quivered with hesitation.

"Don't you have something to tell us, First Ranger?" The Head asked.

Frederica ignored the others again, zoning in on the paper in front of her.

"What did you just read? Tell us," Stefan signed.

Frederica's eyes were glazed over, appearing as if her mind was going both at a snail's pace and a million miles an hour.

"What's wrong with her now?" Quinn asked.

Dagim grumbled. "Frederica, what did you read?"

Frederica finally acknowledged their questions, raising her head. "I've yet to inform you of the most important piece of knowledge I uncovered from the cultists. And I can see on your faces that you're desperate for me to tell you," she sighed. "But I think that instead, it's best you see the next part for yourself."

***

A half-day of travel later, Dagim, Stefan, Quinn, and The Head followed Frederica towards the ruins of an old white building. Such ruins were the least of their concern as they walked through the fields, however. Frederica had taken them to a place none had ever seen before. A part of the land that even The Head, in over fifty years of travelling on Planet Magnae, had seen nothing of. Dagim was the most surprised by their surroundings, having to manually shut his mouth, fastening his gaped jaw.

The fauxangel sanctuary he had seen astonished him, for the columns reminded him of ancient Earthly empires. But this area astonished him more. From the fine white paint that chipped off the columns of the old ruins, to the green grasses around them and the clear blue puddles of water, this area reminded him of Earth itself. It was as if humanity's old home had been recreated right there.

"This place is phenomenal!" Dagim exclaimed.

"It is! It really fucking is!" Quinn agreed, overwhelmed by the beauty around her. She turned in every direction, unsure of what to take in most.

"To think our ancestors wasted a planet where everything looked the way it does here," The Head scoffed, an unending grin on his face.

Stefan gasped as he knelt. He enjoyed the sensations of their surroundings as the winds trickled tufts of green grass past his knees. He passed a hand through a puddle of clear water. He never knew liquid could be so fresh and smooth.

"No way is this place real!" Dagim chuckled, stretching his arms out to bask in its brilliance.

"We can marvel at the beauty of this place later," Frederica dismissed. "For now, let's look at what the cultists told me would be here."

Everyone else fell in line, returning to following her lead as she climbed amongst the scattered pieces of heavy, fallen rock that was once an impressive building fit for royalty.

Dagim and the others expected to go further into this Earth-like plain and explore all its wonders as they uncovered secrets rarely seen by the rest of humanity. They were somewhat disappointed when Frederica stopped the tour at a half-broken polished column. A column of little importance, bar the few interesting images carved into it.

"Did you bring us out here to look at rudimentary art?" The Head asked.

Quinn squinted as she looked over the markings. All she could make out was a series of poorly drawn stick-figure men, with one holding a ball of some sort. "What is this even supposed to be showing?" she asked.

"A group of women passing a circular source of energy. A representation of the passing on of a spiritual torch through a cycle," Frederica answered. "The Theola Cycle."

Stefan tracked his fingers across the markings, traversing the hole of the source of energy.

"The most important piece that we had to see for ourselves, I'm guessing," Dagim said.

"Mhm," Frederica said.

She retrieved a piece of shiny glass from a compartment of her battle wear. She stepped to the side, left and right until she found the right angle in which she caught the sunlight. None knew what she was in the process of doing. None asked, watching, and waiting to see.

Frederica directed the sunlight that gleamed off the glass until it hit the depiction of a source of energy on the carvings. As the sunlight burned into the image of the source, what could only be described as pure magic occurred.

A minuscule bundle of dark fauxangel energy formed out of thin air, filling the hole. A neat little trick that recaptured the wonder the others had when they first arrived on this Earth-like plain.

"How did you know that would happen?!" Dagim exclaimed.

"It's what the spiritual cultist showed me when I asked for proof of their knowledge of Theola and her existence," Frederica said.

"Very impressive trick," Quinn said.

Stefan nodded in agreement.

"This is what proved to me that the information they gave can be trusted," Frederica said. "After seeing that, I hope you'll keep your minds open when I tell you all that they told me."

"Fine, I'm sold. The cultist cunts know more than we assumed," The Head accepted with a scoff. "Now tell us more about this Theola."

Frederica returned the glass to the compartment. She sat down on one of the broken columns at the ruins. With her hands closed and pointed in the way a recruit professor would, she addressed the group.

"Every generation or so, five or so people from our planet report having had a strange encounter with a fauxangel like no other. Greyish skin as opposed to golden, dark energy as opposed to light. Unfortunately, none of them ever had any proof as to what they saw. They get dismissed as the tirades of crazy men until everyone forgets about the situation. Then, after another generation, another few people report seeing the same type of fauxangel woman with the same general appearance but slight differences in expression. Different iterations of Theola," Frederica started. "Either this *Theola* is one person who only shows up for a few years in each generation, or Theola is the general name for this breed of fauxangel that gets reborn every generation. It's said that the few humans per generation who encounter her in some ways are blessed and cursed. More often cursed. Either way, the few who find themselves being the only ones of their generation that witness Theola are said to expect extreme things to happen to them of both a phenomenal and frightening nature. From the moment they first see her, to the end of their natural lives," she continued.

The calm Earthly winds whistled through the air, filling the void of fascinated silence that Frederica's listeners left.

"And we're two of this generation's few?" Dagim asked, breaking it.

"It would appear so," Frederica said.

That fascinated silence held again. This time, it was The Head who had broken it after a while, doing so with one of his loudest bellowing laughs.

"Amazing! I always knew you were special, Devil Child. But you, First Ranger? Quite the surprise."

"As was your father, Keith Best," Frederica said.

"Sorry, what?" uttered The Head, abruptly snapping out of his laughter. Both by the clear insubordination present through the use of his full name, as well as the mention of his father. "What do you mean?"

"I asked around, pleading with anyone who claimed to know Theola to give me a list of names of all the most notable people who had claimed to have been one of their generation's few who saw her. And one name on that list shone brighter than most," Frederica said. "The author, Ryland Best."

XXIV. A MOUNTAIN OF INFORMATION

FIRST Ranger's extensive, gruelling work had paid off. Frederica and the people of the North Magnae Forces had their fauxangel knowledge developed to an extent none would have considered possible earlier in the war. No one could have anticipated learning of Theola herself, never mind the Theola Cycle and what it meant for humanity. Another gathering was held in the bunker meeting room, becoming the most regularly visited room by The Head and the top recruits.

"Before we start, has anyone heard from Foreseer VII? Or Aiza, as some of you recruits like to call her?" The Head asked. "She should have come back from her scouting mission a while ago. Anyone heard anything?"

No one had any answers for him. The Head grunted, annoyed. He decided not to ask any more, starting the meeting regardless of these worries.

"Whilst digging through my family history, I was able to find some cryptic letters written by my father. When I first saw his neurotic, incoherent chicken scratch about a dark woman, I dismissed it as him losing his mind and complaining about his mistress or something. But now I know what it truly is," The Head said. "It's true. My father was one of the few of his generation to have seen Theola."

"What did these letters say?" Frederica asked.

"Most of it was barely legible. What I generally picked up was that he was worried she would be the end of him. He repeated that a lot," The Head answered.

"Maybe Theola had tried to kill him?" Stefan signed.

"That's what I interpreted from it, too," The Head said.

"Probably because of the stuff he wrote in the book that makes the fauxangels seem less important. Like how The Divinity has only existed for a few hundred years," Dagim said. "I'm guessing she succeeded in ending him eventually."

"Which is also why we can't find a single other copy of that glowing book," Quinn said.

"It's all coming together," The Head chuckled.

Frederica let her mind spin for a while before she came out with her contribution to the discussion.

"I reckon your father stumbled upon some hidden historical knowledge. But in the middle of writing it in another book, he was forced by someone to change it. Probably Theola, maybe someone else. But I have a strong feeling that Ekib's absence from the history it tells has something to do with all of this," Frederica explained. "What I can't figure out is why she would remove Ekib's role in history but keep in the fact that The Divinity was only *created* recently?"

"Let's just be happy with how quickly we've managed to find out such a great amount of new info!" The Head celebrated. "Fantastic work so far, Frederica. You've been running yourself ragged to get us this information. Your amazing work ethic and level of dedication have not gone unnoticed."

"Thank you, sir," Frederica said, downplaying the great pride his praise gave her.

There was a weak knock at the door. Dagim glanced over. "Who's that?" he asked.

"Is someone new joining our meetings?" Stefan signed.

"Yes, someone is," The Head said with great reluctance. Something told Dagim he was not going to appreciate what was on the other side of that door.

When it opened and that dreaded figure walked in, Dagim saw he was right to feel that way. His blood pressure skyrocketed within an instant. His curious stare degenerated into an inhuman, loathsome glare. Had he been lighter-skinned, his face would have flushed red with rage. From his expression alone, the others at the meeting table would not have been surprised if he launched himself out of his seat and attacked the man. How else was Devil Child supposed to react when faced with the individual who tried to kill him?

"Morning, everyone," The Vice said nervously.

Frederica had a visceral reaction to The Vice, too. As opposed to Dagim's indignant fury, her emotions ran cold, a quiet pale fear prompting her gooseflesh to rise.

"What the fuck is he doing here?!" Dagim exclaimed.

"I would also like to know," Frederica muttered.

The Vice Foreseer rubbed the side of his face. Many of the bruises The Head gifted him were yet to heal, including his broken nose.

"Dagim," The Vice sighed, sorrowful. "I cannot begin to tell you how sorry I am for-"

"Shut the fuck up!" Dagim ordered, interrupting him. He turned to ask The Head. "Why the fuck is he here?"

The Head leaned forward in his seat with an atypical hint of anxiety about him.

"Listen, he's apologised and explained his reasoning behind why he did what he did. I think they were stupid fucking reasons, but I can see where he was coming from,"

The Head said. "As a peace offering, he has come bearing gifts on what we've been trying to figure out. We need the information he has. Beggars can't be choosers."

"Oh, well, if he's explained himself and brought along his study notes, then all should be fucking forgiven," Dagim said sarcastically.

Quinn remained quiet. She and Stefan silently watched. The Vice stepped forward. "Dagim. Understand that from now until the day I die, I am forever indebted to you. Anything you ask of me, I'll do. I only want the chance to aid humanity again, no matter the cost," he explained with a genuine obsequiousness. "And Frederica. I'm sorry for trying to force you into my devilish schemes."

Frederica shifted with discomfort, unsure of what to make of this. Dagim, however, knew where he stood.

"This is ridiculous," he scoffed. "The man tries to kill me twice, and he's let back into the fold just because he's learnt some new stuff?!"

"It's not ideal, I know!" The Head exclaimed. "But like I said, begg-"

"Yes, yes. Beggars can't be fucking choosers! I understand!" Dagim exclaimed. His eyes shot daggers at The Vice. "Now what's this important information you have to make up for it?! It better be fucking good!"

The Vice bowed with gratitude. He pulled out one of the empty chairs next to Stefan and the interpreter. He sat himself on it gingerly, as if doing so would hurt him. The poised and haughty arrogance he was once infamous for would take a while to return. Every movement of his body rang with the same humility that being exposed and beaten for his crimes had installed inside him.

"As you know, my exile caused me a great deal of shame. It gave me an abundance of time to think. Not only about how my foolish superstitions almost saw me killing our planet's most valuable recruit, but how, through them, I sacrificed my role in the grand scheme of things. I lost sight of the bigger picture. And so, during this exile, I told myself that if I was to ever show my face around the North Magnae Forces again, I'd make myself useful," The Vice explained. "I spent all my time doing all the research I could. Scouring wherever possible for any information I could collect on the glowing book I remembered Dagim having found."

"And what did you find out?" Quinn asked.

"A portion of it is information you've uncovered. Regarding the Theola Cycle at least," The Vice said.

"What goddamn use are you, then?" Dagim exclaimed.

"I'm still sitting on a mountain of information, many things you don't know yet," The Vice said. "Like how at some point in time, Emmanuel Ekib worked closely with this Theola fauxangel."

The Vice's words had already hooked the entire room, and it was time for his actions to reel them in. He opened up his robe to reveal a series of weathered scrolls tucked away. He scattered the scrolls over the table for the others to see. They were paintings. Art so old it was a surprise one could make out their contents.

Each of these five paintings depicted something similar. Different scenarios in which a tall, dark-skinned man with kinky, curled hair and a heavy-set brow fraternised with a fauxangel woman who vibrated with dark energy.

"That's Emmanuel Ekib," Dagim pointed out.

"And Theola," Frederica added. The Vice confirmed with a nod.

"I heard that Frederica asked questions of the spiritual folk on the seedier parts of our planet. I encountered a similar class of people during my exile research period. Fauxangel-energy-science enthusiasts, who were surprised that someone of my background took their craft seriously. But instead of questions, I asked them for directions," The Vice said, pointing at the paintings. "That's what led me to the tombs where these could be found."

"We're in dangerous tomb territory," The Head smirked, excited by where this was heading.

"They were happy to show me the tombs these came from. Their first reason was that they were surprised an outsider was willing to believe their superstitions. The second is that they respected my bravery. You're supposed to just admire these paintings, not try to go deeper into the tombs to take them for yourself," The Vice said. "I risked being caved in by an avalanche of rock to retrieve these."

"Brilliant," Frederica muttered as she admired each of the paintings. "How old are these?"

"Hundreds of years old. Barely preserved by the fauxangel energy in the tomb," The Vice said. "They would have been painted around the period that Ekib was most likely to have been active."

Stefan traced his hand over Ekib's face on one of the paintings. "I think we can all agree on one thing at this point. The history we're taught is false. Just as we suspected, the words of the glowing book are true," he asserted in sign.

No one said anything in response. It could be assumed that all agreed. Especially Dagim and Frederica.

"That's not all," The Vice said. He turned over each of the paintings to paragraphs of writing in a language formed from symbols alone. A language none in the room could understand. He arranged the scrolls around as if to reveal some sort of message, though not a single other person had a clue as to what was being done in front of them.

"Do you know what these say?" The Vice asked.

"Not a clue," said The Head.

"The energy science enthusiasts and I spent quite a lot of time trying to decipher it. At first, I thought they were pulling my leg, and I was wasting my time. But eventually, we were able to figure out what certain symbols meant. Wasn't the best of jobs, but we managed to determine what this *might* say," The Vice told them.

Dagim sat up, being quite literally on the edge of his seat. "What's it say?!"

The Vice Foreseer leant over the table, stretching both arms over the collection of paintings as he read out the message. "Something about how Emmanuel Ekib is a traitor whose ambition ruined any chances of human-fauxangel peace," he revealed. "Then it goes into a tirade of crazed rants, talking about how he was a false God, a fake king, and a man whose existence should be erased from the universe."

XXV. EMERGENCY

NORTH MAGNAE'S forces grew in numbers. Not only were new soldiers recruited, but their ranks were being filled with those from the south and a recently employed class of civilians. Civilians with knowledge of the spiritual, scientific, and fauxangel-based variety. Lab coats and preacher cloaks were becoming as commonplace as crimson battle wear, with these knowledge brokers filling the bunker rooms. A concentrated effort was being made on the part of The Head and The Vice to extract as much knowledge as was available. Even with everything Emmanuel Ekib and Theola related they had learned in the past few weeks, they still felt as if there was much more to be dug up.

Each day, the metal room had become more of a cluttered mess of documents and studies than the clear space it had been upon their first few meetings. As the regulars sat in the black meeting room, they found it hard to move around with the table stacked with papers and surrounded by boxes filled with much more.

The Head grumbled as he watched another pair of scientists and spiritualists burst into the room, leave behind another box of information, and exit the room. "Right, what are we discussing today?" he asked, moving the box aside.

"I think we should condense everything we know about this new history first," Frederica suggested. The Head agreed, gesturing at The Vice, who spread out the documents that were placed in front of him, looking at all ten at once.

"From our understanding, this is the most likely series of events: An unknown force created the first Theola hundreds of years ago. She created The Divinity who created the fauxangels. All of this occurred on the planet Luxurae. Whatever force created both of them filled The Divinity with the compulsion to travel to find and guide lower lifeforms, and punish them if they did not follow his rule. It also filled the Theola reincarnates with the need to attack anything human. And so, with him as the figurehead, the Theola who had created him sent The Divinity and his fauxangels to what was humanity's new home following the technological apocalypse on Earth. Our planet, Magnae," The Vice laid out thoroughly.

"Several decades following the fauxangel's arrival and violent reign, a group of travellers found the pond of energy, realised The Divinity could bleed and began their campaign of conflict against the fauxangels that we carry on to this day. At an unidentified point in history that we're yet to pinpoint on our timeline, Emmanuel Ekib once worked with a version of Theola, only to betray her in some way, leading to Theolas passing on the message through their cycle that Ekib and those like him, meaning humans, are never to be trusted," The Vice continued.

"At another unidentified point, Theola revealed herself to Ryland Best and eventually killed him. But not before he and his fellow scholars were able to write the book that held the truths of our history that had been lost over the years. A book that was altered to leave out Ekib and hidden by fauxangels, with an alternate version of history being passed through the lands instead, the one we know about the flood and the lake," he finished. "Does everyone agree that what I've just spoken of is the most likely series of events?"

He received five acknowledging nods in response. The Head wiped down his chiselled jaw with a quick stroke of his grey beard. "There's quite a few gaps here and there, but yes, that all seems correct," he said.

"Let's get to filling them then," Dagim sighed.

They did just that, their meeting continuing onwards for hours as they attended to the many boxes and papers that had been retrieved for them.

***

Later that day, Dagim and Quinn returned to Hugo's hospice. Quinn cleaned the oat paste from Hugo's mouth as she placed his feeding tube on the stone table to the side. Dagim helped her in stretching out Hugo's limbs to keep the muscles in use and prevent their degeneration.

As they completed their duties in aid of their comatose companion, they received a visitor. A civilian walked into the cold hospital room. A famous civilian at that. Roisin Indermill, formerly known as Recruit Infinity, the former best medic Magnae had to offer.

"Hey, guys!" Roisin greeted.

"Roisin," Dagim greeted back with a smile.

"How are you doing?" Quinn asked.

"I deeply miss being around you and the other recruits every second of the day, but other than that, I'd say I'm doing fine. I'm still staying at the hospital, getting treatment for my arm and whatnot," she told them. "Enough about me. How's Hugo doing?"

Quinn sighed at her unresponsive lover. "It's still not looking like he'll wake up anytime soon," she admitted, her and Dagim sharing a sorrowful look.

"I don't know what you two are so worried about. Hugo's strong. Watch, he'll wake up eventually and be back to the arrogant, charming rogue we know and love a lot," Roisin insisted, maintaining her beaming smile despite her friends' moods.

"Hope you're right, Ro," Dagim chuckled.

"Of course, I am," Roisin said. "He'll be fine. I'm sure." Quinn smiled warmly. "You know, I've missed your optimism. We could use more of that around here."

"It's getting gloomy around here, isn't it?" Roisin asked.

"Gloomy *and* bureaucratic," Quinn said. "It feels like we're always either going to or coming back from a ten-hour meeting every single day."

"It's been useful, though, hasn't it? I've heard some of the stuff you've learnt. A whole version of history that was completely hidden? It's wild to think about!" Roisin said.

"There's something new every day. My head's about to explode from information overload," Dagim said.

"But it's never boring. That's why I don't mind being asked to come back here for a while," Roisin said.

"You're staying here for a while?" Dagim asked. "I thought you were just visiting."

"Some of the new energy scientists want me to help them conduct some research," Roisin said.

"What type of research?" Quinn asked.

"I'm not sure. But whatever it is, I'm glad I can still be of use to you guys. Even though I messed up my arm," Roisin said. Dagim smiled.

He surprised Roisin, enveloping her in a bear hug. A welcome surprise, she thought, as she hugged him tighter.

Dagim released her from his grasp. He held his hands on both of her shoulders, admiring her sheer presence.

"What's up with you?" Roisin laughed.

221

"Nothing, Roisin," Dagim said, sighing with a grin. "Just glad you're with us."

***

Dagim sat on a mattress on the floor in the empty room that was his bunker sleeping quarters. The only possessions he presently had in the room were his great sword and the cloth he used to polish it up and down to pass the time.

The sword vibrated with no energy. Fire, fauxangel-based, or otherwise. It had been quite a while since Dagim had been able to use it other than hunting for food to bring back to the bunker. He missed seeing the vibrant sprays of tyrian that came with gutting The Divinity's people. He wondered when he would next get to do just that.

A metal clang rang sharply in Dagim's ears as his doors burst open. He saw The Head Foreseer.

"Devil Child! Ready your weapons and meet me at the tunnel!" he ordered with an urgent scream. "I need you to gather a soldier squadron for an emergency rover trip to Bambril Nation! Now!"

Dagim had no time to ask questions, but no reason to ask them either. He knew a desperate call to action when he heard one and wasted no time in preparing for it.

***

An hour later, Dagim stood by a rover in Bambril Nation. Below him was a half-mile-long quagmire of blood-coloured mud, moistened further by the nearby Medocra Sea. Surrounding him was The Head Foreseer as well as the twenty-four other soldiers he had gathered for this emergency fighting squad. Every set of eyes projected into the distance, towards what, from Dagim's position, looked nothing more than a moving shadow, hovering in the air. A strange phenomenon, but not what the Devil Child would consider needing an emergency force of soldiers for.

222

"The shadow? Is that the emergency?" Dagim asked.

The Head kissed his teeth. "Telescope!" he ordered.

One of the soldiers grasped the telescope from the back carriage of the rover. The device was handed to The Head, who aggressively passed it to Dagim. "Look into that and tell me what you see."

Dagim put the telescope up to his left eye. The shadow appeared as visible as if he had been right next to it. Upon initial viewing, the shadow still seemed unimportant to him. He kept looking, waiting for something, anything, to happen.

The energy moved as if it were alive. Wisps of dark, cloudy substances emerged from the shadow. The wisps combined to form an image. A laughing face. A very recognisable mocking face.

"Is that Theola's face?!"

The Head nodded. "I think so. Our scouts have seen it marauding through civilian settlements."

"I don't understand. Doesn't she only show her face to a few each generation?" Dagim asked.

"I guess we're all special then, not just you and First Ranger," The Head scoffed.

Dagim rolled his tongue on the inside of his mouth, scowling with discomfort.

"What's our next move?" he asked.

The Head rifled through the carriage and yanked out an item. A great sword, similar to the one Dagim wielded in his scabbard. The first time Keith Best had held a blade he planned to use in years.

"Let's get to its position before it can get to any civilians," he said.

XXVI. DARK TENDRILS

STEFAN kissed a drawing of his darling Anais. He filed it away back into a crevice in his battle wear. A superstition he would always complete before a gruelling battle or dangerous mission. He needed to have done that in this scenario. They were about to reach a shadow of energy with an image of Theola's face emerging from it.

"What's the plan?" Dagim asked as their group of twenty-six energy-bladed fighters came within a few rushing steps of the collection of dark wisps.

"Attack that damned shadow with everything you've got!" The Head said. "Just like our ancestors did with the first fauxangels, we'll find out whether this apparition can be killed!"

As expected, Dagim was the first soldier whose fiery blade hit the target. As soon as the tip of Dagim's great sword sliced through a wisp of the shadow, he was faced with a burst of dark fauxangel energy, as if the shadow had just bled. Just as The Head suspected, the apparitions could be attacked. On his orders, all twenty-four men, including Stefan, joined Dagim in cutting at the shadow. Over thirty blades broke into different parts of the shadow's energy as the face shrank away, being replaced with flailing tendrils.

A pair of soldiers was met with unexpectedly gruesome fates as the shadow energy fought back. Tendrils of the shadow had tangled around them at blistering, near imperceptible speeds, crushing their waists until their bodies exploded. Three more succumbed to the same fate soon after, staining their comrades with their wet blood and fleshy corpse parts. Nervous hesitation passed through the army of soldiers as they continued to cut at the shadow.

"Careful, men! Don't be reckless!" The Head advised, slicing the tendrils that came for him, spilling dark energy over his feet. "Maintain the same caution you do when fighting fauxangels! Treat this as if you're in a battle with Theola herself!"

Stefan kept a rhythmic count in his head. One, two, three, one, two, three. Step, throw, slide, step, throw, slide. His energised throwing knives cut past each tendril that faced him, his steps and slides allowing him to attack from different sides without having to worry about its grasp.

**

Stefan's calves burned, and his arms ached as he continued his step, throw, slide routine. It still proved effective, cutting tendril after tendril. But he thought he could be liable to drop from exhaustion at any moment. The shadow had decreased in size and emitted a screeching noise as it oozed dark energy. As if it had been crying out as it bled away. The soldiers had made good progress in harming the apparition and were close to destroying it. But it had cost them the lives of four more soldiers who saw its tendrils cut around their necks and wrap their chests in collapse.

Silent Memoir was grateful for Devil Child's presence at his side in battle. Just when he felt his legs about to give way, he was hit with a flood of bursting dark energy. He wiped the nasty secretion out of his eyes as he saw what had thrust it into them. Dagim, The Head Foreseer, and three of the enduring thirteen soldiers joined each other in a simultaneous final attack as they slashed into the image of Theola's face. Energy drained from the apparition as it shrank and condensed. Stefan could hear a faint yet intense scream echo from the energy as it collapsed in on itself and disappeared. It was as if that shadow was connected to Theola's main body, and thus, with its destruction, she was crying in pain wherever she was positioned.

Stefan could finally rest, and so could the rest of the soldiers. He lay on the floor, surrounded by energy-soaked mud, panting hard as his comrades re-grouped around him.

"Chin up, men. This is as great a victory as we could have expected on such short notice!" The Head bellowed, out of breath. "Keep an eye out for similar shadows, energies, and apparitions around civilian settlements. Hibernation is over. We're back to our fighting days."

***

Mirroring the screams of Theola's apparition, Frederica curled into a ball in her bunker's sleeping quarters. Her previous record for most pain endured had been well beaten. Her head experienced such pain that a spear through the skull would have been a relief.

She thought she had been making a valiant effort to keep her migraines at bay. A mixture of stimulants and sheer resilience saw her able to cope for weeks on end. But that afternoon, she reached a level of pain that even she could not power through. The thought of ignoring these headaches was but a foolish desire, as at this point, she could hardly prevent herself from screaming in pain.

"What's wrong with me!" Frederica exclaimed, the pains worsening by the second. "Why is this happening?!"

Frederica's head rocked back and forth, hoping and praying she would be spared these attacks to the mind. She received her wish, though at the cost of her sanity. An

226

effervescent light emerged from the corner of her vision. The pain of Frederica's migraines dulled as the light expanded continuously, robbing her of her vision.

When the light dissipated and her sight was granted back to her, she was transported to another visual plane. She stood in terror, forced to experience another vision of supernatural proportions.

Similar to a dream she had once had, she was not a tangible figure within this plane but a vague essence watching from above as if she were a true angel. She soared above what appeared to be a Planet Luxurae forest, the luminous trees and the jagged aureate leaves alluding to such. The forest was both a beautiful sight and an eyesore, its shining light being both gorgeous and irritating to look at. Frederica felt the same about all of Planet Luxurae from speculative images she had seen in books, so it was no surprise to her that her visions gave her this feeling.

She saw a spot of respite for her pained eyes within the forest, deep beneath the tall trees and their gleaming leaves. The only area of the forest in which dark energy was more prevalent than light. The only area like it for miles. Black shadows slowly encircled the west of the forest to create a dark enclosure amongst the trees. Frederica's intangible state floated closer towards the area.

Theola sat there, resting by a tree. Her pale skin had been beaten black, blue, and purple. Frederica counted over ninety bruises, scrapes, and deepening wounds formed all over the powerful fauxangel's body. She was in a bad way, though she smiled as if all was well. Frederica identified the obvious source of her sadistic amusement. It was said that not a single human had been recorded having stepped foot on the fauxangel planet of Luxurae. Yet Frederica counted as many human corpses scattered around the forests as bruises and cuts on Theola. Each of these ninety corpses was perpetually bled out as the sharp tendrils of her dark shadows gored their bodies continuously.

Frederica was sickened by the sight of so many soldiers. She assessed that they must have been captured during a mission and taken off Magnae to torture.

Most of these individuals made her feel guilty as she did not recognise the faces of a great portion of these dead comrades. She did recognise one of the corpses, though she felt worse by the fact.

She had been wondering why Foreseer VII was missing. It was unlike her to be out of the fold for so long, even whilst on a mission. She knew now.

Aiza Armstrong lay dead on fauxangel soil amongst the butchered corpses of comrades.

***

"Are you serious? Genuinely?" Quinn asked. She was standing in the halls that led to the meeting room, along with The Head and The Vice, when Frederica had come to them with the news.

"It's what I saw in one of my visions," Frederica confirmed. "Foreseer VII is dead."

"Your visions?" The Vice asked. "I've heard these being mentioned before. What are they?"

"For a short while, I've been getting these strange flashes of sight. Lights taking my eyes to other lands and other plains to show events happening elsewhere. That's how I first saw Theola," Frederica informed him. "In my most recent one, it showed Theola had captured a number of our soldiers. She tortured and killed a whole legion. Aiza was one of them."

"You sure those visions of yours can be trusted? Maybe what you saw has not happened?" The Head asked with desperate hope. A good question, Frederica thought.

"I wondered the same thing. That's why I asked the scientists and spiritualists about these sights of mine," Frederica said. "They said a small portion of those who Theola appears to first in a generation experience such *symptom visions* as I do. Though they also said none have ever been as vivid as the ones I described."

"And? Can they be trusted as fact?" Quinn asked, concerned.

"The vast majority of the people who got these visions saw future scenarios with their own eyes that followed the events they saw in their visions and dreams in the past. From what they could tell from others who were affected by this ability, what they saw ended up being reality most of the time."

"Right," sighed Quinn. "So that means..."
Frederica nodded before she could finish her sentence.

"There's a good chance what I saw truly happened, unfortunately," Frederica explained solemnly. "There's a good chance all those soldiers are dead. Including Aiza."

Quinn clasped both sides of her temples, her head growing weary. "No way," she sighed in disbelief, her eyes tearing up.

The Head shook his head. "I was wondering where she had gone. I sent her on scouting missions and had the *nerve* to be frustrated with her lack of a return," he sighed, sorrowful. He clenched his jaw. "I can't think of a single force member who deserved such a fate less."

"God rest her soul," said The Vice.
The Foreseers and recruits stewed in collective frustration. Each hung their head in commemorative silence, in honour of the late Foreseer VII, Aiza Armstrong.

Their solemn silence was unceremoniously ruined, interrupted by the slamming metallic sounds of boots clapping down a hallway.

"Quinn! Quinn!" Roisin called out with a level of excitement rare within the bunkers nowadays.

"What?!" Quinn asked, Roisin falling over her as she reached them.

"Come to the hospice, quick!" Roisin exclaimed. "Hugo's awake! Hugo's *finally* awake!"

XXVII. PROMISE ME

HUGO blinked his eyes open, the sensation feeling as foreign to him as flying through Luxurae skies. It had been long since he could move his head and look around a room. He was met with the best sight possible once he did. All of his friends, who, as they looked back at him, seemed as if they had never left his side. Especially Quinn, who he thought had never looked so astonishing.

"Welcome back, Heart Stealer," Quinn chuckled, her eyes glossy with tears. Hugo smiled, stretching a hand out to caress her again. Quinn leaned in to plant a kiss. Hugo pulled her in closer, making out with her with as much passion as his weakened body could muster.

"Long overdue," Hugo quipped after the kiss. Quinn smiled. Her cheeks blushed, and her eyes rolled. Hugo scanned the smiling faces of his friends again, still in disbelief over being awake.

"Oh shit," he chuckled, his voice weak. "How long was I gone for, guys?"

"Too fucking long," Dagim scoffed with Stefan chuckling in agreement.

"So much has happened since you were last awake!" Roisin said.

"There's a lot of information we'll need to get you caught up on," Frederica added.

Hugo sat up, the smile on his face contrasting against his pained groans.

"It'll take a few days for me to get used to walking around. I won't be able to even think about fighting for a while longer," he said. "Until then, you guys can tell me what I've missed."

***

Roisin started the day feeling wonderful. With Hugo having finally awakened from his coma the previous evening, she woke up feeling as if another miracle could occur that day too. That delightful mood she had started the day in was still not enough to calm her nerves as she walked into the 'research room' at the end of the bunker halls.

Roisin had been asked to arrive there as early as possible. She entered the dimly lit room, faced with a highly complex medical table that doubled as a chair, adorned with its metal restraints. Five steel chairs surrounded the contraption. Sitting in these chairs were five stern-faced energy scientists wearing lab coats and blank countenances.

Their cold faces dismayed her. She was about to find out why the Magnae Forces had asked her to join them once more despite her condition.

"Roisin Indermill?" called out a heavy-spectacled energy-scientist. The de facto leader of these cold fauxangel-essence enthusiasts.

"Yes, that's me."

"Take a seat, please."

"Why? What's about to happen?" Roisin asked.

"We're just going to do a few tests on you. Learn more about the disease that plagues your arm," the head energy scientist explained.

"What for?" Roisin asked.

232

The energy scientist adjusted his glasses with a push of his index finger. "I have an inkling about it when it comes to the fauxangels," he told her. "Understanding your condition is the key to opening doors of never-before-realised knowledge."

***

Dagim rested on the old mattress of his bunker room. His body and soul alternated between feeling elated and exhausted. Elation through the news of Hugo having woken up again, and how closer they seemed to get to understanding the full truth of the fauxangels each day. Exhausted by the abrupt return to daily battles that he and his fellow soldiers of Magnae had been subjected to.

He raised both hands out in front of him. Both his palms were stained black from dark energy being splashed over them. The consequences of killing Theola's apparitions all afternoon. Civilian settlement after civilian settlement had to be cleared of these new foes. It was all he did some days, and at times, he would see the dark tendrils in his sleep. He noticed that the more of these dark shadows of energies they had to fight, the fewer fauxangel sightings were made by the scouts. It was as if Theola's forces had taken over from The Divinity. Dagim never thought he would think it, but he *missed* having to fight the fauxangels. They made for a much less tiresome enemy.

Roisin burst into Dagim's room without knocking. She threw herself onto his bed, mounting him without as much as a hello. Dagim wriggled his way out from under her. He sat to one side of the bed as Roisin kneeled on the other side.

"You alright?" Dagim asked.

"I've just learnt a bunch of insane stuff that I need to tell you now!" she said as she closed her fists. Dagim found her

233

face odd-looking at that moment. Her eyes were wide and over-excited, yet an accompanying smile was absent.

"Go on, let it out," Dagim said.

Roisin cleared her throat as she shifted closer. "Do you know the name of the condition that causes my arm to deteriorate without medicine?"

"Can't say I do."

"Neither can I. Neither can anyone. Not even the doctors."

"What? Then how do they treat it?"

"They give me the standard medicine that helps slow down all degenerative diseases. But my disease isn't like any of the standard degenerative ones. That's why the medicine doesn't work at times. That's why I have to get it constantly treated. That's why they've never even come close to curing it," Roisin explained. "Isn't that interesting?"

"It is."

"They did some tests on me today, and you wouldn't believe where my disease originates from."

"Try me," Dagim said.

"Fauxangels," Roisin answered.

Dagim's face tightened into a perplexed lour. "What?" he scoffed. "How?"

"The fauxangel-energy-scientists did all kinds of new tests to inspect me. They even prodded me with some weird contraptions I'd never seen in a medical office before. Like these special syringes with teeth at the end of them that practically cut an inch-wide hole through my arm,"

Dagim grimaced at the thought of Roisin being cut with those devices. "There's a reason that normal hospitals don't like them working alongside their doctors and researchers," he said. "I'm still surprised that they're a serious part of our forces now."

"I'm glad they are. They had very different methods of testing my blood and skin tissue. They were able to find things out that no other doctors could," Roisin explained. "The head doctor said he had an inkling my disease had something to do with fauxangel energy. I thought he was just saying that because he is an energy-scientist and that's their thing. But after he did his tests, he sent my tissue samples and blood to mainland doctors, and they assessed the same thing: Fauxangel energy overexposure at birth. Because of the meteoroid attack on Cavannahtown at the time."

"Fauxangel energy exposure at birth?" Dagim repeated, unsure. "You've lost me."

Roisin rubbed her most affected arm down as her explanations continued. "They say that children whose mothers were pregnant with them in areas most heavily affected by the war or were born around an area with a lot of fauxangel energy experience the same thing. As the wars went on, this happened to a lot of kids. But the majority who were affected badly would die soon after. Only a rare few like me survive into adulthood with side effects."

"That's interesting. Never knew you could get diseases from fauxangel energy overexposure," Dagim mused. "We should be more careful with it then. Surprised none of us have caught something. Putting it all over our blades and in our rovers. Hell, what's going to happen to me if I consume the Ultimatum Source?"

"Don't worry. None of you are likely to catch a disease like mine, no matter how much energy you handle."

"Are you sure?"

"Yes. It's only really an issue if you're exposed to a great amount as an infant, like I was. Or, in exceptionally rare cases, if you were to be hit with a gargantuan amount of it at once," Roisin elaborated. "I think you should be fine if you consume the Ultimatum Source carefully. By the time it passes through your body, it will have been enough time for you to have a fighting chance. But people who have been hit with that amount of energy with no time to process it will have their bodies degenerate rapidly. If they don't instantly die, that is."

Dagim's ears perked up, and his back straightened as he sat up with enthusiasm. "That's happened before? Someone's been hit with energy worse than the Ultimatum Source?"

"A few potentially have. Naturally, there are no official records of it happening," Roisin said.

"Of course. That would be too convenient," Dagim grunted.

"But we do know someone who *could* have been one of the people it happened to," Roisin said. "Someone connected to you."

"Who?" he asked.

Roisin took a brief moment of pause before she responded as if she dreaded having to do so.

"Ade Chibuike. Your father, Dagim," she revealed. "Overexposure to fauxangel energy. That's what they think crippled your father that day. It's part of what made you the Devil Child."

Devil Child felt every muscle within him tighten. Every bone in his body chilled. He clawed at his ear to make sure he had been hearing her correctly. Once he determined he had, his expression changed. His thick eyebrows almost eclipsed his eyes as he glowered at Roisin.

The expression he held frightened her. She had only seen such intensity whenever he was about to engage in battle. She stepped away from him. She knew that as her friend, he would never harm her. But she could not shake the feeling that Dagim was seconds away from a violent outburst.

"This better not be a fucking joke, lie, or half-truth, Roisin. You'd better be only saying what you mean to say," he threatened.

"I wouldn't joke about that, Dagim," Roisin answered.

"You sure that's what they said? Do you swear? You swear they said Ade Chibuike?!" Dagim asked, his emotional state having changed from intense simmering anger to erratic angst and consternation. "You're sure you're not mixing up the name?!"

"Your father's name was Ade, wasn't it?"

"Yes, definitely."

"Then I'm sure," Roisin answered with certainty.
It was clear from a single glance that Dagim's mind was a muddled muss. Eyebrows raised, eyes glazed open, mouth a small fraction open, lips trembling, stiff of being. Like someone had shut down the processing of his body. This was the weakest Roisin had ever seen him. And yet, she did not find it shameful to see him like this. She found it endearing. It was also the most human she had seen him. As much as it concerned her, it was refreshing to see the perpetually brutal and fearless Devil Child experience the same emotional vulnerability that his comrades did daily.

"Are you okay, Dagim?" she asked, resting a gentle arm on his shoulder.

Dagim rested an even gentler hand over hers. "I am, it's...well, there's no other way to put it. What you just said was the last thing I would have ever liked to hear."

"I'm sorry. I know you don't like bringing up what happened to your parents that day, but I had to tell you," Roisin said.

"It's not just that," Dagim sighed. "It's the Ultimatum Source," he said.

"What about it?" Roisin asked.

"The excavation team still haven't recovered it from the wreckage at the cave. And, to be honest with you, I'm hoping they aren't able to retrieve it for a while," Dagim admitted. "I feel guilty about it, and I know I shouldn't feel this way, but I do. I'm fucking *dreading* having to consume it."

"That's not like you," Roisin said, shocked. "Why's the news I gave made you feel that way?"

Roisin saw Dagim's gaze perform a quick darting shift away from hers before returning. Whatever he was about to say, she knew it came with a disinclined demurral. Her gentle hand remained over Dagim's on his shoulder. She held it tighter, encouraging him with a soft caress of her fingers over the back of his hand.

"I never knew that was what crippled my father. Growing up, I'd heard from others around Incoba that he was an explorer, so I thought maybe he had an accident during one of his expeditions," Dagim said. "I never got a solid answer from the man himself when he was alive. In my early life, his mind degenerated as much as his legs had the day I was born. He was also almost blind, kept saying *the light* caused it. Never had a clue what he meant back then."

"I didn't know you had those memories of him. You were quite young when he died," Roisin commented.

Dagim laughed. "I suppose in a way he told me what had happened to him from the start. Just never the full story. The *light* must have been fauxangel energy. Who would've thought?" he chuckled.

"Yeah," Roisin laughed nervously.

"Now that I know what happened, I don't know what to do," Dagim said. "It's making me second-guess a lot."

"Like what?" Roisin asked.

"Like whether I'll be able to handle consumption of the full Ultimatum Source," Dagim said. "That amount of energy crippled my father. What if it does the same to me? What if it does something *worse*?"

"And what if it doesn't?" Roisin asked, taking up a rare position as the assertive one of the pair. "You are the strongest soldier North Magnae has to offer. The best soldier the entire planet of Magnae has. There's not a single person alive who humanity needs to consume that source more."

"Humanity," Dagim repeated in derision. He rubbed down his head, chock-full of stress. "What did the human race do to deserve a person like me as their final hope?"

"Humanity has been *blessed* to have a person like you as our final hope," Roisin insisted. "If anything, I think we're lucky. At a time when we needed it most, the universe granted us with you, a man who embodies the very essence of a warrior."

"And to bring such a man into the world, the universe had his mother die when giving birth to him and his father go mad," Dagim countered. "Seems like the universe has a twisted sense of hope."

"You are *not* some sort of bad omen because of the way you were born. I'd say you are a good omen, *despite* the way you were born," Roisin asserted.

Dagim shook his head with profound disagreement.

"All this time, I've ignored the doubters, the uncertain and all those who have said I wasn't suited to take on ultimate power. I've dismissed their whispers, I've insulted their sanity. But now, I see where they're coming from. If I'm humanity's true hope, then maybe we were never meant to last long as a species."

Roisin removed her hand from Dagim's shoulder. She crossed her arms and pouted at him, furious with his disparaging comments. She had it in her mind to slap some sense into him, but ultimately decided against it.

"Dagim. Does The Head Foreseer believe you are best for this?" she asked.

"Yes?" he answered, not as certain-sounding as Roisin would have liked. She tutted.

"And do I believe in you?"

"I don't know, do you?"

"I do," Roisin confirmed with an aggressive nod. Dagim laughed. "I appreciate your support, Roisin, but it doesn't change-"

Roisin cut him off immediately. "And so does almost every single member of our forces. From the spiritualists to the energy scientists to the scavengers to the scouts to the tacticians to the medics to the soldiers to need I remind you, the fucking *Head Foreseer* himself! We *all* believe that you will save us!" Roisin shouted down at him. "Tell me, Devil Child. What right do you have to claim we are all wrong?!"

Dagim had no response for Roisin. Nothing new to say. He stood there, quiet. Thoughtlessly staring at the ground.

Roisin planted a spontaneous kiss on Dagim's lips. He could not process what was happening as he felt her mouth softly lock with his for what felt like a minute. When she broke off the kiss, she returned to crossing her arms and staring him down with a disparaging glare.

"Where did that come from?" Dagim asked with pleasant surprise. "You've never done anything like that before."

"I didn't know what else to do," Roisin smiled with a shrug. "How else was I going to show you how much you're valued?"

Dagim laughed. "I appreciate it."

"It wasn't for free. I want you to do something for me in return," Roisin said.

"And that is?" Dagim asked.

"Promise me you'll never doubt yourself again. Promise me that you'll accept your fate as our saviour," Roisin insisted. "You have to, Devil Child."

XXVIII. DIVINE DEATH

FREDERICA held her head against the leaden walls of her sleeping quarters. The chilling, hard surface pressing against her forehead was a last-ditch, futile attempt to ease the pains that cursed her head. Frederica was somewhat grateful that the headaches had become so commonplace. She had begun to become used to the constant agony. Not a single painkiller or medication worked, and so she resorted to the only tactic left. Weathering the storm.

"No, not again," Frederica muttered in fearful anticipation.

She could feel it coming. She could see it coming. The momentarily dulled pain would bring forth a light from the corner of her eye, a light that could consume her sight and transport her to a foreign plain for yet another vision. But whilst the feeling that came with it persisted, the light never came. Darkness formed within the corners of her eyes. Blackness consumed her vision in this instance.

Instead of her essence being transported to another plain, a foreign essence was transported to hers. Frederica remained in her room, no longer alone. As dark energy dissipated from her eyes, she imagined the worst-case scenario as to what was imminent. Her pessimistic prediction proved to be an accurate one. Frederica was filled with dread as Theola stood inches away from her.

"Frederica Rasmussen," Theola greeted.

"Theola," Frederica said, her voice so hoarse and weak it was barely perceptible to the ear.

"You people have been talking about me a lot, asking a lot of questions," Theola said as she stepped closer to First Ranger. "Thought I'd show my face in case you wanted to ask any of them directly. From the source itself."

Frederica stepped away from her. "What do you want?" Theola closed the distance again. "To give you a chance to end this war right now," she said.

Frederica fixed an intent look deep into Theola's eyes. What had stunned her most about this encounter was how human she appeared up close. From the flecks of discolouration in her eyes to the subtle imperfections in her bone structure. She was far more human-looking than any of the fauxangels below her, including The Divinity. Had it not been for the dark aura she was constantly engulfed in, Frederica could easily have confused Theola for a civilian. An estranged family member, even.

"Hello? Am I speaking to myself?" Theola asked. "Do you plan on responding any time this century?"

"Sorry, what did you say again?" Frederica asked, frazzled.

"Tonight, I'm giving you the chance to end the constant wars between your people of Magnae and the people of Luxurae," Theola said. "Do you accept?"

Frederica levelled a discerning gaze. "I'm not even going to try and pretend I know what you're talking about, so why don't you just tell me instead of wasting time with cryptic quips?"

"Someone's trying their best to look brave," Theola mocked. "There's nothing cryptic about any of this. I need you to do something for me, and in return, I'll make sure this war is done and dusted."

"Can you get to the point, please?" Frederica groaned. Theola smirked, amused by her insolence.

"Alright, I'll just say it straight then. I'll kill The Divinity and take away every 'fauxangel and apparition' as you call them, back to Luxurae. In return, I want you to kill Dagim Chibuike."

"Again, what on Magnae are you talking about?! Did you come all the way here just to mock me?"

"You recruits are so snappy! You're worse than Devil Child! Can't even get through a conversation without your guard being up to the high heavens!" Theola complained. "And speaking of Devil Child, *no,* I am *not* mocking. I'm telling the bona fide truth. I'll kill The Divinity if you kill him. I *will*."

Frederica studied Theola's expression and body language for any signs of dishonesty, any tell-tale notions of blatant lies from the way she held herself to the number of times she blinked. She could not detect a single one. An entity like Theola could potentially mask such signs, but Frederica felt compelled to believe her anyway. As ridiculous as it seemed.

"Do you not believe me? Am I not trustworthy enough for you, First Ranger?" Theola mocked, irritated by her silence. "Very well, take a look at this."

A black force of energy occupied the space in front of them when Theola waved her hand with savage speed. As Theola conjured up a portal of darkness, Frederica received her second major shock of the evening. The portal vanished, leaving behind its transported cargo in its place. Frederica stepped back again, her head slamming against the hard walls. The blow dazed her, though not nearly as much as

244

what had been brought in front of her. Now, two powerful fauxangels were in her room.

The Divinity crouched down on all fours, grovelling at Theola's feet. His crown shone with the brightest tyrian purple blood Frederica had ever seen. His head had been completely scalped.

Yet that was not the worst of his injuries. Six of the ten fingers on each of his hands had either been severed or mangled to the point they could barely be considered digits. Frederica's eyes tracked down to the tunic trousers the fauxangel was wearing. A bloody spot stained his crotch. She did not wish to imagine what had happened there.

"Spare me," The Divinity coughed, staining the steel floors with specks of fluorescent blood.

"Shut your fucking mouth," Theola snapped at him. She struck him violently against the back of his head, causing a vomiting spill of more purple on Frederica's floor.

"What's this?! What have you brought him here for?!" Frederica panicked.

"Calm down. Now," Theola ordered.
The Divinity cried tears of blood. "Please, I'm sorry I-"

"Close your mouth, younger! Close your mouth, you *impotent* imbecile!" Theola shouted, interrupting his plea with a lightning-fast dark tendril that protruded from her hands and slammed his face against the floor. "I don't want to have to tell you again!"

The Divinity fastened his mouth shut as his life depended on it. He whimpered, letting the blood drip from his broken nose and down onto his lips.

"He had the nerve to follow me back to Magnae. To question what I was doing with my time on this planet when he should have stayed sulking with his useless golden ilk on Luxurae!" Theola shouted furiously as she prodded The

Divinity's bloody head with dark tendrils. "As if I have to explain myself to my creation!"

From the tremble at his lip, Frederica could see The Divinity was compelled to say sorry again. He knew better, keeping his wounded mouth shut.

"Look at this man, Frederica. Look at him! Look at this pathetic excuse of a carrier of my will! A man who is so weak, his greatest attack on the humans left him bloody and bruised! A man who can't even follow simple instructions and stay fucking put whilst I deal with the mess he's made!" Theola ranted in intense bursts of screaming passion. "I don't need him anymore! And since you don't believe I'll do it, I think I might as well end him right here, right now!"

"Theola, don't! Don't I beg you! Don't!" The Divinity broke out in a desperate cry.

Theola did not listen. Ten dark tendrils broke out of her skin as she constructed the architects of his demise. Frederica winced as she watched each tendril attack The Divinity, piercing his body through both his eyes, his ears, nostrils, mouth, and the nape of his neck. Theola's stabbing shadows buried through his body, the head fauxangel's entire constitution bloating with dark energy. Frederica was granted the rare privilege of being the first human to see The Divinity truly suffer and the last to see him alive. The final image of the godly alien who had terrorised Planet Magnae for so long was that of a bloated, blubbering face pulsing with veins and drenched in tears as it exploded into oblivion.

Black smoke and tyrian blood covered every inch of the room from the walls to the doors to both Frederica and Theola's faces. Frederica took a deep, pained breath out, digesting it all. Theola's anger subsided as she returned to her smirking ways.

"You believe me now, don't you?" she chided.

Frederica nodded, making a strange wheezing gasp as she opened her mouth. She had intended for words to come out, but could not even hope to find them.

"Good. So, you'll do as I say and kill Dagim Chibuike?" Theola asked.

Frederica gulped, looking like a jittery mess. "I'd like to understand something first," she said.

"What?!" Theola groaned.

"If you can teleport in here and do all this, why can't you just teleport to Dagim's room and kill him?" First Ranger asked. "If Dagim's death is all you want to end this war and take off, then why haven't you done it yourself?"

"I don't *want* to do it myself. I want *you* to do it for me, no questions asked," Theola said, poking Frederica's chest with a small wispy tendril. "I just got done showing you how I don't like explaining myself to Luxuraeans like our late friend The Divinity. What makes you think I'm about to waste my time explaining myself to a human?"

Frederica grumbled with dissatisfaction. "That brings up another question, then."

"Ask away," Theola sighed.

"Why me of all people? Why did you choose me to show this to? To tell this to? To kill Dagim?" Frederica questioned.

She did not obtain the answer she sought. Theola responded with a smile, a wave of her hand and a conjuring of a dark portal.

"Don't disappoint me," Theola said, walking through the portal. "You were the vessel. Prove you're worth more."

As soon as Theola vanished, all signs of her having been there vanished with her. The dark energy that stained the area had been wiped away. Only The Divinity's remains remained. Frederica crumbled to her bed, desperate to rest. A part of her thought that perhaps all that had happened had

247

just been a dream. She desperately wanted to believe it was so. But she knew good and well that what she had experienced was reality.

Frederica sighed. Once again, she had been asked to kill the Devil Child, a recurring pattern in her life. This time she was urged to by an outside force. And once again, she surprised even herself by how willing she was to consider it. Theola had just killed The Divinity in front of her. The dark fauxangel woman disposed of her most powerful comrade.

Perhaps this war would be finally over if Frederica would just do the same.

XXIX. LORD KNOWS

THE Vice Foreseer handed Devil Child his weapons like a servant would to his master. The Foreseer and the top recruit occupied the middle of the room at the busiest time of the evening. Recruits scattered through the main bunker, rushing from A to Z as they prepared for a mission The Head had not yet detailed. All that was known was that they would require their weapons. All could guess that whatever the mission was to be, it involved the extermination of Theola's apparitions.

Dagim collected the weapons from the second-in-command. He admired the gleam of his polished longsword as well as the shine on the barrel of his Bronze Bullet.

"Whoa," he gasped, impressed. "You cleaned these thoroughly."

"Yes. Exactly to your liking," The Vice said.
Dagim's eyes narrowed. "Can't believe you did every single task I asked of you."

"You seem not to be willing to accept my change of heart, so perhaps acts of service will prove it to you," The Vice said. "I'm regretful of my past actions. All I want is to aid humanity as I was always supposed to do."

"Right. I'm still keeping an eye on you," Dagim said. The Vice sighed, understanding his apprehension.

"Devil Child, are you ready for the nation sweep with your squadron?" The Head asked, having carelessly interrupted their conversation as he barged in between them.

"I've been able to gather a strong starting squad for battle, except for one recruit," Dagim said. "No sign of Stefan. Did you already send him out on a mission?"

"Nope. Did you?" The Head asked The Vice Foreseer.

"I didn't," The Vice said.

"Where the hell's he disappeared to then?" Dagim complained.

"Who the fuck knows," The Head grunted.

He cupped his hands around his mouth as he screamed out a message to the ranks.

"Silent Memoir! Where the hell is Silent Memoir?!"

***

Stefan returned to Vohdkaz Town. He sat on the soft, cropped grass with a large blanket over his back and his sights set on the beautiful constellations above. He enjoyed the stars above him with the best company possible. His sweet love, Anais. The gentle-eyed, impassioned young woman cuddled up to her boyfriend tight enough to have burst him. If it were up to her, he would never leave.

"Do you have to hold me so tight?" Stefan asked in sign language as he laughed.

"You think I'll let you go? Now that I have you all to myself again?" Anais signed back.

Stefan laughed, seeing to match her hold as he gripped her closer and kissed her forehead.

"Only for a short while, my love," Stefan signed. "I'm not even supposed to be away from my duties right now."

"I can't believe you took an unauthorised leave just to see me. How daring," Anais signed. "Just goes to show how much you appreciate me. You're so lovely, Stefan."

250

"You're even more lovely. And, you're worth the risk," Stefan signed.

Anais made herself cosier, letting the blanket drape over her head as she snuggled up to Silent Memoir. Her face suddenly scrunched, a thought coming to mind.

"What made you decide to take the risk? To come and see me even though the war is yet to finish?" Anais signed with inquisitive eyes.

Stefan signed his response. "Things are getting very serious in the war. There's this new fauxangel, Theola. She and her apparitions are stronger than The Divinity and his fauxangels. We're having to guard settlements and fight battles every second of the day," he explained. "I want to see as much of you as possible, as frequently as possible. In case, God forbid, I never get to see you again."

Anais' eyes squirmed as they filled with tears. She gripped his face with intensity, another action of hers in which he matched. The silent couple kissed each other, the Vohdkaz stars above sparkling as bright as their love.

***

Hugo leaned an arm against the stone-studded walls of the battle recuperation room. He propped himself upright with a knee placed on one of the series of cushions laid over the iron benches attached to the walls. He had finally regained the ability to walk without assistance. He still had trouble moving around like he used to.

"Useless legs," Hugo spat as he sat down on the bench. He could not describe how appreciative he was of Quinn and Dagim's aid during his comatose state. If they had not stretched out and worked his muscles during that time, he might not have been able to stand up at all.

He remembered earlier in the war when he despised the idea of having to rush into battle. With the post-traumatic

251

stress that would cripple him every time he faced a fauxangel, and the constant bumps of Granulate P that he would have to snort just to keep up with the other soldiers. He hated having to keep on fighting back then. Now, he felt the opposite. He wished he could join the fight against the fauxangels. He wished he could do his part.

Hugo watched the door open as twenty dark-energy-stained soldiers flooded into the room in no time. One thing Hugo remembered fondly from their early days was that after battles, especially after training battles, the recruits would return in the most rambunctious mood. The passion of battle would still flow through them. He rarely saw any of that anymore. Rarely did they return with any enthusiasm. That day, he saw them return as jaded as they had ever been. No passion for the war they were fighting. No passion for life at all, it seemed.

"Dagim, how's it going?" Hugo asked as he sat by the bench next to him.

Since the Devil Child had returned from battle, he had stayed rooted in that same spot. He sat with his legs wide, arms flat, and eyes absorbed by nothingness.

"Hugo," Dagim muttered. Uttering those words alone drained the little energy he had.

"I'm guessing that wasn't the best of battles," Hugo sighed.

With how Dagim shook his head in response, one would have thought it had been replaced with lead. "It's horrible out there, Hugo," he sighed. "And it's just getting worse."

***

Frederica waded through the dark in the dead of night. She moved through the halls of the top five sleeping quarters, ensuring not a single step made a sound as she crept down. Four rooms lay ahead of her, each room a metre apart. The

252

last room on the left side of the hall belonged to Dagim. Her final destination.

Frederica's inner palm went numb, the feeling drained with how tightly she held her weapon. She had a sickle in her hand. This was the blade she would use to fulfil her end of the bargain proposed to her by Theola. The weapon that would kill the Devil Child.

Frederica could not comprehend what she was doing. It was as if she had no autonomy of her own. Not a single thought ran through her head as she stepped down the hallway. A wild animal would have shown to have more agency and ability of contemplation than the First Ranger possessed in the hallway that night. Her emotions were as dulled as her thoughts. All she could sense within herself was an inescapable impulse. A will to act. A compulsion to go forth with this treacherous mission. To kill Dagim without a second thought.

"Evening, Frederica," echoed a low voice behind her. Frederica dashed to the side, her heart beating fast enough to cause an attack. She had been caught, a figure emerging out of the shadows to confront her. She held the cold steel wall behind her as she awaited him. The Vice Foreseer revealed himself. He smiled at her, then down at her sickle.

"What do you plan on doing with such a sharp weapon at such a late hour?" The Vice Foreseer asked her. Frederica chose not to respond, unsure of what she could say that would make for an appropriate answer.

The Vice motioned towards First Ranger's destination. "I believe that one's Dagim's room," he said. "Were you aware of that?"

"I was," Frederica answered.

Silence. That was all that passed through those halls for a short while after. Pure silence as The Vice's judging eyes of ice struck a pick through her heart. She could not stand to look him in the eye at this moment. But she was too frozen to have done anything else.

"Who better to help us kill angels than a devil?" The Vice asked.

"Sorry?" Frederica muttered.

"Who better to help us kill fauxangels than a Devil Child?" The Vice corrected himself with a laugh.

His humour had been lost on Frederica, the young woman in a blank state of confusion.

"Sorry?" she repeated.

The Vice let out a deep breath. "I can't believe there was once a point in time when I thought his death would be the best for humanity. To the point where I even had other Foreseers on board. To the point where I had even you on board," The Vice said. "Deroren val bovai wrero."

"What does that mean?" asked Frederica. She was not familiar with that phrase in Magnae Second Tongue. Just as she was not familiar with the point and nature of their current conversation.

"You don't know bad until you've seen worse," The Vice translated. "I thought a *devilish man* being given ultimate power would spell humanity's doom. But during my exile, I saw different. With the things that I saw the fauxangels do? The hardships I had to survive as those creatures ran rampant? I understood that not letting Dagim be given ultimate power is what would *actually* spell humanity's doom. We need the bad to deal with the worse."

"That's a different tune from the one you used to sing," Frederica commented.

"A lot has happened since then. My time as a Foreseer had me lose sight of the real problems of our world, the real struggles of Magnae and what the fauxangels had done to it,"

The Vice said. "I applaud The Head for keeping his eye on the ball. Lord knows I didn't."

"That's nice," Frederica said awkwardly.

"It is," said The Vice. "I think you should make sure you don't lose sight of what's important either."

Frederica took a deep breath in as his icy stare dug through her deeper. He cleared his throat in preparation for another thoughtful speech.

"One compliment I can give to Dagim, The Head Foreseer, and people like them, is that they are not deluded about their unruly natures. They are well aware of it, and it's what allows them to fight for what is good and right," The Vice Foreseer told her. "The truly dangerous people in this world are those who think they are above such unruly behaviour but have their actions show otherwise."

"Like who?"

"I think you know who, Frederica."

The Magnae Forces' second in command had nothing left to say. He left Frederica, turning around and walking away measuredly. The Vice disappeared into the shadows of the night, leaving her to think and act on her own.

Frederica backed herself against the hall walls. She slid down until she was sitting, folded within herself. She thought through her actions for the first time that night. The compulsion that consumed her no longer had any hold, gradually fading the more she thought about it.

The sickle in her hand felt foreign and strange. First Ranger glanced at her destination for the final time. She only felt disgust at the thought of completing her mission. She rose to her feet and walked back to her room.

She would leave Dagim be, Theola's deal be damned.

XXX. DEAL WITH

A rare celebration was held within the main bunker room. Fauxangel energy of both a dark and light quality was placed in different crevices around the room to give it a flashing fluorescent glow. The underground containment boomed with applause and aplomb for a party of the ages.

"He's dead! He's dead! The Divinity is dead!" The Head celebrated to the raucous cheers of the rest of the forces. That morning, Frederica had graced him with the most pleasant news. She revealed to him that The Divinity had been killed by none other than Theola herself. She claimed to have seen it in one of her visions. The result of a *dire issue of subordination,* she had called it, where Theola had executed him for his incompetence. The Head did not care how he had died, only that he truly had. Once he could confirm it, once he could send scouts across the lands and report no more sightings of his fauxangels, his mind went ablaze. All he wanted to think about was how to celebrate this joyous news. They did, in the greatest way Magnaeans knew how.

Any soldier who took a single solitary second to consider their situation realised this was a bittersweet victory to swallow. Whilst The Divinity's death was more than enough reason for humans planet-wide to cheer, it had not done much to alter their current position. As of recent times, the main threat to the Magnae Forces had been Theola and her apparitions, with The Divinity's fauxangels being an afterthought and The Divinity himself having not done much after his hibernation. In reality, this news had done nothing to change their current fates. Yet that did not stop the workers and recruits of The Magnae Forces from indulging in drinks, songs, and jubilant dance.

Of the recruits that occupied the bunker, an inverse graph could be made with those who experienced the most battle and hardship first-hand, and those of the lower ranks. Whilst the lower-ranked recruits jumped at the rare opportunity to party with The Head, the top recruits that remained were reluctant to join in on the festivities. As the majority of their companions threw caution to the wind, Dagim and his closest friends sat in a corner of their own, quietly drinking from bottles as they relaxed. Dagim and Roisin sat close to each other, across from Hugo and Quinn, who used his shoulder as a headrest, their arms intertwined.

Dagim's circle of six was incomplete, however. Stefan had not returned, and though they had asked Frederica to join them, she had decided to seclude herself in her room for an early night's sleep.

Dagim took a sip of his drink as he gestured his head towards The Head. He drew the group's attention to their leader, thrusting his arms into the air as he continued his chants of "The Divinity is dead!"

"Have you ever seen him so insanely happy?" Dagim mocked.

"No," Roisin laughed. "I think it's lovely."
Dagim scoffed. "One way of seeing it."

"I'm surprised you're not doing the same," Quinn scoffed back at him. Dagim's thick brows furrowed. Hugo smiled, looking to add to her point.

"Droregen de simvi par vrey! Droregen de simvi par voo! Droregen de simvi par vree! Droregen di mas eh vel schru!" Heart Stealer sang. He pounded his chest as he imitated the style of Dagim's patriotic post-training battle chants from before the war proper. His brief show prompted great laughter from the two girls and a weak smirk from Dagim himself. "What happened to all of that?" Hugo asked.

Dagim's eyes fixed on the floor for a moment. Quinn and Hugo made a valid armour-piercing point. There was a time when he would thrust himself into uplifting chants and dances, just like The Head had been. A while ago, he would have been the one to kickstart the celebrations and convince the others to join him in the most raucous of choruses as they sang about their greatness. This idle solemnity would have been foreign to him a few months ago. The Devil Child was losing his fire. He had been feeling the creeping spectres of self-doubt pouring water over his formerly passionate soul. If he carried on like this, they would extinguish it forever. He knew he could not let this happen. He had to keep the promise that was sealed by Roisin's kiss.

"Fuck," Dagim sighed under his breath. He knocked his head back as he downed the rest of his drink in one long gulp. The others gasped, chuckling with surprise as he smashed the quickly finished bottle on the floor. He rose to his feet and stood in the middle of their group circle like a proud leader.

"Enough of this sulking around in a corner," Dagim said. "The war might not be over, but The Divinity is dead. He's done. Fucking done. If we can't celebrate that to the fullest, then what *can* we celebrate?"

"Did my singing cast a spell on you or something?" Hugo asked.

"Must be the case," Roisin laughed.

"Shut up," Dagim laughed. "Let's go dance with our comrades."

"If you say so," Quinn chuckled as the three of them followed Dagim to the middle of the room. The top recruits implanted themselves into the high-energy festivities that echoed through the bunkers. They made efforts to enjoy their night, allowing themselves for just a few hours, to forget the dire state of their lives, their people, and their planet.

***

Hugo vomited as he drunkenly stumbled from side to side in the corridors of the spare sleeping quarters. He still had trouble walking from his time spent comatose while sober. Whilst drunk, it became a Herculean task. He had wanted to walk to the bathroom but could not find it in time, forcing him to catch the protruding vomit into a spare battle helmet he had found.

"Fucking nasty," Hugo groaned as he wiped his mouth clean. He accidentally dropped the helmet, the crimson headgear slipping out of his shaking hands and coating the section of the corridor with vomit. He was too tired and drunk to even think about cleaning it up. He continued to stumble through the corridors in search of Quinn.

As he walked through these metal halls, he saw many other recruits in the same state that he was. Half-drunk, slovenly, and desperately trying to recover from the hecticness of the ending party as they spilt themselves over the walls and floors.

He saw many things that reminded him of the parties the recruits used to have before this war started. Back when they had only faced prisoners in a yard as opposed to fauxangels on the planetary plains. He saw recruits pass out on top of each other. He saw The Head, The Vice, and older employees gambling and playing drinking games in the private rooms. He saw groups of intoxicated young men spar in duels with metal bars and helmets similar to the one he had thrown up in.

Most interesting of all, he saw Dagim and Roisin lost in the passions of lust. They were drunker than he, kissing as if they wanted to devour the other, pulling and dragging each other into a private room where they would engage in the sloppiest of sexual escapades. Hugo laughed, wondering if either of them even knew what they were doing. It amused him to think about how awkward it would be once they found out in the morning.

As Hugo wandered about, he struggled to find Quinn. He checked many different rooms, winding down one corridor to the next. As he stepped into one of these rooms, he halted his search. He had not found Quinn, just a sorry sight that could sober a man even in his state. Hugo froze as he lowered his eyes to the centre of the hospice room he had just barged.

A man lay on the mattress propped up on the steel mound in the middle of the cold enclosure. Hugo had stumbled into one of the care hospices of the wounded civilians they had taken in to treat. Whatever treatment he had been given failed. His pale skin was stained black with the 'blood' of Theola's dark tendril masses. His body harboured deep wounds that soaked the bandages a dark red from the pools of now dried-up blood. This was a sad sight regardless of who the individual was. It was a sadder sight once Hugo realised that he recognised him. This was a man he did not know well, but could place his face anywhere.

A much older man and an infamous one at that. A former soldier whom a few other recruits would also have recognised. A world-weary man who would often wander around towns, inspiring budding young warriors with his tales. Hugo remembered being a pre-teen and sitting around a campfire with his brothers, Harlen and Hudson, and all the other neighbourhood children as the man regaled them with stories of humans triumphing over fauxangels. It was after hearing one of this man's stories that the young Heart Stealer finally decided he would apply for recruit school and become a soldier for the forces. The living embodiment of his youthful aspirations lay dead in front of him.

"Just what I needed to see," Hugo sighed as he shut the door to the room.

The glassy illusions that the brief respite the celebrations had given him were shattered into a million pieces and cut at his heart. Both of his wobbly feet had been placed back into reality. There was still much they all had to fight for. To make matters worse, his body was too weak to help fight anytime soon. More great men like that one would die, and he could do nothing about it.

Hugo walked away from the room and down the corridor, his legs feeling even weaker. He wandered about the bunkers in solemn contemplation, passing by his drunker recruit counterparts as they continued to relax and unwind. The illusion of celebration was still intact for them.

As Hugo reached the end of the corridor, he stumbled upon his reason for having walked out in the first place. Quinn turned around the corner, greeting Hugo with a cheeky smile that told him she was still a touch inebriated.

"I was wondering where you went," Queen Triumph laughed as she draped her arms over his shoulders. "Did you run off to go vomit in secret?"

"Yeah," Hugo answered, his voice trailing off in a dejected manner. Though her loving eyes searched for his, they would not meet. Hugo would not make eye contact with her, as if a fauxangel had cursed his pupils from raising upwards. Quinn's face soured as she watched the melancholic misery that grew over her boyfriend.

"What's wrong?" she asked, her voice soft and worrisome.

Hugo raised his head. He tried to force a signature cocky smirk back on his face. "This war shit never gets easier to deal with, does it?" he quipped.

Quinn smiled, her eyes holding sympathy for him in conjunction with a sorrow of her own. "It doesn't," she agreed softly. "I realised that this morning."

Hugo's eyes became sharp and alert. "What's happened?"

Quinn took both of her arms off of Hugo and used one to pick out a folded piece of paper she had been keeping in the back of her trousers. She handed it to Hugo, who wasted no time in unfolding and reading it. Once he had read just a few lines of the legalistic written tome, his back and shoulders slouched with despondency.

"The Iqra House Orphanage," Hugo uttered quietly as he finished reading.

"I already knew this was going to happen. This letter just confirmed it for me," Quinn sighed as she took the letter back from him. "It's officially gone. The place that took me in as an unfortunate young girl won't be able to do the same for anyone else. Ever again."

Queen Triumph struggled to maintain a strong, unaffected disposition. Hugo stared back at her with the same sympathy she had levied on him a few moments ago.

He could see the subtle shakiness about her. A clear effort was being made on her part not to be a mess of tears.

"What happened? Was it destroyed, or could they just not afford to keep it running?" Hugo asked.

"It was almost burnt down by fauxangels many weeks back. A few Theola tendril attacks put the nail in the bloody coffin," Quinn explained. "It was a miracle it lasted this long anyway. Money's been running low for too long now. It was already over for them."

Hugo shook his head with dismay. "Quinn," he uttered. He knew not what to say to console his woman, only what he felt was right to do. He held her softly, compressing her body with a hug warm enough to thaw ice. Quinn melted within his hands, resting her head against him in the same way that always made her feel more comfortable. Heart Stealer stared into space as he rocked from side to side, holding Quinn dearly.

He racked his mind for anything he could say to lighten the mood and change the subject with haste. He opened his mouth to reveal the best he could come up with.

"This war shit might not get easier to deal with, but we won't have to deal with it forever. I can already see us winning soon," he smirked. "The Divinity was killed by Theola herself. A Luxuraean killing one of their own shows they've not got it together *at all*. That's a good sign."

"You're right," Quinn agreed, sounding more hopeful as she looked up at him. "It's not too far-fetched to think we could defeat her soon."

Hugo nodded in agreement. "I still can't believe it's all real, though."

"What do you mean? The fact The Divinity is dead?"

"Yeah. Still doesn't feel real at all."

Quinn broke away from Hugo. Her face grew pensive and pondering. "Frederica's visions," she commented. "What *I* still can't believe is that's how we found out. That her Theola-curse visions are an accurate source of information."

"I wouldn't have believed it if it weren't for those fauxangels spontaneously dying near the Austral Settlement. Or the reports from Incoba Nation," Hugo said. "Who knows what really goes on in Frederica's head, visions or not."

"Yeah, she's been acting in the strangest ways recently," Quinn added.

"She's been acting strange ever since this war started," Hugo said. "Though to be fair, so have most of us."

***

Frederica twitched in her bed, her eyes shut hard enough for her eyelids to be pained and red. She had wanted to sleep early and get a good night's rest, but the relaxation it would bring eluded her. The drenched sweat that coated her body turned her bedroom floors into a water hazard as her soul rocked with pain. She had been in this state for hours.

Whilst the entire Magnae Forces celebrated The Divinity's death, from the beginning of the party to its end, she remained in the same place, shaking with deadly discomfort. She wanted to scream for help hours ago. She wanted to get up and stumble out of the room, to let someone, anyone, know of her plight. But whatever was possessing her body with pain and turmoil prevented her from doing so. She could not control a single muscle. She could not make a single sound, but for the quietest of wheezes. For hours, she had been trapped in her own personal hell, unable to help herself or receive help.

Frederica's eyes burst open as she silently cried. She kept pleading with herself that eventually, someone would come looking for her, enter her room, and help her out of this state. But no one came. All that Frederica had to accompany her were the awakened dreams that played all around her, like ghosts clouding her line of vision throughout the night.

Even then, she could not make sense of what these phantoms of fantasy were showing her.

"Centuries have passed. Strength has returned," one of these dark phantoms proclaimed. It seemed to be the silhouette of a tangle-haired woman who lay on the floor, rose, and lay on the floor again in a repetitive fashion.

"My memory is frayed. Many lessons learned have been damaged. All I know is to hold trust. Reserve trust. Keep your trust in yourself. Give your trust to no one, especially not the human," a phantom in the corner of her room kept repeating to itself as they twitched and shook in the same manner she did.

"One over half a dozen. That is me. I am number seven. I am the strongest. I shall use my power to transport and influence. I shall use the fading will of the first. I shall ride this cycle with the most fervour!" the largest of the phantoms screamed as it flash-stepped across her room, plunging it into further darkness as shadowy wisps radiated off of its being.

Frederica wanted to scream, but all she could do was gasp pitifully. She felt her brain tear itself from the inside, experiencing an ungodly pain as if Devil Child had split her skull into two with his energy-charged longsword. Frederica was convinced she would die there that night.

In a way, she was right.

XXXI. OCCIDENDUM

VARIOUS members of the forces scrambled around Frederica's hospice bed. She was in the same state she had been when they found her that morning. Flurries of frothing drool spilt out of her mouth as she convulsed, causing the steel slab below her mattress to rattle and shake from her jerking movements. She was both asleep yet active, unresponsive yet constantly moving. Her eyes were shut firm as she suffered in a catatonic state that the medics who analysed her and everyone who surrounded her at the time could not figure out.

Roisin wiped the sweat from her brow. Dagim and Hugo joined each other in gently holding Frederica's arms down to stop her convulsions from injuring them as they tried to determine what was ailing her. Quinn stood to the side with crossed arms and an anxious glare.

The only member of the main six not present was Stefan, who was yet to return from his self-appointed leave of absence with the lovely Anais.

"You sure she was like this when you found her?" Dagim asked.

"Definitely. It freaked me out when I checked in for her this morning," Quinn said. "I haven't got a clue what happened to her before."

"Maybe she's having another one of her visions?" Roisin suggested.

"Does this usually happen when she has her visions?" Hugo asked.

"I don't know, no one has ever seen her actually have one," Dagim sighed.

"Then what's wrong with her?" Quinn asked.

Dagim shrugged. If the medics, including Roisin, could not come up with a solid answer, neither could he or anyone else, for that matter.

The door to the hospice burst open with a ringing metal slam, shooting every eye away from the convulsing Frederica and towards The Head Foreseer. The bald, muscular man's coarse face hardened, scowled and red from the mixture of anger and fear that told Dagim there was an emergency to be attended to.

"Devil Child, get your sword in your hand and take a squad and a rover out to Golden Mainland Country!" The Head ordered with urgency.

"What's with the panic?" Dagim asked. "Has another Theola apparition attacked?"

"No. From what the scouts said they've seen, it's much fiercer than anything we've ever fucking faced," The Head asserted. Words that would capture the interest of even the most lackadaisical recruit and force them to pay attention. "A rare fauxangel has been sighted. A mangled monstrosity wearing both the face of The Divinity and Theola. A horrible black demon over fifty feet tall."

Frederica's condition had already put the group in a state of fretting and at a loss for words. This news only created a tenser atmosphere. Dagim rushed out of the room, following The Head as the two men made their way towards what was to be the most interesting battle of their lives.

Their racing rovers halted at such speeds it was a surprise no soldier saw himself flung through the camo-coloured hood of the vehicle and onto the gleaming grass. Forty Magnae soldiers and the Head Foreseer arrived at the place of the Demon Giant's sighting.

Golden Mainland Country could have been considered a holiday destination at some point. With its fittingly coloured grass and the shiny specks that floated in the air during especially cold summers and hot winters, it was one of the rare civilian settlements that was a treat to visit. Dagim could see why this was one of the places Theola would send her newest creation to. A creature with the compulsion to destroy would always choose the most beautiful of lands to drag down to their rotten level.

What was once an imposing community centre constructed of fine mahogany had been reduced to piles of blackened wooden debris. The architect of the destruction was standing behind it, applying that same creative destruction to the rows and rows of neighbourhood homes that stood behind it.

As the forces stepped forward, the civilian casualties of such an attack were clearer. Townspeople staggered and stumbled over roads blocked with the bodies of their fellow citizens as they fled in all directions.

"Holy mother of all things godly!" The Head exclaimed, watching the panic as he and his men marched closer to the scenes of despair.

Before the Head Foreseer could give any orders, the two scores of soldiers were forced to take immediate action. The Demon Giant would give them not even a second to discuss quick battle plans as it leapt from its position around the neighbourhood and landed right in their path. Upon its landing, six fleeing soldiers were crushed, with a few more injured in the effort to escape being trampled under the shadowy figure's heel.

Dagim stared up at the face of the demon high in the sky. Both of the mangled faces it wore held joy. The Divinity's half on the left side faintly smirked, as if that side of the creature's face had suffered from a stroke. The Theola half on the right side laughed maniacally.

Dagim swung his energy-laden sword into the ankle of the grand fauxangel. He sprinted away as soon as his attack landed, predicting what would inevitably come next. The sword only created a small slit on the demon's ankle, but this was enough for it to want to thrash out in anger. With just one kick forward, it killed eight soldiers at once.

Dagim ducked out of the way of a comrade's severed head, only to taste the spraying blood of another whose stomach had been cut out of him by the attack.

As the demon's foot slowly returned to its resting position, the entire force of soldiers attacked at once, some synchronising their bladed stabs and cuts as they all hacked away at its left leg. They succeeded in cutting a deep wound into the creature's ankle, which bled with black smoke that formed into the shadows of screaming men. The Demon Giant's balance had been affected to the point that it could not stand straight. The twenty-four remaining fighters decorated both sides of their ankle with cuts and bruises.

The demon lunged down to deliver a crushing blow of its knuckle to the floor. The soldiers needed no warning shouts to tell them to jump out of the way as the demon's shadowy punch created a black crater in the ground. The wind force from the blow knocked a couple of soldiers down, but thankfully, none found themselves underneath the grand fauxangel's knuckles.

Three brave recruits jumped into action, two launching throwing knives at the Demon Giant's Divinity-Theola face and one resorting to the use of his emergency firearm. The one who fired the Bronze Bullet lost their life for it, unable to dodge the second Earth-shattering punch the creature delivered. His death was not in vain. His bullet and the throwing knives of the other two attackers had created a crevice in the middle of the demon's double face.

"The face! It's vulnerable! Attack the face!" The Head ordered. "Fire your Bronze Bullets into that damned creature's fucking face! Make the skies rain with the blood of its blackened, mangled head!"

"You heard the man!" Dagim shouted. "Pinpoint Firework Formation! Now!"

A few of the soldiers continued to strike the creature's ankle with their blades. They prevented it from being able to stand up on two feet again, forcing it to keep crouching down. The rest followed The Head's orders and Dagim's formation suggestion. They ducked, rolled, and leapt out of the way of the giant's crushing fists as they took turns firing at the same location. Each aimed for the middle of the Demon Giant's face, right in between The Divinity half and the Theola half.

A score of bullet wounds to its face later, with twenty Bronze Bullets spent and discarded, the soldiers saw their first sign of victory. The Demon Giant's skin cracked, flaked, and broke apart where all the bullets had struck it. The weaker Divinity-based side could no longer hold its constitution, corroding into a mess of black flesh that slid off and dropped to the earth. The Theola half frowned.

"Fantastic work, men!" The Head cheered as he raised his blackened longsword into the air.

With half of the demon's face having been shot off, half of its strength left the fauxangel vessel it called a body. In clouds of black smoke, the vessel shrank instantaneously. Before their very eyes, it diminished to half its original size.

"Let's finish it," Dagim ordered their men as they bounded forward for more blade-based attacks. "Keep aiming for the face!"

But that was much easier said than done. The Demon Giant's injured left ankle proved to be less of a burden moving forward. Its smaller size made for lighter steps and increased agility. The twenty or so remaining warriors had expected their cutting of the creature to be half its size to halve their work and double their chances of defeating it. The opposite was the case, as they were met with a world of pain delivered by a creature much more erratic, nimbler, and large enough to keep posing a deadly threat.

A spinning kick took down two soldiers, slicing across their necks and chests. A triple set of swift uppercuts slaughtered many more, exploding through human bodies with ease. The remaining soldiers struggled to land a blade on the creature as it took them down one by one.

By this point, The Head had rushed back to the rover. Being over twice the age of most recruits, he was never meant for this much battle. Or any battle, come to think of it. He knew he was not fast enough to keep dodging the demon's constant strikes. He knew that if he stayed in the fold, he would eventually be caught off guard, and Planet Magnae would lose its leader. He resented the fact that he could not continue to lead his men in battle.

"Hold strong, soldiers. Hold," he muttered to them as he rested by the rover, gathering his strength and stamina.

Dagim, on the other hand, was fast enough. But not as fast as he thought. He managed to duck underneath a

271

swinging kick, only for a chopping punch to come right after. He jumped out of the way of this attack, too, but was a fraction too late. It was a strike that would have gutted him like a fish if it had landed directly. Instead, it only grazed him, the wind force it generated sending the Devil Child flying across the battlefield. He landed near the ruins of the destroyed community centre, slamming his head hard against a pile of wooden debris.

"Ah, fuck," Dagim groaned as his head grew foggy and vision grew clouded. He struggled to keep himself conscious, to keep himself in the fold. But he was fighting a losing battle against his body.

What he last saw before blacking out was the heads of two comrades being crushed by the half-faced Theola Demon's giant clapping hands.

***

Stefan arrived at the battlefield, speeding in a rover of his own. He had planned to spend another day avoiding his duties in the forces to extend his quality time with Anais. That was until the news reached Vohdkaz. News that told of how The Head Foreseer, Dagim, and multiple other comrades were engaged in a horrible battle against a giant demon with Theola's face. A battle that they were losing.

Stefan stepped out of the rover with his crimson armour fastened on and throwing blades charged with energy, filling a vibrating artillery belt that made his chest glow. When he had heard the news and rushed to the bunkers to retrieve his equipment, he had heard they were losing. But now, it was clear they had already lost.

Just three soldiers were struggling against the Demon Giant in a futile attempt to prevent it from marching onward to destroy more civilian settlements. The remaining thirty-seven lay dead or injured across Golden Mainland Country.

Of the three remaining soldiers, none were The Head or even Dagim. It seemed they had not only lost the majority of their fighting force, but their two leaders.

Sheer panic would have broken Stefan's mind if the guilt had not done so first. He would have cried out in horror if he had the voice to do so. This had all happened in his absence.

Whilst he was enjoying a splendid time with his girlfriend, his comrades were fighting one of the most important battles of their lives. He should have been there, helping. Instead, he was arriving at the closing stages, watching as the Demon Giant set its sights on more congregations of humanity to conquer. Stefan had never felt less deserving of the title of soldier in his life. He had never felt less worthy of being recognised as a human being. With haste, he took out a pencil and paper from his equipment belt and scrawled down a series of questions and statements. He tucked them away and sprinted across the battlefield.

Before he could reach the Demon Giant and the last few recruits that were fighting it off, Stefan spotted Dagim lying face-first in the dirt. Silent Memoir dashed down towards him. He shook the Devil Child with violent desperation, hoping to God that he was just injured and not yet dead. His hopes were confirmed, the stocky dark-skinned soldier coughing up blood as his head rose upwards.

"Stefan," Dagim croaked as his eyes blinked open. "It's all gone to shit. Where've you been?"

Stefan clenched his jaw, the shame settling in as his muscles tightened. He avoided the question and pulled out the piece of paper that had questions of his own.

"Where's The Head Foreseer?" one of them read.

"I don't know," Dagim answered. "When I last saw him, he was sitting by one of the rovers, taking a breather."

Stefan sighed as he looked around the battlefield. He saw no Head Foreseer and no intact rovers in the general area other than his own. All he could see was the Giant Demon.

When they looked back at it, the pair saw that the few remaining recruits who were chasing after the creature were no longer there. They had been killed and discarded. The Theola-faced dark fauxangel bounded onwards, undisturbed. With speed, it ran west.

Dagim and Stefan burst into a desperate run after the creature on simultaneous instinct. Both knew that just the two of them would be no match for the creature, yet they intended to attack. They would not get to do so, however.

The creature carried out a rapid forward stride, bombing its way to a settlement west of their position. Every time they thought they were getting closer, the creature would take another far-reaching stride forward that would increase the distance between them.

"God fucking damn it all!" Dagim screamed as he stopped for breath. The injuries he sustained during battle left his head too foggy and chest too pained for him to continue running for much longer.

Stefan stopped running too, helping the Devil Child stay on his feet as he cursed at the moment.

"Come back here! Come back here right fucking now!" Dagim exclaimed at the Demon Giant.

The creature did not hear him, nor did it turn around to charge after them. Its only instinct was to search for another large group of humans to slaughter.

As Dagim and Stefan watched the creature escape, they heard the churning mechanisms of a rover behind them. They turned to see that the vehicle had been greatly altered. The entire hood and overhanging section were crudely cut and removed to make an open-top rover, with the driver's head barely peeking over the remains of the front of the vehicle. Dagim and Stefan stepped to the side as The Head pulled over next to them.

"Nice of you to finally join us, Stefan," The Head scoffed. Stefan gave him a meek nod in response.

Dagim glared at the jagged sword marks all over the altered vehicle. "Why on God's red Magnae did you spend all that time cutting the top off of a rover?"

"You'll see," said The Head as he ground his teeth. Somehow, his eyes showed both excitement and trepidation. They locked in on the absconding Demon Giant.

"That creature's going to kill the last remnants of the Golden Mainland if it keeps heading that way. It'll destroy all of Maeynation and parts of the Capital if he continues in the same direction," The Head commented.

"We'd better blow its brains out before that then," Dagim grunted. He climbed the rover, attempting to get inside through its now-opened top. The Head Foreseer prevented him from doing so with a shove.

Stefan attempted to open one of the doors to the rover. He could not manage to unlock it. The Head shook his head as if to warn him not to try again.

"What are you doing? Let us in!" Dagim ordered. "We have to get there!"

The Head shook his head. "*I* have to. You and Silent Memoir have to go back to the bunkers."

Stefan's light eyebrows furrowed in confusion. Dagim's face contorted with the same confusion doubled by anger and frustration.

"What the hell are you doing?!" he demanded to know.

"Don't worry about that, Devil Child. All you and Silent Memoir have to do is go back to the rest of the forces and tell them what you saw today," The Head Foreseer ordered with a smirk. "Tell them their leader did what he had to."

Before Dagim could ask any more questions, The Head Foreseer charged the rover forward, travelling at rapid speeds as he closed in on the Demon Giant.

Stefan and Dagim shared a blank, empty gaze. Both knew what the other was thinking. But neither wished to make it known. Instead, they broke eye contact and silently watched it all unfold.

As The Head's speeding rover came closer to the Demon Giant, the shadowy fauxangel took notice of its presence. It turned around, its instincts kicking in, ready to dispose of the human pest at its feet.

The Head Foreseer circled his rover around the creature's feet. He piloted the vehicle with one hand and used the other to throw knives at its calves and shin to injure it further. The Demon Giant became bridled with frustration, its Theola half-face grimacing. It tried to grab the rover multiple times but was unable to as The Head drove rings around it. The Head Foreseer narrowed his eyes as he watched the Demon Giant prepare to deliver a downward punch. He waited for the perfect moment to stop his vehicle. Never in his life did he need to time something so perfectly. As luck would have it, he did not fail.

The Demon Giant landed a devastatingly powerful blow to the ground, just behind The Head's rover as he timed a drift past the left leg. As this was happening, he retrieved an item from underneath the passenger seat.

The wind force and earthquake combination thrust the rover into the air. At the same time, The Head committed the most audacious action either Stefan or Dagim had ever seen a Magnae fighter take. The Head Foreseer leapt out of the open top of the soaring rover. He too soared for a moment, a

Bronze Bullet in his hand and a look of crazed excitement on his face.

"DROREGEN DI MAS EH VEL SCHRU!" The Head screamed in Magnae Second Tongue with the most patriotic fervour that Dagim had ever heard escape a man's mouth.

He landed on the Demon Giant's head, grasping onto it. The grand fauxangel grabbed him, its hand latching onto the leader of Magnae with blistering speed. As the creature's grasp crushed him, the strength left The Head Foreseer's body along with his life force. He had just about enough strength to shove the barrel of the gun into the crevice that had cracked and destroyed The Divinity side of the face.

He pulled the trigger, the Bronze Bullet firing its way through black flesh, destroying its composition from the inside. The creature's last action was to squeeze tighter, crushing The Head. After this final act, its head burst in an echoing explosion.

The Demon Giant dropped to the floor. It lay dead, a bubbling black mass of smoke and meat in the place where its head once was. Theola's most awful creation would never move or breathe again.

Keith Best, aka The Head Foreseer, lay next to it. His body was destroyed, his upper half and torso completely severed from his legs. He, too, would never move or breathe again. Yet his lifeless face wore a sublime smile.

***

It was a very good thing that the remaining Magnae civilian survivors were not able to see the inner workings of their planet's forces. A glimpse of the current status of the Magnae Forces would drive their morale to the deepest depths. The main bunker room was filled with scores of researchers, spiritual cultists, knowledge brokers, general recruits, new and old, and what remained of the soldier regiment. Even with all of these people congregated in one area, the room held completely silent. All heads faced the floor, all hands rested over hearts. A glance at any one of these faces told a sorrowful story of a thousand words. The disconsolate protectors of the planet were robbed of their guidance. The official leader of their military forces was gone. The de facto leader of the humans of Planet Magnae was gone.

The Magnae Forces could do nothing but stew in a collective concoction of depression and uncertainty as they mourned the death of Keith Best, their former Head Foreseer.

XXXII. UNTOLD STORIES

HOURS later, the silence that held with the mourning respect they had given in the main room carried on throughout the entire bunker. The death of the Head Foreseer weighed on everyone's minds. There was much work to do, but the top recruits decided it was best to take time out of their day to commemorate him further.

The Vice Foreseer called them into a room not typical of their meetings. Dagim, Roisin, Hugo, Stefan, and Quinn stood in a circle around a metal slab that held The Head Foreseer's ashes in a golden urn, burning with the essence of the potent energy inside.

The Vice spoke over the emblem. "There was rarely a man as great as him before he was born, and there aren't any who could hold a candle to him now that he's dead. He always supported me, from our days as recruits to my days as his right-hand man. Even with all my wrongdoings, even after the horrible acts I committed, he welcomed me back. Not just for the sake of forgiveness, but for the sake of aiding humanity in the war effort he has planned all of his life for. I hope that I'll be able to fill his position adequately. I pray that I'll be capable of even *partially* filling the void he left as a Head Foreseer," he said with tear-felt passion. "Keith Best was willing to lose his life in the process of destroying

Theola's demon and preserving this planet. I will gladly give my life to see Theola herself destroyed, saving this planet."

Dagim, Roisin, Hugo, Stefan, and Quinn all nodded with an appreciative solemnity about them. Dagim raised his head, wishing to offer some words too.

"The Head Foreseer, or Keith, as those close to you called you. You were one of the only people who always trusted me. A man who always believed in me. One who knew what it was like to be someone like me. To be a Devil Child," Dagim said. "I'll follow your advice to the fullest. I'll use the awful power within me and finish the work you started. I will secure Magnae for humanity. We *will* win."

The group held their silence, enjoying the collective peace that came with paying respects to their late leader. They would carry on his will, now until the end.

***

Dagim marched down the corridor to the healthcare area of the bunkers. He remained in the stoic and contemplative mood he had been since the moment he and Stefan brought back the news of The Head's death to the bunker. He had just returned from a self-appointed scouting mission. He hurried back to the bunker after being told of some more interesting news that could, if just momentarily, raise his spirits.

Dagim walked into the hospice where he saw The Vice Foreseer, Roisin, Hugo, Stefan, and Quinn standing at Frederica's bedside. She was no longer convulsing and twitching in pain. She was awake, healthy, and able to sit upright, with her stern, alert stare steadied forward.

"Back to normal?" Dagim asked.

"Back to normal," Roisin confirmed with a smile.

"Thank God," Quinn sighed.

"It's not fun being comatose, is it?" Hugo asked, speaking from recent experience.

280

"No," Frederica answered, bluntly. The Vice rested a hand on her shoulder.

"How are you feeling, First Ranger?" he asked her.

"Clear," she answered, cryptic. A pause was taken as if she had more to say. But nothing more came out. She continued to stare forward emptily.

"Clear? How? Your mind's cleared?" Roisin asked her. She nodded. "I have much to tell. Many untold stories."

"Aren't you going to tell us how you got all twitching and comatose first?" Dagim asked.

"They are one and the same," Frederica said. "They're the reason I know it all now."

"All?" Quinn asked. Frederica hummed in confirmation.

"I'm glad we've done such extensive fauxangel research. If we hadn't, I wouldn't have been able to make sense of anything I've seen over the past few days," Frederica answered, sighing as she massaged her forehead. "Analysing those painful cryptic visions has allowed me to fill every single gap in the mountain of knowledge we have on the history of the fauxangels. No stone has been left unturned for me. I've seen it all. I know it all."

The group's eyes rested on Frederica with wonder. It was as if they were in the presence of a true witch of ancient mystic arts. Or as if the highest and most ethereal of fauxangels had decided to take up attitudes of human virtue and join their side.

"Then we shall listen," The Vice said.

***

Frederica took the group to a secluded field a mile behind the hidden entrance to their underground bunker. Before she started her explanations, she wished to get one major update out of the way. She showed them what else her seizure visions had given her other than worldly knowledge.

281

Without as much as a warning, Frederica conjured a ball of light energy within the palms of both her hands. The sight alone caused Stefan to jump back away from her, almost knocking the others over in fear. None could blame him. Each of them thought that perhaps they were experiencing a strange vision or dream, too. Each observed Frederica with silent apprehension for a while before finally putting words to such apprehensions.

"What the fuck?!" Dagim exclaimed.

"Since when were you able to do that?!" Roisin screamed.

"Since my seizures stopped and I was able to wake up undisturbed," Frederica said. Nonchalant, she increased and decreased the sizes of the balls of energy in her palm at will. The others stared at her as if she were an alien freak from a planet far stranger than Luxurae. It took a while for the group to unclench their bodies and unwind their minds.

"Are you part fauxangel now?" Hugo asked.

"Honestly, I considered it. I now have powers similar to a high-level one, but as far as I can tell, I've experienced no physical changes to indicate my being closer to that species," she answered. "This is something similar yet different."

"It's something very odd," Quinn commented.

"Yes, very strange," The Vice agreed.

Frederica shut one of her hands, dissipating the golden energy in it, whilst increasing the amount of golden energy in the other. "Are you ready to hear about all the new things I learnt during my comatose journey?"

"After seeing that?" Dagim said as he pointed to the energy in her palms. "Definitely. Don't leave anything out. Not a single goddamn piece of information. Tell. It. All."

Frederica pulled the golden energy from her palm and used it to make moving paintings that would depict everything she was about to tell them.

"Our universe has a real God, and it's certainly not Theola, The Divinity, or any other derivative alien creature. He has many names in many different languages, the most commonly used title being *The Bestial Energy*. Think of him as a raw manifestation of power and potentiality, but conscious," Frederica said. She spread out the golden energy in her hand to create the image of an ever-moving cloud of crackling smoke and energy, golden and pure. This was the closest she could come up with in terms of visualising the creator. All were intrigued by this revelation. Dagim most of all, who stared deep into the clouds of smoke and energy as if to try and connect with it.

"Though our universe has many galaxies, you'll be disappointed to find out that we are alone. There are no other life forms across the cosmos as intelligent and conscious as we are. Of all the creatures of the universe, we are the most otherworldly it has to offer."

"What about the Luxuraeans?" The Vice asked. Stefan nodded his head down with the same question in mind.

"The galaxy we currently reside in, the MG Galaxy, is one of the most dangerous the universe has to offer. Compare the plains and conditions of Planet Magnae to Ancient Earth, and you'll find that the latter was much more sustainable. The humans of Ancient Earth reached technological heights that we could only ever dream of. But these scientific and artificial heights also caused a technological apocalypse that destroyed their planet and forced them to evacuate in search of another. Here, Planet Magnae, was the only other planet our species could survive on. Though they were barely able to do just that. As I said, the conditions here are far less favourable than those on Earth. So, The Bestial Energy decided we needed help," Frederica explained.

"The Bestial Energy created our alien overseers. The fauxangels. A species intended to be our less intelligent but much more powerful counterparts. Their humble, simple natures and grand powers were meant to guide us, so we would not make the same mistakes on Earth. They destroyed spaceships, processing machines, and anything else that could have us repeat the apocalypse. Because if we destroy this planet like we destroyed Earth, there are no other habitable planets for us to escape to," she said. "But we did not get along with the fauxangels at first. When they first arrived to guide us, they were attacked and seen as freaks of nature due to their lack of true human behaviour. It did not help that these first few fauxangels would often unintentionally mistreat the humans they were meant to help usher into the new world. The more the humans resisted fauxangel guidance, the more fauxangels would try and force them to listen. Eventually, any goodwill held between us was destroyed, and the fauxangels saw it more efficient to rule over us with a violent golden fist."

"Wild," Hugo muttered. He rubbed his head as if this new information was causing his brain to bulge. His eyes danced as he watched Frederica's golden energy show scenes of fauxangels beating and subjugating humans.

"So, they *were* always meant to lead us," Dagim scoffed. "Ironic."

"Still doesn't excuse what they have done," Quinn said. Stefan's lips pursed with contemplation.

"It came to the point where a new generation of humans only knew of the fauxangel's cruelty and grew to despise them far more than humans before. Some young men and women grew up with their only life goal being the desire to

284

enact some form of vengeance. One of these men was the impossibly intelligent, boundlessly ambitious, and highly passionate historical figure known as Emmanuel Ekib."

Dagim's eyes shot wide open at the mention of this name. They narrowed slowly again as he listened.

Frederica's energy conjured an image of a slim but muscular man holding a book up to read in one hand and holding a knife down low with the other.

"The real Emmanuel Ekib, as opposed to what most history books have told us, was an intellectual first and fighter second. He was a rough and raucous young man with a prodigious intellect who would endlessly study the fauxangels in a desperate effort to find a piece of information that could be used against them. Among the many things he learned, three were the most important in terms of serving his plans: One - That Planet Magnae had various naturally occurring, highly potent, and dangerous resources that, through mixture with fauxangel energy, could be neutralised, utilised safely, and used for military purposes. Two - He could alter energy to extend his lifespan. Three - He figured out that though the fauxangels had developed a brutal nature when it came to enforcing the law on humans, they had not yet developed the malicious natures they are now known for. If you showed no fear in front of them and a desire to listen and obey to the point of complete and utter obsequiousness, they greatly enjoyed your human company."

"He used the second and third to make sure he could put the first thing he learnt to use," The Vice assumed.

Frederica nodded with confirmation. "On the surface, Ekib was an ally to the fauxangels, making them believe he would be the key to the humans finally accepting their rule. He used his closeness to them and the use of the repurposed energy to start the first truly equal war between humans and fauxangels. He allowed groups of guerrilla rebels to sneak into fauxangel sanctuaries and off them, whilst harvesting more energy for more experiments," she stated. "It was these experiments that made what we now know as The Ultimatum Source, at the heart of that sacred lake. It was always kept as a reserve in case of emergencies, whilst being slowly added to. Just as it is in the modern day."

"That makes sense," Dagim said with a slow knock of his head downwards.

Frederica's golden beams depicted The Bestial Energy again. "Though our creator is the embodiment of power and potential itself, his actions throughout history show a level of passivity towards his creations. After fixing a problem in a galaxy, he would leave it untouched for centuries, only interfering once extinction became a threat. It wasn't until well into Ekib's war that he decided to do something about the bloody conflicts tearing apart Planet Magnae. He decided to enter an old creation of his into the universe that he had not planted on a planetary plain yet. One that could be considered a dangerous upgrade to the Luxuraeans. A higher brand of fauxangel that would operate more from the shadows and be able to control both humans and other fauxangels more subtly. The first Theola," Frederica said.

Dagim crossed his arms tighter. As opposed to Ekib's, the mention of this name made him wince away and lose interest slightly.

"By this point in the war, the fauxangels had not figured out Ekib was the secret traitor and assumed he was just a humble scholar making efforts to convince his human brethren to stop their attacks. When the first Theola came down to Magnae, however, this changed. She quickly deduced he was the traitor. But instead of attacking him or revealing it to the other fauxangels, this more advanced model of the species decided persuasion and diplomacy were the best ways to move forward. The first Theola and Emmanuel Ekib would make a deal."

"What kind of deal?" Roisin asked.

"All Emmanuel Ekib had to do was get rid of the energy he had created, including the Ultimatum Source, and Theola would take all the fauxangels back to Luxurae, away from Magnae, and away from humanity. She cut underneath her nails and gave her word. Ekib shook her hand, accepting the deal," Frederica answered. "But like most agreements between humans and fauxangels, it didn't last."

"Ekib betrayed the first Theola. Just as the paintings depicted," The Vice predicted where the story was going next. "Then, he used a part of the Ultimatum Source to kill the first Theola. That is why every reincarnation of Theola was implanted with the message not to trust humans."

The others looked to Frederica for confirmation. She nodded. "Ekib did not want peace on Theola's terms. He wanted to continue his crusade and destroy the fauxangels himself, just as he had dreamt of doing as a child. He used the remains of the original Theola to replenish the Ultimatum Source and make the sacred lakes of energy more bountiful. With the first Theola dead, he continued the war, considering it all a fresh start. He hid his betrayal of Theola and told a new story of history to the next generations of humans fighting fauxangels. He created the image of being a great man who started their fight against alien gods, revealing himself as the number one enemy to the fauxangels and securing his spot as ruler of humanity. That was his true goal from the start. He started life as a lowly peasant, and the fauxangel threat allowed him to use his smarts to rewrite humanity's history and become its king."

"You're telling me that humanity could have been free from fauxangels if he had taken the deal? If it wasn't for the fact that the guy who was supposed to be our saviour wanted to be a fucking Godking instead?" Hugo asked, outraged. Frederica nodded, watching that same outrage pass through the rest of them. Hugo sighed. "Great."

"As all humans know and have known, the standard fauxangel power set goes from being able to conjure fires to travelling through light portals and shooting down energy, depending on how powerful one is. Theola, on the other hand, can use dark energy and possesses a low-level version of The Bestial Energy's ability for tangible creation, which she can use to create different types of mindless demons. She used this power to its greatest extent to create The Divinity, the figurehead of the race who would create new batches of Luxuraeans before having this creation ability taken from him. What Ekib and the other humans did not know at the time was that Theola's reincarnate," Frederica explained. "But the reincarnations took a toll on the Theola soul. She might have been an upgrade to the Luxuraeans, but she was still an older and more dangerous model of the species. Each new Theola in the cycle was born with greater power but a more degenerated mind. All they knew for sure was that they were not to trust humans. Humanity and fauxangels would conduct constant on-and-off wars, with Theola leading the fauxangels from the shadows, not desiring to even interact with the humans directly out of disgust and sending the fauxangels, tendrils, and her demons to do the work for her. Only Ekib had real proof of her existence for decades."

"Kept it like that for a while," Dagim commented.

"Eventually, the humans started to lose the war as each new Theola that was killed was replaced with another one who hated humans even more. Their hopes dwindled once

The Divinity was born, too, his new batch of fauxangels aiding Theola's cause. All of this despair led to Ekib's eventual defeat and disappearance," Frederica continued. "But before he vanished, he consumed a portion of the Ultimatum Source. And since my visions did not clearly show me how he died, it's safe to assume that he *might* still be alive on some other plane of existence."

"Interesting," The Vice Foreseer muttered in contemplation. Frederica rubbed her chin as she thought about what else she had learnt from her seizure dreams.

"That brings me to your father, Dagim."
Dagim stepped forward, the deep interest he had been losing during the explanations returning with full force as he glared at Frederica. "What about him?"

"I believe you and Roisin found out about how he got crippled around the time of your birth, didn't you? The same type of energy exposure that can injure infants for life. Such as what happened when Roisin was born."

Roisin rubbed her arm, the mention of her condition seeming to make the often-ignored and endured pain of her damaged limbs more present. "Yes, we discussed it."

"From what my visions showed me, Ade Chibuike was an explorer like no other. He was passionate and active, like you, but instead of for battle, for adventure. He travelled to dangerous areas no sane man would even think about. He always took a token, a part of these lands, to honour his visit to strange places. It seemed that some of these places took a part of him, too."

Frederica stared at Dagim, ignoring the eyes of everyone else. She could tell the discussion was making him uncomfortable, the tales of his father causing a slouch in his posture, avoidance of eye contact, and a tensing of his dark, bearded jaw.

"Dagim. On the day of your birth, a blinding light that was initially thought to be an explosion of underground fauxangel energy took away your father's sight and injured his legs. On that day, he acted in a manner unbefitting even an insane person. Instead of consoling your mother as she died from the complications that came with your birth, he went on another adventure. Though he had no vision and weak legs, he was somehow able to arrive at his destination. He travelled directly to the tomb where Ekib was last seen in Barranae Nation."

Roisin and Quinn gasped. Stefan's eyebrows furrowed whilst Hugo's raised. The Vice Foreseer's eyes slimmed. Dagim stood still, waiting for her to continue.

"An energy possessed him. He kept muttering about how he was to help Ekib, how he was to make a cycle of his own. But all he could do was flail about and utter empty words and promises to himself. Once he left the tomb, unsuccessful in the mission his senile mind was hell-bent on completing, he only grew more senile. His mind became so damaged that he could not even coherently speak out whatever was possessing it. He was nothing more than a crazed man with a fractured brain," Frederica said, looking at Dagim with a newfound empathy. "That must've been hard to deal with growing up."

"It was," Dagim said. A crack in his voice apparent. The prelude of what would have been tears had the Devil Child been a more sensitive individual. He held stern, staring on as if these memories did not affect him. Roisin consoled him with an arm on his shoulder anyway.

"So, what, do you think Dagim's dad was influenced by Ekib's soul that day or something?" Quinn asked.

"I don't know. All I know is that the next Theola in the cycle sought to destroy the tomb. Her rationale being that perhaps Ekib's consuming of the Ultimatum Source gave him similar abilities, and he may one day reincarnate as she had many times," Frederica said. "But after Theola had destroyed the tomb, the very same light that blinded and crazed Ade attacked her with a powerful force. It was as if the tomb itself held Ekib's will. Not only did it kill her, but as she died, she could sense it had affected her in a way an attack never had before. She could no longer feel the driving force at the centre of her heart. She could feel the source of her reincarnation abilities dwindling."

"Her heart. That's her weak point," The Vice muttered, taking a mental note.

"Then what happened?" Roisin asked Frederica.

"In complete and utter desperation, the sixth Theola forced her heart out of her body with a dark tendril, using dark energy to slice it into pieces and scatter it across the planet in search of a temporary host," Frederica explained with building anticipation, growing more excitable with each word. "Most of these pieces were discarded. But one of them landed inside a live organic host on the Pestoech Mountains. It was preserved until the seventh Theola, the Theola we now know, had its body created. And though its stay was temporary, that piece of the heart changed the host forever."

"Where did it go? What was the host?!" Dagim asked.
Frederica suddenly snatched at her chest. The retelling of the visions granted her an abundance of spontaneous physical pain. The others looked on with worry and intrigue as her breath grew laboured. Frederica's body heaved as she struggled to get the words out of her mouth.

"It explains everything. Why I started to have visions once the seventh Theola made herself known. It explains why I was given constant headaches and seizures and saw apparitions dancing about my line of sight. It explains why I have these abilities that allow me to manipulate energy all of a sudden!" Frederica cried out with intensity. "And it explains why I've always had an urge I could never understand. One that went beyond resentment or jealousy or whatever justification I or others gave for my hatred of you. For as long as I can remember, I've always had the urge to kill you, Dagim. This explains it."

Both Dagim and The Vice found themselves astonished, zeroing in on Frederica with an unforeseen focus as First Ranger struggled to finish the revelation.

Dagim's eyes glossed over as he glared at her. A similar urge to the one she described came over him, but vice versa. A million memories passed through his head. He remembered all the attempts made on his life during camp. He remembered his visits from Theola that hurt his mind and increased his self-doubts. He remembered the late Aiza Armstrong, aka Foreseer VII, telling him that no one else but The Vice and some other Foreseers were involved in the efforts to try to kill him. He had a hunch that she was lying. Now that this hunch of his was confirmed. Frederica had been compelled to create the conditions of his death, even before the idea came into the minds of The Vice or anyone else. She had been a danger to him all along.

"What do you mean?" Dagim asked. He made great efforts to control himself, ignoring every urge he had to attack her, so he could hear the conclusion of the various tales Frederica had delivered that day.

Frederica swallowed a lump in her throat so heavy it almost choked her. She took a deep breath and stepped closer to Dagim, despite her instincts telling her this was the most terrible of ideas.

"I am the human vessel who was used to preserve the Theola Cycle as a child. You are the last surviving human connected to Ekib's will, connected to the strange blinding lights that warped your father's mind and almost ended the Theola Cycle," Frederica stated. "We were always destined to be at odds with each other, Dagim. We are the physical embodiments of the historical struggle between Emmanuel Ekib and every Theola."

XXXIII. PAINFUL PREPARATION

THERE was much to think about for the Magnae Forces. They had uncovered all the untouched knowledge one could need on the history of the fauxangels. They knew enough to figure out how the highly sought-after end of the war would be brought to fruition. But no solid plans had been made yet.

The forces were still recovering from the loss of their Head Foreseer. As well as the shock that came with Frederica's revelations about her and Dagim. Devil Child and First Ranger, the physical embodiments of the historical struggle between Emmanuel Ekib and every Theola. Who would have thought?

That night, Alexander Lang, aka The Vice Foreseer, sat on the neatly pressed bed of his bunker room. He quietened his mind as he thought over everything he had seen and learnt in the past few months. The rest of the room was a mess, opened and closed history books and fiction novels scattered all over the floor. The Vice shifted his body, sitting more comfortably in his bed as he stared upwards.

He looked over a painting of himself and The Head Foreseer. The picture depicted the two of them when they were much younger. Years before they were top Foreseers. The days when they were just two recruits. Killbroker and

Ace Lieutenant. The Vice sighed softly as he stared into The Head's painted blue eyes.

"You would have loved to hear what we've learned recently," The Vice said, speaking to him through the painting. "First Ranger was a vessel for Theola, compelled to destroy anything related to the human who betrayed her. And Devil Child's birth just so happened to have the light of Ekib's will shine on it."

The Vice looked down with a scoffing smirk. "To think there was a time I tried to set them against each other. Ironic, isn't it? I still don't blame you for the way you dealt with me once you found out."

He stared back up at the painting. With a blink of his smooth hazel eyes, he looked at the depiction of his younger self in it. He had a serious face in comparison to The Head's boisterous smile.

The Vice smiled. "You had many worries about this recruit class. *Many*. But you also often said that this batch had the potential to be the most special group of individuals the planet has ever seen," he said. "I think you were right about them. Especially those two. First Ranger and Devil Child will save us all."

***

Taking up his new position as the highest-ranked and only living Foreseer, The Vice stood on a metal stage in the middle of the main bunker. Hundreds of employees and recruits of the Magnae Forces met him with silent and stern faces. He was in the process of giving an important speech. One in which the rest of the forces saw themselves brought up to date on everything that he, Dagim, and the top recruits found out. From humanity's arrival on Magnae and The Bestial Energy's initial creation of the fauxangels, all the way up to the significance of Dagim and Frederica's births.

"I know this is all a lot to take in, but take it in you must. And fast. It is of the utmost importance that you retain every piece of information we have given you. We plan on using all of it to win the final stretch of this war. And we plan on doing so very soon," The Vice Foreseer lectured.

Scavengers, medics, cultists, scholars, and battle planners were taking notes on everything The Vice said.

"From what we have learnt, the best chance we have of killing Theola is to strike at her heart. That is her weak point and the source of her power. Our ranks might be thin, but if we play our cards right, we should have enough power to take her out once and for all," he said.

The surviving soldiers of their dwindling ranks paid the most attention. Some took more notes. Others did not bother, wishing to commit all that was to be said to memory.

"Our excavators have almost completely recovered the Ultimatum Source from beneath the cave debris at the bottom of the lake. As soon as it is free, Devil Child will consume it. With him finally fulfilling his destiny of obtaining ultimate power, and First Ranger's newfound golden energy abilities, I see no reason as to why we can't destroy Theola's heart and put a permanent end to her reincarnation cycle and all fauxangel presence on Magnae."

The recruits all looked towards Dagim and Frederica. They observed the hardened expressions of their appointed saviours. Neither of them glanced away from The Vice, ignoring the attention as other recruits murmured with curious discussion.

"Thank you for listening, ladies and gentlemen," The Vice said, concluding his speech. "We're in the final stages of conflict now. Victory is close. Good job and good luck."

As The Vice stepped off the stage, the room immediately burst with energy as all of the forces discussed their next steps forward. A new vitality had been infused within the Magnae Forces. For the first time in a long time, they could see a world in which they would win.

Of all the recruits and Magnae employees who talked feverishly over one another, two remained quiet and forbidding. The so-called saviours of their future themselves. Dagim and Frederica. Both of whom, despite standing close to each other, had not acknowledged the other's presence for all of The Vice's speech. The two powerful recruits stared as the other recruits clambered around them. They gave each other looks halfway between rivalrous glares and signs of budding admiration.

"We've not talked much since I told you about our *histories*," Frederica said.

"What else is there to talk about?" Dagim asked.

"We've both recently found out we were practically destined to be enemies. That our very births were intertwined with the greatest conflict this planet has ever seen. That's *a lot* to talk about," Frederica said. "Especially considering we've never been the friendliest of recruits."

For a brief moment, Dagim lost the staring match, his eyes shifting for a fraction of a second.

"Who cares if pieces of Theola inside you caused you to want to kill me? It's also given you high-grade abilities. Strength and power that our side can use," he said. "You're going to be a great help when it comes to ending the fauxangels. That's all I care about right now."

Frederica studied Dagim as she ran a hand down her raven-black hair. "A surprisingly mature attitude. Not one I would have expected from the Devil Child."

Dagim sighed. "Listen, if you want me to admit I'm not happy with you, then I will. The fact you've always harboured the urge to kill me bothers me. I can't deny that," he stated. "But at the end of the day, you controlled that urge. You could have killed me at any point, but you never did. You denied the will of the strongest ever fauxangel inside you because you knew doing so would help us all. That on its own deserves my respect."

Frederica closed the distance between her and Dagim. A smirk came over her face. Dagim smirked back as he watched her stretch out her hand. She offered it to him, and he graciously accepted. A peace between them was to be established as they shook hands.

This was the closest the pair of them came to being friends since the start of their rivalry as rookie recruits. It was the most united and the strongest recruits of the Magnae Forces had ever been.

***

Theola paced back and forth in a moist cave on Planet Luxurae, lit by light fauxangel energy balls at the centre of the ceiling and a crevice on the ground. Without these lights, the stone enclosure would have been completely dark. The weak lights shone a faint glow over half of Theola's face, her appearance closely fitting her status as a shadowy demon. Just a fraction of her glistening malevolent smile and one wild eye were visible through the darkness.

"I received a series of vague visions last night. The type of visions only given to those new to the cycle, as if I were a younger version. And a tinge of pain in my heart to accompany them," Theola said, seeming to speak to no one in particular. From her perspective, she had the most bountiful of audiences. She could see them as if the weak light had illuminated the entire space. "I believe the vessel has unlocked the sights of all things learned by past Theolas. From The Bestial Energy to the modern day, she knows it all. I thought I might be able to attack from afar. But with this? I think I should show my face again."

Theola looked out of the cave and onto the shimmering golden lands of Planet Luxurae. Not a single fauxangel or Luxuraean strolled through the lands. Not a boy, girl, woman, man, or elder could be seen for miles on end. She was alone, the only fauxangel alive on their home planet. She sighed and scoffed at the same time.

"When the humans killed that beautiful two-faced giant of mine, the last portion of The Divinity's soul left this worldly plain. As did his weaker brethren, their beings leaving with their pitiful creator. I was lucky I was able to harvest the final remains before they returned to the stars," Theola explained to her unseen audience. "But fear not, you will be more than enough to replace them. You will make an even better army than those twinkling, slow-minded narcissists could have ever dreamed of being."

The weak light that shone above and below intensified with heat as she smiled wilder. The light brightened the cave to reveal that the crevice Theola was situated in stretched far and wide as long as a mountain was high. Attached to each inch of the walls around her by black shadow restraints was the audience Theola was speaking to. The forming of black flesh bubbled and churned to create the muscular bodies of smoky demons. Each held a mangled and distorted face that, from a certain angle, resembled The Divinity's at the moment of his death.

"It's time I complete the cycle and reach the ultimate goal. I'll enact the final vengeance on the people of Ekib and wipe Magnae clean," Theola declared. "Those fiery red plains will soon be free from the plight of the disgusting species that betrayed the first of me. The first Theola learnt to never trust a human again. And I, as the seventh, as the strongest of us all, shall be the one who succeeds in erasing them from the story of our universe. Me."

***

Hugo walked into a training room similar to the one he and the other recruits used to frequent back in the days when he would take body parts of prisoners they killed during training yard sessions. The days when he was a cockier, more energetic recruit who had not yet tasted the fear that real war would bring.

He sat on a bench near the blade-sharpening station and the energy-charging crevice next to it. He reached underneath the bench and retrieved what had been left there for him. It was his signature miniature axes. It had been a while since he used them in battle. His hand shook with anticipatory anxiety, unable to hold the weapons still.

"Is your body finally well enough to join the fight again?" Quinn asked, smirking as she walked into the training room to join him.

"Yeah, just in time," Hugo chuckled nervously. Quinn sat down, cuddling up next to him. Her warmth cheered him up. "I heard you're planning to fight, too. Is that right, scavenger girl?"

"We don't have that many *actual* soldiers left. It's the least I can do," Quinn answered with a shrug.

Hugo's smile widened as he felt her hold him tighter. He could feel a slight shake about her chest when she first held him, her body revealing the anxiety she also had but would not voice. But the more she held him, the more her body calmed to a still. Hugo chuckled with amusement.

"I still can't believe how we ended up. If anyone had told me months ago that I would one day share a love with Queen Triumph, I would have laughed in their face."

"As would I, Heart Stealer," Quinn laughed back. She smiled up at him. "Do you want to know the first time I admitted to myself that I always liked you?"

Hugo's eyes widened with intrigue. "Yeah, tell me." Quinn smirked as she sat upright. "It was that day I came bursting into your tent, trying to expose you for taking Granulate P," she said. "I tried to grab you and force it out of your pocket. You grabbed me before I could. Then, out of nowhere, we lost ourselves in each other's eyes. Like we were in some scene out of a rivals-to-lovers tale."

Hugo chuckled. "I remember that day," he sighed with a smile. "Wild times."

All of a sudden, Quinn's jovial demeanour grew sullen by the second. "Speaking of Granulate P…" she uttered with trepidation. "...do you reckon you'll be able to go into battle again without it?"

Hugo's smile left his face. He looked down at his axes as he clenched his sharp, clean-shaven jaw. He cleared his throat to speak.

"I've seen what's happened in my absence. I was comatose and helpless, my legs were too weak to carry me a few steps. I've felt the pain of wanting to help out in battle but not being able to for too long," Hugo said. "At this point, anxiety or not, there's nothing that will stop me from fighting to my greatest ability. For the sake of the planet, Heart Stealer needs to return in full force. And he will."

Quinn looked deep into Hugo's determined, beautiful eyes. She felt a swelling in her heart so pleasurable she could sing, and so forceful it could burst. She pulled Hugo in by both sides of his chiselled, handsome face and gave him the wondrous joy of a woman's flaming kiss. Hugo enjoyed the taste of Quinn's lips as the two aggressively acted out their love with the energetic passion of an Ultimatum Source.

"I'd tell you two to get a room, but it looks like you've got your heart set on this one," they heard Roisin chuckle.

The two broke away from each other to see Recruit Infinity smirking at them with flushed cheeks. They had been so involved in their kiss that they did not hear her enter. A fact that amused them to great laughter.

"Enjoy the show, Roisin?" Hugo asked.

"Yeah, and I enjoyed the dialogue that came before it. I heard all about how you two are willing to fight," Roisin said. "Me too. I'm going to be out on the field, back to my healthcare duties and doing some fighting of my own."

Queen Triumph's eyebrows furrowed. "But what about your arms? They'll deteriorate!"

"Damn my arms!" Roisin spat venomously. "We are in the final stages of the war I've given my life to as a medic, and I'm going to see it through on the front lines. Just like the planet needs Heart Stealer, it needs Recruit Infinity."

Quinn and Hugo locked eyes. The couple had half a mind to argue against her. Both wanted to open their mouths and convince her otherwise.

But they could tell by the wide smile of child-like wonderment and willpower on her face that they would just fail to persuade her. She had made up her mind.

"Glad to hear that, Roisin," Hugo accepted.

"Welcome back to the forces, Recruit Infinity," Quinn said. Roisin chuckled, her rosy cheeks blushing redder.

***

Of all the recruit soldiers who were ready to battle to the death to save their world, none were as ready as Stefan.

The mute warrior's blank face signified the countenance of a man who was willing to risk it all to see his people succeed. To spill gallons of blood on the battlefield if it meant they would win.

Silent Memoir had joined a series of top recruits, including Dagim, excavators, and The Vice Foreseer, in the newly cleared-out sacred cave. They stood behind the lake of powerful water, the source was at the heart of.

The excavators had cleared the lake and uncovered the Ultimatum Source. It was still intact, though it had lost a portion of its energy. With sizable pincers, one of these excavators placed the source of power itself in The Vice Foreseer's metal-gloved hands.

The Vice held it carefully, looking at it with the same awe that captured almost every single pair of eyes in the vicinity. It was a simple but beautiful thing. A pure, hardened ball of tangible golden energy the size of a large fruit that had vibrated with heavenly radiation. It would soon be one with the Devil Child.

But unlike the others, who watched the ritual take place with focused eyes and bated breath, Stefan could only think about fighting in the future. The guilt in his heart still held strong. He should have been in that battle against the Demon Giant. He cursed himself for having arrived late to what had been the most important battle of the war thus far. The battle where a large portion of their soldier force was killed, as well as their Head Foreseer, who gave his life to save the planet from the marching otherworldly beast.

He punished himself internally for having chosen to spend time with Anais when he should have been fighting with his comrades. He would never make such a mistake again. He would only allow himself to see his wonderful girlfriend again once he felt he *deserved* to. Only when this war was done, when Magnae was safe from Theola, would he allow himself to be happy with love again.

Stefan snapped out of his self-imposed trance as he watched the final stages of the ritual commence. Dagim was about to be fed the Ultimatum Source. After all of this time, their best soldier would finally consume the ultimate power.

The excavators had helped the Vice Foreseer piece the source into multiple consumable chunks, which he carefully clasped within his protective metal gloves. Dagim prepared himself physically and mentally, every muscle in him flexed to the point of protruding veins as his eyes shone gold with the source in sight.

"Are you ready, Devil Child?" The Vice Foreseer asked, pacing towards Dagim with the pieces of the Ultimatum Source surging in his hands. Dagim nodded. And so began the feeding of power.

One by one, The Vice Foreseer placed each into Dagim's opened mouth, letting them fall down his throat. Once the dozenth and final piece of the source had passed through Dagim's body, he let out a cough and fastened his mouth shut. He waited, his body twitching through an almost imperceptible worry about him. The onlooking Magnae Forces members looked to be even more concerned than he was, the air in the cave stale from the collective held breaths of all who had gathered there.

Dagim felt a rising in his stomach and an enlightening through his body. The effects of ultimate power were about to kick in.

His mouth was attacked with an awful taste as if he had drunk a gallon of poisoned blood. The inside of his heart stirred, his chest bulging and contorting as if the muscle had been doing somersaults whilst being stabbed by a knife upon each landing. His stomach burned as if he were to be immolated from the inside. It was a horrific pain that many humans had never and would never experience. Yet Dagim weathered it to the best of his ability as he crouched over.

The surrounding Magnae employees encircled him, ready to offer him aid should he need it.

Dagim shut his eyes hard, wincing with unbridled pain. When his eyes opened once more, they had been transformed. They had changed from a blackish-dark brown to fluorescent gold.

His gaze was bright enough to hurt the eyes of any who made contact with the new and improved Ultimatum-Dagim.

XXXIV. THE FINAL STAGE

THE humans of Planet Magnae were ready. Or as ready as they would ever be. They had finally put themselves in a position where an attack on Theola could prove successful.

Their preparations had been just in time. Before they even thought of seeking out Theola, she had decided to attack first. She returned to Magnaean soil with her blackened demon children by her side.

Whether it be by foot or by rover, the forces saw every major civilian settlement they passed by that was still standing being met with a violent demon infestation. Black, shadowy figures tainted the air with spilt human blood. Buildings were pummelled by blackened fists, adding bricks reduced to dust and rotten wood to the blood-stained grounds. Theola had decided to plant the majority of her creations in the Capital Settlement. The biggest congregation of civilians displaced by the war, a grassy mountainous hill with hundreds of homes circling it. The largest civilian district on the planet was to suffer the most from this final conflict. Some of these refugees were permanently engraved into the hilltop itself, their bodies being ground into a paste, scattered across and into the muddy crevices of the grassy mountain. Mothers and fathers struggled to protect their children as dark humanoid devils chased them on all fours.

Some braver civilians decided to fight back, only to have their necks cut open and chests torn out.

These civilians would not have to fight back any longer. The Magnae Forces arrived at these scenes at the Capital Settlement and put an end to them. The final battle against Luxuraeans began as humanity met Theola's shadowy children with blades and bronze.

***

Hugo anxiously stepped out of the open door of a parked rover, following a rank of dozens of soldiers led by Stefan. The squad set out to clear a cobbled road through the side of the hill of all the demons that occupied it. His Magnae crimson armour felt strange on his person. His miniature axe felt foreign in his hands. For a moment, he felt how he did during the earlier days of this war. Like a soldier who could not function without the help of Granulate P. A nervous wreck that was not equipped for real battle.

"Shit," Heart Stealer muttered to himself, almost to the point of tears.

He watched as Stefan flung eight burning throwing knives, one in between each of his fingers, at the faces of two Theola demons. He did not even wait for the smoky children to burn and die before rushing onward to attack another set. The silent warrior moved nimbly, flash-stepping through the streets as he executed twice as many demons as any of the other soldiers surrounding him. A sight that inspired Hugo to unfreeze himself and take a step forward.

Hugo chuckled. "Remember when he used to be two spots below you on the recruit rankings?" he said to himself. "Don't let them show you up, Heart Stealer. It's time to fight for your people again."

Hugo's brief pep-talk spurred him onwards. He approached the first demon he could find and sank the iron-

307

hot blade of his left axe into its skull without thinking. He followed his warrior's impulse and used his right axe to sever the bottom half of the creature's face. The demon attempted to punch and claw at him, but it lost its head before it could lay a finger on his crimson gear. Hugo received his first alien kill in a long time. He smiled, ready to add more to the list.

Stefan spat blood out of his mouth, his punishment for having failed to avoid a punch from one of the demons. He enacted vengeance on the creature, planting four charged throwing knives into both of its mangled eye sockets. As he stepped back following his attack, he received another demon-induced injury, black, scratching nails clawing against his back. He had time to dodge another similar attack, but not enough time to return one as another demon struck his body with a kick. As Stefan fell to the floor, both the demons who had attacked him and a third companion of theirs cornered him. He shot back up on his feet and reached into his armour compartments to find larger and sharper hidden blades to fight with. The demons closed in on him. But before they could attack him or vice versa, the demons vanished. All three of their bodies had been reduced to dark pieces of smoking flesh on the floor by an object moving at superhuman speeds.

Silent Memoir's eyes darted over to see what had so easily destroyed them. Dagim went forth with muscles bursting with coarse veins and eyes of gold. The Ultimatum Source granted him speed and strength far beyond the greatest of soldiers combined. He watched as Dagim ran forward again, pulverising multiple demons with a singular punch and shooting off towards another set. Stefan moved to deal with the demons Dagim had not struck yet as he pulled another set of throwing knives out of his armour folds. He had hundreds more of these miniature blades on his person that needed to be embedded into demons.

He smiled as he watched Dagim work, glad he was able to witness the glory of ultimate power.

***

Quinn and Roisin piloted a high-speed rover, driving around the outskirts of the Capital Settlement and the bottom of the monumental hill. A mile away, a squad of other recruits were taking the civilians and refugees of the settlement into a series of escaping rovers as the two of them dealt with the fauxangel force at hand. They ran over any demon that passed by as they made further preparations inside.

Inside the rover, Quinn's feet grew red and raw as she sat in the driver's seat, pressing hard on the panel buttons on the vehicle's floor to charge it forward as she held the steadying box. In the backseat, Roisin fiddled around with a four-foot-long cylindrical device with two buttons on either side, made from the same material as Bronze Bullets. Once she stopped meddling with one of these devices, she placed it on the seat next to her and reached underneath her seat to prepare another.

"What's that again?" Quinn asked, glancing back.

"Remember those researchers who studied my arm condition? They built these. When I said I'd be helping out on the front lines, they told me to take these with me," Roisin said as she set up the second device. "We're going to use them to shoot some demons."

"What are they? Advanced Bronze Bullets?"

"Basically. Imagine if instead of firing one explosive bullet, they could fire five the size of a large fruit."

"Sounds useful. Are they?"

"Not sure. Let's check."

Quinn parked the rover on the side of the hill. She exited the driver's seat and opened the doors to the back seat. Roisin stepped out of the rover with one of the Advanced Bronzes in her hand. Quinn picked up the other. A group of eight demons sprinted towards their position. Together they aimed and fired. A booming echo sounded across that side of the mountain hill as the Advanced Bronzes' bullets launched forward. Just as they had hoped, the Advanced Bronzes were effective. Their two shots saw the group of charging demons explode into black bloody decorations.

"I drive, you fire," Quinn suggested as she handed her Advanced Bronze back to Roisin. She placed herself back into the driver's seat of the rover.

"Right," Roisin agreed. After locking herself in the rover, she pressed a button which prompted a section of the door to fold downwards, leaving a small enough space for her to watch the battlefield and aim fire. She placed the barrel of the Advanced Bronze in this open compartment. As Quinn drove onwards and ran over the demons in front, Roisin blasted away the demons that surrounded them.

The duo of girls clearing that side of the land of demons soon became a trio. With her new fauxangel-like abilities, Frederica aided Quinn and Roisin's alien-killing efforts.

She closed her eyes, allowing golden energy to vibrate off her body. Using the energy to shoot herself into the sky, she flew among the clouds, her arms stretched out like a god. As she flew, balls of potent energy shot down from the aura surrounding her and burned the demons that ran about the ground one by one.

***

It had been many years since The Vice Foreseer had fought on a battlefield against alien products of Luxurae. He had not even touched a weapon since his recruit days. Unlike the late

Head Foreseer, who, despite his age, would find himself more willing to join the recruits on the front lines at times. It was that habit which led to the defeat of the Giant Demon and his noble death. Whilst The Vice Foreseer did not have the energy and passion to swing a sword about the battlefield as he screamed patriotic Magnae chants like The Head, he did have the willpower to fight alongside his soldiers and the Bronze Bullets to do so.

Days before, he spent a considerable amount of time scouring the lands and sweeping the bunkers for every Bronze Bullet owned by a fallen soldier that had not been spent. He had managed to retrieve twenty-five. He carried a pack attached to the back of his crimson armour with all of these Bronze Bullets neatly organised for quick retrieval. It was heavy and impractical to carry, but it was also the only way he could contribute to the battle and survive.

The Vice Foreseer followed a group of twenty soldiers as they took on an immense congregation of demons, thirty-three. They crossed a river near the south side of the Capital Settlement hill and engaged with the enemy. As the men around him cut into the demons, he retrieved and set off the first Bronze Bullet from his back, blasting through the empty brains of the first demon he was targeting. The same bullet heavily injured another demon, allowing a soldier to kill him with one swipe of a blade through the back of the neck. The Vice felt a swelling of Magnaean pride in his heart as he reached for more bronze.

***

Theola watched her demons work over the horizon. She enjoyed the sights of them terrorising humans as she sat upon a throne made out of the rock in the side of a cliff.

"My children are so resourceful," she giggled.

The fauxangel leader looked down at the lake below her. It was stained completely red and contaminated with the decapitated and dismembered body parts of humans from all over Planet Magnae. The sight made her smile, though weakly, her face twitching with a slight pleasure. She looked into the eyes of one of the decapitated heads, who had fair skin and silky brown hair. The human reminded her of a duller version of The Divinity.

"He's almost as handsome as younger was," Theola scoffed, images of The Divinity's face flashing through her mind. She conjured up a dark energy tendril and stabbed it into the lake, picking up the bloody head. She gave it a mocking look, then gazed up at the sky.

"Can you see, younger? Can you see how I'm finishing the last stage of the war? Can you see how I'm doing your job for you?!" she chastised towards the heavens.

She dropped the decapitated head back into the lake. "Such hubris yet such incompetence. You were one of my worst creations, younger. And *your* creations would never have gotten this far," she said.

Theola thought about the batch of gold-tinted-skinned Luxuraeans that died along with The Divinity. Her face grimaced with disgust. She stared back over the horizon, watching her demons rip apart humans. This brought her smile back.

"My children are far better. They talk less and kill more, like how I should have crafted you in the first place. When we're done, Planet Luxurae and the rest of the cosmos will be populated with their likeness, not yours," Theola announced. "Once I win, we'll make this a Theola galaxy."

***

Recruit Infinity and Queen Triumph were not experiencing the same success they had been when they first engaged in battle. The mechanism that pulled the wheels of the rover had been damaged, torn out of place by clawing demons they had failed to run over. Quinn had only just about managed to drive them far away enough from danger before the rover crashed. Now they were stuck without a vehicle.

Roisin, Quinn, and two male soldiers were cornered, their backs against the rover as the demons descended upon them. Quinn picked up the one unspent Advanced Bullet. Of the ten shots the two of them possessed, they were only down to one. As she did this, Roisin tended to the wounds of the two male soldiers they had passed by. With heaps of gauze, she speedily stopped the bleeding of one's leg, then bandaged the chest wounds of the other twice as fast.

As she finished, she peered up with fretting eyes, seeing how close the group of demons were to them. Just a few rushing steps away.

"Okay, Quinn, I think you should fire now," Roisin said as she stood up.

Quinn sighed. "Let's hope this one doesn't go to waste," she grumbled.

She fired the Advanced Bronze's final gargantuan bullet at the group of demons, eliminating four of them. The remaining twelve continued to press forward, desperate to sink their hands into human flesh and dash it over the rocks below.

"Oh Lord," Roisin gasped.

Before anything could happen to them, they were rescued by a flying Frederica. Without as much as a word, the gold-energy-encased First Ranger flew over their heads and blasted canary-coloured lasers at the group of demons, incinerating them. Before Roisin or Quinn could speak their gratitude, Frederica had already flown off elsewhere. She attended to an even larger group of demons that were heading in their direction. First Ranger engaged in battle with all thirty of them, disappearing over the horizon.

"Let's go," Quinn suggested, picking up one of the injured men and walking in the opposite direction to the legion of demons. Roisin picked up the other injured soldier, dragging him with his arm over her shoulder as she followed Quinn to an escape as they rushed over a mound in the grass.

The two young women had only taken twenty steps before they were met with another roadblock. The path to their freedom was blocked, the entire mound they sought to escape over lined with demons, emerging from the other side of the hill in search of more humans to kill.

"Oh fuck!" Roisin gasped. She and Quinn wasted no time in swivelling and escaping west instead. But they had no time. All of the demons had spotted them and were increasing their pace.

Five demons rushed towards the two of them. Three of these demons attacked Quinn, forcing her to drop the injured man she had been carrying. She was able to avoid the grasp of two with a jump and a skip. Roisin was not so lucky.

"ROISIN!" Quinn screamed as she watched a demon latch onto Recruit Infinity. The warning should have been spoken a second earlier. If so, then perhaps Roisin would have left the battle whole.

As if it had known her weakness, one of these demons had decided to grasp at the more infected of Roisin's damaged arms. It pulled at the right arm that had faced the condition the worst, tearing with all its might until it was completely separated from her body. Fountains of blood sprayed from out of the fleshy red hole where a limb had been. Roisin Indermill's eyes froze with bloodshot shock as the soldier she had bandaged and carried dropped. She tripped over her own feet, falling to the grass as she rolled down the hill. Then, she screamed.

Roisin's screams were so loud and blood-curdling that they deafened Quinn's ears and made her buckle at the knees.

"No! Roisin!" Quinn cried. She dodged another demon attack and sprinted down the hill to catch up with her. "Oh God! Roisin!"

Quinn held Roisin in her arms. The rosy-cheeked redhead had lost consciousness and was losing more blood. The gaping hole from her lost arm leaked onto Queen Triumph as she held her, her tears intermingling with the vile, pouring liquid.

Quinn looked up to see a group of demons having fun with the bodies of the injured men they were forced to drop, tearing pieces out of their torsos. The rest of the demons ran towards the two of them to finish the job.

Queen Triumph gathered all the strength she had, lifted Roisin up, and slung her over her back. She ran with the will of an experienced soldier, desperate to take the injured Roisin to safety.

***

Dagim entered an Ultimatum Source flow state, killing everything in his path. He ran faster than a speeding rover as he dragged his fist across two dozen demons with one epic, lingering punch down the fields outside the Capital Settlement. The immense power he used to waste armies of Theola's demons was much appreciated by the other soldiers in the area, because the demons grew harder to kill, and their numbers seemed to replenish.

Stefan joined him, remaining as nimble as ever, though struggling to keep up the stamina. Many a time, he would have to sacrifice the sanctity of his body, allowing it to be beaten by a demon scratch or kick to buy him enough time to throw cutting knives back.

Hugo's reflexes were also put to the test. Three demons attacked him at once, grazing his skin with their sharp-knuckled punches, a small wound on his cheek being irritated by the burning black smoke that passed by it. Heart Stealer managed to slip out of the non-consensual huddle. With a chopping swing of his left axe and a swift slice of his right in the opposite direction, he killed one of these demons through strikes to the chest, freeing himself to back away.

"Help! Someone help us!" a voice cried. Hugo darted away from the oncoming demons, ignoring them to attend to the voice. Those cries rang an alarm in his head. He recognised who it came from before he even saw who had released it, sprinting in the direction of the voice as he ran around the other side of the mountain.

"Holy shit," Hugo said as he saw Quinn carry Roisin on her back. A series of hastily applied bandages barely staunched a horrific wound on Recruit Infinity. His eyes were stunned wide as they noticed her right arm was gone.

***

The Vice Foreseer shifted from side to side, avoiding the flying bodies of Theola demons and human soldiers alike. The battle that had raged on had become so hectic and scattered that even an analytical mind like his failed to make sense of it. By this point, both forces in their mess of a struggle had travelled out of the Capital Settlement and towards another civilian area. He could see the innocents of war fleeing the area with haste, most being cut down by demons before they could.

Other than this sight, he had no clue where they were situated. He could not even look down at his feet to spot the plain they were standing on. Both sides had swarmed each other in a clustered bundle of blood-spilling conflict. He found it difficult to get a clean shot at any demons. If he stopped moving for even a second, he would be dragged underneath the rabble and trampled. But his legs were burning. His muscles were aching, tiring, and in desperate need of a rest.

The Vice Foreseer yanked a Bronze Bullet out of the pack on his back as he darted diagonally through the unorganised warfare. He angled his shot efficiently, killing one demon and almost killing another as he cleared space to dash forward some more. He reached for another one, using the extra space to settle down and time this shot even more perfectly than the last. This time, the bullet was able to pierce directly through the heads of two, killing them as it lodged itself into the chest of a third. The Vice's efforts cleared the battlefield some more, allowing some of the braver and more capable soldiers room to operate.

The Vice carried out a third perfect shot, leaving fewer demons to deal with and creating more opportunities for soldiers to rush and stab. He looked around, seeing that he was able to stand still and rest for a moment. He watched as his soldiers began to overwhelm the demon ranks in this part of the land. He smiled with satisfaction as he let out a deep breath. They would win this battle, too, he thought.

But his smile of relief would prove to be a jinxing omen. Within an instant, their luck in battle worsened tenfold. A booming explosion echoed through the air. The Vice, his soldiers, and even the demons stared upwards.

An unholy yet godly entity descended upon them. With a wicked smile and a cloud of dark energy surrounding her, Theola joined the battlefield. Her presence alone prompted all humans in the area to freeze silently out of crippled fear. Only The Vice would speak.

"Don't stop fighting now, men!" The Vice exclaimed as he saw the mother of all fauxangels descend from the heavens. He reached into his pack for as many Bronze Bullets as he could grasp. It was empty. Every piece of bronze had been spent.

Before the panic could even set in, his attention was drawn towards the screams of the soldiers that surrounded him. His eyes bolted about the battlefield.

Theola's dark tendrils jutted out of her body, wildly flapping as they took hold of every soldier they could find. In a half-dozen seconds, three dozen soldiers were wiped out. Their bodies were strangled, collapsed, stabbed, and engulfed by black energy.

The Vice was at a loss for words or will. He could not act. He knew not what he was supposed to do. No plans for how he and his soldiers were supposed to escape their fates at the hands of the demon mother. He stood there, watching Theola's tendrils grow as they sprayed the poisoned copper smell of blood through the air.

"Deroren val bovai wrero," The Vice Foreseer whispered, his voice shaking.

Those would be his last words, as a sharp, dark tendril would strike through the mouth that uttered them. It gored a hole into his head and tore it from his neck with a violent thrust upwards.

XXXV. THE FINAL STAGE II

THE humans of Planet Magnae were in the worst of states. Comrades had lost limbs. Demons were overwhelming and killing their ranks in droves. Their Vice Foreseer had been executed, and the executioner, the most powerful being that had ever set foot on Magnae, was on track to do the same to the rest of their species.

The majority of Magnae fighters had either been killed or injured beyond any ability to fight. The sections of the forces that were still standing were holding strong, however. The majority of the remaining Magnae soldiers were able to retreat to an abandoned civilian settlement. A town built upon red concrete that had been cleared of any innocents, now only populated by broken-down stone houses and Magnae soldiers.

These remaining fifty-something Magnae battlers kept their nerve. Mainly due to the combined efforts of the fauxangel-ability-fuelled Frederica and the Ultimatum Source-fuelled Dagim. The two powerhouses protected this final rank of soldiers with speed, strength, and acute bursts of energy.

Frederica soared with the pomp and flair of a golden god. She paused, looking down at the giant army of demons desperately throwing their smoky hands in the air, in a futile effort to pull down the flying soldier. She grunted at them.

"For days, all I had to see were your twisted faces as I was punished by seizures and that awful cycle within me," Frederica said to them. "You may not have the consciousness to appreciate it, but I'm returning the favour. You will all suffer worse than I did."

She made good on her promise, blasting each mangled demon's face with luminescent fire, reducing them to ash.

Dagim sprinted through a large group, fulminating every demon that happened to be in his way. He paused his constant fighting once he caught sight of something at the other end of the battlefield, around where soldiers were preparing new weapons and tending to injured comrades.

Dagim's superhuman speed allowed him to arrive at Hugo and the rover behind him in an instant. In Hugo's arms, he saw the unconscious, sweating, and pale Roisin. Her missing arm alarmed him, the dreadful wound having only just been treated and bandaged. The Ultimatum Source had made Dagim feel the most powerful he ever had, but seeing Roisin in this state made him forget this inner strength, his body hunching over as he crouched down to check on her.

"What happened to her?" he asked Hugo.

Heart Stealer exhaled with solemnity. "I don't know, I only just helped Quinn carry her here and tend to the wound," he told him, running a hand through his dirty blonde hair that was growing unkempt.

A moment later, Dagim saw Quinn exit from the rover they were standing in front of. Her hands were full, spilling over with pills, antibiotic gels, blankets, and various items which she dumped on the floor next to them.

"Our rover broke down, and we were surrounded by demons. One tore off her arm, and once it was off, the others ripped it apart," Quinn recounted.

"Oh fuck," Dagim sighed, wiping a forehead wrinkled with stress.

Hugo and Quinn helped each other arrange the blankets and placed Roisin on them carefully. As they did, they shared a guilty look. They knew they should have tried to convince Roisin not to be on the front lines when she had brought it up before the battle.

Dagim bent down to get closer to Recruit Infinity. "Stay strong, Roisin," he pleaded. He gave her a soft kiss on her smooth forehead. "We're almost at the finish line. We need you there with us."

Dagim and co. were set to deal with more tragedy. The three of them turned away from Roisin as they saw Stefan help a shell-shocked man hobble towards them. The soldier not only had his armour broken, but his shot-open eyes could hardly be seen over the blood that drenched his face. He carried the decapitated head of a dark-haired man with him, the face hidden, turned to face his body.

"Why've you brought that here?" Hugo asked, pointing at the head.

The soldier was too injured to even speak. He coughed up blood and handed the decapitated head to Stefan.

"Who's that and why is he holding them?" Dagim asked. Stefan gave them a look that said "See for yourself," as he nodded down at the head. Dagim took the head off of Stefan's hands and turned it around.

"Oh, my fucking God," Quinn gasped once she saw the face of the dead man. The top recruits stared into the lifeless eyes of their Vice Foreseer.

Stefan reached into a crevice in his armour to retrieve a note he had written before helping the soldier. On it were explanations of what he had stumbled on across the land where he found the injured man. It explained to Dagim,

Hugo, and Quinn what the current situation was. Once they read it, their faces were paralysed by further horror.

"This early?!" Queen Triumph exclaimed. Devil Child and Heart Stealer's heads shook with worry.

Dagim used his speed to zip across the battlefield. He exploded through the next army of demons that Frederica had been dealing with. Once they were all dead from both his efforts and her final series of energy blasts, he stared up at her sternly.

"What's wrong?" Frederica asked him.

"The Vice Foreseer is dead," Dagim revealed. "And Theola's come down to fight us herself."

***

Theola marched through a great portion of Planet Magnae with her wild protruding tendrils, destroying buildings and settlements, kicking down forests, swiping away mountains, blackening lakes, and leaving gargantuan craters in the earth. She used the remaining life force of her demon children, who had not been sent to war, to transform herself.

She now truly looked the part of the God of Destruction, standing at two hundred feet tall. She chuckled with glee, enjoying the sounds of the lakes she stepped in being syphoned, the land she stepped on quaking, and the humans who were crushed underneath her feet.

As Theola broke through a stone hill with just the swipe of a shadow tendril, its absence revealed something flying in her direction. Two things. Her giant smile stretched out mischievously as the speeding flying objects came closer to her. She saw as Frederica flew to her, encased in golden energy. Following her at a slightly lower altitude was Dagim, who was encased in a weaker aura of Frederica's golden energy but held just as equal a face of murderous intent. Theola chuckled.

"First Ranger. Devil Child," she greeted.

She had paused her forward march of rampant destruction, as if she were running errands in the market and had stumbled upon old friends to have a nice chat with.

Dagim vaulted into action, flying in a direct attempt to strike through her heart. He only flew half of the distance between them when the rapid whip of a chest-formed tendril knocked him to the side. He grunted in pain as he retreated to his original position, floating below Frederica.

"Stay where you are. I have something to say first," Theola spat at him in anger. At her new size, her voice boomed with a permanent echo, yet still retained its smooth, devilish pleasure. She directed her attention to First Ranger, springing a fake smile on her face.

"Frederica, darling, this is your final chance. Arguments could be made as to whether you deserve it. But I'm giving it to you regardless."

Dagim scoffed with disbelief. Frederica took a beat before responding. "My *final* chance to align myself with you?" Frederica asked sardonically. "I didn't realise I had been given so many."

"You performed poorly on the tests given. I killed The Divinity, and in exchange, you were to kill the Devil Child. *I* passed my assessment of faith. *You* miserably failed yours," Theola said.

"That's what happened?" Dagim asked. It added more context to what Frederica had told them about The Divinity being killed due to Theola's rage at his incompetence. A deal had been made. Though the thought of it angered him, he was glad she had not gone through with it.

"I never believed your promise of forfeiting the war if I killed Dagim. Even if I did, I wouldn't have gone through with it. Even disregarding my morals, it'd be risking my safety too much to attack him," Frederica explained.

"Glad you have your morals then," Dagim scoffed. Frederica ignored him.

"Yes, First Ranger, you're right to be fair. It's my fault for thinking you might," Theola chuckled. "It's only because I thought you could be deserving."

Frederica's eyebrows furrowed with curiosity. "Deserving? Of what?"

"There was a time I thought you might deserve to be the eighth Theola," the mother of fauxangels answered.

The energy aura that encased Frederica glowed in unison with her wondrous eyes. She knew they should stop stalling, cut the conversation, and attack. But her curiosity was piqued. She wanted to hear more.

"Why would I want to be the eighth Theola?" she asked, though she partially knew the answer already. Theola's eyes sparkled as she lowered her head.

"Usually, when a Theola dies and the reincarnation cycle is to continue, all that happens is a new individual of our likeness is formed out of the clay of the universe. As each Theola is reincarnated, the powers we have are doubled. Or in my case, tripled. But if instead of our essence being placed in another hasty formation from the universe, it was placed into an already existing human being with a pre-existing connection to us? That power would increase tenfold," Theola explained. "If you took up the mantle as the eighth Theola, you would end up as not just the most powerful carrier of our will, but the most powerful entity the universe has ever seen, aside from its creator."

Dagim's eyes were fixed on Frederica throughout the entirety of that speech. He did not like what he saw. He could tell by the subtle contortions in Frederica's stoic countenance that thoughts of wavering were passing through her mind. She would never outwardly express it, but Dagim could feel an energy in the air. One that told him Theola's talk of power would put temptation in her heart.

"I won't lose any sleep over having missed out on that type of power," Frederica said, maintaining her frame as she clenched her fists. "It'd hardly be worth whatever downsides you'd ensure it has."

"There would have been no downsides or tricks. Why would I need them if you aligned with me? The only downsides are the ones you'll get for not siding with me as you should," Theola said. She placed a hand over her heart. "I hope you remember you are permanently connected to us Theolas. If I so choose, I could take out the piece of my heart that was once connected to your birth, vessel. It'd make me slightly weaker, but I would survive. I could roast that piece over a lake of fire and put you in a perpetual state of burning pain until the day you die."

Frederica clenched her jaw. Her stoic and steady eyes narrowed with concern as she glared at her. A reaction that amused Theola.

"But that doesn't have to be your fate. Like I said, Frederica, I am willing to give you a final chance. You can still choose to-"

Theola did not get the final words of her sentence out. Dagim charged himself forward in a burst of near-supersonic speed against her throat, aiming for the voice box and striking it true. With alacrity, he flew out of her range of grasp before she could immediately retaliate.

"Enough of your fucking talking. This is a battle," Dagim scoffed as he floated by Frederica.

Theola coughed and sputtered as if she was about to choke. When she spoke again, her voice was rough and hoarse. "So that's what I get when I try to spare the life of just one human?!" she asked, livid. "Lesson learnt. You'll *all* have to die!"

"So be it," Frederica said.

In that second, the sky burst with light energy, clouds of darkness, and the gale force winds of supersonic flight as the two strongest humans of Planet Magnae battled it out against the strongest fauxangel of Planet Luxurae.

Theola frothed at the mouth with rage, shooting hundreds of dark tendrils out of her body, cutting swipes through the air in a desperate will to kill.

"You are the stupidest human to ever live! I've given you the option to reach your highest potential and align with your fate since birth! Yet you choose to stay aligned with the Devil Child?!" she spat at Frederica. "You could have been the most capable of our line, but instead you battle alongside the progeny of a traitor's will!"

"I don't care about Dagim's connection to Ekib or my connection to the Theola Cycle. We're both still soldiers. Comrades. Humans," Frederica asserted. "And if it's between you and humanity, I'm choosing humanity a hundred times out of a hundred."

She blocked the whipping tendrils with golden blasts as Dagim speedily flew around them. He searched for an opening where he could make another attempt to fire through her heart.

***

As the two powerhouses of the forces engaged in the battle of their lives against a giant Theola, the remainder of the Magnae forces could barely see their struggle over the horizon. But these soldiers had their own problems to deal with. There was still an army of over sixty demons surrounding them, and fewer than forty remaining soldiers to fight them back. The soldiers who could fight needed to protect the injured ones who could not and kill the demons. Or at least hold them long enough for Dagim and Frederica to kill Theola.

Hugo, Quinn, and various other recruits were positioned outside the row of rovers in which the recovering one-armed Recruit Infinity and other hurt soldiers were resting. Between Hugo and Quinn was a mountain of stockpiled Bronze Bullets they fired at demons who came close to the rudimentary, manufactured infirmary area they sectioned.

The rest of the soldiers were scattered across different areas of the deadened fields with swords and axes. Stefan led this battle campaign, his blades completely blackened by demon blood.

They seemed to be holding strong enough for an emphatic loss not to be a major source of worry anymore. Still, one scan of the battlefield would tell you that their soldiers were dropping at equal or higher rates than the demons were dying.

Hugo and Quinn felt cornered as they collected Bronze Bullets, fired them at the demons, discarded them, and collected a new set from the stockpile. A group of demons targeted their area, instinctively understanding the rovers were protecting the most vulnerable of the humans inside. Heart Stealer and Queen Triumph could no longer afford to take any time between shots. As soon as one Bronze Bullet had been sent, they had to reach for another and pull its trigger within the next second. Hugo was the faster of the two, spending the Bronze Bullets as he staved off the demon group, taking no time to think or aim. But in the frenzy of his constant firing and collecting, he noticed something.

Despite how the pile they were collecting from was only sets of an old edition of the standard issue Bronze Bullets, one shot he fired was able to strike through a demon's shoulder. Despite the trajectory of the bullet slowing down, it killed the demon behind that one with a hole through the heart. Not only that, but it sent surrounding demons into a panicked frenzy, with a few even retreating and deciding to attack other humans. His mind flashed like a lightbulb.

Once Hugo came to his realisation, he relayed it to the other soldiers in the field with a booming scream.

"They're just like Theola! The source of their power and pain is their heart! Don't bother cutting them to pieces to kill them, just strike each through the heart and move on to the next!" he told the ranks.

They listened and carried out his plan. The Magnae soldiers in the smoke-surrounded field plunged blades and fired bullets through demon hearts, changing the balance of power as they killed off the children of Theola at a steadily increasing pace.

Stefan rushed across the battlefield, throwing fiery knives through the hearts of multiple demons at once. Animalistic dread set in amongst the mindless monsters.

"Kill them all!" Quinn shouted as she fired Bronze Bullets. She and her boyfriend's pile was starting to dwindle. But they did not fear, for they were starting to outnumber the demons with their wilful heart attacks.

***

With a slamming fist of pure Ultimatum power to the nose, Dagim knocked Theola's giant head backwards. Instead of blood, black smoke trickled out. Frederica fired four energy balls at the injury, buying Dagim enough time to fly out of the clawing grasp of Theola's hand. But the hand acted as a decoy. By choosing to dodge it with such haste, they had also chosen to land themselves in the path of four tendrils protruding from the protective barrier around Theola's chest.

Two of these tendrils grabbed Dagim, entangling him. The other two beat Frederica with a powerful force.

Dagim ground his teeth and applied as much strength as feasible, freeing himself from the contortions of the tendrils and flying away. The beating of the other tendrils had hit Frederica with enough force to almost take her out of flight and drop her out of the sky. She charged her body with more golden energy, steadying herself and preventing a descent into the dirt. She regrouped with Dagim, the two soldiers floating next to each other as they planned their attacks moving forward.

"I go high, head and neck. You go low, legs," Frederica suggested. "We'll throw her off balance with her mind muddled and feet shaking."

"Alright," Dagim agreed, zipping into action as he flew towards Theola's knees.

"Dreadful fucking humans!" Theola screamed out. Her body stumbled as it reeled from the pain of Dagim slamming right at the centre of her left kneecap. As she tilted to one side, Frederica fired energy lasers at her head from the other side.

"STOP!" Theola screamed, her shout echoing across the lands. In one shadow cloudburst, she released one hundred dark tendrils from her shoulder blades and sternum. Each was more powerful than the last.

Frederica flew out of harm's way quicker than she could even think of doing so. Dagim dodged multiple of these as he continued to attack her legs. Fifteen of these dark tendrils combined into one swinging black baton that dealt a catastrophic blow that rang through Dagim's body.

The golden aura energy around the Devil Child faded as soon as the hit landed. He plummeted out of the sky, having momentarily lost his strength and the ability to fly.

Frederica soared into rapid action, catching Dagim and whisking him away before Theola could get her tendrils on him. She flew a considerable distance away from the giant fauxangel. Her breath grew heavy and fast as she held Dagim in her arms and charged him with more golden energy to keep him afloat.

Theola would not allow for their well-needed rest and recuperation. As Frederica recharged Dagim and the Devil Child waited for the Ultimatum Source to heal his broken bones, Theola ran across the desecrated lands of Magnae. She destroyed everything beneath her with every quaking step of her giant feet in a forward rush for blood.

As soon as Theola arrived close enough to attack them, Dagim's recharge was complete. Frederica threw him to one side as she flew away, his new energy aura allowing him to fly in the opposite direction. As Theola's rage grew, so did the speed of her flailing tendrils. All the two could do was fly and dodge in response, the shadowy tentacles giving no room for a counterattack. Though they dodged all direct hits from the tendrils, their sheer size and magnitude meant that each blow would land on them in some way or another, scraping by their heads and knocking past their backs. Their bodies were gaining various cuts and scrapes, and losing energy as they flew around in circles.

"It's over for humanity!" Theola shouted as her attacks pressed on. But her declaration would be shown false just a breath later.

All of a sudden, she buckled over, almost tripping on her own giant feet as she stumbled to the side. Dagim and Frederica capitalised on this opportunity before even realising why it had come by. Dagim took another shot at her heart. With a supersonic hit and run, he was able to create a small but bloody black hole in her chest around where her heart was. At the same time, Frederica was able to fire a focused and potent golden laser at one of her eyes, not blinding it, but scorching it to the point of squinting. The two flew back out of the reach of Theola's tendrils. As they recouped, they finally looked down at the ground.

"They did it!" Frederica gasped with disbelief as she watched all of the remaining soldiers of Magnae arrive at the scene in a dozen rovers. The remaining forty Magnae soldiers poured out of the rovers with their weapons at the ready, willing to risk their lives to help Dagim and Frederica end the war. Four of these rovers had rammed themselves into Theola's right foot, which was what had caused her to slip and stumble. The soldiers of Magnae threw blades and fired bullets up at her legs, weakening her balance further.

Theola's eyes scoured over the horizon as she took in all of the surrounding lands. Not a single one of her demon children remained. The section of Planet Magnae she had used them to beggar had been completely cleared of their smoky menace. Her mouth gaped in disbelief as her eyes flared with red-hot anger.

"It's over for humanity!" Theola screeched with defiant insistence. Her head and neck ruptured with veins, and her muscles tensed violently as she forced harder and sharper tendrils out of her body and towards all human life.

XXXVI. THE FINAL STAGE III

THEOLA'S tendrils stabbed into soldier after soldier, killing a good portion of them before they could even make another mark on her. Her body twitched as she shot out relentless black blades through backs and skulls. Only those who were the most skilled could avoid the attacks and survive long enough to carry out attacks of their own.

As Frederica peppered Theola with energy, Dagim flew through the battlefield, blocking Theola's tendrils from hitting as many soldiers as he could. His golden eyes perused the battlefield to keep track of the top recruits. Hugo and Quinn were stationed on top of a rover, a good distance away from the majority of Theola's knives and their landing position, shooting Advanced Bronze bullets at her legs. Stefan was braver, being one of the soldiers closest to the action, his body was at much more of a risk of being stabbed by a tendril, but his knives were more effective when it came to hitting Theola's legs.

"You humans seem to be under the false impression that you stand even the slightest fucking chance!" Theola raged as she fired hundreds of razor-sharp shadows into soldiers. Frederica blasted another three shots into her face, one hitting her eye.

"You seem to be under the ridiculous impression that we care what you have to say," Dagim scoffed back at her.

"You're going to die very soon. And when you do, we'll dance in the debris of your putrid remains as they wither away. It's not over for humanity, it's over for fauxangels."

Dagim sped forward for another attack on Theola's chest and into her heart. He landed another cutting blow, his knuckles managing to cut the small hole he had opened several inches wider. Instead of flying away to prepare for another attack, he sought to widen the hole that led to her heart with a consecutive blow. Most of the dark tendrils that flayed and shot at the soldiers below and Frederica above were retracted into her body. They reformed around her chest area, creating a thick, squirming aura of shadowy energy that could not be reached.

With another wincing strain, Theola continued to shoot out a further flurry of dark tendrils. These were much weaker and easier to dodge, but were more protective over her body, making their attacks less effective against her.

Regardless, Dagim accelerated forward with fists clenched, looking to use his body as a missile to pierce through the protective chest barriers. He came to sorely regret it. As soon as he contacted the protective barrier, dozens of dark blades struck him at once. He crossed his arms in a guard over his face and curled up into a floating ball to bear the brunt of these attacks. When one blade hit him, it was closely followed by another just a millisecond later. The blades struck him again and again until he could no longer guard himself. He was hit with the sharp end of five consecutive blades to the chest. The second set of Theola attacks to take him out of the air. Dagim hurtled out of the sky so fast he could barely see his descent. In the blink of an eye, he crash-landed like a comet in front of a series of soldiers who were still shooting up at Theola's legs. He was primed to lose consciousness.

Frederica flew down to recharge Dagim's flying aura again. Before she could even fly a quarter of the way to his position, ten tendrils were shot at her at once. Five to the body, four to her legs, and one to her head. First Ranger coughed in pain, her head dizzy as she spun through the air, struggling to regain composure. Once her vision was no longer blurred, she returned to a solid flying state, only for Theola's tendrils to grab a hold of her. Frederica looked into the mother of all fauxangel's pitch-black malevolent gaze as she felt the tentacles wrap themselves around her midriff in a crushing twist.

Dagim's eyes blinked open once more. The Ultimatum Source would not allow him to lose consciousness for more than just a few seconds. But he was still hurt. Not to mention the aura Frederica had replenished that allowed him to fly was broken. He glared hundreds of feet upwards, watching helplessly as Frederica fought a losing battle against the tendrils tied around her, crushing the air out of her lungs. The Devil Child soon noticed that none of the other soldiers were faring very well against the final villain of the alien species either. None of the bullets or knives that were sent towards her legs was causing her any harm, or even tilting her balance in the slightest.

"Shit," he grunted. He looked back up to see how Frederica was faring. She had supercharged her body with golden energy and was protecting herself from being crushed. But the tendrils were still fixed tight around her. There was a good chance the First Ranger could not hold this enhanced energy form. Soon it would fade, and Theola would tear her body in half.

Dagim used his super speed without caution, slamming himself into Theola's feet and ankles over and over again as he zoomed back and forth with pounding bloody knuckles.

The attacks shook her slightly, but they did not hurt her like they once would have.

Theola had used her tendrils to act purely defensively. By directing just half of the strength she was using to shoot tendrils at them to protect her body instead, she had found the most successful battle strategy for herself moving forward. Though her offensive tendrils were less deadly, they still killed enough soldiers to keep her in the game, Magnaean blood pooling at her feet with chunks of blackened human parts floating in it. By sacrificing half her offensive power and applying it to defence, she was able to kill a satisfactory portion of soldiers whilst rendering most of their attacks against her pointless. And, she had Frederica still in her grasp. All she needed was time, and she could crush one of the powerhouses and clear the rest.

If Dagim did not act fast, it all would have been for nothing. If Dagim did not do something soon, they would have to face the reality of a total Theola victory.

The Devil Child ground his teeth hard enough to create white dust as he wracked his brain for any possible battle plan that could turn this all around for a total human victory and be enacted quickly. A pain in his chest developed just from the stress of doing so alone. As his mind did somersaults, he felt a calming hand on his shoulder. Dagim turned to see Stefan turning over a piece of paper to him.

"This better be an idea for how we're going to end this," Dagim scoffed. Stefan nodded with confirmation.

Dagim opened up the piece of paper. He read the plans Stefan had written out. Once he reached the end of the note, his mood changed.

Dagim's demeanour was that of subdued shock. His hands shook, rattling the piece of paper slightly.

"Are you ready for this?" he asked him. Stefan nodded. He looked into Dagim's glazed eyes, his trademark innocent gaze having transformed into a steely and resolute stare.

Hugo and Quinn fired the last of their Advanced Bronze bullets at Theola's leg. Both of their shots had collectively made a small dent that had failed to affect her in the slightest.

"Looks like there's not much else we can do," Hugo sighed. He threw their last spent weapon to the side, clattering on the floor of discarded equipment below the rover they stood on.

"Yeah," Quinn agreed, lowering her head as if the thick curly black hair it sported had made it heavy. As the two of them stood by on the rover, they watched Dagim and Stefan run far away from the battlefield with purpose.

Quinn squinted. "You think they've got a plan for how any of us will survive this?"

"Let's hope so," Hugo answered. "Let's hope to God." He and Quinn took each other's hands, holding them tightly as they prayed together.

"Release me!" Frederica bellowed.
The energy surrounding her exploded in a burst of luminescence, destroying the tendrils that had been trying their utmost to crush her. She felt weak but was free, flying a few metres away. She frothed with fury as she charged more energy into the palms of her hands. Frederica was in the process of sending another burning shot into Theola's eye until her hand was caught by a tendril flying at super speed and wrapping around the wrist.

As Frederica tried to force out of the grasp, twenty more tendrils flew her way, each wrapping themselves around one of her wrists or one of her ankles. Once again, the tendrils held her captive. They pulled at her limbs like she was a criminal on a torture rack, pushing the First Ranger's body to its limits. Frederica cried in agony, unable to use her energy powers to free herself or attack back. Theola observed with delight as sections of Frederica's skin began to tear from the force.

The mother of all fauxangels would have her show interrupted. While all attacks on her feet from the soldiers below failed to injure her, she found herself stumbling over again from a searing pain in her right. Using the strength of the Ultimatum Source to push a rover and the speed to create devastating momentum, Dagim rammed the powerful vehicle into Theola's foot so hard that it exploded. Theola lost all footing. She stumbled again and this time, came crashing down. A quarter of the soldiers below them fell victim to a final crushing blow as Theola landed on the ground. Many casualties were made. But it meant that Theola's unshakeable confidence was shaken, and that Frederica was no longer entwined in her tentacles.

Dagim watched as First Ranger fell. He sped to the left of his position, catching her before her body could be crushed by the ground below. He held Frederica carefully, taking note of the cracks and tears of blood in her skin.

The remaining soldiers watched as Theola picked herself back off the floor. The Magnae earth quaked as she returned to her original stance. She spread out the defensive tendrils, taking the sharp shadows that protected her chest and using them to protect her body in another layer of darkness.

"Charge me! Quick!" Dagim shouted at Frederica. She wasted no time in doing so. Her energy had weakened from its original strength. In quick time, she could only give Dagim enough energy to fly for another few seconds. As soon as the aura replenished around Dagim, he sought to use those few seconds to the best of his ability.

Dagim sped over to a rover across from him. He lifted it above his head with ease and shot up towards Theola, flying with supersonic speed.

As Frederica stepped to the side, Hugo, Quinn, and the twelve remaining soldiers of Magnae joined them in watching Dagim's flying rover gambit.

"What's he doing?" Frederica said.

"No idea," Quinn said. "If I had to guess, he's going to do something wild that will win this war."

"Kill her, Devil Child," Hugo said with a smirk.

Dagim flew at speeds even he would have thought were unimaginable if he had not tried to reach them. He easily dodged every one of Theola's tendrils as his energy aura timer ran out. Once he was close enough to the hole created in her chest that led to her heart, he threw the rover with equal speed. The rover would not reach inside the hole in the heart. It had soared a mere few inches away from the hole when Theola protruded dark tendrils from the surrounding areas to stop it in its tracks. The tendrils wrapped around the vehicle entirely as it began to crush it to pieces. Dagim grunted. In just a moment, Frederica's energy aura would completely fade. He used his last second of flight to its fullest. In his last flight forward, Dagim blasted himself at Theola's eye. He knew he could not kill her this way, but he wanted to waste as much time and cause as much pain as he possibly could.

"FUCK OFF!" Theola screamed as she grabbed at Dagim. Like a man swatting a fly, she smacked him out of her eye with all her might, sending him away from her and towards the ground.

Dagim lost his ability to fly as soon as she had struck him. He laughed with great amusement as he took his third plummet out of the sky of the day.

If it were not for Frederica engulfing him in energy a few inches before he reached the ground, he would have been knocked unconscious. Instead, he glowed gold as he joined the others in staring up at a giant Theola at the peak of her frustration.

"I cannot wait to end this!" Theola snarled as she looked down on the humans. She did not even bother to form any more dark tendrils. She stepped forward. She was ready to crush the last remaining Magnae soldiers under the sole of her feet, with a twisted, mangled smile on her face.

Before Theola could even take that step, her body froze. She gulped down a lump in her throat. She could sense something was wrong with her body before it even started. Once it had started, she felt an unfathomable level of discomfort about her. She clutched at her chest, the source of the great discomfort. She could feel an unfamiliar burning inside her. Beads of sweat poured out of her faster than protective tendrils would.

She wheezed with the voice of an old woman on her deathbed as she held a gripping hand over her heart.

"What's happening to her?" Frederica asked.

"Stefan's carrying out his plan," Dagim said.
Hugo and Quinn's faces drained of colour. Frederica's eyes remained fixed upwards in awe.

"Stefan? He was in that rover you threw?!" Hugo exclaimed. Dagim nodded.

"And now he's in her heart?!" Quinn exclaimed. Dagim nodded again. The top Magnae recruit sported a smirk as devilish as his nickname.

"Silent Memoir snuck his way into another woman's heart. He will go down in history as the hero of this war," Dagim said.

The last few Magnae soldiers watched as Theola wheezed with pain, her eyes bulging out of her head. Frederica felt a small portion of this strife piercing at her heart, her connection to the Theola Cycle as the former vessel causing a great deal of pain.

"Mind over matter," she told herself as she forced her body to withstand the inner burns. "Humanity over Theola."

Inside Theola's heart, Stefan put himself to work. Like Dagim said, he planned to win the war himself. He sliced and cut around the insides of this bloody black muscle, staining himself with the dark vapours of smoky clouds as he destroyed the fauxangel from the inside. He used every single charged throwing blade he had left in every single crevice from his armour to line the inside of her heart, burning and withering away at the meaty blackness that surrounded him. As Stefan continued to destroy Theola from within, he felt the most passion he had ever experienced in his life. Memories flashed through his mind in an instant. All of the most important memories he had on this planet that he was protecting with all his might and will:

The day the fauxangel burnt his tongue, forcing him to change his disruptive ways. The day he met Anais. The day he first became an official member of the Magnae Forces. The day he became a top recruit and was given the nickname Silent Memoir. The day he had missed the battle against the demon and watched The Head sacrifice his life to protect the planet. All of these memories fuelled him to fight even harder, to destroy Theola's heart harder, to throw and kick, and punch, and cut faster and more forcefully than any human ever had. A series of dark tendrils entered the hole of the heart. Before Stefan could even blink, three stabbed him through the gut, skewering him. But even that did not stop him. With his last dying breaths, Stefan threw out the final dozen throwing knives he had kept on him, all around Theola's heart. The energy-laden blades burnt at the muscles, degrading them further and being the final blow that would cause the organ to break and shrivel. As the tendrils that skewered him drained the life force out of him, Stefan watched with satisfaction as pieces of Theola's heart withered and fell. Silent Memoir's final act before he would die was to grasp for the compartment in his armour where he kept his drawing of Anais. He looked at the depiction of his one true love a final time, kissing it as he passed away.

The last surviving soldiers of Planet Magnae sprinted out of the way as Theola's body came crashing down to the floor again. This time, no casualties were made in the fall. The only casualty they saw was Theola, her eyes blank and pupil-less, her chest gored open and seeping with black smoke.

Silence encapsulated the area for what felt like a century. None could believe it, even though it was right in front of them. All of them swarmed to the side of Theola's head. It still seemed unreal. They still expected her eyes to flash with life and for dark tendrils to strike at them.

But that did not happen. Nothing happened. Nothing at all. Theola had truly been killed.

The soldiers did not want to take any chances. They rushed over to the other side of her body and inspected her chest. It had been burnt open completely, blackened with marks from energy blades rather than the smoke of a higher fauxangel. After a while, they allowed themselves to believe the truth that was right in front of them. Theola was gone. Her heart had been destroyed completely, not a single piece flying off to find another manufactured host.

The Theola Cycle had ended. For the first time in history, Planet Magnae was fauxangel-free.

Frederica sighed with relief. The pain she had felt disappeared. Her connection to Theola had been severed.

"We did it! We fucking well did it! Thank God and all things holy! We! Fucking! Did it!" Dagim shouted in a triumphant scream as he thrust his hands in the air.

Frederica used spare knives she tucked away in her armour to blast and burn every piece of Theola's body that tried to float in the sky. Only a few rose, but she took no chances.

Dagim was so relieved that tears poured out of his eyes at an alarming rate. All throughout his life, he had never allowed himself to cry. But he could not stop the tears from pouring down and coating his face this time. The others could not blame him.

As the group celebrated, Roisin stumbled out of one of the rovers on the battlefield. Her body was still weak, not nearly recovered enough to be walking around with a missing arm. But she walked on regardless, desperate to join in on the jubilation.

"Roisin, what are you doing?! You should rest!" Quinn chastised her.

"I'm not going to let a missing arm stop me from celebrating our people's greatest achievement," Roisin said, her face so pale and sickly you could no longer see the blush of her rosy cheeks. She only managed to muster enough strength to join the main group.

As Roisin stopped walking, Hugo had to catch her from falling. "Easy now, Recruit Infinity. It's alright, we've got you," he said.

Roisin smiled at him. Her smile faded once she looked around and noticed one of their friends was missing from the ranks of just over a dozen remaining soldiers.

"What happened to Stefan?" Roisin asked, concerned.

Dagim clenched his jaw as tears continued to trickle down his cheek. "He gave his life so we could win," Devil Child said. "Silent Memoir is the hero of this war."

The group looked back at Theola's withering body. It had melted, degraded, and burnt itself down to the point where they could see Stefan's corpse. His entire body was covered in Theola's black blood, but for the red blood that seeped out of the hole where he was skewered. His hand lay draped over his chest, the picture of Anais grasped within it.

Hugo held Quinn as she burst into tears, shedding a few himself. Frederica lowered her head and clasped both of her hands as she paid respect to her fallen comrade. Dagim knelt down and held Stefan's arms. He laid his head on his chest to honour him.

"Oh, Stefan," Roisin sighed solemnly. "You were always the best of us."

Roisin bent down to give Dagim a consoling kiss on the cheek. She put her one arm around him for comfort. Dagim looked up at her with loving eyes. He put one arm around her, leaving the other resting over Stefan's hand.

The soldiers of Magnae all took a knee in deep appreciation for the life of Stefan Machin, aka Silent Memoir, and how he had given it to win what was once an endless struggle between humans and fauxangels.

Though they were all encapsulated in sorrow, and Stefan's sacrifice would never be forgotten, the sadness would not last forever. At the end of the day, they had won. Planet Magnae had been secured for humans.

They would never have to deal with a fauxangel again.

XXXVII. EPILOGUS

DECADES had passed since Theola died in the final battle that freed the human race from fauxangels forever. The handful of Magnae recruits who had survived were in their late teens and early twenties when the battle itself took place. Now, those who were still alive were in their forties. Their days as fighting recruits were long behind them. Twenty-four years behind them.

They were replaced by days of being the builders of a new, more beautiful Magnae. The skies were brighter, the land was cleaner, and the planet was more populated, with new generations of children who had never known war and would not for a long time. Their world, which was once an empty dystopian hell-hole, had been transformed over the years to become the most thriving human society the universe had hosted in many centuries.

***

Anyone who walked upon the smooth paved roads or passed the tall buildings that made up the schools, churches, and neighbourhood homes, or walked through the safe lands of vibrant flora, would be shocked to know none of it was there just twenty-something years prior. It reminded those who knew of any history of how Ancient Earth might have looked a millennium ago.

Most of this was thanks to Frederica. One of the first things the former First Ranger had done years ago was a thorough ecological study on the plains she had taken The Head and the top recruits to when she told them what she had learnt about the Theola Cycle all those years back. With her knowledge and help from scientists and spiritualists, they were able to treat a great portion of the planet's lands until all of the civilian areas turned into the Earth-like terrain they enjoyed in the present.

If one were to walk down any street in the Capital Settlement, one would hear various voices, from young girls to old men, singing the praises of the top recruits who made them the brighter world they now lived in. From the brave actions of Roisin Indermill, Hugo Stacey, and Quinn Trepanier to the strong fighting spirits of the most powerful duo alive, Dagim Chibuike and Frederica Rasmussen.

You would hear especially high praise for the late Stefan Machin. He was held on the highest pedestal as the man who delivered the killing blow that ended the war, giving his life for the best cause imaginable: Humanity's thriving present.

***

In the middle of the Capital Settlement, a large building had been erected. One with a striking resemblance to the original North Magnae Forces building. Though there was no longer a need for recruits in the fauxangel-killing sense, there was still a need to establish law and order among humans. The first thing any eyes would see outside of the building was that many statues had been erected in commemorative decoration. Impressive pieces of marble honoured dead heroes, including Stefan Machin, aka Silent Memoir, Aiza Armstrong, aka Foreseer VII, Alexander Lang, aka The Vice Foreseer, and Keith Best, aka The Head Foreseer.

In the twenty-fourth year after the war had ended, the *Magnae Protection Forces* was being run by Hugo Stacey, who had taken over in the past year from its former runner, Dagim Chibuike.

This was an even larger mountain of responsibility than the position in society he originally held. Hugo used to help Quinn run the *Trepanier House*. The former scavenger known as Queen Triumph had founded a new orphanage that acted as an homage to Iqra Frazier, the woman whose orphanage had once taken her in as a vulnerable child.

Although Roisin Indermill did not work, she would often visit and offer funds to both establishments. She played a part in allowing the Protection Forces and Trepanier House to continue their work of giving better lives to the children, women, and men of their planet as humanity grew in size and splendour.

***

But not all was well in this life. Whilst tragedies were rare in those days, they had not been eradicated. Roisin and her two children, a teenage boy, and a girl, learnt that the most.

Over the years that Recruit Infinity had aged, her bright red hair had been speckled with spots of grey. Her arm that had been torn off in the final battle was replaced with a golden limb, which, with the advancements of Magnae technology, was almost as useful as an organic one.

The beautiful, brown-skinned twins followed their rosy-cheeked, golden-armed mother into a dark room within one of the newly built churches. They passed by the rows of black and golden pews as they approached a gilded coffin propped up on an obsidian steel mound.

"Father," the boy uttered weakly as they stopped by the coffin. The girl cried too much to utter a word. Roisin placed her organic arm over her daughter's shoulder and her golden arm over her son.

Roisin sighed as she looked over the name engraved on the front of the coffin and the commemorative epithets alongside it:

Dagim 'Devil Child' Chibuike - Humanity's Strongest.

***

Weeks later, a light wind fluttered at Roisin's swaying black robes as she stood at the top of a hill that overlooked a vast open field of green grass. She enjoyed the silence and solitude offered by the calming ambience and the sight of the sun rising over the horizon. Her face wore a mixture of sadness and serenity.

"Roisin," an equally calm voice called out to her. Roisin turned around to see two of her lifelong friends, both walking up the steep grass steps to join her at the top of the hill. They wore the same robes that she did.

"Hugo. Quinn," she greeted the two of them.

The former Heart Stealer and Queen Triumph looked very different to their recruit days. Hugo's dirty blonde hair had darkened to the point of being a deep brunette and had started to recede at the temples. Quinn's curly black hair remained just as curly and buoyant, but showed signs of greying much like Roisin's.

"How are your kids?" Roisin asked.

"The two oldest are starting a business together in Fay Nation," Quinn stated. "The middle's working with me at Trepanier House."

Roisin smiled. "What about the two youngest?"

"They're finishing up school. Both are thinking about joining the Protection Forces," Hugo announced proudly, puffing out his chest. "They want to be fighters, just like Mum and Dad."

"They always do," Roisin chuckled with a joyful smirk. Hugo smiled warmly, though his handsome eyes held a strong sadness in them.

"It's been a while since we've met up with anyone else from the old days, you know," he said.

"Have you not seen Anais? I heard she lives in the Capital Settlement now," Roisin said.

Quinn sighed. "Yeah, we spoke to Anais, but it didn't end well," she revealed. "She still hasn't forgiven us for 'letting' Stefan sacrifice himself in the final battle."

"Right," Roisin sighed. "That's a shame."

The three of them glanced at the rising sun in silence for a few moments.

"I still can't believe Dagim's no longer with us," Hugo commented. "I would've thought he would survive the longest of us all."

"Residue from the Ultimatum Source inside him took a toll on his body's health for the last few years," Roisin said, lowering her head solemnly. "I suppose that's the price to pay for ultimate power."

Quinn comforted Roisin with an embracing hand around her, allowing her to rest on her shoulder. Hugo crossed his arms, trying to maintain composure as memories of Dagim ran through his mind and pulled at his heartstrings.

"First Frederica and now Dagim. The original group's getting smaller and smaller," Quinn said.

Roisin's eyebrows furrowed. "Frederica's been confirmed dead?"

Hugo shook his head. "No, but think about how long she's been missing. No one has seen her for years since she travelled south of the planet in search of more resources," he said. "I think it's safe to assume something happened to her."

"I suppose that makes sense," Roisin sighed. "I just didn't want to believe it."

Another silence was held between the three friends. A silence that lasted for a long while as they mourned Stefan, Frederica, Dagim, and everyone else from the Magnae Forces and from their lives in general who had passed away over the years.

By the time they raised their heads again, the sun had risen from just over the horizon to beaming brightly over them. A delighted smirk came over Quinn's face.

"Think of what Dagim would say if he saw us moping around like this. Hanging our heads. He'd want us to continue our lives with the same passion he would instead. They all would," she asserted. "We should have smiles on our faces. I bet they're all already smiling down at us from above. We owe it to them to smile back."

Hugo chuckled. "That's a wonderful way of putting it, dear," he said, smiling.

Roisin smiled also. "What a lovely thought," she agreed.

***

With a bald head, a thicker beard, and a body both heavily muscled from years of training officers, yet slightly withered from the Ultimatum Source sickness, Dagim woke up with an abrupt blasting of his eyes open.

The much older Devil Child found himself in a space of pure gold. He scowled as he observed his surroundings, unsure of where he was and how he had ended up there. After a few minutes of walking, it came back to him.

The last thing he remembered was passing away in a hospital surrounded by Roisin, their children, and all his closest friends who were still alive at the time. He did not know how long it had taken him to get there, but he knew he was in a place beyond life and after death. He was in the afterlife.

Dagim took a few steps forward through the golden light that surrounded him endlessly. As far as he could tell, he was the only entity in the area.

He eventually stumbled upon another entity. His eyes almost blasted themselves out of his head once they lay on this particular entity. It was the grandest, most beautiful thing he had ever seen. He saw golden wisps of smoke, cloud, and pure energy pull in and out of itself.

He saw a source of energy that was both tangible and solid yet intangible and transparent. That was vast in size, stretching out endlessly, yet at the same time, looked as if it was just a bundle of raw power right in front of him.

"Are you what I think you are?" Dagim asked as he pointed at it.

The source of energy hummed, confirming. "I believe you humans have called me The Bestial Energy," he said. "I am your creator."

Dagim gasped with awe, his mouth opened and quivering as he attempted to shake the light feeling that was forming in his head.

"Is this the afterlife?" Dagim asked.
The Bestial Energy hummed, confirming. "This is not the afterlife that most see."

"What is the afterlife that most see?"

"A return to the heart of the universe to be made anew in another life form," The Bestial Energy answered. "The last thing a soul will ever see is me. Then it is returned to the cosmos to make a new life."

Dagim nodded his head, which still felt cloudy, like he was on the brink of losing consciousness. He could not come to terms with what was happening. He had never thought about what came after death. It was not the type of thing that ever concerned him. If he had, he would not have thought a discussion with the universe's creator would be in his cards.

"So, what is this afterlife then? And why am I in it?" Dagim asked.

"This is where I keep all of my most powerful and volatile creations. The creations whose souls have reincarnated into the most powerful spirits. I may keep you here for centuries or even millennia until I make a creation capable of carrying your will," The Bestial Energy stated. "Just as Emmanuel Ekib's soul was held for centuries until you were born."

"I see," Dagim marvelled, his head and heart swelling with reverence and astonishment.

It was strange. He believed he had always known this intuitively, just not on a conscious level. He was not just possessed by Ekib's will through what happened to his father. He was Ekib. The power-hungry man who had crafted the false image of a saviour, whose betrayal had set the first Theola into a reincarnating cycle of vengeance and lust for human blood, was him in essence. Ekib was what made him the Devil Child. Ekib was what gave him such awful power.

A small part of him was aggrieved by this revelation. But a larger part of him was grateful. This was who he was, this was who he had been. A man with awful power and capable of awful things. But one who used that awful power to improve his planet and its people's futures. The curse of Ekib's light on his soul had always been a blessing.

"Wait, if this is where all the most powerful and volatile souls go, does that mean you keep fauxangels here?!" Dagim asked, worried. "Is this what I see in the gold around me? The holding cells for the souls of the likes of Theola and The Divinity?"

"No!" The Bestial Energy answered sternly as if the question had offended him. Dagim's body quaked, startled by the booming voice from the heart of the energy source.

"They're not?" he asked.

"The fauxangels were my worst creation, and as such, their souls have been destroyed for eternity, never to be set into the universe again. They were a poor choice, designed to fix a 'problem' with my best creation. I should have left humanity be," The Bestial Energy declared. "Your people did not need governance from another species. You could govern each other. You would fail, you would die, but in the end, you would always continue your bloodlines. No famine, genocide, or world-ending threat has ever been able to crush humanity's spirit. I made you the best, and I should have trusted you would stay as such."

"I'm glad you understand that now," Dagim scoffed.
He could not believe he was being snarky and bantering with the creator of all things. The Bestial Energy hummed in response.

Dagim stared into the heart of the Bestial Energy's being. It reminded him of the Ultimatum Source. The same source of energy that gave him the power to help end the greatest war in the universe's history. The same source of energy that corrupted his body during his final years alive.

Dagim stared across the empty gold that surrounded him.

"This is all I have to look forward to for hundreds, maybe thousands of years?" he asked. His creator hummed.

"Yes. Unfortunately, that is your burden," The Bestial Energy answered.

Dagim accepted this with a surprising amount of patience and clarity. He nodded his head as he made himself comfortable, sitting on the floor. "Will I at least have you to keep me company for centuries, creator? I have a lot more questions I could ask you during that time."

"No. In a few moments, I will leave. This is the last you will ever see of me."

"Of course," Dagim laughed with a sigh. "But before you leave, can you answer one final question for me?"

"Ask it."

"What happened to Frederica Rasmussen?"

"Frederica Rasmussen," the Bestial Energy repeated.

"Yes. She was my friend. We fought the greatest of battles together. We re-built the world together," Dagim said. "But years ago, she went missing on the south of the planet. No one has seen her since. Most think she's probably dead, but no one ever found out what happened to her. What *happened* to her?"

The Bestial Energy hummed with the most gravitas it had since the start of their conversation. A flashing light burst in front of Dagim.

Out of the sudden light, Frederica stepped out. Having lived until her forties until her death, her skin was paler and slightly more wrinkled than her recruit days, just like the rest of her friends. But unlike the others, her hair had not greyed. It still kept its raven shine.

Frederica sighed. "Nice to see you again, Devil Child."

"First Ranger!" Dagim exclaimed as he engulfed her in a warm hug. "You died? When?"

"During one of my resource travels through the Cantankerous Sea," Frederica answered. "I suppose that's what I get for trying to reach the Land of Abundance so desperately," she chuckled.

"That's unfortunate," Dagim sighed.

"It is. But look where I'm at now," Frederica said. "My soul is powerful and volatile enough to be held by God for centuries. Just like yours."

"So it is," Dagim laughed.

The Bestial Energy hummed with a land-quaking vibrating force. "I am afraid I have to cut your reunion short. Frederica must be returned to her segment of this afterlife."

Dagim clenched his jaw. He nodded his head again, accepting The Bestial Energy's decree.

Before Frederica was to be flashed away once more, she offered a handshake to Dagim.

"I'll see you when our souls meet again on the mortal plane, Dagim," Frederica said.

"When our souls meet again," Dagim agreed as he accepted the handshake firmly.

The two of them shook hands one last time before a light transported Frederica away. With her, The Bestial Energy left, leaving Dagim alone.

"What a life I've lived," Dagim sighed with a smile.

He sat down and rested, ready to wait out potentially thousands of years of solitude until his soul would be reincarnated.

He closed his eyes and enjoyed the serenity of the golden heaven that surrounded him.

THE AUTHOR

Jason Tejiri Boje is a Nigerian-European author of fantasy, science fiction, thriller, and young adult drama novels. He graduated with a Bachelor of Arts with Honours degree in Business Economics from Lancaster University in 2023, where he had developed his writing skills alongside his studies over the years. He has received numerous awards for several written works, including television screenplays and online novels.

CONNECT WITH JASON VIA:

Instagram: @jasonbojewriting

TikTok: @jasonbojewriting

YouTube: @jasonbtg

www.ingramcontent.com/pod-product-compliance
Lightning Source LLC
Chambersburg PA
CBHW031101030726
47496CB00002BA/329